DATE DUE			
JL 0 8 '96			
JUN 1 9 '96			
JL 22 '96			
JUL 22 '96			
AUG 22 '96			
NOV 2 6 '96			
DEC 9 '96			
2/20/97			

BLOOD OF PATRIOTS

BLOOD OF PATRIOTS

CONGRESSMAN
NEIL ABERCROMBIE
and
RICHARD HOYT

A TOM DOHERTY ASSOCIATES BOOK

New York

BLOOD OF PATRIOTS

Copyright © 1996 by Neil Abercrombie and Richard Hoyt

"Zombie Jamboree (Back to Back)"
Words and Music by Conrad Eugene Mauge, Jr.
TRO © copyright 1957 and renewed 1995 by
Hollis Music, Inc., New York, NY 10011-4298.
Used by permission.

A Forge Book
Published by Tom Doherty Associates, Inc.
175 Fifth Avenue
New York, NY 10010

Forge® is a registered trademark of Tom Doherty Associates, Inc.

Library of Congress Cataloging-in-Publication Data

Abercrombie, Neil.
    Blood of patriots / by Neil Abercrombie and Richard Hoyt.
        p.   cm.
    ISBN 0-312-86166-4
    1. Government investigators—Washington (D.C.)—Fiction.
2. Terrorism—Washington (D.C.)—Fiction.   I. Hoyt, Richard,
1941- .   II. Title
PS3551.B375B56   1996
813'.54—dc20   96-11599

Book design by Richard Oriolo

First edition: May 1996

Printed in the United States of America

0 9 8 7 6 5 4 3 2 1

In memory of Reuel Denney

. . . from two of his grateful students.
It was a privilege, joy, and inspiration.

We began writing *Blood of Patriots* on October 3, 1994, in the midst of fevered appeals to apocalyptic violence and limitless, often secret campaign spending used to manipulate voters through market research and television advertising. We had finished the first draft—all the themes, characters, and plot were in place—when terrorists bombed the federal building in Oklahoma City on April 19, 1995.

Then came more news that mirrored our story: former federal drug prosecutors were charged with working for the Cali drug cartel, and independent expenditure committees were accused of grossly manipulating elections. As for our assertion that the White House is now literally for sale, we had finished the book *before* Steve Forbes announced his intention to invest personal millions in a bid for the Presidency; we were editing the proofs when he began his amazing binge of buying television advertising.

But none of this compares to the revelation— kept secret for months by the FBI—of the words of Thomas Jefferson on the T-shirt worn by Oklahoma City bombing suspect Timothy McVeigh when he was arrested. Fifteen months earlier, we had chosen the exact same passage as the epigraph of our novel and the source of our title, *Blood of Patriots*. We thought the line—written at a time when many Americans felt threatened by the proposed new federal system—reflected the continuing rancorous gulf between America's underclasses and its moneyed elites. But the quotation on McVeigh's T-shirt was incomplete; the blood shed in refreshing the tree of liberty, Jefferson wrote, was its "natural manure."

We believe the called shot of our epigraph may be what the psychiatrist Carl Jung called a "synchrony"—that is, in imagining our story and its protagonists, we found ourselves in a parallel zone with the Timothy McVeighs of our nation.

NEIL ABERCROMBIE
RICHARD HOYT

The Tree of Liberty must be refreshed from time to time with the Blood of Patriots and Tyrants. It is its natural manure.

Thomas Jefferson,
letter to William Stephens Smith,
November 13, 1787

Hall of the House of Representatives

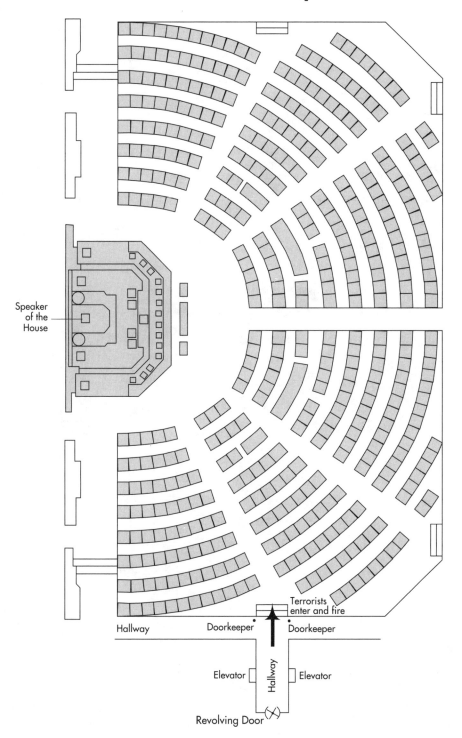

Speaker of the House

Terrorists enter and fire

Hallway

Doorkeeper

Doorkeeper

Elevator

Hallway

Elevator

Revolving Door

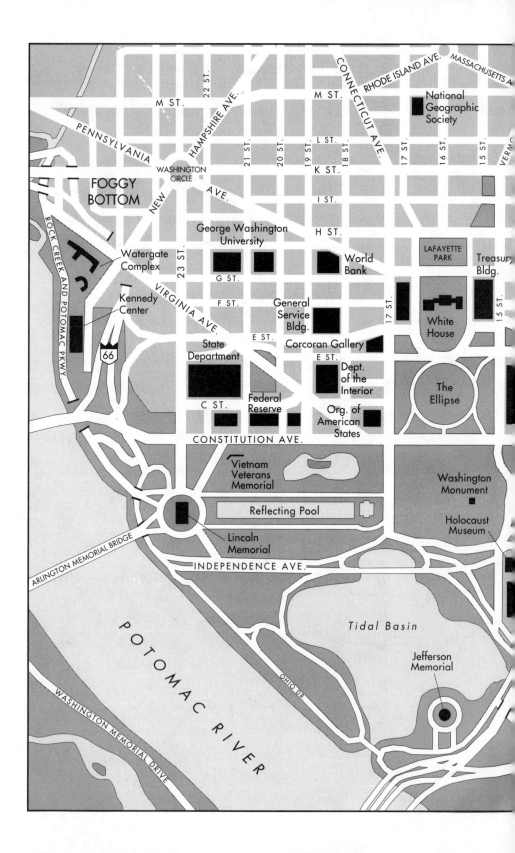

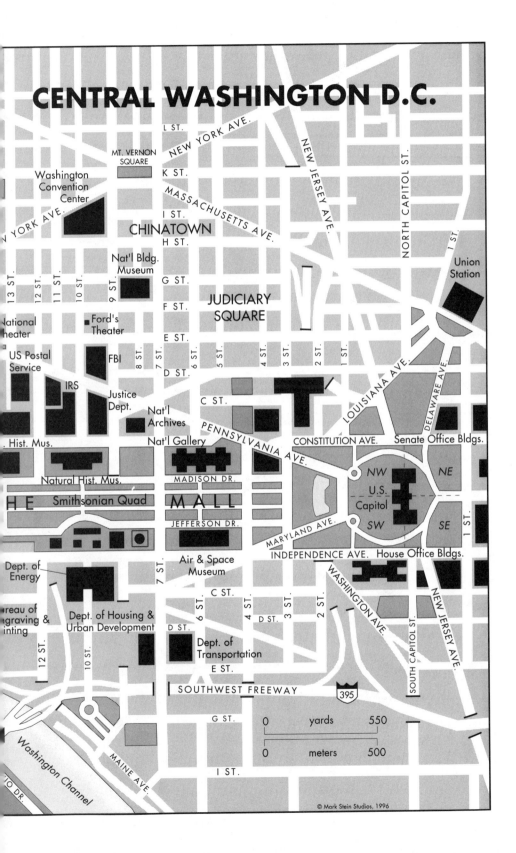

CENTRAL WASHINGTON D.C.

L ST.

NEW YORK AVE.

NEW JERSEY AVE.

MT. VERNON SQUARE

K ST.

Washington Convention Center

MASSACHUSETTS AVE.

NORTH CAPITOL ST.

I ST.

N YORK AVE.

CHINATOWN

H ST.

Union Station

Nat'l Bldg. Museum

G ST.

JUDICIARY SQUARE

F ST.

13 ST.

12 ST.

11 ST.

10 ST.

9 ST.

Jational heater

Ford's Theater

E ST.

US Postal Service

FBI

8 ST.

7 ST.

6 ST.

5 ST.

4 ST.

3 ST.

2 ST.

1 ST.

D ST.

IRS

Justice Dept.

C ST.

Nat'l Archives

LOUISIANA AVE.

DELAWARE AVE.

Hist. Mus.

Nat'l Gallery

PENNSYLVANIA AVE.

CONSTITUTION AVE.

Senate Office Bldgs.

Natural Hist. Mus.

MADISON DR.

NW

NE

H E

Smithsonian Quad

M A L L

U.S. Capitol

JEFFERSON DR.

SW

SE

1 ST.

Dept. of Energy

Air & Space Museum

MARYLAND AVE.

INDEPENDENCE AVE.

House Office Bldgs.

7 ST.

C ST.

6 ST.

4 ST.

3 ST.

2 ST.

WASHINGTON AVE.

NEW JERSEY AVE.

reau of graving & inting

Dept. of Housing & Urban Development

D ST.

D ST.

Dept. of Transportation

SOUTH CAPITOL ST.

12 ST.

10 ST.

E ST.

SOUTHWEST FREEWAY

395

G ST.

| 0 | yards | 550 |
| 0 | meters | 500 |

MAINE AVE.

I ST.

Washington Channel

TO DR.

© Mark Stein Studios, 1996

1

GAMBIT

JANUARY 18, 2000

We have it in our power to begin the world over again. A situation similar to the present, hath not happened since the days of Noah until now. The birthday of a new world is at hand.

—Tom Paine, from *Common Sense*

ONE

No matter how many times they were required to choke that black bird down, Americans always ate crow with extreme reluctance. As in the Vietnam War—after years of being told how essential the fight was—the public was reluctant to admit the war on drugs had been a costly, doomed, even stupid battle from the start. Nobody wanted to hear it.

The controversial hearings on the consequences of ending the drug war were being held inside the Philip Burton Federal Building and United States Court House.

A baby-faced man with an incongruous, vaguely sinister cleft chin listened to the proceedings on a miniature Sony radio with earphones as he walked in the cold wind that blew across downtown San Francisco. He had a certain intense, determined look that was of the saints and the obsessed.

Cervantes' noble but doomed knight had been reincarnated as a woman, Senator Graciela Boulanger, a Montana Republican who bore logic as a lance. Cleft-chin had read articles about the chief critic of the drug war in the news magazines. A *Time* magazine writer had described Boulanger as flying the flag of John Milton, maintaining that truth, put to test against falsehood in free and open encounter, would prevail every time.

Did she actually believe that manure? Cleft-chin wondered.

If it had been summertime, Cleft-chin would have walked a few blocks up Polk Street to gawk at the crazies in the gay bars. On hot summer days, queers on the barstools liked to have the doors open so they could shock and amaze passing breeders and tourists by French-kissing and groping one another's crotch. Cleft-chin believed the alleged AIDS crisis was no crisis at all. It was Malthusian. Queers deserved to die.

But no Polk Street stroll for him. The closed doors to the queer bars were as opaque as the windows steamed over from the heat of overactive hormones.

His stomach growled. He was hungry.

He walked to the McDonald's on the northeast corner of Golden Gate and Van Ness Avenue, a short block west of the federal building. Everybody joked about Big Macs and secret sauces and the rest of it, but there was nothing like loading up at McDonald's before heading for work.

Listening to the testimony, he went inside and ordered a Big Mac, a medium-sized order of french fries, and a cup of coffee. He scored a window seat enabling him to see the intersection of Van Ness and Turk Street one block to the north. The beeper on his hip would tell him when the drivers started the engines of the limousines.

Cleft-chin wanted his rabbits out there in the traffic so the commuters could enjoy the show on their way home from work, and so television stations could share the sport with their viewers.

Cleft-chin could never himself make french fries that were worth a damn. He had wondered how McDonald's did it until one day he read in a magazine that the company cooked and mashed the potatoes first. They loaded the mashed potatoes into a machine that extruded long, thin, perfectly square potato turds that they cooked in hot oil, then froze. At outlets around the world, the potato sticks were thawed and given a final dunking to produce those famous, yum-yum-yummy, golden brown, can't-get-enough-of-'em french fries—a tribute to American ingenuity.

In Cleft-chin's earphones, Senator Boulanger asked a question. She thought she was going to phase out the war on drugs and save the country a bundle. Right! Stupid broad.

Alexandria, Virginia
5:30 P.M.

As the last sliver of sun slipped below the horizon, a man sat in the cab of a tractor double-trailer rig parked at the edge of Quaker Lane, next to the Virginia Theological Seminary. The sides of the trailer and the doors of the tractor cab bore the familiar logo of Wal-Mart, the one-stop shopping market with stores across the United States.

San Francisco
3:00 P.M.

Senator Graciela Boulanger, the chairman of the House-Senate Select Narcotics Committee, looked about at the faces watching her. She had been making the same pitch for close to twelve years. When she first started suggesting the forbidden, the impossible, the reaction of her listeners had been mixed.

A few of her listeners—apparently those harboring fantasies of an Academy Award—managed to look shocked. Boulanger felt amused by those of her listeners who looked embarrassed. On these occasions, she felt like an intellectual Lili St. Cyr, peeling off layers of truth right down to the G-string of her final proposal.

She couldn't count how many times she had presented her case, usually from a dais overlooking a small auditorium or in a room in which her listeners sat around tables just cleared of dirty dishes.

But she refused to quit. She never stopped pressing her case. She believed truth was liberating, and she regarded her pursuit against all odds as an act of patriotism.

Lately, when she faced an audience, she could spot a few people who were actually listening to what she had to say—really listening, not pretending to do so. After all these years of being regarded as a radical on the issue, Boulanger felt each new attentive face was a triumph of fact over myth, intelligence over emotion, and perseverence over resignation.

Thought by many, at best, as politically eccentric—but admired by independent-minded Montanans for her gutsy stand—Boulanger was getting more sympathetic audiences. Sure, this one was in San Francisco, not Middle America, but she nevertheless savored the moment. She had learned that despite outward appearances, many Montanans agreed with her and were acting on the premises at home in Montana's magnificent open-sky vastness.

She said, "Let's get straight to the bottom of it. What if we just said, 'Okay, face it: the war on drugs is a misguided proposition that hasn't worked any better than Prohibition did seventy years ago. Let's do the smart thing and give it up.' What would happen? Want to make a guess?" She looked around the room. Yes, people, perhaps bored by years of fear-mongering by DEA budget defenders, did want to know what would happen.

"Well, first there would be no more drug dealers to kill innocent bystanders during their shoot-outs. Hundreds of thousands of cocaine and heroin addicts would no longer be shoplifting, mugging, and breaking into homes to support their habit. Whatever would we do without our nightly fix of more bad news? I bet we would think of something." She paused with a half grin.

"Seventy-five thousand jail cells would be freed within days. There'd be no more snickering, slick dudes cruising the streets in fancy Jaguars and Mercedes convertibles laughing at us. For the first time in our history, we could begin real drug education.

"Cops, prosecutors, and judges could devote their energies to capturing and convicting violent career criminals who commit theft, rape, or murder about fifty times a year on the average. One year after we ended the drug war, sixteen hundred people would be alive who would otherwise be dead at the hands of criminals.

"To prosecute the drug war, we're now spending about ten billion a year for police, courts, and prisons in all levels of government. We spend this money to maintain a black market so gangsters and drug barons can scam eighty billion dollars a year. For each dollar we spend, we lose seven. Wonderful." She smiled, waiting for the uneasy laughter to subside.

"What do hard-up users do to buy expensive black-market drugs? Why they steal seven and a half billion dollars a year from the rest of us. If you want to really get crass, you can work out the daily toll on that eighty billion."

She cocked her head, looking amused. "The first time I tried to figure the number on my calculator, I was flabbergasted. It works out to two hundred twenty million dollars a day! We willfully waste two hundred twenty million dollars each day while we politically flay one another looking for ways to balance the budget? Think about that for a moment."

Now was the time to lay the numbers on them. Boulanger glanced at her notes, but she hardly had to. She had drug statistics etched in her brain. She said, "You want more numbers, try some of these:

"One hundred fifty people are killed each year in busts for a drug—marijuana—in which there is not a single recorded instance of death by overdose. About thirty-five hundred Americans die from AIDS each year because of unsterile heroin needles; in Hong Kong, where needles are legal, there are virtually no infections by needle. Here's one I really like: When we send a drug offender to jail for one year, we free a violent criminal to steal twenty-five cars, rob forty people, assault seven victims, and commit one hundred ten burglaries. It would take a twelve hundred seventy-five–percent increase in the use of legal drugs to produce as many deaths as now die of AIDS, murder, and bad drugs.

"And as for the corruption of the system . . . well!" Boulanger flung her hands upward in complete disgust. "We had hints for years, but five years ago we learned that former prosecutors in the Justice Department were in the pay of the Cali drug cartel. What can I say? What can anybody say?"

Boulanger was amazed at the mental gymnastics of those who were crippled by fear of admitting the failure of a policy in which there had been invested so much blood, treasure, and rhetoric. She felt her opponents were mostly people who felt uncomfortable with ambiguity—they wanted specific yes/no rules of moral conduct—and the immediate players, drug war bureaucrats and soldiers, and those who grew, smuggled, and sold drugs. There was another odd faction that she had discerned: there were apparently large numbers of people passionately dedicated to remaining ignorant.

And there were the inevitable lunatics who had publicly threatened to kill her because she dared be rational. And a woman to boot! A skirt! That fact gnawed at some of them, she knew.

Boulanger's stomach growled. She was hungry. She hoped there wouldn't be too many questions but, this being San Francisco, she knew there would be.

Washington, D.C.
6:00 P.M.

The idea for replacing paper money with plastic currency would have remained forever suppressed had it not been for Speaker Jim Purdy's decision—in the face of criticism that Republicans were all white males—to appoint Republican Barbara Laine, of Connecticut, chair of the House Banking Committee.

Unknown to Purdy, Laine, who had been a parole officer, was fed up with mobsters and drug barons. Laine immediately moved to hold public hearings on the proposal with C-SPAN viewers looking on. Not even the powerful and outspoken Purdy, who felt he had been ambushed, could stop her.

It was a simple enough idea: Replace the hundred-dollar bill with a counterfeit-proof plastic bill—modeled after the successful printing of plastic money in Australia—and require citizens to turn their old bills in within sixty days or use them for wallpaper. Once the hundreds were in, the fifties would be recalled, followed by the twenties, tens, fives, and one-dollar bills, which saw the heaviest use.

The current cotton-paper bill cost 3.8 cents to print and lasted about eighteen months; a plastic bill cost 2.2 cents and lasted years. The Treasury Department spent two hundred million dollars a year to replace worn-out hundred-dollar bills, and even more to reprint and recirculate worn-out bills in smaller denominations.

The makers of cotton-based paper, suppliers of ink, and printing unions found themselves allied with the Mafia, the drug cartels, and less visible and inflammatory beneficiaries of the underground economy, who did not want hundred-dollar bills to be replaced in a sixty-day period, right out there in front of God, DEA investigators, and IRS agents.

Some of this unreported, untaxed cash was used to support congressmen, senators, and political causes; to openly argue against the proposal was to have one's own campaign contributions questioned.

To dodge a protracted public argument over the merits of Laine's bill, opponents agreed to bring the proposal to a vote on the floor, where they could simply vote no without having to tell voters why. The Rules Committee had decreed that no amendments would be offered, debate would be limited, and Speaker Purdy set a specific time for the vote.

Purdy privately assured opponents that a quorum call would be issued to ensure maximum attendance on the floor before the vote. Representative Laine was not to be deterred, but also not to be helped one damn bit more than absolutely necessary.

TWO

Carter Commission Report

From the preface:

The United States Capitol, housing both the House of Representatives and the Senate, is situated on a slight hill, hence the term "Capitol Hill" frequently used to describe the action at the heart of the government.

The west facade of the Capitol overlooks a grassy mall that runs from Third Street and continues nearly two miles west to the Lincoln Memorial, on the banks of the Potomac River. This is correctly the National Mall, but is more commonly referred to simply as "the Mall," and is flanked by the national museums and archives, the headquarters of government agencies, and the White House.

The Capitol's east facade faces a parking lot reserved for congressmembers and senators, then two irregularly shaped oval lawns, each six hundred feet long and five hundred feet wide. The north lawn is between the Senate and the Supreme Court; the south lawn is between the House of Representatives and the Library of Congress.

The House chamber is located on the second floor of the southern wing. The east entrance to the second floor, approached from the Capitol parking lot by four decks of granite steps, is a revolving door located between the fourth and fifth of eight Doric columns. These stairs and the revolving doors at the top are off-limits to everybody but congressmen, their guests, and staff members.

6 : 1 5 P . M .

Officer Terry Donahue of the Capitol police, who worked for a modest wage, and who did not have hot money tucked away in his attic, was posted in front of the revolving door. Donahue's ambitions were simple enough. He dreamed of taking his girlfriend to Chincoteague Island in Virginia, where they would dig clams in the marshes, and rent an aluminum boat so he could fish for flounder.

At eight o'clock, Speaker pro tempore Tim Nichols was finally scheduled—after all the predictable last-minute wrangling, bickering, and passionate objections—to call for the vote on Representative Barbara Laine's proposal.

When the fateful hour arrived, Nichols would give members not already answering the quorum call seventeen minutes to get to the House floor and vote. The congressmembers streaming in—many of them accompanied by staff members—would make the entrance to the chamber a hubbub of confusion and activity.

In 1995, Speaker Newt Gingrich had briefly allowed cameras to pan the floor and to cut from whoever was speaking to reaction shots on the floor, and the members went bonkers! Yawns, inappropriate yapping, inattention, nose-picking—all there for the cable masses to savor—in effect allowed the director to make editorial comments;

the House went back to essentially static shots with some creative angles, but the action remained on whoever was speaking or on the floor podiums in front of the speaker's main dais.

When the official fifteen minutes to vote had expired and the House floor was jammed with 435 congressmen and -women plus assistants, House employees, and other assorted political camp followers, including former congressmen, who were allowed on the floor, Nichols would tack on an extra two minutes to allow stragglers to vote. Only after latecomers had been given their chance would the voting be closed.

After the two minutes of grace had expired, it was Purdy's chore to calm the inevitable mewing and yelping of the congressional herd so he could announce the result and push on to adjournment or other business. Those members who felt they had voted in the best interest of their constituents, if not the Republic, were inevitably in a jubilant, celebratory mood. Those who felt their constituents had been given the sharp end of the stick rarely accepted defeat in stoic silence.

As all C-SPAN junkies knew, close to half an hour was required to vote and announce the results, during which time the assembled members gossiped, plotted, and milled around. It was during this period that the Capitol police were faced with the maximum security problem.

After the Oklahoma City bombing, security had been strengthened for a time. This consisted principally of attempts to restrict parking on the streets near legislative office buildings. Suggestions for fencing off the Capitol grounds were rejected out of hand. The Capitol had always been accessible to the public. This openness was the hallmark of American democracy, and members of Congress were damned if they would let terrorists triumph by restricting the public from wandering in the halls of the Capitol and their office buildings. Staff IDs were checked a little more carefully and metal detectors received slightly more intense scrutiny. Eventually cars, even those of members and staff, were forbidden entrance into the east facade parking lot at night. Vehicle bombs were the great concern after Oklahoma City.

Officer Donahue's cousin had smuggled two banana trees out of Puerto Rico, and Donahue was keeping them in his apartment under a grow-light. As he waited for the action, he thought of building a hot-house on the diminutive balcony of his apartment so he could use the grow-light in the winter and nature's own in the summer.

Then, in the future when snow howled down over Washington, he and his girlfriend would have fun picking delicious little bananas.

6:20 P.M.

Directly behind his desk was a blown-up photograph of him, his head encased in a stocking cap, standing in a snowstorm by the front door of his restaurant in Buffalo, Mitch Webster's Buffalo Chips Literary Bar and Damn Fine Eatery.

The walls of Buffalo Chips—now being run by Congressman Webster's sister, Angela—were lined with first editions plus autographed photographs of famous Buffalo sports figures; Webster had first editions of Harriet Beecher Stowe's *Uncle Tom's Cabin*, Upton Sinclair's classic, *The Jungle*, exposing the meatpacking industry, John Steinbeck's *Grapes of Wrath*, and Ralph Ellison's *Invisible Man* and James Baldwin's *Go Tell It on the Mountain*, plus autographed photographs of famous Buffalo sports figures. Buffalo Sabres hockey players were well represented, but most of the athletes were famous football Bills—as were the pictures on the walls of Webster's office in the Longworth House Office Building; these included the quarterback Jim Kelly, the big defensive end Bruce Smith, and running backs Thurman Thomas and O. J. Simpson.

While Webster had been dismayed by Simpson's involvement in wife-beating, the jury had found him not guilty of double murder; Webster could not bring himself to remove O. J.'s picture from the wall. Neither could he bring himself to remove a picture of himself and a grinning Danny Rostenkowski, despite Rostenkowski's fall. The loyal Webster would protest, "You know what Danny said? He said, 'They changed the rules on me. They changed the rules.'" Webster even had a two-volume set of *Papers of President William Jefferson Clinton*, although he felt Clinton had abandoned the

Democrats' chief base, working people and minorities, to pursue the affections of suburban suits who didn't want to spend a dime on anybody but themselves.

But Webster's prize was a photograph of himself arm in arm with the white-haired Irishman, Thomas P. "Tip" O'Neill, former Speaker of the House.

Now Webster was kicked back in his swivel chair, his feet on the desk; beside him, his administrative assistant shuffled through papers relating to the proposal to print new hundred-dollar bills— out of plastic. Plastic!

When Webster had first heard of Barbara Laine's idea, he had thought it was absurd. The public would never accept plastic bills. But when he actually laid his hands on an Australian plastic note, he began coming around. There was nothing crazy about it at all. He had thought, Good on ya, mates! Why not? Just what was so holy about paper money anyway? Why waste all those trees in addition to all the tax dollars that could more productively be spent elsewhere? All the talk about cut, cut, cutting the cost of government. Why not save money in places where it made sense instead of whacking services of people who desperately needed them?

While Webster was no particular fan of Laine, who was one of Gracie Boulanger's good friends, he agreed with her on this one. So did his AA. Webster was the ranking minority member of the House Select Committee on Campaign Reform, and he was for any bill that would help check the traffic in hot money. For reasons that were not good, in Webster's opinion, nobody really wanted to do what had to be done to tax the underground economy.

6:30 P.M.

They sat in a gray four-door Ford Taurus sedan three abreast, front and back, parked at the intersection of North Carolina and Pennsylvania Avenues, five blocks southeast of the Capitol.

The man calling himself Oscar had high cheekbones and a distinctive wide jaw. He wore a dark blue suit and polished wing-tipped oxfords. His hair was neatly trimmed—one of those every-ten-days haircuts preferred by compulsive suits.

The woman answering to Luisa sitting next to the driver had the same high cheekbones and wide jaw. She looked like a clone of Oscar, only younger and female. She wore a dark blue suit of the sort worn by female executives in television ads and in the movies. The shoulders were padded, and the red tie was wider and softer than that worn by men, but it sent the unmistakable message that this was a smart, educated professional woman.

There were three similarly dark-complexioned, black-haired men in the backseat. They too were impeccably dressed in suits and all had roomy, high-collar trench coats in their laps.

All six people in the Taurus wore plastic tags that contained their photographs; this was the form of identification worn by congressional staff. They also all wore gloves, which was not unusual; it was a cold January day in Washington.

They chatted in Spanish as they listened to a radio transceiver on the front seat between the male and female look-alikes.

The transceiver was delivering the audio of the proceedings on the House floor being telecast by C-SPAN.

San Francisco
4:10 P.M.

Public hearings had become an odious chore for Senator Graciela Boulanger. The same sides came trooping up to give testimony, which was nearly always predictable. This was a form of political theater so that the public could rest assured that all sides had been heard and considered. All sides were heard, it was true. But truly considered?

She wondered, casually, if the drug warriors were kept in business by some kind of odd conspiracy, the nature of which was so pervasive and subtle that she was blind to it.

Her rump was sore from sitting; her mind was numb from the predictable, dumb, and poorly informed objections to any change whatsoever. Boulanger glanced at her watch. The hearing was to adjourn at five o'clock after which she was scheduled to eat dinner with Mayor Margot Lewis at Victor's at the top of the St. Francis Hotel. She wished her friend Mitch Webster could go with her.

Boulanger was in love with Mitch, although she felt he was attached to a worn-out past in many ways. But she believed he, too, put the interest of the Republic ahead of his prospects for being re-elected. A liberal Democrat, a man who believed in affirmative action and minority set-asides, and she was in love with him! How had that happened?

They had felt an instant physical chemistry when they had met ostensibly as opponents on a League of Women Voters panel called "The New Century—Same Old Congress?" He had said afterward that while he couldn't agree less with her conclusions on most issues, he felt her convictions were the result of a true independence that he admired. She said she felt the same about him, and she added that as long as they had one thing to agree on, how about dinner to see if anything else could be discovered?

Not only had he accepted, but he confessed to her later that night—after their first frantic bout of lovemaking—that, as he'd gone to speak, he'd been practically flailing about trying to find some excuse to ask her to go out with him; the independence angle just spilled out. The wonderful irony of it all, they decided months later, was that they both meant it; they were drawn together by their singular cast of mind.

In a world where everyone they met wanted something from them, and where an honest word was as rare as a kind thought, they could and did open themselves up to each other. The love they felt was a source of joyous wonder to them both.

THREE

The paunchy, baggy-eyed House Speaker Jim Purdy, Republican of South Carolina—speaking from the Republican lectern in the well of the chamber—tugged at his belt and gazed imperiously to his right toward the Democratic minority. The chamber was too small to accommodate everybody on a major vote, and Purdy had once joked that on these occasions, the members looked like restless cattle awaiting slaughter.

In his distinctive, now famous voice, Purdy said, "May I remind my esteemed colleagues y'all have agreed to vote on this bill tonight? Y'all have been arguing this proposal for weeks now. We've had open debate on this. Nobody has been shut out. Y'all've had every con-

ceivable chance to make your position abundantly clear. If your constituents don't know where y'all stand, it's nobody's fault but yours.
All y'all had to do was speak up! Now that we've had a quorum call I
think—"

Above him, Speaker pro tempore Tim Nichols banged the gavel.

"Will the gentlemen in the rear please refrain from talking, please?
Please take your conversations to the cloakroom." He pounded the
gavel again.

In the well, Purdy said, "No more can possibly be added to what
has already been said about this proposal. As per our earlier agreement, both proponents and opponents have twenty minutes of jawing
time remaining evenly divided. People are watching this debate on
television, wondering if we can actually do anything except talk. At
exactly eight o'clock, we will show them we can do it. By golly, we *will*
get on with it. We will conduct the business of the Republic. We *will*
proceed according to our agreement: We will delay no longer; yes sir,
we *will* vote."

Alexandria
7:40.05 P.M.

Upon hearing Speaker Jim Purdy's announcement, the driver of the
Wal-Mart truck by the Virginia Theological Seminary turned the key
to the diesel engine. He waited, watching a red light above the ignition. When the red light turned green, he turned the key the rest of
the way and the engine rumbled to life.

Washington, D.C.
7:42 P.M.

Oscar, Luisa, and three of the four men in the Ford Taurus parked
on North Carolina Avenue got out. They gave their gloves to Luisa,
who put them in her handbag.

The remaining man stayed behind the wheel of the Taurus and drove off.

Oscar and Luisa and their three companions, chatting in Spanish and stopping to inspect menus in the windows, strolled past the Capitol Hill eateries and small grocery shops on the southern side of Pennsylvania Avenue—here running northwest-southeast as it approached Capitol Hill from the John Philip Sousa Bridge over the Anacostia River.

The group walked up the left side of Pennsylvania. As they did, Oscar and Luisa went first.

The remaining three men gave them a twenty-yard head start before they followed, chatting in Spanish.

Oscar and Luisa stopped at Trover's, a clean and well-stocked bookstore. The window display featured biographies of President Thomas Erikson, Maryland governor John Danneman, and West Virginia senator Chet Gorman, plus the current nonfiction contender, Hal Cowley's *Failure of the Republican Revolution*, subtitled *Congress in Crisis, Democrats in Disorder.*

Looking at Cowley's book, Oscar said, *"Cucarachas. Todas son cucarachas. Todo el sistema está podrido. No son nada que cucarachas."* (Cockroaches, all cockroaches. The whole system is rotten. They're nothing but cockroaches.)

A young blonde woman and her male friend, who obviously both understood Spanish, turned their heads.

"Cucarachas!" he said scornfully. He held out his elbow, which his female companion accepted, chin up. They swept on down the sidewalk.

They entered the Flying Burrito Brothers takeout and studied the menu on the wall. Oscar, eyeing the young woman taking orders, looked peevish. He said, *"Cucarachas! Toda ha llegado para esto, Luisa. La comida aqui es propia nada mas para las cucarachas."* (Cockroaches. It's all come down to this, Luisa. The food here is fit only for cockroaches.)

Luisa gave him a look of reproval. "Oscar!"

Oscar grabbed Luisa and exited.

Alexandria

7:48 P.M.

The Wal-Mart rig pulled onto Highway 395, the Shirley Memorial Highway, from the Quaker Lane on-ramp. The driver arched his back.

He passed the Army-Navy golf course on his left.

Ahead and to his left, he saw lights in the Pentagon.

Dead ahead: the city of Washington.

7:50 P.M.

Representative Barbara Laine sat behind the leadership table on the majority side, waiting for the Democrat minority, in this case led by Representative Jerry Anderson of California, to close the opposition. When Anderson finished with his blather, Laine would use the final five minutes to close the debate, which was her prerogative as chairman of the Banking Committee.

The amazing thing was that any single member would oppose the bill. But no, there they were, offering pious and high-minded reasons why the proposal would be everything but a death knell for the Republic.

Plastic money?

The very idea.

Laine supposed that members of the Australian foreign service watching the debate on C-SPAN must be knocking back the Foster's lager and having a good laugh as they watched the silly Americans debate printing money that they'd used for years.

Laine had read about a Japanese word, *kuromaku*, used to describe powerful people who called the shots from a distance. The word literally meant "behind the velvet," referring to the velvet-covered screens from behind which puppeteers, unseen by the audience, worked the strings of their puppets.

In the case of the House, Laine liked to imagine an invisible puppeteer's hand stretched across the chamber, working silk-like strings so fine they couldn't be seen on C-SPAN's cameras. Of course, not all congressmembers were directed by American *kuro-maku*; there were honest men and women on both sides of the aisle, but with each increase in the battle of campaign dollars, the honest ones fell, one by one.

There were those whose strings were pulled who would deny it vigorously and might have even convinced themselves of their integrity. Yet in those most secret and private moments when they considered a vote, they thought obliquely of where they got their money.

Certainly no bloc of concerned voters pulled Anderson's strings on this vote.

When it was time to close the argument against Laine's proposal, Anderson's puppet master pulled the strings attached to his puppet's shoulders, and Anderson stood.

The puppet master pulled the strings attached to Anderson's arms and hands, and the congressman struck a righteous pose.

In another half hour Laine would know the result of all her efforts. She had tried to reckon the vote but, while it looked like she would probably lose, it was still too close to call. She had a chance. If she won, her next assault on the bastion of power and money would be yet another attempt to substitute a consumption tax for the income tax to encourage savings and to make sure everybody paid his fair share, not just people working for a paycheck. This, she had been told, was certain political suicide.

Years earlier, Congressman Al Ullman, an Oregon Democrat, then chairman of the Ways and Means Committee, had the bad judgment to admit that he didn't think it sinister or outrageous to consider dropping the income tax in favor of a value-added tax. Ullman said it was possible to write a VAT law that lessened or eliminated taxes on food and other basics. Fancy spenders, however they came by their money, paid fancy taxes. Those who saved did not.

The puppet masters failed in their attempt to rig Ullman with their invisible strings. The next election, the congressman's opponent was the sudden, unexpected beneficiary of an avalanche of independent expenditures—paid for by tax lawyers, tax avoiders, and those who profited from the underground economy.

Richly informed by television ads erroneously portraying VAT as favoring the rich, eastern Oregon voters chucked the quixotic Al Ullman out of office.

7:55 P.M.

At Independence, Oscar and Luisa, jabbering in Spanish, made an oblique left, crossing Second Street.

Here, Pennsylvania Avenue jumped a half mile over the Capitol grounds, returning to its northwest-southeast path at the Peace Monument west of the Senate wing of the Capitol.

Oscar and Luisa passed between the Jefferson Building—the original Library of Congress—on the north side of Independence, and its annex, the Madison Building, on the south.

They walked past the Cannon House Office Building on their left.

They crossed New Jersey Avenue.

They were now at the principal aboveground route used by congressmembers and their staff walking to the House floor—the intersection of New Jersey Avenue and Independence Avenue, directly in front of the Longworth House Office Building.

San Francisco

5:00 P.M.

At last . . .

Senator Graciela Boulanger, determined not to prolong the repetitious testimony, glanced at her watch and said, "It's now five o'clock, and inasmuch as we're all tired after a long day and have a full slate of folks to hear from tomorrow, I think common sense dictates that we should adjourn in a timely fashion." She banged her gavel. "This hearing is now adjourned. We will meet here again at nine o'clock tomorrow morning."

Boulanger rose to stretch her legs. She wanted to raise her hands above her head and stretch properly, but restrained the urge. She was glad the day was finished. All the babble. All the palaver. Never mind that it was a rehashing of old arguments that she and the two senators with her had all heard before.

To argue that no amount of treasure was enough to fight the holy drug war, a modern version of the medieval Crusades, was to be good and to be above criticism. To argue that common sense and a limit to the taxpayers' pockets suggested alternate policies was to risk unstated intimations that one was "soft" on drugs, somehow in favor of their horrors.

She had long ago learned that it was never possible to simply leave one of these meetings and go eat. First there would be ten or fifteen minutes' ritual jawboning and a self-congratulatory shaking of hands by friends, supporters, and well-wishers.

Her eye on the distant exit, Boulanger began the drill by shaking hands with her Justice Department hosts, saying what a good and productive meeting it had been. Boulanger had not been elected to the Senate both as a Democrat and as a Republican simply by being blatantly honest; to be successful in politics, you had to be smart and tough as well. She was both. People saw it and respected her enough to vote for her despite differences on an issue such as drugs.

When their duties were at last completed, the three senators would walk downstairs where, inevitably, three black limousines would be waiting to pick them up.

The voters had expected hearings, and hearings they had gotten. If the senators were in any way vulnerable to psychopaths, the disaffected, or those obsessed by the logical extreme, there was not a hint of it in the ceremony of departure.

FOUR

Tim Nichols bashed his gavel hard four times and said, "The gentlewoman's time has expired. All time has expired. The question is on bill number thirty-five seventeen. A recorded vote has been requested. All those in favor will vote aye. All opposed will vote nay. Members will record their vote by electronic device. This will be a seventeen-minute vote."

Nichols tapped his gavel to begin the countdown during which each member used a laminated, perforated card to vote. When poked into a slot and the vote punched, this card—with the congressmember's picture on it—triggered a colored light by his or her name on an electronic tote board displayed on the wall above the press gallery, above and behind the Speaker's dais. A green was for "aye," a red for "nay," and an orange meant "present."

As the vote was counted, members milled about in front of the dais, in the semicircle of the well, gazing at the board trying to determine trends in voting.

Which way did one's foes vote?

And how about one's friends?

8:00 P.M.

The elevated dais of the House Speaker faces north, beneath which are two levels of seats containing clerks, parliamentarians, and the sergeant at arms. Beneath this is the floor, or well, where members of Congress address their colleagues in debate from one of two podiums.

The Republican majority generally sits to the speaker's left, the Democrats to his right; each party occupies three sections of seats separated by two aisles. The chamber is surrounded by a balcony, with seats for visitors behind and to the sides of the floor; journalists sit behind the speaker.

The principal east Democratic aisle, glutted by members during major votes, opens onto a hallway. When a vote is called, the door to this aisle is opened outward and locked.

The chamber door faces a sixteen-foot-long passage with two elevators on each side and a heavy revolving door at the end. The revolving door—used by members walking from the parking lot four decks of granite steps below—is the main eastern entrance of the House wing. There are no metal detectors or inspection stations.

At 8:00 o'clock on the night of January 18, 2000, the chamber door and passage were guarded by two doorkeepers and two uniformed Capitol police officers armed with .38-caliber revolvers. They were expected to recognize members and check identification. Members jammed the elevators, bursting from them as they opened. They poured through the revolving door, all fearful of missing a vote that could haunt them in a thirty-second attack ad. As a result, the

chamber passage was the one entrance to the House entirely depen-
dent on human protection.

8:02 P.M.

By 8:00 P.M., all 435 congressmen and -women had gathered to see if
one of the country's first actions in the twenty-first century would be
to begin the process of phasing out paper money for plastic bills.

Mitch Webster good-naturedly muscled his way toward the
east entrance to the floor. The doorkeepers stood, one on each
side, supposedly checking for the lapel pins that signified the wearer
as a member of the House. In truth, the members were well known
and the inspection of legitimacy was virtually instantaneous. The
unarmed doorkeepers were nonetheless watchful.

The card slots on the back of the seat benches immediately
inside the entrance caused members, invariably Democrats, to bunch
up, many pausing to speak to the floor assistant, Jim Loomis. Members were often at a loss to know what they were voting on. Jim
Loomis always knew. Those in the gallery would have been shocked to
hear members ask him what the vote was about and was it a yes or no.

Webster bellowed over the din of assembled members. "Jim,
better 'fess up to all those hundred-dollar bills you've got stashed
away."

"I'll contribute them to your campaign, Mr. Webster," Loomis
said, grinning.

"Just what campaign finance reform needs, Jim. Why am I
so blessed?" Webster headed for a seat beside his friend Charlie
Toguchi of Hawaii.

8:03 P.M.

The driver of the Ford Taurus followed North Carolina around two
small parks, Seward Square and Folger Square, then took a fork left,

southwest, less than half a block to E Street at the corner of First Street.

He was two long blocks south of the Cannon Office Building and the Longworth Office Building.

At South Capitol, with the Capitol Building four blocks to his right, he turned left.

8:05 P.M.

The driver of the Wal-Mart rig crossed the Potomac River on the Arland Williams Memorial Bridge. The Pentagon was on the west bank; the Tidal Basin—shaped like a round-cornered square—was on the east, across a narrow spit of land.

The illuminated white dome of the Jefferson Memorial was on the south shore of the Tidal Basin. In the interior of the memorial, just below the dome, was chiseled Thomas Jefferson's immortal vow:

I have sworn upon the altar of God eternal hostility to all forms of tyranny over the mind of man.

A thousand feet northeast of the Jefferson Memorial, across the shallow basin, lay the Bureau of Engraving and Printing, where high-speed presses printed the Abes, Grants, and Benjies that fueled the furnace of desire.

The driver of the Wal-Mart tractor-trailer glanced to his left; beyond the Jefferson Memorial he could see the Washington Monument, topped by a blinking red light, and farther still, the White House, bathed in a soft white light.

He passed the headquarters of the Department of Housing and Urban Development, a building that took up an entire city block. The elevated Highway 395 here was four-fifths of a mile due south of the Capitol—E through C Streets, capped by Independence.

A short block away from the House wing of the Capitol, South Capitol Street formed a T with Independence Avenue. The Longworth House Office Building was on the left of this intersection, and the Cannon House Office Building on the right.

8 : 0 6 P . M .

The driver of the Ford Taurus, driving south on South Capitol, passed under the Highway 395 overpass where on-ramps and off-ramps were woven together like concrete snakes.

A thousand feet later, he turned right onto K Street and parked on the side of the street.

8 : 1 2 P . M .

The Capitol dome, the epicenter of the American democratic experiment, was bathed in spotlights, brilliant and lovely. The symbolic dome, glowing virginal white against the cold black night, was very nearly surreal, an awesome sight to the most cynical and sour of the country's citizens. For in spite of everything, America remained a country of hope.

A black male cop in a dark blue uniform and wearing an orange safety vest was assisted by a similarly dressed female white cop. Using electric night-batons that glowed red, they had stopped traffic at the corner of South Capitol Street. When a vote was called, police stopped traffic on Independence to help those congressmembers who wished to walk to the House floor instead of taking the underground tunnels.

At the corner of Independence and New Jersey, Oscar and Luisa, encouraged by the female officer's glowing baton, crossed Independence, shoulders slightly hunched as the cold breeze gusted against their billowing trench coats.

They were now four hundred feet from the steps leading to the House wing of the Capitol.

On the north side of Independence, they walked straight ahead on a sidewalk on the left flank of a stretch of road between Independence and the pavement that fronted the Capitol. This entrance contained In and Out driveways marked in each lane by two sets of steel spring-loaded yo-yo barriers with a huge STOP on them designed to block an assault by vehicles. These lanes were bordered by gigantic concrete flower-urns—nine on each side and nine down the middle. These urns funneled both pedestrians and vehicles past two guardhouses.

The first guardhouse, sixty steps from Independence, contained two guards; the nearest guard checked their staff ID and waved them ahead. It was impossible for the guards to remember the faces of the staffs of 435 congressmen and -women, especially in winter coats and hats.

In another sixty steps, they came to the second guardhouse, surrounded by a low clump of bushes in hibernation. A single guard sat behind enclosed glass, the controls for the barriers in a panel before him.

On the transceiver in Oscar's shirt pocket, a male voice said, *"Cinco minutos y contando."* (Five minutes and counting.)

"Está nuestro hombre en San Francisco situado en su lugar?" the male staffer asked his shirt pocket. (Is our man in San Francisco in place?)

"Sí, el está. Todo está listo." (Yes, he is. Everything is go.)

Having passed the barrier-control guardhouse, they were thirty yards from the bottom of the four decks of granite stairs that led up to the base of the columns in front of the House wing of the Capitol. Behind these columns, directly in front of the east entrance of the House chamber, was the revolving door.

Behind Oscar and Luisa, the three trailing bogus staffers dropped back. Perhaps they had work to do back at the office. With a major vote on a controversial bill due up, the Capitol was a busy place.

8 : 1 4   P . M .

The driver of the Wal-Mart rig glanced briefly in the direction of the Capitol, but his view was momentarily blocked by the backside of House Annex Building No. 2 and by the swoop of Virginia Avenue and coil of off- and on-ramps.

It was a half mile to the exit onto South Capitol Street.

Watching the traffic in his rearview mirror, he began slowing the tractor. He pulled a lever on the panel of the dash, and the electric motor of a pneumatic pump began to hum; the pump operated two power lifts, one in each of the trailers.

As the motor hummed, he checked his mirror again. The trailers were topless, and helicopter blades began rising above the sides and into view of the traffic. The blades belonged to dark blue helicopters, civilian versions of Kiowas, small, fast helicopters used by the army for reconnaissance missions and for moving commanders quickly about a swiftly moving front.

He picked up the transceiver from the seat beside him and slowed the truck even more. Glancing left over Third Street at Capitol Hill, he said, "*Arrancalos.*" (Rev 'em.)

The blades began going *pop, pop, pop!*

The driver watched the mirror.

The blades revved.

"*Buena suerte!*" the driver said.

The choppers rose as one and were off, looking like big, quick mosquitoes.

The driver, following the off-ramp to the southeast, said, "*Vaya con Dios.*"

On his transceiver, a voice said, "*Necesitamos toda la ayuda que podamos obtener.*" (We'll need all the help we can get.)

8:17 P.M.

Mitch Webster and his friend Charlie Toguchi stood well to the right of the east entrance. The previous night they had not gotten home until nearly midnight. They had not had a chance to get more than a sandwich at the cloakroom's snack bar that day, and both were hungry.

They discussed the relative merits of Mitch's Buffalo wings as opposed to Toguchi's Hawaiian-style teriyaki chicken while they watched the gaggle of members engaged in what seemed like mass slam-dancing.

They decided that after the currency vote was tallied, they would have chicken wings at Bullfeathers, two blocks from Mitch's one-hundred-year-old town house on North Carolina Avenue.

Toguchi, who would ordinarily take the Metro to his suburban Maryland home, decided he would crash that night on the couch in Webster's pad, which he often did after a long, tiring day.

San Francisco

5:17 P.M.

A beeper went off on Cleft-chin's hip. He belched and punched a button on his transceiver.

A male voice said, *"Está encendido."*

(It's on.)

FIVE

The two Kiowa helicopters, flying single file and twenty feet above the tops of the cars and trucks below them, circled counter-clockwise. They flew over a snarl of roadways that were principal southern ingress and egress from the Capitol—the shortest route to the refuge of white suburbs beyond the Beltway.

Once clear of the freeway ramps and overpasses, the helicopters, with the Capitol's power plant on their right, barely cleared the tops of cars as they flew north on South Capitol Street, toward the national Capitol.

They crossed E Street four hundred feet later.

Dead ahead: the splendid dome.

They negotiated an overpass.

Then passed D Street; four hundred feet ahead of them, left to right, were the three buildings housing offices of the 435-member House of Representatives—the Rayburn, Longworth, and Cannon.

They passed C Street, between Rayburn on their left and Long-worth on their right.

The southern wing of the Capitol Building—containing the House of Representatives—was six hundred feet dead ahead.

San Francisco

5:17.30 P.M.

Although to the masses the wealthy and famous and powerful were as gods peering from the covers of magazines and newspapers and being interviewed, featured, and even worshiped on television, deities they were not. They could not be painlessly beamed from one place to another in the manner of an away team on *Star Trek*.

They all had to walk to and from oil-stained parking garages. For all politicians except the President, parking garages and sitting in traffic were a large part of their lives.

True, life was easier in the case of Senator Graciela Boulanger, as a car waited in the underground garage of the Philip Burton Federal Building. It was just after five o'clock, and, yes, there would be rush-hour traffic in downtown San Francisco. But Boulanger would not have to drive. Somebody else would do that.

Washington, D.C.

8:17.45 P.M.

Oscar and Luisa trotted up the four decks of granite stairs leading to the east entrance to the House of Representatives.

Two guards stood on the second level, swiveling their heads as they nodded to members and glanced at staff identification cards peeking from their coats as people streamed by and up the stairs.

Luisa reached the top deck and strode between two columns. She walked past three straggler staffers on their way out, and pushed a panel of the revolving door. Two Capitol guards stood just past the elevators on either side of the ten-step alcove that formed a T with the hallway just outside the east wall of the House chamber.

To the left down the hallway was the door to the Speaker's lobby behind the dais.

To the right were stairs that led up to the visitors' gallery on the third floor and down to the members' dining room on the first floor. Just past the stairs another hall connected from the left, leading to the Democratic members' cloakroom, and the entrance to the Rayburn meeting room on the right.

Dead ahead was the entrance that led directly to the eastern end of the chamber—the parliamentary left, facing the Speaker's dais—where the Democrats sat.

A uniformed Capitol policeman in front of the door glanced at their staff identification cards as they pushed through the revolving door, Luisa first, followed by Oscar.

As they disappeared inside, their trailing colleague started up the granite steps behind them. One of the two guards on the lower landing raised the collar of his jacket against the chill.

8:18 P.M.

The driver pulled the Wal-Mart tractor-trailer to the curb of South Capitol Street just yards from the intersection with K Street. He turned off the ignition and hopped lightly to the street.

Without looking back, he walked quickly around the corner, striding west on K Street.

8:18.10 P.M.

Oscar and Luisa strode confidently past the elevators on either side of the alcove that led from the revolving door to the hallway flanking the east side of the House chamber.

It was another ten strides from the alcove across the hallway to the narrow double doors guarding the three stairs up to the chamber floor. The doors were opened outward and locked into place as always.

A doorkeeper on each side of the entrance checked for the identification pins members wore on their lapel to keep unauthorized staff and the public from entering the chamber. During the often long periods between furious activity of members hustling to or from the floor, the doorkeepers sat in permanently fixed leather chairs.

Just past the three steps lay the confusion of members on the Democratic side of the chamber.

Oscar, opening his coat, started across the hall.

The guard on the right turned slightly toward him.

He said *"Hazlo ahora"* into the transceiver in his shirt pocket. (Do it now.)

San Francisco

5:18.12 P.M.

Senator Graciela Boulanger slipped onto the backseat of the Cadillac limousine, and the African-American driver, in front of a bulletproof screen, said, "We're in for some traffic, ma'am, would you like some music? I've got a good collection of CDs."

Boulanger, who ordinarily liked quiet, also was aware that politicians often distanced themselves from the lives of ordinary people; she felt it was a good thing, now and then, to share in their pleasures. "Sure," she said. "What've you got?"

The driver, following a yellow arrow to the street exit above, said, "A little of this. A little of that."

"Whatever you like. That's what I want to hear."

The driver laughed. "Yes, ma'am. That'd be reggae."

"Reggae's fine by me."

"Bob Marley? Yellowman?"

"Either one."

He said, "Yellowman, then."

The car was flooded with a rolling beat, and Boulanger found herself moving to the music. She couldn't help herself.

As they entered the bottom of the concrete ramp that led uphill to the street, she saw, in the rearview mirror, that the driver was grinning.

He said, "They say this music is best enjoyed with a spliff of ganj, ma'am." He assumed the lady senator who had proposed ending the war on drugs would know *spliff* was Jamaican lingo for a joint, and *ganj* was short for ganja, or cannabis. Then he added, "But I wouldn't know anything about that."

Boulanger laughed. "I bet you wouldn't."

At the top of the ramp, the driver eased the car into the traffic going north on Larkin Street. As they turned onto the street, Boulanger saw Gateway Croissants on the corner of Larkin and Golden Gate in front of the federal building. Her stomach rumbled. She was hungry.

The driver took a quick turn onto Turk Street, a one-way street going west. As he turned, she saw a passport-photo place across the street. Boulanger had rarely seen a customer in those places, and she had long wondered how the demand for passport photos could keep so many of these establishments in business. She had thought the same thing about health-food stores selling obscure capsules and vitamins until Mitch Webster told her both businesses were popular fronts for laundering hot money.

The traffic inched down the backside of the federal building, until the driver, following the limousines carrying Senators Jacoby and Huff and their wives, stopped at a red light at the corner of Turk and Polk Streets. The California Culinary Academy was located on the northwest corner of the intersection. The marquee outside advertised prime rib nightly at the grill.

Boulanger's stomach growled again. . . .

In front of her, the two limousines exploded, bursting into mushrooms of orange flame.

Boulanger's driver leaped out as the door nearest her popped open. He looped a long, strong arm around her and yanked her to her feet.

He muttered, "Jesus Christ!"

She held on tightly as he ran through the tangle of traffic, carrying her like a bag of potatoes.

When they got to the sidewalk, the driver put her down, and they both stared, transfixed, at the two burning vehicles.

Their own car sat unharmed, reggae still wailing from its CD player.

SIX

The bogus staffers trailing Oscar and Luisa, having crossed Independence Avenue, walked north toward the Capitol, then quickly split. One strode briskly toward the main guardhouse; the second veered between a clump of bushes and the rear of the enclosed barrier-gate guardhouse. Visitors were always struck by how short, open, and easily traversed the distance was from the street to the Capitol steps.

On the south side of Independence, the traffic officers, grateful for the break from having to stand in the street, headed up the steps toward the warmth inside the Longworth Building. They couldn't see the guardhouse because of the shrubbery.

The two guards in the main guardhouse, their attention on Independence Avenue, didn't see the man with the silenced automatic pistol.

Behind them, the single guard in the barrier guardhouse noticed a man holding something. What did he have in his hands?

He saw his friends in the first guardhouse crumple without a word.

He was rising from his chair when the bullets crashed into his back, driving his face into the glass above his console.

8:18.15 P.M.

After the rush of members and staffers had swept by them, the two guards on the Capitol steps had moved to talk about the upcoming Super Bowl; that's when they heard muffled explosive sounds in the direction of the main guardhouse.

As they turned toward Independence Avenue, glass shattered just beyond the steps.

They crouched, going for their guns—totally unaware of the presumed staffer moving rapidly up the steps from below and behind them.

He sent them sprawling with his silenced automatic pistol. He raced upstairs toward the revolving door, his eyes on three actual staff members.

One staffer seemed to be doing a jerking dance, unable to decide what to do. The other two stared, arms stretched forward, as the gunman shot them too.

As he threw his left shoulder into the glass panel of the revolving door, he drew an Uzi machine pistol and popped a thirty-shot clip into its bottom.

8:18.16 P.M.

In front of the elevator foyer, Oscar and Luisa fired their pistols point-blank at the doorkeepers and guards, hitting Officer Donahue in the midsection as he turned on hearing the first shots, and Officer Susan Rise in her heart and lungs.

After killing doorkeepers Jim Madison and Leeza Dorry, they yanked ski masks down over their faces; they bounded up the three granite steps and through the entrance to the floor of the House of Representatives.

8 : 1 8 . 1 7 P.M.

Luisa retrieved an Uzi machine pistol from under her trench coat; Oscar pulled a Model 29 Smith & Wesson .44 magnum revolver with an eight-inch barrel from under his trench coat.

Oscar shattered the skull of Speaker Jim Purdy at the Republican leadership table and picked off Representative Barbara Laine next to him.

Holding the monster pistol with both hands and moving it in a smooth sweep, he then quickly picked off the guards just inside each door of the gallery. He squeezed off each shot with dispatch, yet each was deliberate and well aimed. Not once did he break his lethal rhythm with a miss.

Luisa fired point-blank into the House members gathered in the aisle directly in front of her.

When Oscar was finished with the guards on the gallery perimeter, he glanced up smiling as the guard posted at the gallery door above and behind the chamber entrance peered over the rail. With a smooth half pivot he shot the guard in the face. Then, swiftly exchanging his revolver for an Uzi machine pistol, he swiveled into action.

8 : 1 8 . 1 7 P.M.

She fell forward on the Republican leadership table.

She felt the warm blood. A pool drained out onto the table. Lying there, listening to the bursts of gunfire and the screaming, she could feel the blood spread under her. She tried to move but couldn't. She willed her arm to move, but nothing happened. She was paralyzed and she was bleeding heavily.

Who was doing this?

Sprawled on the table beside the corpse of Jim Purdy, Laine thought she knew. She had actively supported the right of women to have an abortion, which had resulted in an avalanche of hate mail, including four death threats from self-righteous antiabortion zealots.

What Barbara Laine thought as she lost consciousness amid the chatter of automatic weapons was:

It's them.

8:18.18 P.M.

Crouching just in front of Oscar, firing her Uzi in bursts, Luisa caught Speaker pro tempore Tim Nichols with his gavel in the air, uncomprehending and suffused with a rising anger at the unwarranted commotion among the Democrats to his right. If they wanted to horse around, why didn't they go to the cloakroom?

The impact of the bullets lifted the scowling Nichols off his feet and slammed him back into the Speaker's chair. But Nichols rose, looking like a maddened bulldog, eyes bulging with rage. He then pitched forward, plunging headlong over the dais, sending his gavel sailing into the well below.

8:18.18 P.M.

As the screams of terror erupted, the chief page of the minority, Sheila Markowitz, looked up from her desk against the far right wall. Markowitz, the stern mother-surrogate to the teenage pages, stood as if conducting a small chamber group.

"Everybody on the floor. Now! Do it!"

The pages had developed a deep respect for Mrs. Markowitz's devotion to the House and its traditions and would have been mortified to fail her in her quest to meet every member's need, no matter how mundane. They had long since learned to leap to their feet immediately when she told them to jump from their low benches.

"Flatten out!" she commanded.

They flattened out.

When the last page was down, Mrs. Markowitz started to join them, yelling, "Don't look up! Don't look up!" They obeyed her without question, saving their lives as she gave her own.

8:18.19 P.M.

The trailing gunman, pushing past the revolving door into the alcove, shot three people unlucky enough to step out of the left side elevator at precisely the wrong time. The operator was next.

The elevator door on the right opened. The bogus staffer stepped smartly in front of it and sprayed a burst inside, dropping four people and the operator.

He quickly stepped into the hall in front of the chamber entrance and turned left. The Speaker's lobby entrance doors were in front of him and to the right.

When a uniformed guard stepped out from the Speaker's lobby, the gunman pulped his heart with a quick burst from his machine pistol and coolly replaced the clip.

8:18.20 P.M.

Oscar and Luisa, standing shoulder to shoulder, fired a relentless barrage into the members choking the aisle in front of them. The passageway was so narrow that members literally could not walk down it side by side. First-time visitors to the gallery were always surprised to observe how *small*, how *little*, how *narrow* everything was.

Oscar and Luisa took different firing lanes, Luisa to the left, Oscar to the right. The firepower of their thirty-bullet clips was stupefying.

The impact of the hail of bullets slammed bodies together, and the wounded members and corpses directly in front of Oscar and

Luisa—thrust together in macabre embrace—literally had no room to fall.

When the firing started, many members had stood looking at the aisle entrance instead of diving on the floor to take advantage of whatever protection was offered by their steel-backed seats. Others flung themselves over the armrests of the seats, leaving their backs and the tops of their heads exposed to the gunfire.

The eyes of the dead looked surprised, confused, and confounded.

8:18.22 P.M.

Mitch Webster, hearing the gunfire, dived for the floor.

He felt something warm and hot on his face. Blood.

His friend Charlie Toguchi, lying beside him, had been hit in the carotid artery, and his blood was squirting wildly.

Webster grabbed at Toguchi's throat in an effort to stop the blood.

8:18.24 P.M.

The narrow House cloakrooms—one for the Democrats and one for the Republicans—were located behind the sides and rear wall of the House.

Kenneth O'Keefe, the manager of the Democratic cloakroom, and his two chief assistants were at the counter of the cloakroom behind the east wall of the chamber floor. The entrance was to the immediate right of where the terrorists now stood. This stretch of cloakroom had two banks of telephone booths that were always in use by members.

When the shooting started, O'Keefe was watching the vote count on C-SPAN.

He looked out the door facing the chamber toward the Democratic entrance.

Seeing Oscar and Luisa, he stepped to the middle of the banks of telephone booths. He cupped his hands around his mouth and called, "Get down! Get down! They're shooting. Get down!"

He then careened up the passage between the phone booths to the stainless-steel snack bar.

He bounced off the snack bar and turned left into the part of the cloakroom—to the rear of the Democratic side—that contained ancient blue leather chairs and equally ancient couches upon which members of the minority could doze—if they were able to shut out the constant din of conversation.

Several startled members crouched on the floor. They had been watching a NASCAR stock-car race on ESPN while they waited for the total to be announced and the crowd to clear, but the volume was too high, and the zooming of the stock cars competed with the shooting on the floor just outside the door.

Now they looked up at O'Keefe, blinking, their faces asking, What is happening?

"They're shooting out there," O'Keefe shouted. "We just stay put and shut up. They might not know we're back here."

8:18.30 P.M.

Taking care not to trip over a corpse or a wounded member or slip on the already blood-soaked carpet, Oscar and Luisa fired down the narrow aisles at the trapped members.

As they fired, swiftly replacing spent thirty-round clips with fresh ones, they shouted: *"Las cucarachas, las cucarachas!"*

Emptying and replacing thirty-round clips, they slaughtered *las cucarachas.*

They killed and maimed. . . .

And killed and maimed some more. . . .

SEVEN

The driver of the Ford Taurus parked on K Street, having picked up the driver of the Wal-Mart rig, circled the block, and turned south onto South Capitol from L Street.

It was five blocks from L and South Capitol to the Frederick Douglass Memorial Bridge over the Anacostia River.

Oscar and Luisa retreated from the chamber, joining the man who stood guard over the dead and dying in the hallway and alcove; they pushed through the revolving door and started down the granite stairs, taking the low, wide steps in quick time as the two helicopters settled softly down on the oval-shaped lawn fifty yards away.

The two men who had killed the guardhouse policemen waited at the edge of the lawn, thirty yards from the bottom of the stairs.

8:18.40 P.M.

Leo Carney of Oregon, a self-styled "people's" conservative elected in the statewide shakeup following Ron Wyden's senate victory in 1996, was caught by C-SPAN's cameras as he passed behind the Republican leadership table. There was some irony in this; Carney was known for his vigorous opposition to any limit on the right to keep and bear arms.

Carney, soaked with blood, screamed, "Bastards!" and lurched— falling over the bodies of his dying colleagues—through the entrance into the hall.

Carney pushed through the revolving door and headed for the top of the stairs, where he screamed more invective at the retreating terrorists before he stumbled down the stairs in hopeless pursuit.

The dramatic action on the stairway was videotaped by two camera-bearing tourists, Bill and Anne Terwilliger, from Carson City, Nevada. This was the Terwilliger Tape, later to become as famous as Emil Zapruder's famous 1963 taping of bullets striking John F. Kennedy in the shadow of the Texas Schoolbook Depository.

8:18.50 P.M.

All five terrorists sprinted forty feet across the oval lawn to the waiting helicopters and scrambled aboard; Oscar and Luisa got into one helicopter while their associates took the other.

The helicopters, led by the one containing Oscar and Luisa, rose in tandem and darted between a sugar maple planted by House Speaker Champ Clark of Missouri on May 1, 1912, and an American beech planted by Representative Joseph Walsh of Massachusetts on April 15, 1920.

They flew straight at the four decks of granite stairs leading up to the eight Doric colums. As they got to the bottom, they shot straight up and over the roof of the House of Representatives.

San Francisco

5:19 P.M.

The baby-faced man with the cleft chin turned his back to the cold wind blowing in from the Pacific. He listened momentarily to the wail of sirens converging on the intersection of Polk and Turk Streets, then punched a number on a cellular telephone.

A man answered, "Yes?"

"Matt Underhill?"

"Yes, it is. If you'll excuse me for a moment, I have an intersection coming up and . . ."

The cleft-chinned man, humming the opening bars of Beethoven's Fifth Symphony to himself, tapped 8887 to the beat of the music. Smiling, he hung up.

He dialed a second number.

The phone rang four times. Then a recorded voice said, "This is Matt. I can't answer the phone right now, but you can leave a message at the beep."

He waited.

The phone beeped.

He quickly tapped 9998.

He slipped the phone back into his coat pocket and pulled the collar higher around his neck. Still humming Beethoven's dramatic bars, he continued walking away from the black smoke. He was quite pleased with himself. Fun to plant goodies in advance then zap them by phone. The twit who called himself Matt Underhill, little Mr. Hot-Damn Internet man, had literally lost his head to an exploding cellular phone when he had punched 8887. Cleft-chin grinned. Then he'd sent the nerd's house up in flames by popping a loaded answering machine. Hee-hoo!

EIGHT

Carter Commission Exhibit 18-Jan-G3

Statement taken on 19 January 2000, by FBI Special Agent Foster Dunn, of Carl Meyer, clerk of the U.S. House of Representatives; re: his actions following the attack on the House floor.

MEYER: I was downstairs in my office doing some paperwork when the attack started. I had C-SPAN turned on, of course; you may not know it, but we recieve a direct transmission from the floor, so there is no sound—no commentary or music—as there is on the public broadcast. So when he called me, I didn't know what he was talking about. When I looked up, it took me several moments to grasp what was happening.

DUNN: You say "he" called you. Who called?

MEYER: A man's voice. I'm not sure who. I looked up, as I said, and there was this terrible jumble of scenes. The cameras are fixed, and there are only a half dozen or so angles of viewing—the Speaker's dais, the majority and minority tables where those controlling the debates stand, and the majority and minority rostrums in the well. There's no director on the floor. The mikes are voice-activated, and the cameras focus on whoever is speaking.

DUNN: When did the call come?

MEYER: At exactly 8:17. I remember because I looked up to check the clock. As I saw those horrifying images on the screen, I knew every detail would later be important. So I can say with certainty that it was 8:17.

DUNN: What did you do then?

MEYER: I was transfixed by what I saw. At first I thought maybe a fight had broken out. Members were stumbling in and out of the picture, and banging into one another. Some dove to the floor of the well while others seemed flung or slammed toward it. Tim Nichols was sprawled over the dais. The aisle next to the minority table was jammed with members with their mouths wide open and their bodies at crazy angles. I saw blood spurting and silent screaming. I didn't know what was happening, and I didn't want to get stuck in the elevator when I was needed. For all I knew, we were in some kind of siege situation. Silent screaming!

DUNN: Take your time, Mr. Meyer.

MEYER: I knew my duty. I had to get to the floor as soon as possible. If something happens to the Speaker and the majority leader the rules of the House provide that I take the chair until a new Speaker is chosen. I would be temporarily in charge.

DUNN: What did you do then?

MEYER: I ran for the door. I ran down the hall. I ran upstairs to the House floor. The scene was chaotic, as you know. The floor was littered with dead and dying members and there was blood everywhere. The aisle directly in front of the entrance was an absolute tangle of bodies. The . . .

DUNN: No hurry, Mr. Meyer.

MEYER: They . . . they . . .

DUNN: This is hard for us all, Mr. Meyer.

MEYER: The dirty sons of bitches.

DUNN: [Pause.] You were telling me about arriving on the House floor. . . .

MEYER: One minute you've got people calling one another "craven curs" and "running dogs for the rich," and the next minute they're down there in that blood doing their best to help their comrades. It . . . I . . . I'm okay. I really am. [Clears his throat.] I went straight to the Speaker's dais, which was my responsibility. I called for a motion for adjournment and got one. I can't tell you who offered it. My hands were shaking. I . . . I called for ayes and nays. I said the ayes have it and banged the gavel stand. I couldn't find the gavel itself. The floor before me looked awful, I can tell you. That was the single worst moment of my life. All those members bleeding and dying. The Capitol physician and his staff were already on the floor, but they were overwhelmed. All we could do was wait for the ambulances to arrive.

DUNN: What was the time when you banged the stand?

MEYER: I checked my watch. It was twenty-five minutes after eight. I also fixed the time on the wall clock opposite the dais. I immediately set about trying to see if I could find any of the leadership alive, but I couldn't. It was paramount that we reestablish order. Then I called the White House hot-line number on my cellular phone.

8:19.30 P.M.

Oscar piloted the lead helicopter.

As he passed over the roof of the House wing of the Capitol, he glanced to his right at Thomas Crawford's bronze statue, *Freedom*, atop the Capitol dome. This formidable lady wore a helmet with a fierce-looking eagle's head on top and large stars, rather like thorns, around her brow.

"*Ella se ve con frio,*" Oscar said. (She looks cold.)

"*Preocupada*," Luisa added. (Worried.)

Oscar steered the helicopter across the tops of the meeting rooms on the west front of the Capitol. Keeping the chopper barely off the ground, he piloted it over the frozen turf directly at the Capitol reflecting pool six hundred feet dead ahead.

He split the five-hundred-foot space between the peace monument on their left and a statue of James A. Garfield on their right and was immediately over the base of the fan-shaped reflecting pool.

Slightly over one mile dead ahead lay the Washington Monument. One and one-fourth miles to the northwest, behind a block-deep, six-block-long triangle of federal buildings on the south side of Pennsylvania Avenue, lay the White House.

Oscar aimed the Kiowa straight ahead, due west, toward the Washington Monument.

8 : 20 P . M .

Carter Commission Exhibit 18-Jan-C12

Statement taken on 19 January 2000, by FBI Special Agent William Fung of Officer Lasondra Williams of the District of Columbia Police Department.

WILLIAMS: Me and my partner, Officer Harold Morse, were conducting a vehicular patrol of southwest Washington on the evening of January 18. Officer Morse was driving. We were on First and P Streets near Fort McNair when we got the call.

FUNG: What time was that?

WILLIAMS: At eighteen minutes after eight o'clock. We were told we had a Situation Beta.

FUNG: An attack on the Capitol.

WILLIAMS: Yes sir. If it's Alpha, it's the White House. Beta is Capitol Hill. We were to proceed to South Capitol Street and block off all southbound traffic. Beta calls for all streets surrounding Capitol Hill to be sealed off. We were just six blocks from South Capitol, so it didn't take us long. As we pulled up to the street, we saw that a large Wal-Mart truck had been abandoned at the curb on the west side, blocking one lane of outward-bound traffic.

FUNG: Had you been told that helicopters had been launched from a truck?

WILLIAMS: No sir, we had not. Situation Beta had just gone out. I'm not sure our people knew anything about the truck then. We were told to block South Capitol. That's all.

FUNG: What happened then?

WILLIAMS: We decided to block the street at the point where the truck had been abandoned.

FUNG: So you could use the truck to help you with your work.

WILLIAMS: Yes sir. That was the idea. We pulled the squad car sideways to the traffic and pulled on our vests as we got out.

FUNG: Your bulletproof vests.

WILLIAMS: Affirmative. I got out with my flashlight to wave the oncoming cars to a halt, and Officer Morse ran over to check the truck. This was a Situation Beta, and we didn't know what we were up against. The truck was at our backs.

FUNG: Did you suspect that it might have been part of the attack on the Capitol?

WILLIAMS: We didn't know. We didn't see any driver. It was illegally parked, and apparently abandoned, although we didn't know for sure. We did know that it was blocking traffic and we had a job to do.

FUNG: You had no idea who you were dealing with or how the Capitol had been attacked.

WILLIAMS: That's right, sir. Nobody had said the House of Representatives had been fired on. Only that an attack on the Capitol had taken place. When we get a Beta, our job is to do what we're told. There was no time for discussion.

FUNG: I see. Okay. Go on.

WILLIAMS: Well . . . [Clears her throat.]

FUNG: Take your time.

WILLIAMS: I . . . He . . .

FUNG: No hurry.

WILLIAMS: We were part of something real big, we knew that. We wanted to do good. We wanted to hold up our end. The department had been taking a lot of heat the last several years, and we didn't want to let people down.

FUNG: You didn't do anything wrong. Nobody's to blame. I'm just trying to find out what happened. Maybe you saw something that will be useful.

WILLIAMS: You see, there wasn't anybody in the cab, and we were rushed and trying to think of everything we should be doing. What happened was, Harold just hopped up on the running board of the truck to take a quick look into the empty cab when . . .

FUNG: Easy, easy.

WILLIAMS: [Pauses.] The whole rig evaporated like it'd been nuked or something. The blast just shot out, taking everything in its path. If I hadn't been shielded by our squad car, I'd have been gone. The shock was incredible. Lucky I was facing the traffic. The blast knocked me off my feet, and I got ripped across my back with flying glass. If I hadn't been wearing my vest, I'd be out of here.

FUNG: But you saw no people?

WILLIAMS: No, sir.

FUNG: Was there anything at all about the truck that made it stand out?

WILLIAMS: No, it was just a big Wal-Mart truck. You see them all the time. Wal-Mart's a comfortable kind of place, you know. You can relax there. The prices are okay. No pretense, if you know what I mean. Hassle-free.

8:20 P.M.

Carter Commission Exhibit 18-Jan-C24

Statement taken by FBI Special Agent Raymond Vannest on 19 January 2000 of Marine Corps Captain Leonard Collins, duty officer

*at the Pentagon's Emergency Command Center from 1700 hours
18 January to 0100 hours 19 January.*

VANNEST: What we're trying to do here, Captain Collins, is
establish a precise chronology of what happened, and when it
happened. This is not to lay blame, but to establish a foundation
for our investigation. Will you tell me what your responsibilities
are and what you did?

COLLINS: Yes sir. We play a key role in Situation Beta, which
is the coordinated federal and local response to any possible
attack on Capitol Hill. We have helicopters serviced, fueled, and
available at all times together with pilots in the ready room. I received a call from the District Police at 2019 hours saying we had
a Situation Beta. Two helicopters bearing terrorists were fleeing
west over the Mall.

VANNEST: I see. Go on.

COLLINS: I called the ready room and told Lieutenant Boylan
and the others to get their buns in the air immediately if not
sooner.

VANNEST: Lieutenant Boylan being?

COLLINS: Lieutenant Dan Boylan. He was the senior pilot on
duty, sir. He flew the lead helicopter. A big, fast Sikorsky AH-64
Apache. He was the first one off the ground.

VANNEST: And what time was it when you told Lieutenant
Boylan and his crew to scramble?

COLLINS: That was exactly 2020 hours, sir. I can be certain
of that because Situation Beta requires us to keep a precise log
of our communications.

8:22 P.M.

President Thomas Erikson, who wanted Representative Barbara
Laine's money bill to pass in order to fight money laundering and
spare trees, remembered well the fight over introducing one-dollar
coins in the mid-nineties. So he had made a point of watching
C-SPAN coverage.

When the shooting had begun, he, too, was initially stunned as Ferde Grofe's *Grand Canyon Suite* masked the confusion.

The President was instantly surrounded by staff members and military attachés issuing urgent orders and inquiries into secured transceivers.

Outside the White House, Secret Service agents and District police officers raced into the streets with guns drawn.

Within a half minute or less, the House had become a cauldron as the classical music played on.

Wounded and dying congressmembers lay twisting and writhing behind the Democratic leadership table. In back of them, several of their anguished colleagues were draped across the backs of seats, spurting blood. Bloody, shocked members, weeping, crying out, crawled and stumbled over their fallen comrades.

The beeper went off on Erikson's Capitol Hill hot line.

Erikson, his mouth dry and his hands shaking so badly he could hardly keep the receiver at his ear, listened.

It was the House clerk, Carl Meyer.

"I saw it on C-SPAN, Carl."

"Speaker Purdy is among the dead, Mr. President. And the majority leader, I think. I'm not sure I . . ."

"Then you're in charge of the House, Carl."

"Yes, Mr. President."

"We both keep as calm as possible and do what we have to do."

"Yes sir, Mr. President."

"Tell me what's been done."

"The Capitol police have issued a Situation Beta. Ambulances are on the way."

"I want nobody to leave the building except the wounded. Nobody."

"Yes sir, Mr. President."

"I will call General Samuels and put Contingency Delta into effect."

"Superseding Beta."

"Correct," Erikson said.

NINE

Five thousand feet short of the Washington Monument, Oscar passed between the East Building of the National Gallery of Art on his right and the headquarters of the Department of Health and Human Services on his left.

Four thousand feet shy of the Monument, he passed between the National Gallery of Art on his right and the National Air and Space Museum on his left.

Three thousand feet from the monolith, he passed between the National Archives on Pennsylvania Avenue and the round Hirshhorn Museum on Independence Avenue.

Two thousand feet away, Oscar passed between the National

Museum of National History on his right and the Smithsonian Institution on his left.

He passed between the National Museum of American History on his right and the Agriculture Department on his left.

He was now less than a thousand feet from the Washington Monument looming directly ahead.

He glanced to his right—to the northwest—past the corner Commerce Department building at Fifteenth and Constitution: a half mile away, the White House.

Oscar abruptly changed his bearing, breaking the Kiowa sharply to the southwest at a forty-five-degree angle.

He looked toward the northwest shore of the Tidal Basin, fifteen hundred feet dead ahead.

8:22.30 P.M.

Lieutenant Dan Boylan, pilot of the Sikorsky Apache, was above the middle of the Potomac River when he first spotted the fleeing helicopters. Boylan spoke into the voice-activated mike around his neck, a device designed to keep both hands free in the heat of battle.

"This is Roger Six here. I have the rabbits under observation. Two dark blue choppers on the northeast side of the Tidal Basin. They look like Kiowas, but it's hard to tell because of the fog over the water. They're flying ten to twelve feet off the ground and coming right at me, headed for the Tidal Basin."

"Keep them in sight, Roger Six."

"Should we smoke 'em?" Boylan's Apache was a powerful attack helicopter, giving him the advantage over the smaller, slower Kiowas.

"Negative, Roger Six. They are to be forced down, and the occupants captured alive. We have more choppers in the air to give you assistance. Keep them under observation until you have help."

"Got it," Boylan said. "There's nowhere they can go, anyway. They're dead meat."

Oscar saw the helicopters dead ahead. They were flying without running lights, but he could still see them in the fog, looking like large insects hurrying through the night. *"Se ven derecho, amigos. Se están acercando rápido."* (Look straight ahead, friends. Closing fast.)

"Estamos lejos sobre el lado del Potomac," said the pilot of the second helicopter. (On the far side of the Potomac.)

Oscar said, *"Nos falta una milla, exactamente."* (Almost one mile away exactly.)

"Suerte que estaba con nosotros. Quien se hubiera imaginado?" the other pilot said. (Luck is with us. Who'd have dreamed?)

"Tenemos treinta segundos," Luisa said. (We've got thirty seconds.)

Oscar said, *"Si trabajamos correctamente, nosotros estaremos casi directamente sobre el centro del Tidal Basin. Disminuye tu velocidad."* (If we work it right, we'll be almost directly over the center of the Tidal Basin. Cut your speed.)

"Viente y siete segundos." (Twenty-seven seconds.)

"Necesitamos regresar aquí." (We need to come back here.)

Luisa licked her lips. *"Veinte y cinco segundos y contando."* (Twenty-five seconds and counting.)

Boylan's Apache, now above the bridge over the inlet connecting the Tidal Basin with the Potomac River, was on a collision course with the approaching Kiowas.

Boylan had his orders. He swung wide to let the terrorist helicopters pass. "Gunners at the ready. Our orders are not to fire. If we're fired upon, we'll back off. Do not fire back. Hold your fire."

Boylan closed on the Kiowas as they passed over the northeast shore of the Tidal Basin.

"I see a pilot and two passengers in the lead chopper."

"Got it, Roger Six. Be careful."

Boylan said, "The second chopper has a pilot and three passengers."

The lead helicopter made an oblique left, headed straight for the Jefferson Memorial.

Boylan followed. Did the idiots really think they were going to outrun him? Boylan had flown this same chopper in the Gulf War. Boylan was a very, very good pilot, quick and aggressive, and he knew it. No fucking way these assholes were going to lose him.

He flew on their right flank, so he could keep an eye on both helicopters.

8:23 P.M.

Marine Corps lieutenant general Jeremiah Samuels had trained for this very situation. He had reviewed the lengthy documents outlining his responsibilities under Contingency Delta until he could almost recite them. He knew precisely what had to be done, by whom, and when. This was a career moment, beyond all question.

Speaking in a deep, throaty rattle, Samuels, commander in chief of Contingency Delta, said, "Mr. President, have you . . ." He cleared his throat.

"I watched it on television, Jerry, and I talked to the House clerk, Carl Meyers. Jim Purdy is dead and Meyers is in charge. He's got ambulances on the way."

"I'm informed that the terrorists are fleeing northwest in two helicopters. We have Apaches from the naval station in hot pursuit. This is a Contingency Delta."

"Absolutely," Erikson said.

"We have a helicopter on the way to pick you up. Your pilot will be informed where he is to take you after you're aloft. You are Able Flyer today. Vice President Gregg is Green Mountain. I am Gopher Two."

"Able Flyer. Green Mountain. Gopher Two. Got it."

Contingency Delta—the largest federal response to an attack on the city—was an automatic contingency plan, giving specific, systematic instructions to the military services, the District police, and the FBI. Under Delta, the city was in effect put under martial law. Specified buildings and areas were to be sealed, including all those on Capitol Hill—the Capitol, House and Senate office buildings, and the United States Supreme Court—plus the White House, the Pentagon, the FBI buildings, and the CIA complex in Langley, Virginia, across the Potomac River from Washington. Until Delta was modified or canceled, all American armed forces throughout the world were put on battle alert.

"I want the terrorists captured alive. The nation can't take ambiguity in something like this. We must know precisely who is responsible."

"Those are their instructions, sir."

8:23.50 P.M.

The driver of the Ford Taurus parked the car behind a rusting 1982 Chevrolet Cavalier sedan, originally an off-yellow color, now mottled with patches of green and brown primer. Its left front fender was crumpled, and the door was caved in on the passengers' side. The hood and trunk were covered with brown primer, and the handles were missing from the rear doors.

The Chevrolet had gone past the stage of "good transportation" or "fixer-upper." It was one step from recycle time.

The driver got out of the Taurus. The cold night air was electric with the wailing of sirens. He and his passenger stood for a moment looking back over the Anacostia River toward the Capitol.

The driver removed a set of keys from his pocket, slipped behind the steering wheel of the Chevrolet, and turned on the ignition; the Chevrolet's engine fired right up and ran steady and true.

As the driver pulled from the curb, he said, *"Adios, cucarchas."*

8:24.10 P.M.

Boylan and the crew of his gunship were looking right at them despite the veil of fog. They were flying serenely along, scarcely above the water—the pilots seemingly oblivious to his presence on their flank.

They were six hundred feet in front of the domed marble memorial to Thomas Jefferson when the two helicopters exploded simultaneously, blowing machines and passengers into the Tidal Basin.

TEN

arl Meyer looked out over the sea of blood and the dead and dying as doctors went about the grisly task of determining which wounded congressmembers needed help now, and who could wait.

This was medical triage. The members who had the best chances of surviving would be taken first, so as not to sacrifice probability for prayer. There was no distinguishing among party leaders and freshmen members of Congress here.

The most seriously wounded would be taken to the recently reopened Capitol Hill Hospital six blocks east of the Hart Senate Office Building on Constitution Avenue. So as not to overload Capitol

Hill's emergency facilities, the less severely wounded would be taken to other Washington-area hospitals.

Those requiring extraordinary surgery would be moved from Capitol Hill Hospital to Walter Reed, the U.S. Army Medical Center, on Georgia Avenue at the northern tip of the city limits. Here was where President Dwight Eisenhower was taken after his heart attack in 1955; a quarter of a century later, President Ronald Reagan was taken to Walter Reed after he was shot.

The parking lot in front of the east entrance of the House wing was a clutter of ambulances, from which piled paramedics, doctors, and nurses. The Capitol area wailed with sirens.

Overhead, the air was filled with helicopters.

9:17 P.M.

Elphedius Williams, aka Speedy Bill, grinned. He had a nice set of ivories, everybody said so. "Leeyou, Leeyou, will you take a look at that." He turned the key. "This mothah works. See there. No problem."

"Speed! Speed! My man! My man! What kind of dumb mothah fuckah would park a brand-new Taurus in a place like this?" Lucius "Leeyou" Benson shook his head. Benson was small, but all muscles. He glanced up the street. "Ain't nobody to be seen, that's a fact."

"Some dumb mothah," Williams said, as he opened the door and slid onto the driver's seat.

Benson scurried around the back of the car and threw open the door to the passengers' side. "Left a brand-new Ford Taurus in the dark like this. Imagine."

"Maybe one of these here keys of mine will fit in the ignition. Do you suppose?"

"Do it, Speed. Do it. Do it. Try it out."

"Well, will you look at that? Just slides right in there smooth as a working girl's pussy."

"Let's have us a little fun."

Speedy Bill turned his wrist and the abandoned Taurus exploded with such force it left a huge divot on the side of the road.

8:30.15 P.M.

At the height of the Cold War, the government had kept an elaborate underground command and communications center in the Virginia mountains for use in a national emergency. But with the fall of the Soviet empire and the dismantling of the ICBMs, that had been abandoned as too expensive to maintain and not secure—its location was an open secret to local residents, and any terrorist could read the stories written about it in the *Washington Post* and the *New York Times.*

Advances in computer and communications technology had enabled the Pentagon to maintain a secret system of shifting command sites for national emergencies, one for the President, another for the Vice President. One month the President might go to Virginia, the next month to Maryland, Pennsylvania, Delaware, or West Virginia.

Now President Thomas Erikson, grim-faced, stared out of the window of the presidential helicopter at the lights of the Virginia suburbs below.

Erikson was being ferried west to the current emergency command, a corporate retreat in Shenandoah National Park. This was in the Blue Ridge Mountains of Rappahannock County, in western Virginia. Another helicopter was flying Vice President Gregg to another retreat sixty miles northwest, near Hanging Rock, in the Shenandoah Mountains of Hampshire County, West Virginia.

The President, dry-mouthed, found the floor as interesting as the lights below. He rested his chin in the heel of his left hand, waiting by the communications panel for word from Gopher Two.

Marine helicopters had been in hot pursuit of the fleeing terrorists. Erikson prayed most fervently that General Jeremiah Samuels's people would be able to catch the terrorists alive and keep them alive. The lesson of the murder of Lee Harvey Oswald was that anything else would be a disaster for the country.

Both incoming and outgoing communications from the presidential helicopter were automatically scrambled and descrambled by onboard computers, but in order to demonstrate all possible care, they still used old-fashioned, romantic personal codes.

"Able Flyer this is Gopher Two. Able Flyer this is Gopher Two. Do you read me?"

Erikson licked his lips. "This is Able Flyer, come in Gopher Two."

"I regret to tell you, Able Flyer, that the two helicopters carrying the bandits have exploded above the Tidal Basin, killing all aboard."

"Exploded! What do you mean?"

"On their own, Able Flyer. Directly in front of the Jefferson Memorial. No shots were exchanged. Our people returned to base with their rations of ammunition intact and their barrels cold."

"Dead." Erikson sighed. "We needed them alive, Gopher, we really did."

"I know. I know."

"A suicide attack?"

"Could be. But why would they go to all that trouble to plan and execute an attack and then blow it like that? They got the jump on us and had a chance to escape."

"You did your best, Gopher. Have you had any other activity?"

"No sir. We've established two perimeters, a capital city defense around the Beltway, and a line around the Capitol. The Capitol perimeter runs from the Potomac east on K Street to Eighth Street, Eighth south to M Street, and M west to the Potomac. We're also looping a perimeter around the Pentagon on the west bank of the Potomac."

"After we land, I'll broadcast word that the government is proceeding as usual and is in no immediate danger, although the armed forces are on combat alert as part of the routine security drill. People need to know there hasn't been a coup or anything like that, and that there is no reason for alarm. I'll tell everyone to remain calm, that we will find out who did this pronto, and et cetera. I'll promise a full report tomorrow night with hourly briefings by my press office in

the meantime. That will give us a full day to find out what we're dealing with."

"Good idea, Able Flyer."

"When something happens, I want to know about it. If we don't
get any evidence that this is the first step of a larger attack, I want to
return in the morning. The public needs to be assured that I judiciously retreated after the attack and returned to take charge when
the danger passed."

"If they hit again, it will likely be quickly, before we have our
people in place. I'll have Dobermans around your pad before dawn,
Able Flyer. I'll keep you posted."

ELEVEN

Looking back, Thomas Erikson supposed the act of memorizing was a foolish exercise. The Japanese school system was famous for requiring schoolchildren to memorize things, but Erikson supposed few countries outside of Asia did it anymore, and certainly not the United States.

But the principal at little Thomas Erikson's school in the western prairies, a Southerner and a former officer in the marines, believed in the practice. So students at all grades in his school had memorized something. They memorized their multiplication tables. They memorized capitals of all the states. And they memorized the dates and places of American history, especially the Civil War battles.

The principal, explaining this in his annual pep talk before the student body, said America was bonded by the blood shed in the Civil War. To forget that forfeited blood was to dishonor those who had died, and so, from Antietam to Vicksburg, students in his school were forced to remember the dates, places, and terrible numbers of the dead, wounded, and missing.

Now President Erikson, looking out of the window of the presidential helicopter, peered down at the fields and fences and cottages and country roads of Virginia where so much patriotic blood had been shed.

Three of the first four presidents, George Washington, Thomas Jefferson, and James Madison, were Virginians. Washington had gotten the country through the first critical years of the new Republic. Jefferson, who had been ambassador to France, secretary of state, vice president, and president, wrote the Declaration of Independence. Madison, the fourth president, had written the most critical and insightful of *The Federalist Papers* that had shepherded the Constitution into existence.

What would those determined Virginians be thinking if they were here with him now, riding in the presidential helicopter?

General Jeremiah Samuels, calling from Washington on the scrambled security radio band, interrupted Erikson's thoughts. The daily list of codes having been changed, the President had become Rambo Man. General Samuels was now Bucko Boy.

"Rambo Man, Bucko Boy here."

Erikson ran his hand down his jaw. "Go ahead, Bucko Boy."

"Your pad's secure, Rambo Man."

"Just a second, Bucko. Let me look at my map." Erikson unfolded a map of the District of Columbia. "Okay, go ahead, Bucko. Tell me what it looks like."

"Our jarheads have established a perimeter at Nineteenth Street on the west, K Street on the north, Twelfth Street on the east, and Constitution Avenue on the south."

"And the Capitol?"

"We've got that secured too. That's a seven-sided zone as provided by Delta."

"And that is?"

"Running clockwise from the ellipse in front of Union Station to the north, we've secured Massachusetts Avenue southeast to Stanton Park."

"Just a second, Bucko." With his finger, Erikson traced Massachusetts Avenue from the ellipse. "Got it. Go ahead."

"Fourth Street south to North Carolina Avenue."

"Okay."

"North Carolina southwest to E Street."

"I see that."

"Canal Street from E Street northwest to Independence Avenue."

"Got it."

"And Third Street north to Constitution for a slight jag east, then Louisiana Avenue northeast back to the ellipse."

"Yes."

"We've got people going through every room of every building inside those perimeters."

"Good thinking," Erikson said. "Until we get a handle on who these people are, we don't know what they're up to."

"How long before you will be arriving?"

Erikson glanced at his watch. "The pilot's following Delta to the letter. He says about twenty-five minutes."

"I don't think we should deviate from Delta, Rambo Man. You're right. Until we know who's out there and what they're up to, we have to be careful."

Momentarily forgetting codes, almost whispering, Erikson asked, "Jerry, what's the body count?"

"Dozens, dozens, Rambo Man. We're still putting it together."

"Bucko, has it occurred to you that if this is a domestic conspiracy, we could have another civil war on our hands? We can't forget Oklahoma City. We were sailing along, pretending those screwball militias didn't exist until *boom!* The militia movement never went away. We've still got 'em out there in the mountains reconstituting themselves. They're still paranoid. The attorney general tells me if anything they're more virulent than ever."

Samuels said nothing for a moment. Then he said, "Yes. I've thought of that. But I don't think it's likely. This is the year 2000, not 1861."

"The public has become infected by the idea of a political millenium. It's been building for the last five or six years. People want big change. They're not sure what they want exactly, but they yearn for change, dramatic stuff, not just politics as usual."

Samuels said, "Out of chaos, rebirth. Out of the ashes, Phoenix rises. Jesus is crucified and is resurrected. Out of the misery of the Great Depression, Franklin Roosevelt gave us the New Deal. Out of the chaos of the Weimar Republic, Adolf Hitler spawned the Third Reich."

Erikson sighed. "Springtime's just around the bend. Seedtime. I'll see you when I get back to camp, Bucko."

"Yes, Rambo Man. Signing off."

On the intercom, the pilot said, "That's the Manassas battlefield below us, Mr. President."

Manassas. They were now thirty miles west of Washington.

The second major engagement of the Civil War—following the earlier carnage at Shiloh, Tennessee—had been fought at Manassas on July 21, 1862, a day in which the Virginia brigade of Confederate general Thomas J. Jackson, earning his nickname "Stonewall," had come to the rescue of General P. G. T. Beauregard.

The Confederates were defeated that day, but they returned on August 29 and 30 for what Southern historians called the Second Run on Manassas. Then General Robert E. Lee, aided by a legendary flanking movement executed by Stonewall Jackson's valiant Virginians, defeated a Federal army of forty-five thousand men under Union general John Pope.

So much struggle, Erikson thought.

So much blood.

Erikson sat back, his shoulders hunched. Ahead, he knew, there would be a firestorm of blame laying, and ultimately, fairly or not, he would be held responsible. Certainly, if he did not lead the country with confidence and obtain results, he would be held accountable. Nothing else mattered now. Only this. His presidency and his place in history depended on it.

After Aldrich Ames and the other spies unearthed in the intelligence bureaucracy in the previous twenty years, Erikson knew he and Vice President Gregg would have to exercise extreme care in the days to come. If the attack on the House turned out to be part of an internal conspiracy, who knew where the traitors lay? Erikson knew he and Gregg would be well advised to get their own man, someone outside government. He would check it out with the former presidents before he decided, but he already knew whom they would likely recommend: James Burlane, who was currently an independent operative using the nom de guerre of Major M. Sidarius Khartoum.

2
PLAYERS AND PIECES

AUTUMN 1999

"What is truth?" said jesting Pilate;
and would not stay for an answer.

—Sir Francis Bacon, from *Of Truth*

ONE

Outside the little stone house, the unusually early snow, twisting and furling down from the blackness, settled softly on the cold branches of leafless trees. Inside, James Burlane, formerly a soldier of the Central Intelligence Agency—long since sacked as being an untrustworthy loner—twisted the gray tip of his Wyatt Earp mustache. He used a slotted spoon to scoop the golden spring rolls from the churning oil in the bottom of his blackened wok. He put the rolls on a mat of paper towels, and carefully began lowering another round of four into the oil.

Ara Schott, a scholarly-appearing crew-cut man with thick-rimmed glasses—formerly deputy director of counterintelligence for the CIA—responded to sharp knocking at the side door that entered into the kitchen.

There stood Jane Griffin, the infamous Cyberfox, enthusiastically stamping the snow from her boots on the doormat. "Yo, dudes!"

Burlane, observing with approving bemusement that Griffin was indeed a fox under her indifferent uptown grunge, said, "Well, well, well . . . Ms. Cyberfox! We ought to call you Commander Z. *Zorro* is Spanish for fox, isn't it?"

Griffin rolled her eyes. "Right!" Griffin, in her midthirties, with short, shaggy auburn hair, wore outsize spectacles over her large brown eyes. She also wore old hiking boots, patched blue jeans, and a blue nylon ski jacket with yellow paint-drips on it. She wore no makeup. She was about five-six and weighed no more than ninety-five to a hundred pounds.

"Little snow tonight," Schott said.

"What goes up, must come down," she said. "Say, what's this?"

"Spring rolls. Hot and fresh. The best." Burlane held out the platter.

"You make these?"

Burlane nodded.

"All right! I like a man who can cook. You do toilets, too? I hate to clean toilets. Yuck!" She cocked her head.

"When I'm forced to," Burlane said. "I like to spare the porcelain by going outside whenever I can. You can take a farmboy off the farm, but you'll never get the farm out of his system. Good for a man to air his equipment out once in a while."

She gestured over her shoulder. "You go outside to pee in this weather?"

Burlane said, "That's when it's best. It's more soulful to relieve yourself in a snowstorm."

She groaned. "I should have asked if you did windows."

Burlane handed her a squeeze bottle of hot ketchup. "I like to dip spring rolls in ketchup laced with Louisiana hot sauce. It's not traditional Chinese, I know, but it still tastes good."

Griffin did as he suggested. "Okay!"

Schott said, "Well, are you going to come to work for us?"

Griffin munched on her spring roll, looking disgusted. "You guys are too much. I come over here to pick up my check, and you're at it again. What part of 'no' don't you understand?"

Burlane grabbed another spring roll. "We've got some brandy in the living room."

Griffin brightened. "Brandy and spring rolls, a classic Chinese combination. Sure."

Burlane loaded up another plate on his way into the living room. He sat on one of the chairs beside the fireplace. "Ara's good on a computer, but not in your league. Mixed Enterprises has to keep up with the times or go out of business. We need a hacker who can work internationally. We're after a number one pick, the best hacker on the market."

She laughed. "A Jackie Joyner-Kersee of a hacker."

"That's it exactly," Schott said. "James and I can't do everything. He does the field stuff. I work my contacts in Langley and the government. We need a hacker. We have more than enough work to keep you busy."

"If we can keep you out of trouble," Burlane said quickly.

"Me? Stay out of trouble?" She giggled, holding her glass up for a hit of brandy.

"What do you say?" Burlane said.

"I don't want to be anybody's wage slave. I'm an independent kind of person."

Burlane said, "We're not after a wage slave. You'd be a full partner. Our investigations encompass the globe, so it's fascinating work. You'd have a full vote. Stock options. Bonuses. Name it."

"Right!"

"But first, you have to take care of your . . . uhhh, problem. How is that going?" Burlane asked.

Griffin looked disconsolate. "I've got myself a macho lawyer. Isn't that what you do after goons from the federal government come trooping into your living room?"

"Is he any good?" Schott said.

She shrugged. "They all say they're good, don't they? They have to justify their fees."

Schott looked concerned. "What will happen? Will you be okay?"

"My lawyer says with a little luck we can win on appeal, otherwise I'll get three years. If they could get away with it, they'd lock me up and throw away the key. They should have given me a medal."

Burlane said, "The mob has too many friends in high places to let some hacker put a list of their bank accounts on the Internet for the whole wide world to see. You embarrassed the FBI."

"Do you think you've got a realistic shot on appeal?" Schott said.

"We'll see," she said. "I'm Cyberfox the computer bandit queen, so they might think they have to make an example of me. You're right, I hurt their stupid pride. Don't be so stingy with that stuff." She held up her glass for more brandy. "Let me tell you, James. These guys aren't talking about their really big fear. In all that crapola on television and in the news magazines they didn't mention their real fear, not once. It was amazing."

"What fear was that?"

"It all started when I got sore because I couldn't afford medical insurance. So I started tracing the flow of money in and out of for-profit hospital chains. I found billings for patients that didn't exist and billings to insurance companies that didn't match reports to the IRS and billings to companies incorporated in Delaware that were really owned by doctors. For example, I found an AIDS patient who was being charged fifty thousand dollars a week for what amounted to routine medical services. I thought, wow, and kept trucking. It turned out the mob, having observed the physicians turning a sweet buck, moved into the medical supply business as a way of laundering money. Both of them were using this freebie dough to invest in politics to protect their interests."

Schott said, "I thought curiosity was supposed to kill cats, not foxes."

Griffin grinned. "That really got my interest up. I started poking around the accounts of nonprofit educational foundations associated with national politicians. I asked myself, Where was this money coming from?"

"What did you find?" Burlane said.

"It's not that the politicians specifically know they're being financed by hot money or even suspect it outright; it's more that they just accept what's given them and don't look too closely. The result is the same. They're essentially for sale."

Burlane shrugged. "I hadn't thought about buying a politician recently. What I need most is a new set of tires for my Cherokee."

"Well, if you have need of a congressman or senator, there are people out there buying left and right. I was working on the IRS data banks to see if I could figure the percentage of the money that's actually being taxed by them. That's when they caught me."

"Wonderful," Burlane said.

"It was close. They had to have dry mouths. If they let me go unpunished, I might infect the entire population with the truth. Can't have people get even a hint of the complete, disgusting story, can we?"

"I don't think you should hold your breath while you're waiting for it to happen."

"Here I thought I was being patriotic, and they go and get huffy. They were sore because they didn't have anybody good enough to catch me."

Burlane said, "Bureaucrats don't like to be laughed at. I thought calling yourself Cyberfox was a nice touch, though. The uncatchable fox."

"I got the idea from my hair. Same color as a fox's, don't you think? Also, isn't that what foxes do, steal into the chicken coop in the dark of night and have fun? The farmer sits up all night with a shotgun waiting to separate me from my fur, but I sneak right by him all sly and quick and cunning."

"Whatever happens, our offer still stands. Full partner. Fascinating work. Thirdsies," Burlane said.

"We'd take turns with the coffee and cleaning the stupid toilets?"

"That's right."

She cocked her head. "And would spring rolls come with the job?"

"You got 'em," Burlane said.

"Talk to me if I beat this rap, and we'll see." Griffin took another spring roll.

TWO

A gusting east wind sent sandwich wrappers, paper cups, and beer cans skittering and tumbling across Manhattan's early-morning streets; mirroring the city, it was a "*Cosmo* woman" kind of wind—high-heeled, all bones and edges, smart and temperamental, but with languid, Forty-second Street lips.

The small brick warehouse off Twelfth Avenue on the lower West Side contained refrigerated rooms used to store specialty meats for the New York delicatessen trade. Just to make sure that nothing went wrong—owing to miscommunication or a thousand other possible stumbles—uniformed officers of the New York Police Department had gathered before dawn, discreetly cutting off all routes to the warehouse. As the hour of the bust arrived, they were joined by narcotics detectives and members of the Drug Enforcement Administration.

The NYPD narcotics officers would have made the hit themselves had not the DEA—working through its network of informants in South America—laid the details in their lap.

The contraband, said the DEA informants, had been shipped by riverboat down the Rio Negros and the Amazon to Belen, at the mouth of the great river. There it had been repacked, concealed in a shipment of flash-frozen Brazilian beef, destined to be soaked in chemicals and repacked as corned beef in a mob-owned cannery in Hoboken, New Jersey.

The DEA agents would have made the bust by themselves had this not been New York turf. War was war, and public support went to armies that scored success in the field. So when stories of the bust hit the networks that night and the newspapers the next day, both the NYPD and the DEA would take credit.

Now the uniformed NYPD officers, narcotics detectives, and DEA agents waited in their bulletproof vests, staying out of the cold wind, coordinating what was to be done over their transceivers. What they were after was inside the warehouse—of that they were confident. What went in had to come out.

Then, as planned, four police helicopters appeared overhead, just to make sure that nobody was able to escape.

With the police about to rush inside, the sliding front door of the warehouse rattled up and a truck came rumbling out at high speed, its driver shifting gears with grinding abandon.

The truck, with *Carlucci Meat Products* painted on the side, slid around the corner on the wet pavement.

The NYPD narcotics officers and DEA agents took this calmly enough.

Lights flashing, squad cars converged on the truck, which unexpectedly pulled to a stop.

The driver, a long-nosed, beefy man with baggy eyes and wearing a New York Mets baseball cap, dirty khaki chinos, blue nylon windbreaker, and Nike basketball shoes jumped out of the cab, jaw distended, gesturing frantically.

When the officers approached him warily, shotguns thrust forward, they saw that he was bleeding from the mouth.

He was trying to talk, trying to say something, but couldn't.

As they drew closer he jabbed at his midriff with his finger, still trying to talk, but no words came, only eerie unintelligible sounds as the blood gushed.

He wiped blood from his mouth with his right hand as he dug at his shirttail with his left.

Then, suddenly, he exploded before their eyes, raking the stunned officers with blood and what remained of his torso.

5:20 A.M.

While his colleagues searched the truck and closed in on the warehouse, NYPD sergeant James Connelly found the head of the decimated driver on the sidewalk.

The eyes of the driver had been open when he exploded, and they remained open, looking terrified and stricken.

Connelly had seen blood pouring from the driver's mouth when he had unexpectedly stopped the truck and jumped out. He had pumped wildly at his midsection, and for good reason, it turned out; his torso had been wrapped with explosives.

Connelly didn't dwell on the dead man's spooky eyes. The mouth was the thing. There was a reason his speech was so garbled.

Somebody had cut out his tongue.

Seeing the ghastly stub of tongue, Connelly, a Roman Catholic, quickly crossed himself and muttered, "Sweet Jesus."

From the back of the truck, another cop called, "Empty."

The man from the DEA said, "It's still in the warehouse, then."

5:30 A.M.

Close to ten million people lived or worked on Manhattan Island, thirteen miles long from the tip of Battery Park on the south, a block away from Wall Street, to the northern tip, where the Henry

Hudson Parkway crossed the Harlem River. For most of its length—from Broome Street and Kenmare/Delancey Street to the south, three blocks up from Wall Street, to 125th Street to the north—the island was roughly two miles wide.

Editors, writers, designers, producers, directors, business executives, and gamers of every description toiled in immaculate suites of offices in midtown and downtown skyscrapers that aspired to the heavens, while on the streets below, a Third World herd milled about, lost, disheartened, and maddened.

At the southern tip of the island lay the capital of the international financial system; hundreds of millions of dollars passed through Wall Street each day, dispatched electronically throughout the world, to and from London, Paris, Frankfurt, Rome, Zurich, Hong Kong, and Sydney.

This moving and massing of money was so routine that the managers and executives in charge had become bored with what money could buy—food to be consumed or mistresses to be entertained—and came to regard it as a form of combat in which sums of money were points scored.

Underneath all this creativity, moneymaking, excitement, and despair on Manhattan—supporting the cauldron of activity—lay the aged sewers that cleared hundreds of tons of excrement and millions of gallons of urine and flushed water each day. Few New Yorkers understood how these sewers functioned or even who maintained them. As long as the toilet flushed, what went where and how it got there was a matter of total indifference.

What to do with the waste?

How to manage it?

How did the elaborate system of sewers function, really?

During July and August 1999, New York's sewage system had essentially plugged up and stayed that way for six smelly weeks. Caught in a horrific health and environmental crisis, furious New Yorkers shouted at one another and a circus of blame laying ensued. What monumental idiots had allowed this to happen? Why hadn't anybody attended to the obvious? Who was to blame?

On January 1, 2000, James Barfield of the *New York Times*—
looking back on the disaster—would observe that New York's aging,
complex, and rotting sewers shared a problem with Washington.
Sewers moved excrement; the old, poorly understood, and decaying
political system in Washington extruded money. The crisis in both
cases was what to do with too much of something flowing through a
broken-down system.

Barfield wrote, "Any five-year-old country boy knows there are
dangers in trying to hog down a table full of cherry pies in one sitting. Try running that load through our political alimentary canal."

Barfield said surfeit was the problem in both cases. "Up close,
both New York's sewers and Washington's politics are wretched con-
fusions, smelly venues to be avoided by civilized company. Viewed at
a remove—by candlelight and with one's nose tightly pinched—they
can likewise both be regarded, in a mischievous manner of speaking,
as artful."

Now beneath Canal Street, in a sewer tunnel made of bricks and
built in the mid-nineteenth century, two men and a woman, wearing
dry suits and breathing oxygen from tanks on their backs, guided
three airtight, cigar-shaped aluminum tubes into the darkness. While
the underground passages were nearly full, there was yet room for the
imaginative trio to maneuver their cargo of white powder.

The voyagers had studied the sewer in advance of their adventure.
They had mapped its innards carefully and marked the way with
arrows of fluorescent yellow—these fastened to the ceilings—that
told them precisely which way to go at every turn and fork of this vast,
fetid, disgusting subterranean labyrinth. As they proceeded, they removed the fluorescent arrows and sent them adrift in the fluid.

THREE

The combatants agreed on a five-game match of one-hour timed games—three on a Saturday afternoon and two more the next day, to be played until draw, mate, or one of the players ran out of his allotted thirty minutes. As was the practice in speed chess, players kept time on individual clocks topped with start/stop buttons.

The producers had decided the games should be played in what looked like the book-lined study of a gentleman or an intellectual. Viewers could simultaneously watch the game and learn from international grand masters explaining the action on a chessboard insert in the corner of the screen.

The pieces in the insert gave off wiggly little waves in soothing art deco pastels to show their fields of power. When a knight landed, he was immediately surrounded by blinking squares demonstrating that power.

The Las Vegas oddsmakers, chary of getting carried away on a contest that had only two sedentary combatants, had nevertheless posted the Russian nationalist, Ivan Kafelnikov, as a three-to-one favorite to win all five games, making the outspoken Louisianan, Lamar Gene Cooper, a sort of chess-playing Rocky.

Kafelnikov was the man who had promised to regain the empire squandered by Mikhail Gorbachev and the white-haired drunk Boris Yeltsin. A lean, passionate man with penetrating, slate gray eyes, Kafelnikov had found the white horse of destiny to be a difficult mount, skittish and unpredictable.

A memorable phrase by V. I. Lenin—"Chess is a gymnasium of the mind"—had the effect of creating a nation of chess fanatics, spending cold winter nights hunkered over chessboards. Kafelnikov, an accomplished player, had told the *New York Times* that "in chess the attacking and defending pieces have different powers and abilities. One coordinates an attack with diverse pieces. In this it mimics both politics and war."

When he was a college student, Lamar Gene Cooper had fared well enough in tournament play to have been rated an expert, one step beneath a master. A folksy oil millionaire with thinning red hair, cowboy boots, and a colorful Bayou drawl—championing his special Lamar Gene's Blackened Catfish—Cooper had been an on-again, off-again presidential aspirant since Ross Perot had dithered and dissembled, ultimately not running in 1996. Now, flying Perot's faded colors of populist champion and forever gadfly, Lamar Gene Cooper once more faced the question.

Would he run for president or would he not?

The Louisianan was no stranger to the art of political theater; in a move that would have made Huey Long proud, Cooper had challenged Kafelnikov on Larry King's show: "My kind of folks like a man who's not afraid to try. They don't cotton much to whiners and quitters. He hasn't given up on his country, has he? That tells you something."

Having challenged Kafelnikov, Cooper did the gentlemanly thing and offered the Russian white for the first game. Among good players, playing white—moving first—was a decided advantage. However, the superior Kafelnikov had shown his disdain and contempt for Cooper by choosing black.

As a spectator sport, chess had all the thrill of watching paint dry, but the players were the thing. Television made money off drama, not chess. The hype had predictably jacked the players up to a mythological level. Lamar Gene Cooper was a never-quit American, Huck Finn kind of patriot squaring off against the ice-in-his-blood Ivan Kafelnikov, evil genius of the Russian empire. Cooper's challenge had grabbed the nation's attention. The media, ever eager to promote anything that promised confrontation, leaped on the dramatic potential much as Dennis Connor's competitive fire had yanked what had been a boring rich man's luxury pastime—yachting—into fevered center stage with the America's Cup races. The down-home millionaire and the relentless Russian. People who didn't know chess from pickup sticks tuned in.

Cooper didn't play games he didn't think he could win. In this case, it didn't matter how badly Kafelnikov beat him in chess, Cooper still won by coming out as the never-say-die people's champion. In fact, the worse he was beaten, the better it was for his reputation as a game competitor. But he couldn't roll over and tank it; his supporters had to see that he was trying.

As he waited at the edge of the set, Cooper thought about his options. He hadn't played chess or thought about it in years, but he hadn't completely forgotten his college passion.

If he led with the pawn in front of his queen, the game would tend to be strategic—that is, careful and defensive, with blocked positions.

If he led with the pawn in front of his king, the game would likely be tactical, with the action quick and fast.

Cooper didn't think he had the skills to play a strategic game with a player as good as Ivan Kafelnikov—especially under pressure of a ticking clock. Better play the rough-and-tumble tactical game and take his chances. Even grand masters made a blunder once in a while.

Cooper had done his best to be calm, but his mouth was like cotton and his heart thumped as he waited for the floor director to tell him it was time.

Arms wide, the floor director waggled his fingers at the players, who waited on opposite sides of the set. "We're ready, gentlemen. In a moment. Quiet, please! Quiet, please!" He held up hands. "Enter the room when I signal you with my hands. Quiet, please. Enter now!" He made a downward, chopping motion with the edges of both hands.

Cooper walked onto the book-lined set and shook hands with Kafelnikov.

Chess fans across the country were delighted. The match didn't promise very good chess, but as high-ratings, prime-time theater it was wonderful. Nothing like this had happened to American chess since Bobby Fischer took the world championship away from Boris Spassky in Reykjavik, Iceland, in 1972.

The spunky Louisianan, Lamar Gene Cooper, licked his lips and moved his pawn to the fourth rank in front of his king. In chess this square was noted as E4. It was likely going to be a tactical game, filled with early action and pieces going down.

Cooper quickly punched the button on top of his clock.

The second hand began sweeping its way around the face of Kafelnikov's clock.

Tick, tick, tick . . .

FOUR

A pack of Democrats was pursuing the nomination in the year of the American political millenium; in that regard they were more like baying hounds than braying mules. The genteel yet vigorous Governor John Danneman of Maryland, a successor to the retired Paris Glendening, was the leader—popularly regarded as a "bridge" between conservative South and liberal North.

Glendening had barely made it as governor in 1994 against a no-chance crank. When a taxpayer revolt loomed over the Cleveland Browns' move to Baltimore, he decided his family needed him more. Danneman stressed his credentials as a moderate centrist and endlessly crossed the North-South bridge. Combining an understanding and reflection of Southern traditions and values with Northern virtues and aspirations, he managed to appeal to all sides.

Bill Clinton's loss in 1996 had removed the obstacles to Vice President Al Gore's ambitions, but he was tainted by his association with Clinton, and John Danneman had become the Southern moderate Democrat du jour.

It used to be, Take your mark, get set, go.

Now it was, Take your mark; the race is over; where were you?

Running in place, Gore, a sensible man, had lately been talking of returning to the Senate.

What mattered in the long stretch was organization and plenty of money for television spots, and Danneman, who had managed to distance himself from what he regarded as the mush-brained idiots on the extreme left of his party, had both in abundance. He had husbanded his resources like Schwarzkopf eyeing Hussein.

He was being hailed by Democrats whirling in the maelstrom of Clinton's defeat as someone who appealed to economic conservatives uncomfortable with the hard-line populism of the Christian right, and was tolerated, if not welcomed, by moderate Democrats as a pragmatic, sensible candidate who could challenge President Erikson on his own political ground and keep the country from swinging too far to the right. A next-generation Bill Clinton—this time with convictions!

Unless he unaccountably stumbled, the nomination, it was popularly conceded, was his; John Danneman would fly his party's colors in the first presidential election of the twenty-first century.

If Danneman had anything to worry about—a nagging source of anxiety like a spot on his skin that wouldn't heal—it was . . . well, a couple of episodes with women several years earlier.

Danneman was trim and well built with a square jaw and salt-and-pepper hair. He was more Bobby Kennedy–trim than Gerald Ford. He had even features, sincere gray eyes, and a good mouth with full lips that were sensual without making him look like Mick Jagger. Women voters liked him and trusted him.

He had found early on that his sexual attraction rose in direct proportion to his power. Men running for public office had to keep their fly zipped or face inquiry by shocked reporters who envied anybody like himself who might have a sex life. When they were on the prowl for sexual gossip, they seemed hardly more intelligent than squirrels, whose sex life they no doubt admired. He had come to feel that the public insisted on zipped flies as a form of torment, a test for anybody who aspired to be president. You want to be Mr. Big? Sure, pal, go for it—drop your pants for a short-arms inspection, and let's have your IRS forms for the last twenty years.

Danneman wanted the White House too much to continue his secretive escapades and so had knocked off the adventure in the name of ambition. No untoward surprises for Danneman, thank you. No on-the-make bimbo calling a press conference like that hank-of-hair did to Bill Clinton, or the women accusing Senator Robert Packwood of playing grab-ass.

He had no choice. Pursuing the presidency was an Odyssean quest, and Danneman was determined not to respond to the bewitching call of any seductive sirens. He would be satisfied with an occasional coupling with his wife, Mary. The First Lady of Maryland, a former English professor at Johns Hopkins, was an intelligent, companionable woman with presence and courage. She was no Hillary Clinton, but had a wit that charmed rather than grated, and it was easy for people to picture her as First Lady of the United States.

Reasonable time having passed, and there having been no public repercussions from his earlier transgressions, Danneman now felt safe.

Danneman's speech, scheduled for prime time in New Hampshire, was over by ten o'clock, and the candidate, feeling good, was in a handshaking mood as he emerged from the Concord Elks' Lodge. Well-wishers, wanting to tell their friends that they shook hands with the future president of the United States and he was not a bad guy, crowded around, crunching on frozen snow, paws extended. They breathed in frosty puffs and had hearty smiles on their ruddy faces. Stalwart citizens were these worthy Hampshiremen and -women.

Danneman slipped onto the soft, plush rear seat of his limousine, enveloped by the warmth.

It was a brand-new vehicle and still had the new-car smell. Danneman liked that. He remembered the memorable lines that Francis Ford Coppola had given the character played by Robert Duvall in the movie *Apocalypse Now:* "I love the smell of napalm in the morning. It smells like victory."

That's how John Danneman felt about the smell of new cars. They smelled like victory.

Sitting there enjoying that wonderful odor, he noticed that he had blood in the palm of his right hand. He had somehow cut himself in the process of shaking hands. How had that happened?

He looked at the wound. He hadn't felt a hint of pain, and yet there it was, blood and quite a bit of it.

He pressed his handkerchief against the cut.

As the car sped off into the cold New Hampshire air, he took another quick peek at the cut. He had heard of handshaking actually leading to burst vessels, but this looked like a fairly deep cut. Some fool must have had a ring with a jagged edge or maybe a diamond had done it. Whatever the origin, it was like a slice, and it had begun to throb.

FIVE

Bob Bailey waited for the commercial for Mother Gilpin's, home of the Original Gilpin's Chicken-crispins, to end. He unzipped his pants to relieve the pressure on his gut. He wiggled his toes and scratched his armpit. He dug at his balls and adjusted his Mickey Mouse boxer shorts. Life was good.

Bailey scooped up some more Fritos. Sitting in the privacy of a radio station, surrounded by calendars featuring women with remarkable breasts—huge tits, little pointed boobs, and crazed numbers with outsize nipples—was a hell of a lot more fun than television. He was aware that he had a melon belly on a broomstick body, an outsized Adam's apple, and not much of a chin, but he was convinced he had something that the most JFK-handsome liberal alive completely lacked: a functional brain.

In a radio studio, nobody knew what Bailey looked like. He had a deep, confident voice that reverberated over the airwaves and he was skilled at lampooning obvious morons. His listeners loved it. Bailey could sit around in his Mickey Mouse boxer shorts if he wanted and have a little one-on-one fun with his listeners. The liberals were so damn serious and humorless they were easy to skewer. More fun than poppin' frogs with a pickup truck. The libby-wimps were oh so loving and caring and giving—with other people's money. They were political ostriches; their motto was to never let the facts stand in the way of high-minded theory.

Bailey thought it was a real kick jerking them around; the more they howled in righteous indignation, the more he rubbed it in. He felt he had their number dead square on, namely that altruism was a social and political tactic, and anything else, despite all that emotion and those woeful, teary eyes, was hypocrisy. A little hypocrisy he could live with. "But, you can't criticize me because I'm oh so very very gooooood" big-league pretense was enough to gag a maggot.

The radical feminists, most of whom Bailey suspected really wanted to be men, were the most fun, followed by the queers, and Bailey had developed a faggot lisp that never failed to amuse his listeners. On radio, he could do his imitations of Amos 'n' Andy—"Well, helllllllll-ohhhhhhhhh the'h, Sapphi'h honnnn-ey!"—but on television, for some reason, that was out.

Bailey, watching the sweep of the second hand on the studio wall, washed down the Frito remnants with a hit of Wild Turkey and Dr Pepper and licked his lips with anticipation. Alligator lips, his wife called them, the better to chow down on them *flaaaaaaavorful*, wrigglin' libby-wimps. They were finger-lickin' good, and that was a fact. Dippin' 'em in rhetorical hot sauce was a special treat.

The red ON THE AIR light went on.

Bailey said, "Welcome back to the Bob Bailey Show. That's me, Bullet Bob, the human Kalashnikov, over here in Reston, Virginia, mowin' 'em down for your commuting satisfaction. I'm here every Tuesday through Friday night from five till eight, and from eight to eleven on Saturday night slaughtertime. I can hear 'em weeping and moaning now. Just stay tuned and you'll be home to the wife and kids before you know it.

"Well, here we are in the sixth day of the twenty-first century, and it's the same old crapola. I see by the polls this morning that President Erikson's poll numbers dropped to twenty percent this morning, breaking the record lows previously set by Jimmy the Peanut and Billary the Incompetent. The only one doing worse is Dimwit Danneman. It's easy to understand Billary's numbers, and the Peanut had to deal with the Ayatollah Assholla. Only sixteen percent think Erikson's doing a satisfactory job. Wonderful. And yet some Republicans say Chet Gorman is unelectable because he opposes the right of women to casually murder their children in the womb. Talk about the politics of expediency!

"Did you read where sagacious Mr. Weintraub in the *Washington Post* is comparing Chet's challenge to Huey Long's bid to unseat Franklin Roosevelt in 1936? Huey's crime was to claim Roosevelt wasn't going far enough with the New Deal. Not far enough! Imagine! Roosevelt couldn't get his way with the National Recovery Administration so he tried packing the Supreme Court with more members. Remember, this is the great liberal hero who gave Democrats their New Deal coalition they cling to like it was Linus and his blanket. This is the year 2000, and they're still pretending it's 1932. The libby-wimps need to wake up. The world moves on while they're stuck in reverse. Ever notice how labels flip-flop? The libby-wimps call us the conservatives, but they're the ones who live in the past. They're the ones who refuse to face the future. We're the progressives, not them. But everybody knows they're oh so kind and sharing and loving. They're so, so very *gooooooooooood*, Mother Teresas every one. Part of one big happy multicultural family. Diversity. *Riiiiiight!* As long as somebody else foots the bill.

"Franklin Roosevelt didn't go far enough? I say spare us the Huey Longs of the world. Sometimes assassins have more brains than they're given cr—" Bailey stopped, letting his listeners fill in the sentence.

"Ooops! I almost said 'more brains than they're given credit for,' but that would be a terrible thing to say, wouldn't it? Very politically incorrect. I better keep my mouth shut before the FBI comes calling.

"Remember when Oklahoma City happened? Remember how the libby-wimps, all the America-lasters blamed the conservatives for that? Remember how they tried to shut us up, cut us off? Remember how Billary and his head persecutor Jerky Janet Reno tried to come from political Death Valley by jumping on us? Well, they didn't shut us up then, and they won't now—not as long as ol' Bullet Bob is beaming at you. And not as long as we have a great champion like Chet Gorman to fight for us. Let's all pray that nothing happens to Chet Gorman, he's the only hope we've got against those sellouts in the White House. Thomas Erikson is like a screw with stripped threads; mighty tough to get him out of there, but it can be done. It's ten months and counting to the election in November, it's never too late if voters with half a brain wake up to what's going on.

"Speaking of crapola. . . . Here's a juicy one for you, gossip fans, old Bullet Bob got an anonymous tip on his fax machine that the ever popular Governor John Boy Danneman has regressed to his good-timing old ways up there in New Hampshire. Just can't resist those groupies, eh, John Boy? Must be those cold winter nights. But we all remember what happened to Gary Hart, don't we? They say he was stopped six inches short of the presidency, although I bet that's stretching the distance. As I recall, he did have a large nose. Of course, there might not be anything to this rumor, in which case no harm done, eh, John Boy? Just having a little fun at your expense. This is what the libby-wimps call hate radio. Anything they don't agree with they call hateful. *Dooooo* accept our apologies. Ooops, time for the folks who're paying our bills. When I come back, a chat with Congressman Leo Carney."

While another deep-voiced man urged Bailey's listeners to stop by Mother Gilpin's on their way home from work, Bailey thought, What the hell, and drew himself a line of coke. He sure as hell couldn't do that on a television show; that was a fact. Lampooning the libby-wimps went better with coke.

SIX

If Detective Sergeant Roy Hanna thought he was going to fit right in at the Giddyup Saloon and Sporting House on Santa Monica Boulevard, he was wrong; he might as well have worn a three-piece suit as to wear net stockings and a tutu in the Giddyup.

Of course, this was Los Angeles, not Des Moines; for most of America, life was pretty much the same as it had been a week earlier. The celebrants, determined to defend L.A.'s reputation as the craziest of crazy cities, continued ringing in the twenty-first century—wearing whips and hoods and tails and silver studs and showing as much skin in as outrageous a manner as possible. They were as dreams floating up from the spookier regions of the subconscious.

Their baby-boomer parents, who in their own time had strutted their stuff sans bra and smoked many a lid, now muttered in disapproval at such brazen exhibitionism.

The eve of the new century had seen repeated clashes, represented in the extreme by those longing to lead *Leave It to Beaver* lives and those who wanted to do whatever was next. The carping critics, calling up images of self-indulgence and decadence, said Los Angeles was an American Rome, perched on the lip of the abyss.

A voluptuous young woman wore a fetching Day-Glo orange G-string and yellow spray paint that shimmered in the lights. Her shapely friend sported a fluorescent rattlesnake; the pale green rattle was tied to her ankle. The snake, with orange diamonds and wee, tiny orange scales, wound up her left leg, looped over her hip and down under her crotch, then up over her waist; it coiled around her bare left breast, and continued up over her shoulder; its malevolent head, with sapphire eyes, mere slits, rested by one ear.

A man was stylishly attired in skintight leopard-skin nylon, with a bare patch to display his hairy buns and a long tail that he twirled as he slinked along, one foot in front of the other in the manner of a fashion model. Another gentleman wore a two-foot-long plastic penis that happily banged and flopped against his legs as he walked.

Hanna, looking for his partner, weaved through dancers leaping and grinding in the sweeping glow-lights. He snuck a quick glance at his wife's wristwatch. It was so small and the light was so dim that he could barely see the time: 2:57 A.M.

He edged toward the door that led to the storage room behind the bar. Eyeing a fetching young lady attired only in rings—in her ears, nose, nipples, and vaginal lips—he paused by a photorealistic plastic vagina as the dancers gyrated to the Top Ten hit by the rock group that called themselves the Republicrats—a retro version of "Zombie Jamboree," the Kingston Trio hit folk song of forty-five years earlier:

> *"Back to back, belly to belly,*
> *We don't give a damn 'cause we done dead already."*

Hanna found it hard to take his eyes off the girl with the rings.

Next to him, a huge drag queen with monster tits and outsize lips painted on her face peered down at him. Mimicking Mae West, she said, "Hey there, big boy. Give a girl a light?"

Hanna looked up, horrified. Did the drag queen want to dance? God!

The drag queen said, "Get your eyes off the lady with the rings, Hanna. We got work to do."

"Huh?"

"It's me, Roy. Wiggens."

"Wiggens? Jesus!"

Wiggens, looking coy, pulled back the edge of his bra, and Hanna could see the butt of a .38-caliber service revolver. He said, "My sister helped me with the outfit. I think the bouncer likes me. Can you imagine? I played hard to get."

"God, I bet you did."

Wiggens said, "Just once, I'd like to make one of these busts in a sports bar or a Thank God It's Friday." He examined Hanna's outfit. "Where you packing your piece?" He looked confused.

"In my jock."

Wiggens grinned. "Probably not much of anything down there anyway. Right? Perfect place to hide it."

Hanna ignored him. "Is the stuff here?"

"The snitch says it's a go. Got 'em cold," Wiggens said.

"Everything in place?"

"Tanaka and his partner'll take care of the lights. We've got the place surrounded. No way they can get that crap out of here. None."

Hanna licked his lips. "What a place!"

Wiggens grinned. "Bitch, bitch, bitch. Jesus! This is the twenty-first century, man. Grow up. Get with it. You can't stay in the past."

The lights popped on.

Hanna muttered, "Uh-oh. Showtime!" He went for his crotch.

Wiggens drew from his bra.

Yelling, "Police! Police!" they whipped out their badges and headed for the kitchen and behind that, the room where their snitch had said they would find the goods.

SEVEN

It hadn't mattered at all that Ivan Kafelnikov had won four straight games in his chess match against Lamar Gene Cooper. The gritty Cooper—never quitting, aware that millions were praying for him not to screw up—had managed a stunning win on the last match after a horrible blunder by Kafelnikov on his ninth move caused him to lose a bishop, two pawns, and control of the center.

Two months later in Atlanta, Cooper held a town-hall meeting during which he played a dozen mediocre players while taking questions. All the while, he offered jokes, anecdotes, and down-home wisdom. For example, he liked to observe that a quality chess piece was a pleasure to hold; lifting a queen with heft and weight was the intellectual equivalent of holding a .357 magnum. Any kid who had ever hunted squirrels ought to appreciate the power of a queen.

His randomly selected opponents were actually shills; Lamar Gene didn't like surprises when he played chess or anything else. The experiment worked. When Cooper was ambushed with a question he didn't want to answer, he either pretended to be distracted by one of his games, or he gave his questioner a little lesson in chess.

Cooper thought fair was fair—all the reporters wanted to do was carve gotcha-notches on their laptops; people who went to town-hall meetings wanted to learn something from and about Lamar Gene Cooper.

The media pros tormented Cooper as part of their job and resented this tinkering with the rules of the kill. Cooper refused to play their game. If they wanted to impress their colleagues and editors with their journalistic head-hunting, his was one scalp they would be denied.

If his army of passionate followers ever thought, Oh, cut the chess crap, Lamar Gene, and give us a straight answer, they never said so out loud. Cooper said he didn't give twaddle what the gotcha-corps liked; folks were tired of the game in which politicians, understandably defending themselves, had come to regard the truth as a poisonous serpent and avoided saying anything specific.

Lamar Gene Cooper stepped up to the next board and studied the pieces. Then, with a slight grin, he moved a knight. That Cooper would win, there was no doubt. The chess stunt, a reminder that Cooper was not afraid of a challenge, was also meant to convey that he was smart, smart, smart. Lamar Gene Cooper, a chess master who knew the parts of speech, was a hyperswift winner and an unembarrassed patriot who gave a damn about his country.

He pointed to a pretty high-school girl with neat bangs on her forehead who waved her hand from the fifth row back. "Yes, miss?"

The girl with the bangs stood. "My name is Terri Lynn Mackey. I'm a high-school senior here in San Antonio. What I would like to know, Mr. Cooper, is when are you going to end the suspense? Are you going to run for president?"

Cooper laughed. "A good chess player learns early on the foolishness of moving his queen too early. While an amateur flashes a check here and threatens to check there, a skilled player defends and develops his pieces at the same time."

Cooper grinned. "What with all the rumors and speculation about the upcoming election, nobody seems to be looking at the board. When I'm teaching my little granddaughter how to play chess, one of the first things I tell her is that she has to learn how to see the board."

"See the board?"

Cooper said, "A chess player has to worry about how many pieces he has, how much of the board he controls, and if he has his pieces developed, that is, if he has time to win. In primary politics, money is material, delegates won is space, and the days remaining before the convention is time."

"Politics and chess sound like war."

"Oh my, yes," Cooper said. "Chess mimics warfare and politics, like Kafelnikov said. It's foxes after chickens. General Giap after Saigon. Politicians after the White House."

"Foxes after chickens?"

"Sure, sure. You see, a bishop on B2 is like a farmer sittin' in an open window with a shotgun, watchin' the chicken pen at a distance. A real smart fox will check out those windows before he gets too confident about snagging himself some supper. You get my drift?"

"But are you going to run for president?" the girl said.

"Say, I bet you're going to journalism school, aren't you?" Cooper laughed. "Well, the answer is maybe. Maybe. I'm keeping my eye on the center while I develop my pieces. If you don't open correctly, you'll develop weaknesses, and a good player will ambush you in the midgame. Always remember, the object is to win, not just put somebody in check. A lot of people don't understand that."

"So there's no hurry in making your announcement," she said.

Cooper grinned broadly. "No hurry at all."

EIGHT

Lots of cities had beaches. Waikiki Beach in Honolulu was perhaps equally as famous, but it called up images of Diamond Head, rum drinks, and little old ladies in leis mingling with Japanese tourists—the Japanese having lately pretty much bought the place. But there was something about Miami Beach that was special in the American imagination, never mind that a good portion of the sand had been trucked in, making it almost, but not quite, a wonder of nature.

Miami Beach was distinctly more carnal than Waikiki, if less intimate because of its vast size. It was more than a mile and a half long and two hundred yards wide, the better to accommodate the refugees from the winter cold fronts that pushed down out of Canada. Just inland from the beach there was a short wall, meant to block the drifting sand, and then a narrow park, a hundred yards wide, with sidewalks where roller skaters glided and rumbled, flashing their stuff on fashionable and expensive new blade skates. Here skilled young men flew kites in primary colors. The kites whipped and buzzed and roared and zoomed, like colorful dragons riding the breeze off the Atlantic.

On the east side of Ocean Drive, facing the park and beach, was the famous row of cafés, eateries, and nightclubs. It was here that Al Pacino and his partner in *Scarface* had cruised in their convertible, music rumbling from the tape deck.

The graceful, curved art-deco style, dating from the glory years of Miami Beach in the 1920s, was what made Ocean Drive a true marvel. Here were the justifiably famous and extraordinary buildings with their pastels, fuchsias, hot pinks, off-purples, teal greens, and azure blues. Here also was sun, color, and splendid architectural detail—the rounded corner of a window here, an arched doorframe there—that made Miami Beach a mecca for fashion photographers. Their portable darkrooms, fashioned from RVs, seemed everywhere. Everywhere, too, were the extraordinary, long-legged young women whose perfect faces, suppressing any hint of soul, stared out from the pages of magazines in grocery-store checkouts.

For men in the winter of life, perhaps even more than those in the springtime of their cycle, there was a joy and delight in watching the coltish stride of young and beautiful women.

It was because of the fashion models and the women in string bikinis that the elderly gentleman from Cali, Colombia, Diego Rodriguez, liked to go to Miami Beach. Señor Rodriguez had been to the beaches in Rio de Janeiro, where the women were likewise wonderful in the extreme—and with string bikinis hardly wider than dental floss—but there one had to put up with dangerous gangs of feral kids.

Señor Rodriguez was said to be the good friend of El Hombre himself, Guillermo Peña de la Banda-Conchesa. Because of this association, Rodriguez was assumed to be a kingpin of the Cali drug cartel, although he never said or did anything the Drug Enforcement Administration could use against him.

Rodriguez, who prided himself on his education and taste, was an admirer of art-deco architecture as well, and so he was a regular visitor to Miami Beach. What were life and success, after all, if not to enjoy?—even if he was discreetly followed each time by agents of the DEA.

In the late afternoon, Rodriguez and his companions, elegantly dressed in light gray slacks, colorful ascots, and navy blue blazers, took a hike on the beach to check out the string bikinis. Then, the sun having set, they strolled down Ocean Drive to enjoy the fashion models. They stopped several times along the way to drink scotch whiskey, laughing and talking in their Colombian Spanish, which was said to be the most pure in Latin America.

Later, they would have supper at Aldo's, a fashionable restaurant on Ocean Drive that was Rodriguez's favorite. The food critic of the Spanish-language edition of the *Miami Herald* had said Aldo's was "a five-star can't-miss" for visitors from South America who wanted to enjoy the very best gringo food. The bill, he added, "is not for everyone."

9:00 P.M.

It was civilized having all the money one could conceivably want to spend, and the elegant Diego Rodriguez never paid any attention to price when he ordered food at a restaurant—or when he bought anything else for that matter. Rodriguez felt having to consider cost was lower-class and debilitating, a sign of failure, and he wondered how people managed to do it day after day without going crazy.

For soup, Rodriguez ordered the chef's special seafood chowder—close to bouillabaisse, made from live fish, lobsters, prawns, scallops, and clams he picked from an aquarium wheeled to the table for his inspection.

For salad, he was modest, choosing a simple dish of cold white asparagus marinated in tomato vinegar spiked with bruised cilantro.

Among the entrées of the evening, Aldo's chef offered a rack of elk roast studded with cloves of wild garlic and served in a bed of white truffles—the elk having been flown in from Alaska, and the truffles dug up from the bases of oak trees in southern Oregon. The elk struck Rodriguez as exotic, thus perfect. He disregarded the two-hundred-dollar price.

Rodriguez's companions knew what he would later order for dessert. Key lime pie. Never mind that Key lime pie was considered too touristy to be included on Aldo's offerings. The moment he had stepped through the front door, the chefs at Aldo's began to make The Pie. Not just any pie. A pie properly made from limes grown in the Florida Keys.

Rodriguez—having finished his chowder and asparagus and roast elk—was contemplating dessert, pretending, for the amusement of his companions, to be interested in something other than the upcoming Key lime pie, when two unfashionably dressed gentlemen stepped in from the sidewalk.

They had ski masks pulled over their faces, which, like hats, were considered déclassé in a proper supper club.

They also carried Uzis.

They strolled over to Señor Rodriguez's table, and almost casually—with startled DEA agents looking on—opened fire.

They killed the four Colombians at the table, plus a waiter serving a table behind them and the waiter's customer, a real-estate broker. The broker's girlfriend, a former runner-up in the Miss Florida contest, took two slugs in the mouth.

And then, just as casually, the boorishly dressed gentlemen returned to Ocean Drive, piled into a Buick convertible, and squealed away, blue smoke rising from the rear tires.

The Metro Dade police later found the Buick parked half a dozen blocks away. It had been stolen earlier in the evening.

Of the identity of the men who had slaughtered the diners from Colombia, there was not a clue, although the police did not suspect this was a lovers' quarrel. Ocean Drive, an exotic, enduring part of the front line of the war on drugs, had seen its share of cocaine skirmishes. It was not for nothing that Brian De Palma had chosen it to open the dramatics of *Scarface*.

NINE

Jim Lehrer, eyeing the digital clock ticking off the seconds to airtime, sat on a stool behind the counter of the redesigned set. He could have been naked from the waist down and nobody would have known the difference. Before him, the floor was a mass of cables, spread out like a clump of seaweed. Above everything, like so many hot suns in a science-fiction sky, were the lights.

Beyond the lights, technicians and floor assistants watched from the darkness.

In a few seconds, Lehrer would address a red light above a camera lens. Out there, beyond the red light—across America, in Walla Walla and Winnemucca, and in Pocatello and Peoria, in what had become a ritual five nights of the week—tens of millions of people watched Jim Lehrer and his colleagues deliver the news.

Two weeks earlier, in a series of programs summing up the political and technological changes of the twentieth century, a professor from Columbia University had told Lehrer there was no known record in the proceedings in Philadelphia that any of the men who had written the Constitution ever dreamed politicians could one day transport themselves and their supporters into the living rooms of the voters.

The professor said the Founding Fathers would have predicted that a price tag would inevitably be attached to the magic of sending pictures flying through the air. If the Founding Fathers had but known, he said, they would have written a different Constitution.

Lehrer said, "Tonight, our subject is once again the primary campaign being waged in New Hampshire—kicking off one of the most bitter, controversial presidential campaigns in memory.

"After six years of indecision, intraparty bickering, and the loss of the White House, two big questions remain for the Democrats: Can the party of Franklin Roosevelt's New Deal, faced with continuing defections at century's end, ignite their old coalitions and reassert control for the coming years, or will they go the way of the Whigs? Can the centrist Maryland governor John Danneman reclaim Dixie for his party, or will the Democrats finally yield the old Solid South to the Republicans and lay to rest the ghost of Abraham Lincoln?

"And the future is no less certain for the Republicans, whose dramatic takeover in 1994 was later stained by right-wing extremists linked to the bombing of the federal building in Oklahoma City. Former House Speaker Newt Gingrich is running for an unexpectedly open seat in the Senate. As President Erikson's poll numbers continue to slide, will West Virginia senator Chet Gorman succeed in his challenge from the party's right?

"Or, sensing a Democratic party in hopeless decline and a widely disliked Republican incumbent, will the chess-playing Louisiana populist Lamar Gene Cooper, heir to Ross Perot's discontented followers, step in to steal Republican and Democratic votes as a third-party candidate?

"These are the questions we will be asking tonight of our guests: Pam O'Neil, White House communications director; Robert Azar, political adviser of Governor Danneman; William Toone, supporter of Lamar Gene Cooper; and Senator Chet Gorman, speaking to us from Manchester, New Hampshire. Thank you, gentlemen and Ms. O'Neil, for being our guests tonight.

"Ms. O'Neil—you first—what about the public dissatisfaction with the President? What is the President's feeling and is there anything he can do to reclaim his popularity in the coming months?"

The blond, bespectacled O'Neil paused, thinking about her answer. She said, "The President regards poll numbers much as he does the rising and falling of the tides. When they fall, there's nowhere for them to go but up. President Erikson has the core support he needs to win renomination, and he's not an extremist. As Election Day approaches you'll see voters turning to Erikson as the sensible choice. He is firm but fair."

Lehrer said, "This question is for you, Mr. Azar. Over the last three decades the Democrats have lost the Solid South. The decline of labor unions has cost them their core of industrial blue-collar workers, and the urban Catholics deserted them over abortion and other issues, leaving them with passionate liberals and African Americans, who have a poor voting record. Is there any way for Governor Danneman to fashion a new coalition to recapture the White House for the Democrats?"

Azar said, "People don't vote lockstep depending on whether they belong to this or that coalition. The Republican Party has always been the party of rich people and Wall Street. If you're a small businessman, or you work for a salary, or you're a single mother with children trying to get and keep a job, and you want to vote for your best interest, you vote for the Democrat."

Lehrer furrowed his brows. "What about ethnic and racial minorities?"

Azar looked surprised. "What about them? If you're a Hispanic or African American millionaire, I assume you'd vote for the Republican candidate. If you're retired and have to live on a fixed income, if you're concerned about company layoffs, or if you're looking for work, you'd be better off voting for Governor Danneman. Governor Danneman sees this as a nation of individuals seeking opportunity, not of competing groups."

Jim Lehrer said, "Ms. O'Neil, back to you for a moment, before we call on the senator from West Virginia. What does the President think of Senator Gorman's chances?"

O'Neil responded, "President Erikson thinks Senator Gorman is unelectable owing to his position on abortion and his association with right-wing extremists. The President believes if the absolutists insist on an antiabortion plank, it will cost Republicans reelection."

Jim Lehrer said, "Senator Gorman, your supporters have been working feverishly in every hamlet in New Hampshire, and you're fattening your campaign treasury with the largest, most sophisticated direct-mail operation in American political history. Yet you heard Ms. O'Neil, she says President Erikson feels you're unelectable because of your stand on abortion. What do you say to that?"

Senator Chet Gorman was on the screen, a big, burly, ruddy-faced man with dark hair and passionate blue eyes. "Listen, I was a prisoner of war in Hanoi for seven years. Never, ever, not once, in all that time, did I give up. I don't acknowledge the word *quit*. They said I was unelectable when I ran for the Senate in West Virginia, but they were wrong. As to the abortion issue, polls are polls. The most important thing to the people is having a president with guts and spine."

Lehrer said, "Finally, Mr. Toone, it's your turn to offer a word on behalf of Lamar Gene Cooper."

"Mr. Cooper has not yet announced his candidacy for the presidency, so anything I say is just my opinion."

Lehrer smiled. "But you do hope he'll run."

Toone laughed. "Oh yes, indeed I do."

Lehrer said, "The polls are telling us the public wants no part of President Erikson, Governor Danneman, or Senator Gorman. We've been reading for weeks that Mr. Cooper has been gearing up to begin his campaign sometime this month. Is that true?

"People look to Mr. Cooper because all Erikson and Danneman have done is create *more* disillusionment. Mr. Cooper is tough and smart. If he moves, he'll go like gangbusters."

"Tell us, Mr. Toone, if Mr. Cooper doesn't run for president, what would be his likely advice to those two gentlemen to boost their low public esteem?"

TEN

ames Burlane, with his friend Ara Schott lurking over his shoulder, watched Robert Toone on television while he kept an eye on the two cups of milk and water and a half cup of oil warming on the stove. Lehrer had asked a good question. Just what would the great chess player advise?

Robert Toone adjusted his spectacles. "If Mr. Cooper were in the President's shoes, or even Governor Danneman's, I believe he'd most likely try a gambit."

"A bold, risky move."

"Yes, I think that is what Mr. Cooper would advise."

Burlane punched off the set and poked his finger into the mixture in the pan. "Don't want it too hot or it will kill the yeast. Ready?"

Schott took a sip of coffee from a Baltimore Orioles cup. "Anytime you are."

"You got the eggs boiled?"

"Boiled and peeled," Schott said, "I'm hungry enough to eat the south end out of a skunk going north."

Burlane said, "Why don't we listen to some music while I work? Maybe a little Pink Floyd or something."

Ara Schott rolled his eyes. He and James Burlane had watched Jim Lehrer's story on the New Hampshire primaries. Whenever the talk was of money, his freethinking friend liked to listen to the jingling of cash registers on "Money" from *Dark Side of the Moon.* Pink Floyd's inspired song was, in Burlane's opinion, the single best pop music single ever cut.

Burlane watched Schott's reaction. "Okay, I won't force Pink Floyd or Talking Heads on you. How about some Dixieland? A little Jack Teagarden, say."

"I'll put some on," Schott said quickly. Schott was cool to Pink Floyd but shared Burlane's interest in Dixieland, if not his love of reggae. Schott had stocked almost all the Dixieland CDs he could find.

Burlane scooped six cups of flour into a stainless-steel bowl, then added a couple of largish pinches of salt and two packets of fast-rise yeast. Stirring this with a wooden spoon, he poured in the contents of the pan.

From Schott's stereo, the gravelly-voiced Teagarden, the ragged timbre aged in whiskey and cigarette smoke, sang:

"*I shall not, I shall not be moved.*
I shall not, I shall not be moved.
Just like a tree standing by the wa-ha-ter,
I shall not be moved."

Burlane began kneading the wad of dough that had formed in the bottom of the bowl. When he was satisfied with his handiwork, he put a towel over the bowl and took it into the living room and put it beside the fireplace where Schott had a fire crackling. Burlane scooped up Schott's current issue of *Time* magazine and took it with him back to the kitchen. The cover article was about the rising influence of Chinese Triads, or tong gangs, as they were sometimes called.

Seeing the magazine, Schott said, "They say that in the last thirty years that Triads have moved into American businesses bigtime. They own international freight-hauling companies, commuter airlines, construction companies, restaurants, and brokerage firms."

"All those enterprises are useful for what?" Burlane flipped through the magazine, reading headlines and picture captions.

"Useful for moving drugs and laundering drug money," Schott said.

"Heroin," Burlane said. He threw four chicken breasts and a half dozen pork chops into a large pan. He added a cup of water, a chopped onion, three healthy slugs of Kikkoman soy sauce, a couple dashes of vinegar, a small hit of sugar, two goodly pinches of salt, and a generous grind of black pepper. He put the lid on the pot and turned up the heat. "We'll let this reduce while the dough rises."

Schott, watching in amazement, said, "How much is that you added?"

"Oh, I don't know. What feels right."

"Why don't you measure?"

Burlane grinned. "I've made these things for years. Why should I measure? Besides that, if I measured everything, I might be a success. I might actually own something. You ever stop to think of that? Nothing to do now except wait while the meat cooks and the dough rises."

They went into the living room, cups of coffee in hand, to listen to the music.

As they settled in, Schott said, "Speaking of heroin, Jimmy— when they made that big bust in Los Angeles a week or so ago, they confiscated two tons of dope, ninety percent pure."

"At the Giddyup Saloon and Sporting House."

As Burlane mentioned the Giddyup Saloon, Jack Teagarden sang where he wanted to be. . . .

"Oh, I want to be
Part of that number
When the saints go marching in."

Schott said, "Well, my Langley friends say the Giddyup heroin came from Colombia—processed in a Cali lab. The Colombians have been growing their own poppies for about ten years." Schott frowned. "A few days after the Giddyup bust, one of Pena's pals was gunned down in Miami."

"And the conclusion being drawn by your friends at Langley?" Burlane looked curious.

"That the Chinese were sending word to the Colombians to lay off moving heroin on the West Coast."

"Ay!" Burlane pulled off a golfball wad of dough with his hand, which he pressed into a thin six-inch round.

Ara Schott watched this with enthusiasm. "*Sio pao.* Boy, I love 'em!"

"You won't have to go to China to eat right." Burlane and Schott usually froze the extras, popped them in the microwave, and zapped them for three minutes.

Schott said, "You want to watch the weather and find out how long we're going to have this snow?"

"Sure, go ahead." In the middle of the round of dough, Burlane put a couple of tablespoons of the cooked chicken and pork that he had removed from the bones, plus two-quarters of a boiled egg.

Schott used a remote to click off his stereo and turn on his smaller kitchen television set. On the screen, a woman explained the weather using a complicated vocabulary of highs, lows, fronts, and air masses. She had a map of the United States that was covered with arrows and abstract clouds, and neat little symbols for ice, snow, and rain.

Burlane pinched together the bottom of the first *sio pao* and put it on a small square of waxed paper. He set it aside and began forming another round of dough.

Schott punched the remote. The weatherwoman was replaced by two political journalists shouting at one another. He clicked the remote again.

Schott ran the palm of his right hand over the stubble of his crew cut. "Maybe the Blazers are playing. That'll cheer you up."

Burlane, forming another round of *sio pao* dough, looked disgusted as Schott paused briefly at the image of Senator Chet Gorman being interviewed.

Schott tapped the mute button.

Burlane said, "You know, every time I listen to that asshole Chet Gorman, I always wonder about his heroic Hanoi story."

"Well," Schott said, "he sure parlayed it into a hell of a political victory. When Byrd left the Senate not even Senator Rockefeller could have matched his avalanche of Christian bucks. How about a little brandy, Jimmy? Good on a cold winter night."

"Sure." He accepted a glass from Schott and took a sip. "Gorman's story is that he spent the last five and a half of his seven years of capture in solitary confinement, which means that none of the other prisoners saw him, right? That would be from February 1967, when his Air America plane was shot down, until June 1972, when he was returned in an exchange of prisoners of war."

Schott blinked. "Well, right, I guess. But there doesn't seem to be any doubt that he was there when the North Vietnamese released the prisoners. He's there square in the middle of all the pictures."

Burlane smacked his lips. "Say, that's good brandy, Ara. . . . Air America pilots routinely ferried heroin out of the Golden Triangle for Diem's generals." Burlane turned up the heat under Schott's steamer and returned to his chore.

Schott, a counterintelligence officer in the Company during the Vietnam War, was aware the Company had regarded Golden Triangle poppy growers as a buffer against the Chinese to the northeast. Waiting for Burlane to continue his story, Schott topped off their drinks.

Burlane said, "Uncle Ho was cooperating with the Chinese Triads too. He needed money to fight the war."

"I remember the reports," Schott said.

Burlane pressed out another round of dough. "Not long after Tet, I met a guy in an expat bar in Rangoon who claimed he knew Chet Gorman. He said he had served with Gorman in the marines and had seen him up-country."

"By 'up-country,' you mean the Golden Triangle."

Burlane nodded. "He was puzzled because he had heard Gorman had been captured. In March 1968, Gorman was supposed to have been in solitary confinement."

Burlane now had six complete *sio pao* buns, and Schott's steamer was ready. He took the lid off. He quickly arranged the filled buns inside and returned the lid. "These'll take fifteen minutes to steam, and we'll eat like Chinese emperors, Ara."

"Was the Rangoon guy telling the truth, do you think?"

Burlane pulled off another wad of dough. "At the time, I believed him, yes—figured it was probably some misguided Company business. I certainly remembered the story when Gorman popped out of nowhere to declare himself a candidate for Robert Byrd's old seat in the Senate. If it wasn't Company business, then whose business was it?"

ELEVEN

He had been living in a residential hotel in New Orleans until the day after Christmas, when he drove his Ford Bronco west on State Highway 90, looping down through bayou country, down through Houma and up through New Iberia to Lafayette, where he spent three days.

Then he drove around the Gulf of Mexico to the Mexican border, staying one night in Galveston, Texas. He stayed two nights in Brownsville, where he spent New Year's Eve drinking beer and watching a rented sex movie on the tube, then one day each in McAllen and El Paso, and two each in Nogales and Yuma, Arizona.

An athletic-appearing man in his late forties—slight yet muscular—he had oddly plump cheeks, a dimpled chin, pale blue eyes, and a roundish, fleshy mouth. He ordinarily wore running shoes, light tan cotton chinos or blue jeans, and a light sports jacket. He was suntanned and always wore a limp white tropical hat and aviator's sunglasses. Also, he was fluent in Spanish, and liked to joke and tell dirty stories with the Mexicans and Mexican Americans in bars along the border. He was not Hispanic himself; he was a gringo with pale gray eyes.

On January 7, he checked into Sharon's Ocean Getaway in Pacifica, California, a motel overlooking the Pacific Ocean six miles south of San Francisco. He settled his bill each morning, paying in cash.

On the night of January 17, he walked to a deli down the street and bought a ham-and-cheese sub with extra peppers, a package of Fritos, and a six-pack of Corona beer, which he took back to his room. He sat squat-legged on the carpet and opened a bottle. He ate the sandwich and watched the news on television.

The talk was the same everywhere. Congress was set to vote on a controversial proposal to save money by printing plastic bills, an idea also touted as helping the government foil counterfeiters and flush out hot money.

The man with the cleft chin imagined the rhetorical combatants as horseless riders and riderless horses in pitched battle. He giggled. He chewed on his sandwich with appreciation. He thought it was delicious. The beer was good, too.

He flipped to a Spanish-language program. The talk there was the same.

A female journalist asked her guest, the mayor of Matamoros, Mexico, if the proposal would seriously harm the drug trade.

The mayor looked amused. This was an American program, produced for Hispanic Americans, and he wanted to show off his good English. "You mean put the Colombians out of business?"

"*Sí.*"

The mayor burst out laughing. "*Ay! Caramba! Señora.* Ha, ha, ha! Oh, no, no, no! We both know that won't happen."

3

ON PLAYING THE QUEEN

JANUARY 19, 2000

"It's good information, that's all I
can tell you about it," the man said.
"There was one other thing . . . the
money is the key to this."

—Washington, D.C., lawyer,
quoted by Carl Bernstein
in *All the President's Men*

ONE

James Burlane had spent a long night watching television reports of the assault on the House of Representatives, and was lying in bed thinking about the terrorists and their motives when his cellular phone rang.

"Mr. Burlane?"

Burlane recognized President Thomas Erikson's voice immediately, and just as quickly suspected he knew just what the call was all about.

"Me, Mr. President."

"Mr. Burlane, I've been talking to former presidents and getting their advice. If ever there was a bipartisan moment, this is it. The

Vice President and I have no idea who might be behind this or where they might have friends in the government. You see our problem."

"After Aldrich Ames, I can understand the paranoia."

"Your name popped up in every conversation I had, Mr. Burlane. The Can-Do Man. You obviously know how to keep a secret. I had no idea Justice Shive's daughter had been kidnapped until I talked to Jimmy Carter."

"Carter told you that story?"

"He didn't know the details. He suggested I talk to Justice Shive. Under the circumstances, Shive felt the truth was in order. You never broke your vow of silence, and he respects you highly for that. The country owes you one, Mr. Burlane."

"It was fun pulping the crotch of that Yakuza soldier, that's a fact. Pornography is one thing. Sex slavery is another. I laid five straight shots square on his nuts, did Shive tell you that? Satisfaction."

Erikson made a noise in his throat. "Not to mention executing the most powerful godfather in Japan and leaving him in the embrace of a blow-up sex doll."

"Humping a sex doll. He deserved it. He was a prick. By the way, did Justice Shive say how Linda is doing?"

"Yes, he did. He said she's doing just fine, all things considered. She had recurring nightmares for a while, but she seems to be getting over the experience. He recommended that we talk to Senator Boulanger, and we did. I always wondered who was the mystery man behind the marimba coup. Good work!"

"Thank you, Mr. President."

"You were the hillbilly sharpshooter who helped the Brits kick those Arabs off Gibraltar."

"One of my personas."

"And you helped the German detective run down the Tigerman serial killer."

"Another asshole, if you'll pardon the vernacular."

"Mr. Burlane, the Vice President and I are in the market for a private can-do kind of man on this case. Would you be interested in the job?"

"I'd dearly love to kick the butts of whoever did this, and I've got a maximum-smart partner as you know. By the way, I'm now called Major M. Sidarius Khartoum, Mr. President."

"Major Khartoum it is. If you and your friend Mr. Schott will please stand by, I'll get back to you. In the meantime, I ask you not to repeat this conversation."

"Will do, Mr. President." Burlane hung up the phone and lay back in bed, thinking.

Burlane knew that most of the Company classics, those smooth, well-born suits with degrees from Ivy League universities, had taken a peek at his dossier. And now President Erikson had, too. They all knew Burlane was one part Euell Gibbons, one part Henry David Thoreau, and one part James Bond.

Bond was British Empire; his manners and the crease of his trousers were impeccable as the uniforms of advancing redcoats. Burlane was an independent, thoroughly American kind of spook, a Westerner by imagination and habit—more Davy Crockett or Daniel Boone than an agent of any bureaucracy. In fact, for sentimental reasons, he owned a Pennsylvania long rifle and had won prizes firing it in competition. He liked to cook, and carried a wok around with him. Those who had read his dossier knew an ultralight fishing rod was part of his traveling kit; he liked to hunt and dry mushrooms and wild foods; he was a reader.

Also, Burlane had, through long practice, developed an extraordinary ability to imitate birds. He had done this in building his persona of Larry Schoolcraft, a whistling wildlife photographer, in which guise he was able to carry telephoto lenses and parabolic microphones across international borders without raising undue suspicion.

Burlane suspected that while the classics were partly amused at his interests, they secretly feared anybody who thought about value, rather than how much everything cost.

It was a Company classic, Aldrich Ames, an American Judas, who had sold the country out—a man who, for mere money, had led honorable men to their deaths for no more reason than owning a Jaguar and a fancy house. Burlane believed that when the receipts of life were totaled by the final cashier, coins were a pathetic currency; the gold lay in memories of life fully lived.

In the end, the Company had sacked Burlane because his loyalty was to his country rather than to cant, dogma, or an institution. He could not, in his wildest nightmare, imagine an educated farmboy pulling an Aldrich Ames or conspiring to slaughter members of Congress gathered in the House chamber to represent their nation.

7:30 A.M.

Frank Coyle watched in thoughtful contemplation as FBI technicians scoured the chamber for spent slugs. After Puerto Rican malcontents had opened fire on the House floor from the visitors' gallery in 1948, a layer of bulletproof steel had been added to the backs of congressmembers' chairs, so slugs that had hit armored chairs ricocheted, some of them striking members. To make sure the terrorists hadn't had help on the inside, the FBI had to count bullets to make sure they matched the number of spent cartridges on the floor.

Coyle was a short, wide black man with broad shoulders, large hands, and a powerful body. He had been a star tailback at the University of Southern California, on the brink of a Heisman Trophy, when—on a long-ago, awful day in Seattle—a terrific hit by a Husky cornerback had torn apart the ligaments in his right knee, ending his dreams of the NFL.

Coyle was no stereotypical dumb jock; he put the tragedy aside and hit law school with the same passion and determination that he had once displayed ripping through a hole off right tackle. And after law school, he entered the FBI. He was a team player and felt comfortable working as a part of one. He was a competitor. He never quit.

Coyle, looking around the House chamber, wondered if those members who had voted against restrictions on fully automatic assault weapons might now be having second thoughts.

Coyle was suddenly aware of voices being raised, then shouting.

He looked up to see a stout, thick-shouldered man striding his way, followed by Capitol guards trying to restrain him. But he would have none of it, and bulled his way through all opposition.

He was headed for Coyle, who saw that he had a congressman's pin on the lapel of his jacket. A stevedore maybe. But a congressman? He was extremely agitated and not about to stop—at least for the moment.

A Capitol security guard trailed him, pistol drawn. "I know your orders, Mr. Coyle, but he just barged in here. We couldn't stop him."

Pleasantly, Coyle said, "Who are you, sir?"

"I'm Congressman Mitch Webster. I was elected by the people of Buffalo, New York, to be here. I have a right. I don't mean to be rude, but who are you?"

Coyle showed him his FBI boxtops. "I'm Special Agent Frank Coyle."

Webster studied the identification. "Frank Coyle, the football player?"

Coyle nodded.

"Jesus, you were good. Are you in charge of this investigation?"

"I'm temporarily in charge," Coyle said.

"Temporarily? Will you be permanently in charge?"

Coyle said, "I have no idea. That will be up to the director and the President, I suppose. We're trying to keep people out so we can collect evidence without contaminating it. That's why you were told you couldn't come in. You can understand that."

Webster looked about the bloodstained chamber. "There was supposed to be a revolution in 1994. That's what they said—all those smart-ass Republicans. I remember one of them was asked what his constituents wanted him to do in Congress. 'Three, two, one—blow it up,' he said. Can you imagine? The bastard had probably never been in a fistfight, and we wonder why some maniacs would even think of coming into the House chamber and just slaughter everybody in front of them. We invited them in here!"

The guard looked at Coyle, wondering if he should do something.

Coyle held up his hand. "Hear him out. Let him get it off his chest."

"People died for two hundred years to make this country safe for assholes like him, filled with wisecracks and hot air. Goddamn it, this is not just the floor of the House of Representatives; this is the People's House! The floor of the House of Freedom! You think that's corny? Sappy?"

"No sir, I most emphatically do not," said Coyle, who was himself the great-grandson twice removed of Africans brought to North Carolina as slaves.

Webster glared across the chamber, then began weeping. "We won't be able to get the goddamn blood off the walls and the chairs. We're going to have to burn the carpets! They're soaked with the blood of my friends. Look at this. Look at the blood. That aisle is less than twenty steps long. It was *stacked* with my dead friends."

The security guard said, "Mr. Coyle?"

"I said we'll hear him out." Coyle gave the guard a cool look. "It won't hurt us to listen to what he has to say. Respect what he's been through."

Looking around at the shambles of the House floor, Webster said, "All the overheated rhetoric, the puffed-up macho posturing. You'd have thought we would have learned after those fucksticks blew up the federal building in Oklahoma City, but we didn't. We went right back to the same old ways. We all pretend we don't know what's got them so worked up—all that hate. Well, think about it for a moment. Look at what's behind their rhetoric about the Trilateral Commission and their complaining about alleged secret deals made by the Rockefellers and the Rothschilds."

Coyle blinked. "And you're saying, bottom line?"

"I'm saying what people really don't like is democracy by the highest bidder. They're angry to the bone, which anybody should be who has half a brain. But we kept it up. Wouldn't stop. We were *asking* for this. We were *begging* for it. No wonder they called us cockroaches." Then his eyes watered up again and his chin bounced up and down.

"When I was elected, I wept with gratitude. I felt as if I'd been given the rarest gift imaginable, trust freely given by men and women I didn't know. They walked into a polling booth and punched a hole by my name." He wiped his eyes with the sleeves of his jacket. "My grandfather was a teamster. Do you know what that is?"

Webster plunged onward. "He drove an eight-horse hitch. Eight horses pulling a beer wagon to saloons in Buffalo. He got to be foreman by being able to whip any man who challenged him. My old man worked all his life to own one of those saloons. My mother started her day throwing fresh sawdust on the floor after she cleaned up the beer slop from the night before. They thought working and breathing were the same thing."

Coyle said, "Easy, easy, Congressman."

"When I opened my joint, my father, Big John Webster, who was named for John L. Sullivan, took my mother's hand at the doorway and told her, 'Our Mitch has done it. This is not a bar. This is a restaurant.' They had tears in their eyes. I was making a dream come true for them. My old man didn't want to eat chicken wings with his fingers because he didn't want to dirty the napkins. 'Real napkins, Helen,' he said. He told me, 'There's only two places in this world where you'll find true democracy, in the ring and in the grave, and the grave is the only one they can't fix.'"

Webster fell silent, his eyes filled with tears again.

Coyle said, "Maybe it wasn't militiamen. Maybe it was raghead nutballs. Followers of jihad looking to get saved."

"Arabs didn't do this."

Coyle shrugged his shoulders. "We'll see. We'll take our time and check everything out and eventually we'll run the scumbags down. We'll find who did it and why."

Webster said nothing for a moment, then looked at Coyle straight on. "When I raised my hand in that well down there, my heart was pounding. My mom and dad were up there in that gallery." He pointed to the balcony behind the Speaker's dais. "I swore to uphold and defend the Constitution of the United States." He gripped Coyle by the shoulder and squeezed hard. "Here is where you vote, Frank. Here is where you speak out. Here is where it counts. For every coward, there's a Wayne Morse telling the truth about Vietnam. For every scammer, there's a Tip O'Neill, who knew it was an honor to ask your neighbor for a vote."

Coyle put his arm around the distraught Webster. "It'll be okay," he said.

Webster said, "This is the People's House, Frank. If we can't get through this, it won't be okay. We risk losing it for good."

Coyle said, "I hear what you're saying. I love it, too, Mitch. I truly do."

"Will you get them for me, Frank? Will you do that?"

"I always played to win at USC," Coyle said. "I still do."

TWO

President Thomas Erikson knew there would be no shortage of critics and jaded journalists brandishing the advantage of hindsight as though it were equal to brains, who would be eager to let as much blood as possible. To them, truth was a kind of blood. Erikson regarded them as crazed pit bulls out to shock and amaze the credulous masses by drawing as much of that blood as possible with their teeth.

Reporters hadn't always been such barbarous cretins. When Erikson was a young man, television reporters had regarded themselves as journalists with serious responsibilities. Those were the golden days of CBS's national father figure, Walter Cronkite; ABC's straight-talking Howard K. Smith; and NBC's nightly duo of solemn Chet Huntley and serious young David Brinkley.

But the coming of cable television and intense competition for viewers had changed all that. Now, Erikson felt, television news was public theater. The networks now used the blood sport of spiking and bashing of political careers as a way to bolster their ratings. They were celebrity attack dogs, famed for baring their smiling fangs as they brought their prey to ground.

The most famous among the high-priced canines met on Sunday-morning talk shows, political High Mass. Erikson's friends in Congress said one of the regulars, a serious-faced, pontificating woman, was an imperious, haughty bitch as she prowled the halls of Congress. One of her comrades in these spirited jousts on the "issues" was an alleged liberal who sneered at Erikson's earnest efforts to address the needs of the middle class. This man had famous arched eyebrows in the form of inverted Vs. Erikson told his friends that judging from the vacuousness of this journalist's many forcefully stated opinions, his trademark eyebrows were larger than his brains.

But the Doberman journalist who really got under Erikson's skin was a silver-haired, right-wing ideologue who couldn't contain the spittle on his eager lips. This man, for whom few politicians were Republican enough, had been furious when Erikson had come from nowhere to supplant the faltering, suddenly aging Bob Dole in the 1996 Presidential race. House Speaker Newt Gingrich had responded to Dole's woes by jumping into the race himself. But Dole's supporters, regarding Gingrich as unelectable, rallied behind Erikson when Pat Buchanan fell on his extremist sword and "outsider" Lamar Alexander was revealed to be another rich hustler. Steve Forbes ended up flatter than his tax plan. Colin Powell amazed everyone by keeping his word and would not run.

The Doberman journalist, baring his polemical fangs on television, had urged Gingrich on. Temperate observers later said going with Erikson rather than Gingrich and his bloated egoism had enabled Republicans to beat Bill Clinton with a victory that Dole never would have been able to achieve.

* * *

The White House contained four floors. The President and his family lived on the top two floors; state dinners and Presidential receptions and other functions were held on the ground and first floors; tours of these rooms, conducted from 10:00 A.M. to noon, had been suspended under the security provisions of Contingency Delta.

The familiar grand columns over the main entrance to the White House faced Pennsylvania Avenue and Lafayette Park across the street, closed since the Oklahoma City bombing in 1995. The rear of the White House overlooked the mall and the Washington Monument.

Erikson ordinarily held meetings of his cabinet or the National Security Council in the Cabinet Room in the West Wing, overlooking the Rose Garden. But for this first meeting of the fifteen government and military figures who would take the first steps in guiding the national response to the assault on the House of Representatives, Erikson chose the Green Room for the meeting—so named because of the pale green silk that covered the walls. Through the right window of the Green Room—beyond the President's Garden and the Washington Monument—the President and the emergency committee could see the Tidal Basin over which the terrorist helicopters had exploded.

The men and women Erikson had chosen for this awful task gathered in the Green Room with cups of coffee in hand. They took turns in front of the window on the right side of the room, overlooking the south portico.

Even now, the morning after the tragedy, FBI dive-barges were moored on the Tidal Basin, two hundred feet shy of one mile distant.

When President Erikson entered the room, they retreated from the window and took their seats. Erikson helped himself to a cup of coffee from a silver urn atop a wheeled serving tray that the White House staff had rolled into the northeast corner of the room.

Then, with Vice President Gregg to his right, Erikson sat on the green-and-white-striped settee on the west wall beneath two oil paintings, Alvan Fisher's 1849 *Indian Guides*, in a heavy, gilded frame, and Ferdinand Richardt's mid-nineteenth-century *Independence Hall* in Philadelphia. In front of this settee was a polished sofa table with drop ends, flanked by green-cushioned side chairs.

General Robert Bach, chairman of the Joint Chiefs of Staff, took the chair to Erikson's left. Sanford Zalburg, the Attorney General, sat in the chair on Gregg's right.

Wes Mills, director of Central Intelligence, and Paul Barnhouse, National Security Advisor, sat in the Duncan Phyfe chairs between the sofa table and the fireplace on the east wall.

Claudia Merman, Chief Justice of the United States Supreme Court, and FBI director Edward Woolbright sat in chairs that flanked the Italian fireplace mantel.

Dennis Fuhr, Secretary of Defense, and Senator David McGrath, Senate majority leader, shared the mahogany bench in front of the left window. Senator Harold Untermeier, Senate minority leader, and Representative Charles Zacharia, the House majority leader, still suffering from headaches resulting from a neck wound in the *cucaracha* attack, took the matching bench in front of the right window.

Representative Edgar Poorman, the acting House minority leader, having been the Democratic whip, and Marine Lieutenant General Jeremiah Samuels, the commander of Contingency Delta, took the green-cushioned chairs on the north wall under George H. Durrie's 1858 painting *Farmyard in Winter*, depicting a Connecticut farm circa 1825.

Erikson licked his lips and took a deep breath. Looking up at the huge portrait of a pensive Benjamin Franklin hanging above the fireplace mantel, he said, "I thank you all for being on time this morning. I decided we should meet here this morning instead of the Cabinet Room because we have a view of the Tidal Basin. In the future we will meet in the Cabinet Room."

Erikson took a sip of coffee. "Before we address the many questions of the crisis at hand, I think we ought to consider the possibility of taping this morning's meeting. In the future, when all the many books on this tragedy have been published, the very least we can offer is an accurate record of what actually happened. We know from our experience with the Kennedy assassination that ambiguity is the fertilizer of conspiracy theories." Erikson looked around the table.

The matronly Justice Merman, a former member of the Federal Court of Appeals in San Francisco, said, "I agree, with a reservation. Ultimately, the record should be complete and accurate for the benefit of scholars. But until we know who or what we are dealing with, we need to be able to speak openly and candidly."

Erikson asked, "Others?" He looked at the FBI director. "Mr. Woolbright?"

Woolbright, a jowly, good-natured man who smoked a pipe, was a former chief of the Chicago Police Department. "I agree with the Chief Justice. We tape the meetings, but seal the tapes until this thing has come to some kind of resolution."

Erikson looked around the table. "There being no objections, we will tape our meetings with the understanding that the tapes will be locked under seal until such time as I and the attorney general mutually agree to move them or release them. Pray God sooner rather than later. Agreed?" Silence. "Doug?"

Vice President Gregg rose and left the room. Erikson shuffled papers, saying nothing.

When Vice President Gregg had returned and taken his place beside him, President Thomas Erikson stood. "There's really nothing I can add at this point that isn't already on the news. I'm told we now have one hundred seventeen congressmembers dead, and eight members in critical condition." He motioned with his head toward the window.

"I spent the night at my Contingency Delta location in Virginia. I flew back here early this morning after security perimeters had been established around the White House and the Capitol." He looked around the table, then bit his lower lip. "Charles?"

An eight-term Republican, the serious-minded majority leader Charles Zacharia—who had grown up on a wheat farm—was a broad-faced, muscular man, highly respected as a political deal-maker. "Do we have any idea if this is a domestic conspiracy or whether it is foreign-based?"

Erikson shook his head. "We don't. And to tell the truth, I don't know which would be worse. A domestic conspiracy would rip the country apart and a foreign conspiracy would likely lead to war. The public would demand it."

Zacharia shook his head. "Is a civil war any better?"

Erikson said, "Either way, there'll be no shortage of critics. I think there's one thing all of us in this room can agree on: There's no room here for out-of-control egos or partisan politics." Erikson bit his lip. "General Samuels tells me the terrorists were obviously skilled, trained professionals, yet they and their helicopters blew up. We don't know whether they were suicide volunteers or were double-crossed."

"We're starting at zero," Samuels said.

Erikson said, "We're faced with two immediate problems. We have to address the unfinished business of the House, and we need to calm and unite the nation behind a rigorous investigation."

Justice Merman said, "The Constitution provides that governors appoint replacements for a deceased senator, but not members of the House. Their seats must be filled by special election."

Zacharia said, "We obviously can't do business with a fourth of the seats vacant." He glanced at Poorman.

Poorman, a Democrat from Los Angeles, was famous for his quick wit, political courage, and rumpled suits. Poorman, it was said, looked like his name. Poorman said, "We shouldn't do it."

Erikson said, "I think the fairest solution would be to adjourn the House until we can elect new members. I will urge all the governors in the strongest terms to call their legislatures into session to draft emergency bills calling for special elections within sixty days. That would give candidates time to campaign, yet get the House back to work. I realize that a majority of the presidential primaries fall during that period. I don't know how that adds up or if it does. I just don't see any choice. Congressman Zacharia? Ed?"

"I agree," Zacharia said.

Poorman said, "How about if Charles and I and what's left of our leadership in the House get together this afternoon and talk this over? Charles?"

"We'll do it," Zacharia said.

Erikson said, "We can learn a lot from the experience of the Warren Commission. The public should be reassured from the start that there will be no lingering secrets from this investigation. Secrets are a debilitating political virus. There will be no such secrets here. Director Woolbright?"

"One thing we know for sure. This was no psychopath acting alone as in the case of Lee Harvey Oswald. This is clearly a conspiracy, and I think General Samuels is right. We're dealing with professionals. Whether this conspiracy is foreign or domestic in origin, we've got some extraordinary security problems. I think the Director of Central Intelligence would agree with me on this."

DCI Wes Mills, white-haired and spit shine correct atop bird-thin legs, was a retired Marine Corps general. Mills, sitting seemingly at attention, replied, "I certainly do. We caught the Israelis spying on us, and they were supposed to be our allies. We all know about Aldrich Ames and how the KGB wormed their way into the National Security Agency. We should make every effort to be very, very careful about how we proceed."

Erikson thought about that for a moment, then said, "Until we know who the conspirators are, no government agency should be above suspicion of harboring their friends. Can we all agree to that?" He checked around the table. There were no dissenters. "Director Woolbright?"

"I agree."

"Wes?"

Mills said, "Yes."

Erikson said, "Our investigators will have to work in a firestorm of rumor and speculation. A select group of distinguished Americans should be invited to join those present as the nucleus of a national commission to oversee the investigative task force." He checked the table, inviting questions or objections.

"In the case of the Kennedy assassination, President Lyndon Johnson chose the Chief Justice of the Supreme Court, Earl Warren. If he will accept, I propose to appoint Jimmy Carter. Since leaving office, President Carter has achieved a level of credibility in the minds of the American people that I believe is beyond question." Erikson paused. "Are there any objections?" He waited.

He continued. "FBI director Woolbright has recommended that a chief investigator be appointed immediately while memories of eyewitnesses are fresh and there is physical evidence to be collected. Do you have a recommendation, Eddie?"

Woolbright said, "Yes, I do; Frank Coyle, the man who was on the scene this morning and temporarily in charge. He's a veteran agent, widely respected by his colleagues."

Merman raised an eyebrow. "The football player."

"Former football player. He's currently in charge of special and extraordinary inquiries. When we've got a tough one, he's the one we call. He was second-in-command of the investigation of the explosions under the World Trade Center in New York, and was one of the first investigators on the scene at Oklahoma City."

Erikson said, "Unless there are objections, I think we should immediately name Coyle as the chief investigator. The public needs to be reassured that the government is acting quickly and responsibly and their best man is already on the job. Objections?"

There were none.

THREE

A cold wind was blowing across the Tidal Basin from the north-west and Frank Coyle, standing on the shore in front of the Jefferson Memorial, fastened the top button of his mackintosh trench coat. In front of him, FBI divers were slipping into the cold water.

Coyle was grateful that the marine chopper had confronted the terrorists when it did. Another half mile and the fleeing Kiowas would have been over the Potomac River, and the divers would have had to work in a current.

The terrorists had attacked the Capitol from where it was the most vulnerable, from the south, a four-block jigsaw of on-ramps and off-ramps and the Capitol power plant. The Mall afforded them a six-hundred-foot-wide avenue to begin their escape; if they had made it to the Potomac, which flowed from the creeks and streams of the Allegheny Mountains of West Virginia, they would have had a broad expanse of water for the final leg of their escape south to the Chesapeake Bay.

As was learned in the bombings of the Pan Am flight over Lockerbie, Scotland, the World Trade Center, and Oklahoma City, conventional explosives don't evaporate their targets. They just blow them apart. With patience and hard work, the Bureau divers would be able to put the Kiowas back together, if not the remains of the terrorists themselves.

Coyle decided that he would have night-lights installed around the Tidal Basin so divers could work twenty-four hours a day.

Coyle looked across the water and the grass past the Washington Monument at the White House. Was a worried Thomas Erikson watching from his bedroom window?

11:30 A.M.

Carter Commission Exhibit 18-Jan-B2

Taped interview by Special Agent Frank Coyle of Marine Corps helicopter pilot Lieutenant Dan Boylan, of Kalamazoo, Michigan. Deposition taken in the pilots' scramble room of the Emergency Command Center, the Pentagon.

COYLE: I want to go through your pursuit of the terrorists on Wednesday night, Lieutenant. I want to know everything, minute by minute if possible. I say again, I want to know everything, even if you don't think it's important.

BOYLAN: Sure. I'll never forget that night, that's for sure. When the call to scramble came, I and the other pilots on duty were watching the old Burt Lancaster movie on television, *The Professionals*, and talking about the New York Knicks, who were due up after the movie. The horn went off and we popped to our feet, and the duty officer said there had been an attack on

Congress, and the terrorists were fleeing to the northeast in helicopters.

COYLE: How did he do this, the duty officer, I mean?

BOYLAN: On the intercom. We always keep at least four pilots on duty in case of just such an emergency. That's SOP. When the call comes in, the duty officer relays it to us on the intercom, and we're off and running. Our mission is to get in the air ASAP.

COYLE: Did the duty officer tell you how many helicopters?

BOYLAN: Yes, he did. He said two.

COYLE: Go ahead, Lieutenant, tell me what you did.

BOYLAN: My copilot and I . . .

COYLE: His name?

BOYLAN: Lieutenant Charles Beaver, sir.

COYLE: Okay.

BOYLAN: Charlie and I ran to our Apache and got aloft as quickly as we could.

COYLE: How many helicopters did you put aloft?

BOYLAN: Ultimately, six, sir. But Charlie and I were the first to get into the air.

COYLE: What happened then?

BOYLAN: The air-control officer said the unfriendlies were flying west down the Mall.

COYLE: And your instructions were?

BOYLAN: To close fast on them, and to observe them, but not to fire. We were to force them down at a designated area.

COYLE: You were armed, I take it.

BOYLAN: Yes sir, to the teeth. We could evaporate a target if we wanted.

COYLE: When did you first see them?

BOYLAN: When we were about halfway across the Potomac. They were running without night-lights, but I could see them as they passed through patches of fog.

COYLE: Where? Where were they when you first spotted them?

BOYLAN: On the far side of the Tidal Basin flying just above the water, ten or twelve feet, say.

COYLE: By the far side, I take it you mean the northeast side.

BOYLAN: Yes sir.

COYLE: What happened then?

BOYLAN: I closed on them almost in the middle of the Tidal Basin so I moved to one side to let them pass. We were under orders to hold our fire.

COYLE: Could you see the pilot and passengers?

BOYLAN: I could see people in there, a pilot and passengers, but no details. It was dark. Everything happened very quickly, and I had to fly my chopper in foggy conditions.

COYLE: I'm told they were Kiowas. Tell me about Kiowas.

BOYLAN: They're reconnaissance helicopters manufactured by Bell Helicopters for the army. I think they're capable of holding six people. The army uses them for flying commanders around. They're fast, but no match for my Apache, which is an attack helicopter designed to carry marines into combat.

COYLE: What else? Tell me what you saw and what you did.

BOYLAN: They were flying single file without running lights.

COYLE: [Interrupts.] Specifically, how many pilots and passengers did you see in each helicopter?

BOYLAN: A male pilot accompanied by a male and what appeared to be a female in the lead chopper. A male pilot and two male companions in the second. It all happened so fast. I had to worry about being fired upon. I had a crew to protect.

COYLE: Exploded. Boom. Just like that.

BOYLAN: Yes sir. Into incredible bursts of flame.

COYLE: Simultaneously or one chopper at a time?

BOYLAN: Simultaneously. One second they were on my flank, and the next second, *pow!*

COYLE: Did you see the terrorists throw anything out of their helicopters?

BOYLAN: No sir, I did not.

COYLE: Could somebody have jumped out?

BOYLAN: Sir?

COYLE: You said they were flying just above the water. Ten or twelve feet, you said. You said there was a patchy fog, so you could still see them from some distance. I assume they could see you as well.

BOYLAN: Yes sir, I assume they could.

COYLE: So they had some warning. Would it have been possible for someone to jump out of one or both of those choppers into the water?

BOYLAN: Into the Tidal Basin?

COYLE: That's right.

BOYLAN: Sure, I suppose. What's a jump that low? Nothing.

COYLE: But you didn't see anybody jump.

BOYLAN: No sir, I didn't.

2:00 P.M.

Frank Coyle walked slowly along the lines of yellow nylon strings being stretched above at the site of the exploded truck at South Capitol and K Street just south of Highway 395. South Capitol had been blocked off so the forensics technicians wouldn't have to deal with traffic, gawkers, and passersby.

Examiners in white smocks, rubber gloves, and plastic booties were attaching strings to neat rows of stainless-steel pegs that had been driven into the pavement in an enormous circle surrounding the blast site.

Aware of the traffic zooming by on the freeway one block to the north, Coyle knelt beside Skip Roberts, the forensics investigator in charge. Roberts, a thin blond man with a largish nose, sat on a canvas director's chair at a folding table, entering data into an IBM laptop computer.

Forensics examiners had needed only hours to find the identification number of the van that delivered the explosives to the parking garage below the World Trade Center in New York—eventually leading to the arrest and conviction of the Muslim terrorists who had planted the bomb. And they found the axle with the telltale numbers within hours of the bombing in Oklahoma City.

NEIL ABERCROMBIE & RICHARD HOYT

But in both New York and Oklahoma City, the blasted evidence had landed on concrete. Here they had to deal with dirt and gravel.

Roberts and his forensics examiners would slowly and carefully recover everything at the blast site, from cigarette butts and bottle caps to shards of glass and pieces of metal and plastic. They would photograph each item and, using the FBI's mainframe computer, they would reassemble the shards and pieces—much like an elaborate jigsaw puzzle—to yield the make, model, and year of the exploded rig.

Seeing Coyle, Roberts paused in his chores. He looked up, adjusting his eyeglasses. "Hello, Frank."

"Skip."

"We've just started on the grids. One square foot for each square. We'll take a photo of each grid and have it blown up in the lab before we clear it with magnifying glasses."

"Before and after photos to make sure you've got everything."

Roberts nodded.

Coyle glanced up at the sky. "What if it snows?"

Roberts pursed his lips. "Rain is as bad or worse than snow and the wind is even worse. After we get the grids marked, we'll clear some paths so we can pitch a tent. It's the best we can do under the circumstances. But it will help to keep the place secure and we can work around the clock that way."

"How long will it take, do you think, Skip?"

Roberts shrugged. "Hard to tell. If we luck out like we did in New York and Oklahoma City, we could score in a day or two. If not, it might take a week or more even working around the clock. It's impossible to say for sure. These shits didn't use firecrackers. They did a real number on the truck."

Coyle sighed.

"We've got our best people on the job, Frank. We'll work around the clock, but we can only go so fast. If we try to hurry it, we risk screwing up."

Coyle squeezed Roberts's shoulder. "Do your best, Skip, nobody can ask any more than that."

Roberts clenched his jaw. "Eventually we'll figure it out, Frank. We won't quit until we do."

3:15 P.M.

Frank Coyle stopped briefly by the spot on Bangor Street in the Anacostia District, one mile east of the Firth Sterling Gate—the northernmost entrance to U.S. Naval Station Washington—and three-fourths of a mile northeast of St. Elizabeth's Hospital, where the poet Ezra Pound had been incarcerated for years in an effort to save him from prison on charges of collaborating with the Italian Fascists in World War II.

The Firth Sterling Gate was a half mile northwest off the Anacostia Helicopter Facility where the presidential helicopter was kept and maintained, and one mile north of the Defense Intelligence Agency Analysis Center.

Chief Forensics Examiner Katherine Nevy was in charge of the reconstruction of the destroyed car, using the same computer-assisted reconstruction techniques employed by Skip Roberts on the South Capitol site.

Nevy's team, like Roberts's, was in the process of clearing space to erect a tent over the blast site. They, too, would work around the clock.

Although an automobile was a less complex assignment than a truck, Nevy told Coyle it would take days if not a week or more for her team to identify the car so it could be traced.

7:00 P.M.

Carter Commission Exhibit 18-Jan-B3

Taped interview by Special Agent Frank Coyle, of William and Anne Terwilliger, of Carson City, Nevada. Deposition taken at the J. Edgar Hoover Building, Pennsylvania Avenue at Ninth Street, Washington, D.C.

COYLE: I want to thank you for taking time out to talk to me tonight.

W. TERWILLIGER: No problem. No problem at all. If there's anything we can do to help.

A. TERWILLIGER: Anything.

COYLE: I want to know where you were and why you were there and what you heard and saw.

W. TERWILLIGER: We were the guests of Congressman Bill Bernhart—one of those who were killed. We had been volunteers in his campaign from the beginning. He was going to meet us right after the vote. We'd wandered down the Capitol steps toward the center of the plaza to shoot some video of the statue of Freedom on top of the dome.

A. TERWILLIGER: Congressman Bernhart was the one who got the guards to let us video the statue of Freedom.

W. TERWILLIGER: We were just returning when we saw the terrorists running down the stairs.

A. TERWILLIGER: [Pause.] Hard to believe what happened.

COYLE: Take your time.

W. TERWILLIGER: We were standing at the bottom of the steps in the parking lot when we heard what sounded like a string of firecrackers going off in the Capitol Building.

A. TERWILLIGER: At the top of the granite stairs.

COYLE: What happened then?

W. TERWILLIGER: Just as we heard the firecrackers, or what sounded like firecrackers, two helicopters came swooping in and landed at the lawn on the far side of the parking lot.

COYLE: Go on.

W. TERWILLIGER: The firecrackers stopped, and a woman and two men with little assault rifles came running down the stairs.

COYLE: "Little assault rifles"?

W. TERWILLIGER: Machine pistols, I think they call them. They had masks on. You know the kind. Skiers wear them.

COYLE: Did they see you?

W. TERWILLIGER: If they did, they didn't pay any attention to us. They ran across the parking lot, and a couple of seconds later, the two helicopters took off.

COYLE: Did they say anything?

W. TERWILLIGER: The man kept repeating a word, but I don't know what it was. It was in a foreign language.

A. TERWILLIGER: Spanish, I think. He kept shouting it to the woman as they ran.

COYLE: Did you see anybody else run for the helicopters?

W. TERWILLIGER: No, we didn't. But our attention was on the noise and the people in masks running down the stairs.

COYLE: After the helicopters took off, what then?

W. TERWILLIGER: Then I remembered my camera.

A. TERWILLIGER: This man came down the stairs, screaming and shaking his fist. He was covered with blood.

COYLE: Representative Leo Carney of Oregon.

W. TERWILLIGER: We didn't know he was a congressman then.

A. TERWILLIGER: He was just an enraged man covered with blood. Bill took his video.

W. TERWILLIGER: Everybody wanted it. The *New York Times*. The *Washington Post*. Everybody. But I gave it to the Associated Press so everybody could use it.

COYLE: You gave it to them?

W. TERWILLIGER: This isn't something to make money off of, a tragedy like this. They said they'd file for a copyright in my name.

A. TERWILLIGER: I'll never forget the look on that man's face.

COYLE: Representative Carney's.

A. TERWILLIGER: [Pause.] It was like he was crying and screaming at the same time. And the blood. He was covered with blood. We knew something horrible had happened inside. It was awful.

FOUR

President Thomas Erikson waited, studying his notes. He checked his watch. Five minutes to go.

Behind him on his left, the presidential flag; on his right rear, the stars and stripes of Old Glory.

In front of him, technicians were adjusting the lights on either side of the pool television cameras that rested atop the gold-and-white seal of the United States.

He took a drink of water.

Feeling suddenly old beyond his fifty-eight years, and tired, he glanced up at the presidential seal in relief on the ceiling.

Erikson's left shoulder ached from the arthritis that he had inherited from his mother and which plagued him with every change of weather. Now he was hit by a needle of pain.

The floor director said, "Three minutes, Mr. President."

Erikson nodded.

The fall and winter were the worst for the arthritis, and lately, with one storm front after another swinging southeast out of Canada and across the Great Lakes, he could hardly lift his arm. Another stab of pain.

On the far end of his office, behind the cameramen and technicians, Rembrandt Peale's round portrait of George Washington in the uniform of the Continental army hung above the white marble fireplace mantel.

He sighed and looked at the Frederic Remington bronze cowboy atop a rearing bronco in front of the small window on the east wall of his office. After four years in office he had become used to the White House portraits and the statues that reflected his country's rich heritage and traditions, young as it was. Now, when the United States was in grave peril, he was overcome by love of country.

Erikson was president. Somewhere out there, far beyond the television cameras resting on the great seal, real cowboys still rode the high country. These cowboys, along with more than 260 million of their fellow citizens, had put their trust in him in an electoral ritual as close to sacred as a secular society could allow. Not all of them agreed with his politics, but he was their president and his responsibility was awesome. They were counting on him and he, dear God, on them.

The lights snapped on, hot in his face.

The United States had its faults, that was true. But it had its accomplishments as well. It had given the world representative democracy as outlined in *The Federalist Papers* by Alexander Hamilton, James Madison, and John Jay, plus jazz, and the private-detective novel. American soldiers had whipped fascism and American determination had brought the Stalinists to ruin. Not bad.

The floor director said, "One minute and counting, Mr. President."

This wasn't the first time Erikson had gone through the drill of addressing his countrymen on national television, but never on an occasion of such gravity.

He looked straight at the camera, determined to do his job and do it well. He would give them the awful numbers: 117 dead and 36 wounded in the House chamber with 8 in critical condition at Walter Reed Army Hospital; 23 Capitol police and congressional staff killed and 14 wounded; 12 killed in the gallery, hallways, and elevators, plus 1 District of Columbia police officer and 2 unknown males. In San Francisco, the count was 2 dead Senators and their wives plus 2 drivers.

He would tell them about the Carter Commission and the need for the states to hold special elections to restore balance to the House of Representatives.

Rally the country. Lead it forward.

"Thirty seconds, Mr. President."

He tried to swallow. He drained a glass of water.

A bolt of pain ripped through his shoulder.

He thought of Tom Paine: *"These are the times that try men's souls."*

The red light went on.

"Good evening, my fellow Americans . . ."

Fifteen minutes later, he shifted forward in his chair.

"In the last several years, our national political and cultural dialogue has been dominated by the question of what sort of country we will become in the twenty-first century. We are at the end of a political millenium. What course our future would follow promised to be at the heart of this first Presidential election of the new century. As we stood on this cusp of American history, just days into the year 2000, we were struck by this obscenity.

"We will not let terrorists or conspirators defeat us. We will defend our national honor, and we will not, under any circumstances, allow it to be taken by assault weapons. We are a valiant people, a people of vision, come together from all continents and the most diverse of cultures in pursuit of a common dream of freedom. That is our historic legacy. It is our inevitable destiny. Of that there is not now and never will be any doubt.

"God bless the United States of America."

The red light went off.

President Thomas Erikson, suddenly fighting back tears, stared past the cameras at George Washington's portrait.

FIVE

The White House

11:30 P.M.

When James Burlane arrived in President Erikson's private office on the second floor of the White House, escorted by a marine sergeant in dress uniform, Erikson and Vice President Gregg were watching a portable Magnavox television set, where the story of the hour was of the President's message from the Oval Office.

The Oval Office was intended largely for public functions; Erikson retreated to his private office to read and study the issues before him. The President, seeing Burlane and his escort, tapped the mute button on the remote.

The marine said, "Mr. President, sir, Major M. Sidarius Khartoum."

Erikson said, "Thank you, George. That will be all."

The marine came to attention and saluted. "Mr. President, sir." He pivoted and left.

Erikson punched a button on the white telephone and intercom transceiver on his handsome desk and said, "We are to be left alone until further notice or unless it's a hot-line call or there is a new development about the terrorists. There are to be no other interruptions. None."

On the intercom, a male's voice said, "No interruptions, Mr. President. Will do."

"When I say none, I mean just that."

"Yes sir, Mr. President. Got it."

Burlane looked about the richly appointed room.

The President eyed the long-haired figure standing before him. Burlane had a gray handlebar mustache and his curly gray hair fell in a tangled mane about his shoulders.

Burlane said, "I expect Andy Jackson had a few of the rabble like me in here, too." He smiled. "He was the champion of common people, right."

Erikson extended his hand. "Major Khartoum."

Gregg said, "You look more like Wild Bill Hickok than a Company man."

Burlane said, "Sacked Company man, Mr. Vice President. I don't want to be confused with suits. A necktie is a hangman's noose, no offense. An honor to meet you both. By the way, Mr. President, I thought that was a first-rate speech tonight." He glanced at the screen where former president George Bush was being interviewed. "What're they saying?"

"That this surpassed the attack on Pearl Harbor as a national day of infamy, and that the president's performance was right up there with the best of presidents under crisis—Abe Lincoln, Franklin Roosevelt, et cetera," said Gregg.

Burlane looked at the set. "The television ratings are soaring. The networks must love it."

Erikson said. "Would you like a little Wild Turkey and branch water while we talk?"

Burlane nodded yes. "In view of what's happened, I think one is called for."

Erikson poured Burlane a drink.

Burlane gestured at the Magnavox. "This room was imagined in the Age of Reason. A television set looks like a tumor in here."

Erikson grimaced. "Won't you take a seat, Major Khartoum?" He sat in an easy chair with rounded arms upholstered in a flowered chintz that matched the curtains.

Burlane sat in a mahogany chair upholstered in a pale blue.

Gregg poured a drink for the President and one for himself, and sat down in a chair matching Burlane's.

Erikson sipped his drink and said, "Let me get straight to the point, Major Khartoum." He gestured at the television set. "You watched my address tonight, and you know speculation is already rampant that drug barons are likely behind this attack, what with the money bill and the attack in San Francisco."

Burlane nodded yes.

"It's bad enough if we're dealing with drug barons, if that's who was behind it. At least they're based in Colombia. What if the drug cartel isn't involved? What if it's an internal conspiracy?"

Burlane took a sip of whiskey. "The first step in an attempt to take over the government. Indeed. What if?"

Erikson said, "Just last year we had to jail two federal prosecutors who were working for the Cali drug barons. You tell us, is it smart for the Vice President and me to totally trust our so-called professionals with an investigation into this business without some kind of fail-safe? Who knows where the conspirators' friends are?"

"Under the circumstances, you should be careful. I agree."

The three men fell into silence, thinking. Burlane was struck by how small Erikson and Gregg seemed. On television, bearing the trappings of power, they seemed larger than life. Civil gods. Now they looked tiny and vulnerable. Frail. A little scared.

Erikson said, "Tell us, Major Khartoum. What are your politics? The Vice President and I are both political men, and under the circumstances we feel compelled to ask you about your politics."

Gregg smiled. "You appreciate our curiosity."

Burlane said mildly, "Sure, I understand why you ask the question, and I suppose I don't blame you. I'm not a Republican, if that's what you want to know."

"No?" Erikson glanced at Gregg.

"No. And I'm not a Democrat either. But if I told you I was an Independent, you wouldn't be satisfied, would you? I'll have to be more specific than that."

"I think so," Erikson said.

"I don't want to be flip at a time like this, but I think the best way to understand politics is to watch nature films of bower birds and eland antelopes and so on."

"Bower birds?" Erikson cocked his head.

"Male bower birds compete for females by building elaborate nests. The females watch them and judge. The fancier the nest, the more likely they are to score. Zoologists call this 'display' on the part of the males."

"And the elands?"

"The male eland who stakes out the safest territory with the best grazing gets his end in and reproduces himself. The losers live at the edges, inviting attack by hyenas. Surely you and Vice President Gregg have witnessed similar behavior by your political friends and acquaintances." Burlane looked at Erikson, then at Gregg.

Gregg, glancing at Erikson, smiled.

"We humans are cooperative predators. Our ancestors roamed in packs, working together to bring down animals that were stronger and faster than they were. Republicans and Democrats are packs of predators pursuing money, modern meat."

Erikson laughed. "Really, that's how you look at it?"

"Greed is a legacy of our genetic inheritance, Mr. President. The Founding Fathers anticipated Charles Darwin when they wrote the Constitution. In the end, we'll find that whoever attacked the House of Representatives did it in pursuit of some form of meat."

Burlane, looking bemused, said, "In the Caribbean, there's a bird ritual in which a senior male and a younger apprentice dance on a curved bough that is inherited and passed on from generation to generation. They dance for up to ninety percent of the daylight hours, nine months running. A female watches, and if she is pleased, she may grant her favors to the senior bird. She's quite fickle given the time and energy invested in trying to impress her."

Gregg glanced at Erikson. "Can the senior bird deny the apprentice the bough if he chooses?"

"Yes, he can," Burlane said. "The apprentice has to get the dance right. If the senior bird is pleased, he may surrender the bough and retire."

Erikson said, "What kind of animal are you most like, Major Khartoum—other than a human?"

Burlane thought about that for a moment. "Probably an orangutan. I'm fairly smart for a primate, and I prefer privacy and solitude over parties and crowds. Once in a while, when I spot a comely female in estrus, I do my best to fulfill our mutual craving, but I watch the trumpeting and braying of elephants and donkeys from the shadows."

He took another sip of whiskey. "I regard myself as someone who genuinely loves his country, although I would never fly a flag in my front yard as proof of it." He squatted before Erikson's heavy, solid desk, and ran his hand over the carved American eagle on the front.

President Erikson, watching him, said, "I take it you admire the desk."

"It's truly extraordinary. Having a desk like this is almost worth running for president."

"One of the perks," Vice President Gregg said. He looked rueful. "I had my shot at it, but came up short." Glancing at Erikson, he looked amused. "I'm still learning the dance."

Erikson said, "If we don't pin these terrorists, we'll both have to surrender the bough."

James Burlane, having finished discussing the details of the President's assignment, started to go, then stopped with his hand at his forehead, looking puzzled. Had he just remembered something? He started to speak, then closed his mouth.

Erikson, watching him, said, "Tell us everything on your mind. We need everything aboveboard."

Burlane smiled. "As you know, Mr. President, computers have made greed a spoor that's easily masked. In the bad old days there were paper trails to follow. My partner and I have decided we need to add a special talent to help us follow the scent of money through silicon cul-de-sacs and detours. We've been trying to recruit an exceptional candidate. Now is when we might need her the most, depending, uh, on whether or not she can be made available." Burlane cleared his throat.

"Depending on whether she can be made available. Will you explain that?"

"She's a superhacker, Mr. President. Maybe the best. Ara and I have been trying to recruit her to be a kind of electronic bloodhound for Mixed Enterprises. It's the modern world."

"Oh?"

Burlane said, "Her accomplishments are widely acknowledged, if not universally admired. Cyberfox, Mr. President."

Erikson looked surprised. "Jane Griffin? Isn't she in . . ."

"She's doing three years in the federal correctional facility in Allenwood, Pennsylvania. But she's no criminal, and everybody knows it. She was just trying to see what she could do twisting the tail of a few mobsters and some uptight bureaucrats. It was a form of challenge."

"Sure it was."

Burlane shook his head. "She got three years for exposing the mob. American justice."

Erikson said, "She's an obvious anarchist!"

"That might be taking it a bit far, Mr. President. She is high-spirited, I agree, but not out of control. We both know if she hadn't yanked the FBI's chain along with the mafia's or if she'd worn a necktie and hired fancy lawyers, she'd have been put on probation. We all know her real crime was eyeing the flow of political money. So now we've made her Saint Joan of the hackers."

"Jane Griffin!"

"Mr. President, if it turns out that we really need Cyberfox, do you suppose you can arrange a parole or leave or whatever? Ara and I would give her a job, no problem. Her mind is being wasted where she is now. Let her earn her freedom by helping her country."

Erikson said, "Major Khartoum, if you think you need her, you just check back with me and tell me why. I'll listen. If Jane Griffin helps us pin the people behind these attacks, yes, I'll write her a pardon."

SIX

President Erikson and Vice President Douglas Gregg joined Frank Coyle in front of the window of the Green Room. In the far distance, they could just see FBI divers working from a platform anchored on the Tidal Basin in front of the Jefferson Memorial.

Erikson eyed Coyle over the brim of the coffee cup. "So who do you think is most likely behind this, Mr. Coyle?"

Coyle bunched his face. "I have no idea." He smiled grimly. "The usual suspects."

Erikson stared at the ceiling for a moment, saying nothing. Then he said, "A domestic conspiracy involving people inside government? Is that possible?"

Coyle glanced quickly at the Vice President, then back at the President. He cleared his throat. "Hard to forget Oklahoma City."

Erikson said, "Tell us, Mr. Coyle, what is the ordinary motivation for people who betray their country?"

Coyle didn't hesitate. "Sex, money, and ideology, Mr. President."

The President raised an eyebrow. "And power."

"Money is power, Mr. President. The more money you have, the more power you can buy. The more power you have, the more money you can bank."

Gregg said, "NRA nutballs are fueled by ideology."

"Ideology, yes," Coyle said.

"Antiabortionists."

"Religion would fall under ideology as well."

"In the case of the mafia or drug cartels?" asked Gregg.

"Money."

Gregg said, "And the Puerto Ricans who attacked the House in 1948?"

"Ideology."

Erikson asked, "What about Alger Hiss?"

"Ideology," Coyle said.

"And Julius and Ethel Rosenberg?"

"Ideology, Mr. President."

"Lee Harvey Oswald?"

Coyle cleared his throat. "We think ideology, but perhaps money as well. But since Norman Mailer's *Oswald*, pathology also. Pathology, ideology. More often than not the same thing."

"Aldrich Ames?"

Coyle's face tightened. "Money."

The President said, "And if you were to bet the odds in this case?"

"Ahh, money." Coyle took a sip of coffee.

"Which means the mafia or drug barons." Erikson leaned forward.

"Or, uhh . . ." Coyle licked his lips.

Erikson said, "Say what's on your mind, Mr. Coyle."

"Or somebody after political power."

Erikson sighed.

Gregg, glancing at the President, said, "Which of the motives are easier to deal with?"

"Greed is more predictable than sex or ideology," said Coyle.

"Mr. Coyle, do you remember the case a few years back where an investigator hired by the Senate Select Narcotics Committee exposed the chief legal counsel as working for the Cali drug cartel?" asked the President.

Coyle said, "Yes, I do. He nailed one of our people, too."

"Working for the Cali cartel."

Coyle looked chagrined. "Unfortunately."

Gregg said, "Do you know the name of the committee investigator?"

Coyle eyed the Vice President, then the President. "No, sir, I don't. As you can imagine, there was much speculation in the bureau, but his identity was never made public."

Erikson said, "The investigator made eighteen million dollars flying Colombian coke into Miami, and turned it all over to the committee. Do you recall that?"

"Yes, I do," Coyle answered. "It was extraordinary. A troop of Boy Scouts and Girl Scouts dumped the money in a pile in front of C-SPAN's cameras."

Erikson smiled. "Do you know the name of the Company man who was assigned special duty as a field agent for the National Security Council before Colonel Chet Gorman's tour of duty?"

"A man named James Burlane."

"Do you know what happened to Burlane?"

Coyle said, "He was sacked because he objected to proposals to fund the Nicaraguan contras secretly."

"And why did Burlane object? Do you know that?"

Coyle nodded. "The story is he had the balls to tell Casey that Congress specifically denied funds for the Contras. To fund them secretly was a violation of the Constitution."

Erikson said, "Vice President Gregg and I want task-force ID cards issued to Major M. Sidarius Khartoum, Burlane's current nom de guerre, and his associate, Ara Schott. Do you know who Schott is?"

"He is the former Chief of Counterintelligence for the CIA, a first-rate security officer."

Erikson said, "Burlane and Schott together form their own investigating firm, Mixed Enterprises. The names of Burlane and Schott are not to be found on any task-force budget or personnel lists. The Vice President and I will take care of Mixed Enterprises' fee from our own budgets."

"As insurance against a mole in the task force," Coyle said. "Not at all a bad idea."

"If Burlane or his nom de guerre appears in any newspaper or television report, the Vice President and I will hold you personally responsible."

Coyle said, "Understood, sir. With the sums of money available to the drug cartel and its mafia allies, any number of people are potential moles."

"The President and I expect you to give Burlane all possible cooperation," said the Vice President.

"Yes, of course. That goes without saying," Coyle agreed.

Erikson said, "The Vice President and I expect you to give us periodic private briefings on the task-force investigation. Khartoum and his partner will be doing the same regarding their inquiries."

They fell momentarily silent, watching the divers work in the distance. Some trucks arrived and workers began erecting what looked like light poles on the curved shore of the Tidal Basin.

Coyle said, "I ordered lights erected so the divers can work around the clock. They've got high-powered underwater lights that can make the bottom of the Tidal Basin look like the top of a kitchen table."

Erikson said, "What goes down stays down."

"Everything that went down with the explosion we'll eventually find," Coyle said.

Erikson said, "Just as long as the truth comes with it, Mr. Coyle. "

9:30 A.M.

Frank Coyle and James Burlane sipped coffee while they waited for breakfast at a spartan yet comfortable and cozy place called the Florida Avenue Grill. Burlane was the only white face among the customers packed into the cramped floor space.

"Your grits will be good, and there'll be plenty of them," Coyle said.

"I bet there will be," Burlane said, looking around.

"The lady in the kitchen knows how to cook an egg over easy, guaranteed. When the white turns solid, she gets 'em off the heat pronto."

"These people know you're with the FBI?"

Coyle smiled. "Oh yeah. They know who I am. They're proud of me. I'm beating the white man at his game. By the way, Jesse Jackson and Natalie Cole are regulars here, too. Also Mayor Berry and the fight promoter Rock Newman."

"The coffee's good, I'll give 'em that," Burlane said.

"They started out with three seats and a kitchen in the basement. Now, they've got a kitchen here on the first floor plus thirty-nine seats. This is North Carolina soul food, Major. You can get first-rate baked ham or roast chicken for lunch. I like to eat here once in a while to remind myself that I don't have to hang out in the sun to get a good tan."

Burlane said, "No offense, but I always thought the USC Trojans were raging pricks."

Coyle cocked his head. "Oh?"

Burlane smiled. "I graduated from the University of Oregon."

Coyle laughed. "The Fighting Ducks! What do you expect? You might as well call yourself Artichokes or Earthworms."

"I hated it when you got your knee fucked up, that's a fact. You had a real future in front of you."

"Like they say, shit happens. And it turns out I had a real future after all, didn't I?"

They stopped talking while the waitress served their breakfast.

Coyle, smearing butter on a biscuit, said, "For whatever it's worth, we know the car that exploded in Anacostia was a Ford Taurus. The truck that went up on South Capitol Street was a GMC. They both had the numbers scrubbed from their blocks. That means we'll have to account for every single model of those vehicles that was ever manufactured."

"Can you do that?"

"We can try."

Burlane said, "They still could have been stolen. The scrubbed numbers could simply have been a red herring designed to mislead."

"Unfortunately," Coyle said.

"Who are your suspects as you see them now?"

Coyle said, "There's a new proposal in committee for the registration of handguns. We could be looking at NRA malcontents. We've got some real cowboys out west."

Burlane thought about that. "What about the handgun registration in the works? Was it likely to pass?"

"They tell me no way," Coyle said. "That's a one-issue vote for too many people. If you have a rural constituency and want to keep your seat, you vote the right way on that one."

"Hard to see a motive there." Burlane retrieved a pad from his hip pocket and made a note. "They were talking about antiabortion zealots on the radio this morning. They on the task-force short list?"

Coyle said, "Some asshole might get carried away and ambush a doctor arriving at an abortion clinic, but a group of them mounting an attack like this?" He shook his head.

"It does sound unlikely," Burlane said. "What about the drug cartel? What's your thinking there?"

Coyle said, "On the surface, motive in the extreme. The more money involved, the bigger the motive."

Burlane held up his cup for a refill of coffee.

"Because of the layout of the House floor with respect to the entrance, it's impossible to tell whether the victims were targets of opportunity or whether the terrorists were specifically out to kill Democrats. Maybe the Republicans were lucky."

Burlane said, "What if a genuine hard-ass, a mobster, say, used laundered money to deliver an election to Congressman A, with the understanding that A would prevent a certain measure from coming out of committee, but Congressman A, feeling pressure from his constituents, reneged. And what if Congressmen B and C, say, had also received the same laundered money and also finked out. Wouldn't this be a demonstration that one should not receive without giving something in return, even if one is a United States congressman?"

Coyle frowned.

Burlane said, "If that were the case, you'd have to go through the past campaigns and voting records of more than a hundred dead congressmen looking for a motive, wouldn't you?"

"For starters."

"What if the aggrieved party slaughtered a hundred congressmen as a cover for the killing of one or several specific targets?" Burlane pursed his lips.

"God!"

"Can't rule it out," Burlane said. "There have been cases where a murderer blew up a whole airplane or derailed a single train to kill one person."

"I know. I know."

Burlane fell silent for a moment, thinking, then said, "Our best bet is to follow the snouts."

"The snouts?"

"That's what a representative democracy is all about, isn't it?—managing snout space at the public trough."

Coyle smiled.

"Nobody anonymously spends millions of dollars in election campaigns because they're worried about the future of the country. They do it in expectation of return. Who knows the most about the washing of drug money? The DEA, I take it."

"You should talk to a man named Glenn Allard. We've already talked to him, but go ahead, take a shot at it yourself. I'm sure Allard won't mind going over the same territory if it helps the cause. You should also talk to David Enright, the CIA's chief drug watcher."

"Also, I want to talk to somebody who knows how political money is washed."

Coyle said, "Representative Mitch Webster, the ranking minority member of the House Select Committee on Campaign Reform. You could talk to the chairman, of course, but Webster has fire in his belly."

"What's the best order?"

Coyle thought a moment. "I'd think Webster and Enright, then Allard."

SEVEN

They walked west on Independence Avenue as they talked, their breaths coming in soft white puffs. James Burlane had longer legs, but Webster was fit and knew how to walk himself. Until the government learned more about the cockroach terrorists, the Capitol was still under Contingency Delta and Independence was very nearly deserted.

Webster bit his lip as they passed by the Rayburn House Office Building, with the Capitol on their right. "The situation is so screwed, it's hard to know where to start."

Burlane said, "How about the political action committees that everybody is always arguing about? Tell me about the PACs."

Webster rolled his eyes. "The PACs!" He groaned. "PACs were established in 1974 to eliminate the influence of individual contributors, which had become a scandal. In order to disperse political influence, we banned individual contributions of more than a thousand bucks and created political action committees, but like all efforts at reform, there were unintended consequences."

Burlane smiled. "'The best-laid plans of mice and men . . .'" They started downhill, the monument to James Garfield on their right.

"Anybody can establish a PAC," Webster said. "All you have to do is register a name with the Federal Elections Commission, and you can contribute directly to a candidate or simply campaign for a candidate or issue on your own. It's all just a matter of defining the money. 'Hard money' goes to candidates directly. 'Soft money' supports issues allegedly 'independent' of candidates, hence the term 'independent expenditures.' Soft money doesn't have to be reported to the Federal Elections Commission. The reality, of course, is that hard and soft money work together."

"So the money really isn't secret, but it might as well be for all the control the public has over what it buys."

"Correct."

They were at Third Street. Burlane paused. "Shall we walk down the Mall?" He looked across the Reflecting Pool at the western facade of the Capitol.

Webster said, "The American Chamber of Commerce can support their favorite cause with soft money; so can the National Potato Growers Association, or the American Dental Association. You name the group or the issue. Keep in mind that many voters cast their ballot on the basis of a single issue. And so-called hard PAC money, which supports a candidate directly, doesn't have to come from a candidate's district or even his state."

"You're saying a combination of hard and soft money, judiciously spent, essentially allows an individual or a group to covertly buy a House or Senate seat."

"Or the White House. Absolutely," Webster said.

They walked in silence for a minute, then Webster led the way across Third Street, and they were headed west on Jefferson Drive, flanked by leafless trees.

Webster said, "What it comes down to is, there's no way for the public to know who 'owns' a politician. 'Independent expenditures' of millions of dollars are not contributions, Major Khartoum. They're investments. At least in the bad old days we knew who owned which politicians."

Burlane looked to his left at the National Air and Space Museum, which was closed as part of Contingency Delta. Inside was the *Enola Gay*, the B-29 which had carried the atomic bomb that was dropped over Hiroshima.

Burlane smiled. "Could the mob or the drug cartel use laundered money to buy politicians?"

Webster cocked his head. "Well, of course, foolish man. If associations of doctors, lawyers, and accountants can do it, what's to prevent El Señor Pedro Fuckstick of Colombia from doing it? Nothing. The voters have brains enough to know that elections are for sale. Why do you suppose people are not bothering to vote?"

They crossed Seventh Street with the round, ultramodern Hirshhorn Museum and Sculpture Garden on their left.

Burlane said, "I know you're a Democrat, but the truth is both parties are playing the same game, aren't they?"

Webster said nothing.

The Smithsonian's main museum, a redbrick castle featuring a mélange of towers, cupolas, and Victorian architectural bric-a-brac, was coming up on their left. Jefferson Drive curved slightly to the north to accommodate the castle, which was a favorite of kids visiting the capital city.

Burlane agreed with the kids. He admired what he regarded as the lunatic architecture of the castle. He paused before the castle. "Don't you think this is a hip building?"

Webster, regarding the building, smiled. "It's just obscene being able to buy people who are supposed to be representing the best interests of their constituents."

"Well, like you said, it's a form of investment, isn't it, like buying shares of stock."

Webster sighed. "When PACs were originally established, the Republicans thought they'd benefit the most because of their ties to businesses and corporations. And it did work that way for a while. Then the Democratic majority began arguing that it was stupid to give money to the Republicans when the majority party actually passes laws."

"Then the Democrats started getting the most PAC money."

Webster nodded yes. "The Republicans tried to eliminate PACs until 1994, when they won majorities in both the House and the Senate; then they shut up and started phoning people who had given money to Democrats, asking why were they being so foolish. Investing in the Democrats was like throwing money away."

The two men followed the curve of Jefferson Drive past the Freer Gallery; Webster led the way north on Twelfth Street toward the center of the Mall. He crossed Twelfth Street. The Washington Monument was about four hundred yards dead ahead.

Webster said, "But the PACs and millionaire candidates are just part of the horror. Consider this, Major Khartoum. If your organization is strictly nonpartisan and just involved in voter education and getting out the vote, you don't have to report the expenditure to the Federal Election Commission."

Burlane said, "The League of Women Voters, say."

"Correct," Webster said. "The real beaut was Chet Gorman's Senate campaign in West Virginia, which copied Ollie North's run for Chuck Robb's Senate seat in Virginia, in 1994. Gorman's backers set up the Brigade of American Patriots under section 501(c)(3) of the IRS code. This is for nonprofit charitable organizations such as the American Cancer Society and the Red Cross. A 'nonpartisan' organization gets a forty percent break on postal rates, and donations are tax-deductible."

"The real purpose of the Brigade was to promote Chet Gorman," Burlane said.

"Of course. It was Chet did this, Chet did that, every month. Chet was even president of the Brigade, and his company, which sells stun guns to police departments, rented office space from the Brigade. But the organization just shrugged off complaints as coming from partisan malcontents."

Burlane laughed. "Oh, well, sure."

"When Gorman announced he was running for the Senate, he resigned as president of the Brigade, but he kept its mailing lists, which were the basis of his direct-mail efforts that brought in twenty-five million dollars—surpassing even Ollie's numbers. The Brigade of American Patriots remains a legal fraud. It's not a non-partisan organization under the IRS code, but because of political reasons—"

"Fear of the Christian right," Burlane said.

Webster nodded. "Correct. Since nobody has the balls to challenge their scam, they just do it, screw the law. Now, unless President Erikson can finger the terrorists who attacked the House, we just might be looking at President Chet Gorman."

They stood before the Washington Monument, looking up.

They were momentarily silent, then Burlane said, "Shall we walk over to the Tidal Basin and watch them work? I've got Carter Commission boxtops."

"Sure," Webster said. He started walking to the southwest in the direction of the Tidal Basin. "You want to know what the heavy hitters do, Major Khartoum? Since the telecommunications bill in '96, they reserve their time well in advance so that their opponents can only buy spots in the middle of the night when nobody is watching the tube. Plus, the media people don't want to give up all that advertising revenue. Reform would cost them heavy bucks. The result of that bill was to let the media, especially TV, spread its crocodile jaws and absolutely devour money."

Webster quickly fished a card out of his wallet and scribbled a number on it. He said, "This is my private number. Those cowards killed several close friends of mine, and I want something done about it."

They were drawing near the Tidal Basin, where FBI divers were working from barges anchored in front of the Jefferson Memorial. Webster pointed to a large granite-and-marble building just off the east shore of the Tidal Basin. "That building right there is the heart of Washington, Major Khartoum, did you know that? From it courses the lifeblood of all this political struggle."

Burlane looked puzzled. "It is? What is it?"

Webster regarded the building. "That's the Bureau of Engraving and Printing. The cockroach helicopters exploded directly in front of the mint."

1 : 0 0 P . M .

Carter Commission Exhibit 19-Jan-3K

Partial transcript of a taped call received at 1612 hours, 20 January 2000, by Special Agent Clarissa Thomas, the on-duty Carter Commission hot-line operator.

THOMAS: This is the task force hot line for the Carter Commission. We are taping all calls for possible use by our investigators. My name is Clarissa, I am a special agent with the Federal Bureau of Investigation.

FEMALE CALLER: Special Agent Coyle said on television that we should call if we saw anything on Wednesday night that might be of help.

THOMAS: He sure did. What did you see? It would help us if you can be specific.

CALLER: It was my boyfriend and me, actually. Mr. Coyle said the task force was interested in hearing from anybody who thinks they might have seen the man and woman who opened fire on the House.

THOMAS: Yes, he did.

CALLER: A few minutes before the attack, my boyfriend and I were on Pennsylvania just down the street from the Capitol area, and we think we may have seen the man and woman who were the cockroach terrorists.

THOMAS: Please tell me your name, and how can we reach you?

CALLER: I'm Elisa Johnston and my boyfrend is Barry Morrison. Our phone number is 545-2777.

THOMAS: Tell me what you saw.

CALLER: A Hispanic-appearing man and woman. We saw them twice, actually. We saw them in front of Trover's Bookstore talking about the books on display in the front window. They were wearing those plastic staff tags. I work in the Library of Congress annex so I'm familiar with those tags.

THOMAS: They spoke Spanish?

CALLER: Yes, they did. My boyfriend and I met each other in Honduras when we were in the Peace Corps, so we both speak Spanish too. We assumed they worked for a Hispanic member of Congress. Someone from California or Texas maybe. New Mexico or somewhere.

THOMAS: What did they say?

CALLER: The man looked angry. He said the system was rotten and was run by cockroaches. He obviously didn't like the food, either. When they passed Flying Burrito Brothers, he said it was only fit for cockroaches. We couldn't help hearing them. The man, especially, spoke so harshly.

THOMAS: Did he say what he meant by "the system"?

CALLER: No, he did not.

THOMAS: Did either of them use a name?

CALLER: She called him Oscar once.

THOMAS: But he didn't mention her name?

CALLER: No, he didn't.

THOMAS: Is there anything else that struck you as unusual about them?

CALLER: Well, I called them a man and woman rather than a couple because they were obviously brother and sister. They looked so much alike that they could have been twins, except that he was older.

THOMAS: Not father and daughter?

CALLER: No, they were too close in age for that, I think. The man was in his late forties maybe. The woman was in her late thirties. Neither one of us can remember exactly what they looked like, only how strikingly similar they were.

1 : 3 0 P . M .

Carter Commission Exhibit 20-Jan-R4

Excerpt of an interview by Special Agent Frank Coyle of Spec 5 Harry Andrews, Communications Center, the Pentagon, conducted at 1330 hours, 20 January 2000.

COYLE: For the record, Specialist Andrews, where were you on the night of the cockroach attack?

ANDREWS: I was on duty at the big board at Communications Command.

COYLE: And what happened?

ANDREWS: At 2024 hours we received a Situation Beta. There had been an attack on the Capitol. When that happens we put on the scanners to monitor all communications in or near the capital. The idea is to intercept and record any communications by unfriendlies.

COYLE: And did you do that?

ANDREWS: Yes, we did. We recorded an over-the-air conversation in Spanish about one minute before we intercepted the helicopters over the Tidal Basin.

COYLE: The transcript of the conversation that I have here?

ANDREWS: Yes sir, that's the one. No hysterics or yelling. Just brief conversation in Spanish. Then nothing. Then *boom!*

EIGHT

Bob Bailey, wearing his favorite Mickey Mouse boxer shorts, and with his usual Wild Turkey and Dr Pepper, watched the second hand on the control panel while his listeners were treated to a taped message from Mother Gilpin's Chicken Crispins.

The red light went on.

Bailey said, "Once again, Bob Bailey, the human Kalashnikov here at the mike mowin' down the libby-wimps. The subject again tonight is the murder, by ambush, in cold blood, of one hundred and seventeen congressmen. Have you been paying attention to what's been going on in the last ten years or so, folks? I mean really staying on top of it?

"Listen to me. In 1989 Comrade Gorbachev understood that the Imperial Soviet Union just wasn't working. People in Georgia and the Ukraine resented the bureaucrats in Moscow telling them what to do. They resented Russian carpetbaggers running their lives. Estonia, the most productive of the Soviet states, found that the wealth it produced was being used to develop Siberia. And Soviet scientists couldn't keep up with the West because they didn't have computers and the wonderful comrades didn't trust them to think for themselves. So Gorby finally threw in the towel. He had to. He had no choice.

"Then, friends, in 1994, a remarkably similar thing happened here in the United States. Newt Gingrich, who was tired of the dewy-eyed liberals dictating everything from Imperial Washington, staged an electoral revolution and took over Congress.

"But the *oh so goooooooooooood* libby-wimps, who just loved all that power and all those perks, tried to pretend this was a coup staged by a cabal of rich people. And old Bill Clinton, trying to save the Democratic hide, did the unthinkable. Oh, the libby-wimps! The libby-wimps! Poor babies! While Newt was jerking their caucuses and other scams they used to finance the good life on the taxpayer's tab, Billary pulled a Gorby and pretended to dissolve the Great Society so the libby-wimps could stay in power.

"It's hard not to feel a trifle sorry for Billary. I'll call Billary 'she' because that contains a 'he' too, doesn't it? That ought to satisfy everybody. It was like Billary had been elected to go to a political prom, and she wanted oh-so-badly to be popular. Billary thought if only she wore the same dress everybody else was wearing then everybody would love her. First she tried a beehive hairdo like when Lyndon Johnson was president. But when people told her that looked stupid, she changed into one of those chic little yuppie cocktail dresses. You know, basic black, with a single strand of pearls— the libby-wimps just went crazy. Nothing, just nothing, seemed to fit Billary. What should she wear?

"Well, now. It's taken us close to six years to realize that Thomas Jefferson was right. The best government is the least government, but the libby-wimps are still at it, yearning for the good old days when they got to waste all those taxpayer dollars in the name of a greater good. That worked while we still had a workforce of industrial blue-collar workers, but when the libby-wimps tried to cobble a new coalition, it just didn't fly.

"What did they learn? Well, they learned, or should have learned, that blackie-wacks don't vote. That queers only comprise six percent of the population, not ten percent. That women have more brains than feminist dykes give them credit for. That Asian Americans and Hispanic Americans understand that 'minority' is code for blacks, not them, and 'civil rights' is anything having do with blacks, not the rest of us. That white males resent being portrayed as villainous devils. That people don't like their tax dollars wasted on bubble-brained social-engineering projects. That people want their legislatures to write the law, not judges. And that people resent emotional attempts by birdbrains to rewrite history in textbooks.

"Remember the Communist apparatchiks? They, too, hated to give up the power and the good life. When geneticists told Joseph Stalin it was impossible to mold the perfect socialist man in one or two generations, he banned the study of genetics. Sound familiar?

"And what did the defeated comrades do?

"Well, in 1991, they tried to stage a coup. This was, of course, in the name of 'the People.' Right. By this time Boris Yeltsin was in charge, and he didn't let them. He sent in the tanks.

"But we don't have a president with Boris Yeltsin's guts, do we? We've got good old cautious Tom Erikson. Did you hear his speech last night? We needed Winston Churchill. Who did we get? Mr. Sellout. Mr. Careful. Mr. Cautious. He says we have to take our time bringing the terrorists to justice before we get on with the business of deciding the country's future. Well, I wouldn't think he has to look far to find the guilty.

"Just who is behind the assault on Congress and the murder of the two senators in San Francisco? The Cali drug cartel, they're saying. All by their lonesome? Ask yourself who pals around with drug dealers. Law-abiding, God-fearing citizens or . . .

"Ooops! Time for another word on behalf of the wonderful folks at Mother Gilpin's. When I get back, I'll take some calls. I'm sure there's an offended libby-wimp or two out there to come up with the old deny, deny, deny. And they'll be oh so offended. They're so very *gooooooood*! Above criticism. Right."

Bailey, off the air for the commercial, giggled and did another line of the chalky white powder on his console.

White Deer, Pennsylvania
6:30 P.M.

James Burlane, shaking his head, punched off Bullet Bob Bailey as he slowed for the hamlet of White Deer, four miles south of Allenwood.

Burlane agreed with Bailey that middle-class Democratic voters thought the left wing of their party had blown them off in favor of complaining African Americans and mouth-off feminists. But Bailey conveniently overlooked the fact that this perception was warped by journalists lusting for the sensational and outrageous.

And for Bailey, in the middle of a horrific national crisis, to suggest that treasonous Democratic liberals were attempting to stage a coup by wholesale murder was poisonously irresponsible. Pouring gasoline on a bonfire.

Burlane passed the city limits of White Deer and was into Pennsylvania countryside covered with a six-inch layer of snow.

Ever since Newt Gingrich strutted onto center stage, the Republicans had been urging all incoming House members to read *The Federalist Papers*. Well, Burlane, too, had read *The Federalist Papers*. And he was familiar with James Madison's famous Federalist Number Ten, where Madison had said liberty is to factions what air is to fire.

Burlane sided with the honorable socialist Murray Kempton, who dedicated his last book to the conservative William F. Buckley, Jr., whom he called a kind and generous man. The aging Kempton, looking back over the years of struggle on behalf of working people, was disgusted by the quarreling, Manichaean, us/them, black/white scoring of political points by the extreme wings of both parties.

A sign up ahead pointed the way to the federal correctional institute.

7:00 P.M.

Jane Griffin, opening the box of *sio pao* on her side of the glass partition, looked delighted. "All right."

"I don't imagine having them x-rayed will ruin the taste."

"Now if we just had some of Ara's brandy for another classic Chinese combo. Thank you for coming up, James. Most people say they'll come, but they never find the time to actually make the drive."

Burlane glanced about the visiting room. "Well, how's life? Do you hear the ghosts of Nixon's men stalking the corridors at night?"

Griffin looked chagrined. "There's a computer in the library they let me play with, but it's just a toy, and it doesn't have a modem. I guess if I had one word to describe this place, it would be noisy. I don't know about the men's side, but the women in here don't have anything to do but talk, talk, talk, and watch stupid television all day. I don't have any time to just kick back and think."

Burlane sighed. "I don't know how I could take it."

"Two months and I'm going bonkers, that's a fact. Little Bobby Dickens did time here, did you know that?"

"Yes. I knew that."

"One of the most talented hackers who ever lived. Dark Star, he called himself. How's that for brass?"

Burlane said, "He should have stayed well clear of the Company's computer banks. That was a no-no."

"They let him out on condition that he never again have anything to do with computers. He can't own one or even borrow one. They might as well have executed him. Put him out of his misery. You know why we drive the bureaucrats and politicians nuts?"

"I'm listening."

"Everybody is equal on the Internet. We talk all the time about equality, but we don't really like it in practice. It doesn't make any difference if you're male or female, old or young, hot-looking or ugly. All that matters is what you can do with your machine and how well you can write. You use pseudonyms to ensure your anonymity, and there are no rules to enforce hierarchies. There are no borders or bureaucratic thought-police to enforce official ideologies."

"Intellectual kick-ass time," Burlane said.

Griffin slapped her thigh. "No excuses. Precisely. The Democrats should like that, shouldn't they? No discrimination and all that. Well, you know what they want to do? They want to regulate us so some by-the-book bureaucrat can tell us what to do."

Burlane smiled. "Tell me."

"In cyberspace nobody knows if you ride a bike or drive a BMW. Who cares if you went to Yale or a community college in Yakima? Age, race, sex, creed, and national origin are all unknown. All that matters is the quality of your cortex. That's what they can't take. They talk about equality but they secretly hate it. Pinheads, they are."

"Listen, Ms. Griffin, when Ara and I tried to recruit you before, you said no. We're still interested. If we could get you out of here on parole, would you be willing to do some work for Mixed Enterprises? We have a complicated job, and we need help."

Griffin brightened. "Really? On parole!"

Burlane nodded.

"How? How would you get me out on parole?"

"Thomas Erikson."

"The President!" Griffin blinked.

"Maybe even a pardon if we do good-enough work."

"A pardon? Why would he do that? Last summer, the Attorney General was calling me every name in the book."

"Times and circumstances change, Jane. Ara and I need you to help us find the people who opened fire on the House floor."

Griffin brightened. "Really? I'd do anything to help nail those idiots, James. Anything. But I'd need equipment that's up to the job. A computer with real memory."

"We need to follow money that has been moved one or more times, possibly in and out of banks in the Bahamas or the Cayman Islands."

"I'll need the right gear and software."

"Can you make us a list of what you'll need?"

"Sure, I don't have anything else to do."

"Don't be afraid of the cost. If necessary, we'll make Tom Erikson pay for it. You'd stay at Ara's place. Ara has an extra bedroom, and you'll have your own office with everything you need."

"Hey, no problem." Griffin grinned broadly. "You're rescuing me, James. Do you know that?"

"We need you."

"You know what happens after the guy rescues the girl, don't you? It's *very* romantic. We watch the whole movie knowing at the end, the hero and heroine are going to jump in the sack together. Hope and rebirth and all that. Confirmation."

Burlane arched an eyebrow. "Do you object to those endings?"

She tilted her head. "Oh no, not at all. All the romance I'm going to get in this place is by watching the movies." She hesitated. "Do please talk sweet to President Erikson. And *do* hurry back, big boy."

Burlane laughed.

Griffin turned serious. "Please, please do it. I'm good, I really am. I'm low-maintenance. All I need are some cornflakes and fresh fruit for breakfast and a good computer to play on. Just get me out of this jabber, jabber, jabber."

"Will it take long to pack."

Griffin beamed. "Oh, you'll do it. The cavalry arrives bearing *sio pao*! My rescuer."

9:00 P.M.

Senator Chet Gorman was so handsome he could have qualified as a Marlboro man, and, if the polls were to be believed, there was no doubt that women thought he was just wonderful. As a presidential candidate, he came off as a take-charge kind of guy, standing tall for God, country, and family values—not to mention his antiabortion views, which troubled many women who were otherwise enthralled by his masculine good looks.

And now, standing before the glare of television lights, Gorman, his forehead carefully powdered, his suit color-coordinated, was solemn in the extreme.

He looked at the camera straight on, his lips firm, his eyes determined.

"My fellow Americans. A quarter of a century ago I spent seven years in prison in Hanoi, much of it in solitary confinement. I survived on a diet of rice and bugs. The only light in my cell came through a rectangle hole the size of a playing card. In all that time, as the hours stretched into days, days into weeks, weeks into months, and months into years, the only thing that kept me going was my faith in God and a deep and abiding love of my country.

"Each day, I did push-ups and sit-ups to keep my body from deteriorating. To keep from going insane, I retraced the events of my childhood in West Virginia—playing halfback for my high-school football team, fishing in the Ohio River, and hunting whitetail deer with a bow and arrow. I ate imaginary Thanksgiving dinners, remembering the taste of turkey gravy on mashed potatoes and my mother's stuffing."

Gorman paused, looking choked. Was he about to cry? He clenched his jaw and continued.

"And each day when my card-sized hole turned dark and it was time to sleep, I resolved that if I survived that awful ordeal, I would return to my motherland, the United States of America, the land of the free and the home of the brave, and dedicate my life to preserving those values that had nourished me and enabled me to endure. I have done exactly that, and that is why I am campaigning for president in this first election of the new century.

"Just before I came here tonight, I took some quiet time in my study to reflect on the events of the last few days. I turned to my Bible and it opened, as though guided by the hand of Providence, to

Isaiah, chapter six. Those of you familiar with the Bible will know that as the scene where the prophet Isaiah is touched by an angel and made righteous. Yet Isaiah lived among an obstinate, unclean people. Someone had to save the nation of Israel. But who? Who would this be?

"'I heard the voice of the Lord,' Isaiah tells us.

"God said, 'Whom shall I send? Who will go for us?'

"And Isaiah replied, 'Lord, here am I. Send me.'"

Gorman fell silent, then he said, "My fellow Americans, last night you all heard President Tom Erikson, our commander in chief, ask us to set aside our differences and unite so that we might bring to justice the heinous, despicable terrorists who ambushed and murdered the people's representatives conducting the people's business. We need to do this, he said, so that we can reaffirm the strength of our nation's values, and get on with the important business of deciding our future. I agree.

"I ask you all to heed President Erikson's call for unity. I ask you all, whatever your age, your race, or your politics, to join him in this national effort. This is no time for Democrats and Republicans or blacks and whites. This is time for Americans. During World War II, we rationed meat, gasoline, and rubber, among other essentials, and women joined the industrial production lines to build tanks and airplanes so the men could fight at the front; Rosie the Riveter joined forces with G.I. Joe. Thus united in common purpose, we defeated the Nazis and the Japanese Imperial armed forces. Despite all that has happened since that stirring and noble triumph, at the cost of so many lives, we remain the same, essentially good people. And, as President Erikson says, in time of crisis, we will do what has to be done.

"President Erikson has asked the governors to call for special elections within the next three months to fill the seats of those congressmen and -women who were murdered. I agree with that. In the spirit of national reconciliation, and to demonstrate our resolve, my fellow Americans, I further ask you tonight to consider the possibility of canceling the upcoming primary elections so that

President Erikson, our commander in chief in this time of crisis, can concentrate on securing the safety of the Capitol and identifying the conspirators. They may be foreign or they may be domestic. As the President says, at this point we just don't know.

"It is not fair of us to ask our President to simultaneously lead the investigation into this tragedy and seek reelection at the same time. And it is unseemly for those of us who have honorably challenged him to campaign against him in this time of crisis. Is not the fairest solution, to President Erikson and to the Republic, to set aside politics as usual and wait until the national conventions in August to choose our candidates? Well, who will choose the delegates, you ask? Of course, it will require effort, but I find it hardly credible that our parties can't choose their delegates through local caucus or by convention, as was routinely done in years past. The question before us all is simple enough: Do we continue to argue and bicker and score political points, or do we join together and back our commander in chief in our national hour of need? . . . I say the latter."

NINE

David Enright, a Martha's Vineyard, Yale University kind of man, and James Burlane, onetime farmboy out of Umatilla, Oregon, walked along the banks of the Potomac.

David Enright wore sturdy brown walking shoes, at once utilitarian and stylish, khaki chinos, a bluish green herringbone Harris tweed jacket, and an Irish walking cap. He had close-cropped silver hair, and his silver beard was neatly trimmed.

He carried a gnarled walking stick that he used to poke and prod at trees and weeds as he and Burlane walked along the Potomac River. Burlane was clad in an olive-colored leather jacket, given to him by a hashish smuggler in Amsterdam, blue jeans, and well-worn New Balance running shoes.

Enright, examining Burlane as they walked, said, "You're from Oregon. I would have thought you'd wear Nikes. The Nike headquarters is in a Portland suburb, isn't it?"

Burlane rolled his eyes. "It might as well be in China. Also, I buy shoes, not advertising. I buy American, and I'm for the underdog. New Balance is both."

Enright grinned. "By the way, we always suspected it was you who exposed Peña's mole on Senator Boulanger's committee."

"Me? You think it was me?" Burlane looked amused. "And you guys think you're running an intelligence service?"

"Whoever it was did a hell of a job," Enright said. He looked out over the water. "To answer your question, Major Khartoum, the Colombians have long known they have to expand their markets if they are to make more money. About ten years ago, they moved into Europe and former Soviet-bloc countries. For years, the smoking of nonaddictive hashish, made from cannabis resin, has been, de facto, legal."

"No shit, Red Ryder."

"The Europeans and Scandinavians had to deal with heroin from the Middle East, but the plague of cocaine was an American problem. The Russians didn't realize what the Colombians were doing until they intercepted a ton of cocaine on its way from Finland to St. Petersburg." Enright poked the ground with his walking stick. "The breakup of the Soviet empire created a demand for capital, but the Western banks were afraid of repeating the debacle of the petrodollars they had loaned to the Third World."

"But the gentlemen from Colombia had plenty of money to invest," Burlane said.

"They had to do something with that currency, and advances in technology enabled them to encrypt their fax and telephone communications and use electronic fund transfers to deposit their money in dummy companies around the world."

Burlane said, "In places where Western banks feared to tread."

"Most of the Soviet-bloc countries had yet to adequately replace the Stalinist regulatory void. Ten years ago there were no laws against fraud, money laundering, or organized crime, and no functioning institutions to regulate business. The Russian crime lords stole and sold anything they could lay their hands on: precious metals, arms, and even weapons-grade plutonium from old Soviet stocks. Of course, they sold whatever drugs they could lay their hands on, the more addicting the better."

"Have they been working with the Italians and Colombians?"

Enright said, "There's been nothing to enforce a contract between crime gangs except raw power. They stake out and defend territories. They work together when it's to their advantage, but that's it. If I were you I'd talk with somebody who has been keeping track of money laundering, and somebody who knows about changes in the heroin traffic over the last six or eight years."

"Glenn Allard at the DEA?"

"He'd be good. Senator Graciela Boulanger of the Senate Select Narcotics Committee has been following developments in the heroin trade, but you know her already, don't you?"

Burlane didn't say anything.

Enright said, "She's been in charge of that committee for years, both as a Democrat and now as a Republican, and is privy to current data from the DEA and other agencies."

Burlane said, "What if the illegal cocaine and heroin market were somehow eliminated?"

Enright considered Burlane's question. He said, "It would put the Cali cartel out of business. You remember all those old gangster movies. That was all over illegal traffic in alcohol. All the resources of the government, including the heroic and determined Elliot Ness, weren't enough to defeat the gangsters of the 1930s. It took the repeal of the Volstead Act to do that."

TEN

ames Burlane was amused by the pretension of the Drug Enforcement Administration that the location of its headquarters needed to be kept secret—its existence being routinely deleted from maps of the Washington area. The intrepid warriors apparently believed that crazed drug dealers stalked the city bent on wreaking havoc with their tormenters, but were so monumentally stupid that if they couldn't find the building on the map, they'd be foiled.

This romantic paranoia extended even to inquiries by members of Congress, which were met with evasion and suspicion. Burlane assumed the pretense of a clear and present danger was part of the DEA pitch for more money come budget time: they had to be paranoid because they were so effective, see; they had the drug barons on the run.

For years the Central Intelligence Agency complex in Langley, Virginia, several miles to the north, had pretended it was invisible, apparently to foil KGB numskulls who couldn't find their butts with both hands. But after having the location of its headquarters detailed in numerous spy novels, the CIA finally gave it up. In the end, it turned out, not only did the KGB know where the Company was located, it had employees working on the inside.

The DEA high-rise in fact had risen up like a steel-and-glass mushroom from the grass between Army-Navy Drive and the edge of the south parking lot of the Pentagon. All a curious out-of-towner had to do was drive east on Highway 395 toward Washington, take the Exit 9 off-ramp, and start looking for what looked like the corporate headquarters of an insurance company.

Burlane, having used his Carter Commission boxtops to negotiate the cameras, guards, and the rest of the security apparatus on the ground floor, talked to Glenn Allard in his tenth-floor office which faced east—overlooking the Pentagon, the Potomac River, the Tidal Basin, and, two miles distant, the Washington Monument.

Glenn Allard, taking a sip of coffee, looked thoughtful as he considered Burlane's opening question. "I understand why you're curious, Major Khartoum, and under the circumstances, I'll give you the truth, not the official DEA pitch. Internationally, the profits of the drug traffic are said to be a trillion dollars a year, which is half the annual federal budget. Did you know that?"

Burlane said, "Plenty of motive to slaughter a couple of senators and a hundred-odd members of Congress."

"Motive and then some," Allard said. "The U.S. is the Cali cartel's most profitable market. I've been on the trail of hot drug money for twenty years, so I'm speaking from a biased point of view, but the truth is for years the war on drugs was fought bass-ackwards."

Burlane cocked his head. "Backwards?"

"About twenty years ago, the Colombians switched exclusively to cocaine, which was addictive and so more profitable than marijuana, and far less bulky to smuggle. For a while, they tried to do business in the United States personally, but after several biggies got busted, they directed their empire from Medellín, and later from Cali. Their money went further in Colombia, and that's where their producers were. Trying to intercept drugs at the borders is downright stupid. We've tried to do that for twenty-five years, and it doesn't work. That is *not* the right way to do it, never was."

"What is the right way?"

"To stay in business, the Cali drug lords needed to swap dollars for Colombian pesos. The question has always been, How can we stop this flow of money? By the way, they're currently moving about twenty-five billion dollars a year from the United States to Colombia."

"Stop the money and you stop the trade, is that it?"

"Over the years we've had forty-two agencies involved in attempting to stop the traffic in hot money. The DEA currently has more than two hundred agents working full-time on money laundering."

"How much does all this cost the taxpayers?" Burlane asked.

"The agents following the money or the drug war?"

"The full tab."

"Nobody knows for sure. But say eighteen billion a year, ballpark. Depends on how you count the costs."

"Oof!"

Allard said, "People don't write checks for drugs. Thirty years ago we required banks to report every transaction involving ten thousand dollars in a single day, then we required a customs report for every overseas shipment of ten thousand dollars in cash. Unfortunately, when we put our finger in one hole, money just squirts out of another." Allard sighed.

"Greed is a liquid concept. Money flows like water. Then what happened?"

Allard said, "The yuppie bankers were the first to step forward, bless their hearts. The suits felt they weren't shit unless they were driving BMWs."

Burlane gave Allard a lopsided grin. "They, too, knew the cost of everything, but the value of nothing."

"They discovered that the cartel was willing to give them a two percent nick for letting unreported cash slip through their accounts. Move two million a week through your accounts and you could quadruple your week's salary—that's in addition to your nick in transaction fees and overnight interest. And you didn't have to report the two percent to the IRS."

"A predictable turn of events," Burlane said.

"After we busted a few fuzz-cheeked suits, and they actually had to do jail time, they backed off that little scam." Allard looked amused.

"But the Colombians always found a way to wash their money."

"Oh, sure."

"And the situation now?"

"We can't stop the dope from getting in, and owing to electronic fund transfers, we can't do anything about the hot money going south."

Burlane thought about that for a moment. "If you can't stop the smuggling, and you can't eliminate the money washes, what do the drug barons really fear? Anything?"

"No."

"There's nothing at all we can do?"

"To achieve something that can be described as victory?" Allard shook his head. "Absolutely nothing, I hate to say it, working for the DEA and all, but the truth is that the moralists using the war on drugs as a political card are keeping the Colombians in business."

ELEVEN

Senator Graciela Boulanger had for years been an irregular patron of Sherrill's, a Capitol Hill beanery on Pennsylvania Avenue a few doors down the street from the Library of Congress. Sherrill's reminded Boulanger of Piccolo's, a simple eatery in Missoula, Montana, where she had grown up, and she felt all of the people's representatives needed to occasionally remind themselves whose dollars ultimately stocked the political cash register that was Capitol Hill.

Mitch Webster was close to being a regular at Sherrill's, where he sought refuge from the pretentious trappings of the power lunch where, over trout or lamb chops and overpriced wine, political favors were routinely bought and sold. Above the elegant clink of silver against china, the taxes of workingmen and -women—who ate in places like Sherrill's—were bartered and spent.

But the cowboys and ranchers and loggers who had elected Graciela Boulanger to the Senate both as a Democrat and a Republican were not chic; they were just hardworking people.

Sherrill's, established in 1922, had a decor that appeared unchanged from the 1930s—with the exception of a color television set in the front window. Sherrill's contained two rows of wooden booths opposite a long counter topped with glass display cases of cakes and pies. Three ceiling fans slowly churned the air overhead, and there was an illuminated electric clock at the far end.

When they first met years earlier, James Burlane had greeted Boulanger with a thumbs-up grip that she associated with black athletes and Mitch Webster's friends. Later she learned he did this deliberately to figures of authority as a form of tease and to demonstrate his independence.

Boulanger remembered clearly Burlane's description of himself when she had hired him as an investigator of the Senate Select Narcotics Committee, which she had chaired these many years. He had said he found no succor in cant or dogma, and he avoided identification with groups. "I ignore agreed-upon social and political lies, Senator Boulanger. I accept the nature of the beast."

Boulanger had been conditioned by the movies to believe that any operative worth his salt was an anal retentive impeccable dresser. And yet, as she would never forget, Oliver North—a marine with a spiffy haircut, shined shoes, and a chest covered with colorful campaign ribbons and medals—had, under oath, casually lied to Boulanger and her colleagues.

Now, she was pleased to note, Burlane was working for the Carter Commission task force investigating the cockroach terrorists.

Burlane again gave her a hip handshake as he showed her his Carter Commission identification. "Senator Boulanger, good to see you again. It's been a while."

She liked him. Perhaps it was because they were both from the Pacific Northwest. "Major Khartoum, the marimba man," she said. *Marimba* was Miami slang for the drug trade; a marimba player smuggled or sold drugs. As an investigator for the Narcotics Committee, Burlane had played the marimba for Graciela Boulanger.

Burlane smiled. "Playing the people's tune."

"I hope you're as good this time out as you were for me."

"I'll do my damndest, Senator. You know that. With your help maybe I can nail the people who tried to take you out in San Francisco."

They ordered lunch, a club sandwich and iced tea for Boulanger and a BLT and Rolling Rock beer for Burlane. When their food came, Boulanger took a sip of tea and said, "Now then, Major Khartoum, what can I do to help?"

"David Enright said I should talk to you about some spooky new developments in the drug trade, namely with respect to heroin. Can you tell me about that, please?"

"Enright the CIA drug watcher."

"Yes."

"Of course," Boulanger said. "Tell me, what do you think of when somebody says 'heroin'? What's the image that comes to mind?"

Burlane smiled. "He's got the touch with a deck or a cue."

Boulanger looked puzzled.

"Give me an eighter from Decatur."

Now Boulanger understood. "Frank Sinatra in *The Man with the Golden Arm*."

"Nelson Algren's book," Burlane said. "More recently I think of HIV and AIDS being passed through infected needles. I also think of New York."

"You should think of HIV. And at least half the users are in New York, that's true. There are real problems with heroin addiction portrayed in *The Man with the Golden Arm*, but let me come to that. First, how many users are there in the U.S., do you suppose?"

Burlane shrugged. "I have no idea."

"Nobody does, and that's a major part of the problem. A half million is the usual figure. The scary development is in the demographics of the users."

Burlane looked puzzled. "The demographics?"

"The users are ordinarily young, between twenty-six and thirty-four, and there's always been a class stigma associated with heroin.

The middle- and upper-class drug of choice has been cocaine, so that's the drug that's gotten the attention of the media and the government. Heroin has been a drug for poor blacks and Latinos so nobody cared. Remember, it wasn't until cocaine became fashionable among the middle class that it reached epidemic proportions."

"But the middle class doesn't like the idea of needles."

"No, it doesn't, and for good reason. What's interesting is the popular stereotype of addicts driven wild by an insatiable need for the next fix—the image of tortured junkies twisting in sweaty agony as they go cold turkey to shake the devil's craving." Boulanger sighed. "It turns out that forty to fifty percent of the users use it occasionally, on weekends."

Burlane looked amazed.

"They're called chippers, in the lingo. They chip at it. They don't feel a need for treatment so they don't show up on the statistics. A heavy user of coke will burn out in a few years, but a heroin user can maintain a casual habit for decades. Do you see the awful logic unfolding?" Boulanger cocked her head.

"I think I do, but I'm not sure."

"The DEA tells us that the nationwide purity of heroin marketed on the streets ten years ago was thirty-seven percent. That was up thirty percent since 1980. The heroin sold in New York ran at fifty-four percent, and in Boston it was averaging nearly seventy-four percent. The heroin was adulterated, so you had to shoot it with a needle."

"And risk HIV infection from dirty needles."

"Correct. But if the heroin is clean enough, and on the streets it currently is, you can smoke it or snort it, and the results are the same as shooting. No need to share needles."

Burlane said, "They cleaned it up so they could sell more."

"Exactly," Boulanger said. "Heroin is a derivative of opium, which come from the poppy plant. India legally markets five hundred metric tons of opium used for morphine and other legal painkillers. Another four thousand tons is used to support the habits of opium smokers and heroin users. Most of the heroin has historically come from poppies grown in the Shan Mountains in an area bordered by Burma, Laos, and Thailand. I bet you know all about that story, eh, Major Khartoum?"

"I know the Company protected the interests of the poppy-growing warlords as a buffer against the Chinese."

"Historically, Golden Triangle heroin commanded about sixty percent of the U.S. market, but about fifteen years ago, Mexican brown, or black-tar heroin, appeared on the West Coast," said Boulanger.

"Called black tar because it was so dirty it had to be cut and shot by needle."

"Correct. The Mexicans started with about twelve thousand hectares of opium poppies, and then the Colombians got into the business and were soon cultivating about thirty-five thousand hectares, and their production has been growing ever since."

"Oops!"

"The Colombians are now the second largest producers of opium poppies in the world. And they aren't producing black-tar heroin, either. The quality of heroin produced in Colombian labs some time ago surpassed that produced in Afghanistan and Pakistan. It's now the best in the world."

"All the better for middle-class snorters and smokers."

Boulanger nodded yes. "The Colombians learned from the cocaine trade that real money lies with the middle class. A kilo of coke will now bring from twelve thousand to forty-three thousand dollars wholesale. A kilo of high-quality heroin will bring from eighty thousand to a quarter of a million bucks. And now we have the interesting phenomenon of cocaine dealers giving away free samples of pure heroin."

"That can be snorted or smoked."

"That's right," Boulanger said. "I realize this is all circumstantial evidence, but do you want to guess as to what the Colombians have in mind now, Major Khartoum?"

Burlane cleared his throat.

"Do you remember reading about a big heroin bust in the famous Giddyup Saloon in Los Angeles? Two tons of pure heroin."

"Yes, I do."

Boulanger grimaced. "That was Colombian heroin. The Colombians switched from pot to coke because it was more profitable. It looks like they're switching again."

Burlane said, "Do you think the Colombians would open fire on Congress if they thought the black market might be eliminated?"

"With the amount of money at stake if the public ever woke up? . . . Yes, I do," Boulanger said. "Absolutely, Major Khartoum, you bet, yes I do."

1:00 P.M.

Carter Commission Exhibit 22-Jan-M12

Excerpt of an interview by Special Agent Frank Coyle of Alice Reid, linguist and Hispanic affairs analyst, the Central Intelligence Agency, Langley, Virginia, conducted at 1300 hours, 22 January 2000.

COYLE: I take it you've had time to study and analyze the tape, Ms. Reid.

REID: Yes, I have.

COYLE: And your conclusions?

REID: First, you should know there are sharp regional variations in Spanish. Puerto Rican and Cuban Spanish are both extremely slurred. The Spanish here is not slurred. I think it's possible that one male and the female learned Spanish as a second language. They were apparently both in the lead helicopter.

COYLE: Possible?

REID: I wouldn't state it as a certainty. It's a feeling I have, that's all. They're both extremely fluent.

COYLE: What else might you deduce?

REID: That they're from Colombia.

COYLE: Would it be possible to fake a Colombian accent?

REID: Sure, with practice. In this case, they sound like Colombians, but I can't state that as a one hundred percent certainty.

TWELVE

They stood by the window of the Green Room, looking down past the Washington Monument to the Tidal Basin, where divers were continuing their labors. The pressure of the ordeal had obviously gotten to President Erikson, who had a distracted, distant look in his eyes. The Vice President, too, looked haggard and drawn.

James Burlane took a sip of coffee and then drew a deep breath. "While the terrorists seem to have blown themselves up, I'll withhold judgment on that until the FBI has finished its search of the Tidal Basin."

Erikson looked surprised. "You don't think they were blown up? The pilot physically saw them a matter of seconds before their helicopters exploded. Did you read the transcript of their communication?"

Burlane said, "Frank told me about it."

"Spanish with a Colombian accent."

"That's what they say. I find it hard to believe professionals would kill themselves. Even Colombians. They may have been volunteers, but suicidal? That's tough to swallow."

"Mmm," Erikson said.

"Mr. President, let me be straightforward here. There is an inclination to be so respectful of the office of the President as not to tell the whole truth. I do respect you, sir, but too much blood and too many tears have been shed for me to be anything other than honest."

"Be as candid as you see fit."

Burlane glanced at Gregg, then returned his attention to Erikson. "A prosecuting attorney needs means, motive, and opportunity to prove a murder case, and that's what police officers are trained to look for. Murder is sometimes committed out of sexual passion, but just as powerful a motive is money. For money, you should understand that I also mean power, which is what money buys. Money, remember, is the meat of the hunt, and it is at the heart of politics."

Erikson smiled. "I almost forgot. You and Darwin."

"Only a fool ignores the genetic legacy of the beast, Mr. President. Wishing and passionate assertions to the contrary won't make it otherwise. We are what we are. We may become something different, but it will take centuries, not decades."

Erikson cocked his head. "And in this case the beast has done what?"

"Incumbent politicians of both parties use untraceable money to buy office and remain there. 'Soft money' is the euphemism. The majority party has the greatest advantage. You Republicans have done your damnedest to cut everything except the cost of campaigns. When the Democrats were in power, they were no different, I grant you."

"Surely, Major Khartoum . . ." Whatever Erikson was about to say, he let it drop.

Burlane said, "The same officeholders who argue that no money should be kept secret from the IRS and the DEA are loath to knock off soft political money. They say they're sick of eternally having to beg for money, but if that were really the case, they'd do something about it, wouldn't they? No damn wonder people started pushing for term limits."

"And the short of this is?"

"The short of it is that anybody with enough money could theoretically have hired Colombians to carry out the slaughter on the House floor. So we don't know for sure if it was drug-related, do we? What if it wasn't? Soft political money multiplies the number of possible conspirators and makes identifying them almost impossible. But I bet both of you have thought about that, haven't you?"

Erikson said nothing.

Burlane said, "The people at the Constitutional Convention in Philadelphia went to extreme lengths to thwart greed. Now it's possible to secretly buy a seat in the House or the Senate. The current cost for a House seat in a district of six hundred thousand voters is a half million bucks at the low end. In some districts members are paying twelve to fifteen dollars a vote."

Erikson, watching Burlane, remained silent.

"I bet you Republicans would do just fine on a level playing field. No problem. Just go out there and talk to people. Or does that prospect seem a little too intimidating?" Burlane looked disheartened. He closed his eyes and sighed, exhaling between puffed cheeks. "Sorry, Mr. President. I apologize."

"Accepted," Erikson said, "Major, I don't need a lecture on the evils of money in politics. I also accept that politicians, me included, have just come to feel we can't do anything about it. Maybe we really don't want to, as you say. Perhaps it takes a crisis like this to bring out the truth. Put your fury to good use, Major Khartoum. Plow ahead. Don't give up. Run these bastards to ground, and we'll stomp on their privates most properly, guaranteed."

"Truly we will," Gregg said. They were the only words he had spoken in the entire conversation, and James Burlane knew he meant them fervently.

"When you took me on, I told you about my interest in Jane Griffin."

"Cyberfox."

"With all this money involved, Mr. President, the only real shot we have of getting to the bottom of this is to spring Jane from Allenwood. Let her put her supercharged cortex in the service of her country."

"You mean, bend the law." Erikson looked uneasily at Gregg.

Gregg said, "Surely if there was ever a national emergency, this is it!"

Erikson considered that. "Executive privilege."

Gregg looked at Erikson. "I say yes. Spring her."

"Plus we'll need money to buy her the computer gear she needs. I'm not sure Ara and I have enough money in reserve."

Erikson stared at Burlane, then said, "Okay, Major Khartoum, done. I'll get your talented Ms. Griffin out of Allenwood on parole or leave or whatever, plus I'll put her equipment on my budget. If she finds something to help us avenge this outrage, I'll pardon her within two minutes."

"Thank you, Mr. President."

THIRTEEN

Diver Norm Montiegal, thirty-one, of Bethesda, Maryland, bearing a net evidence bag in his hand, surfaced from the Tidal Basin.

He pulled his mask from his face, staring straight at the marble visage of Thomas Jefferson watching him from the shadows of his round monument.

Montiegal held up a bag that contained a partial human hand and three-fourths of a lower jaw.

Grinning, he shouted in triumph, "This is for you, Tom!"

Arlington, Virginia

6:00 P.M.

Winter bass weren't easy to come by. In the summertime, they lay low in deep water so they could keep cool, but there was no figuring them in the winter, especially if the fisherman didn't have a boat.

Jonas Faulkner liked plain old bank fishing; all a person needed was a bucket of worms or something that smelled like hell. Catfish, which were scavengers, went for liver that had been allowed to get a little rank or a wad of pork fat. Fancy folks looked down on fishing for catfish, but there was something peaceful and tranquil about sailing a hookful of worms *kerplunk* out in the water and putting your rod in a forked stick in the mud.

Faulkner knew, without putting too fine a point on it, that the more expensive the fishing, therefore more exclusive, the higher the status. At the top were fishing for marlin or salmon or tarpon, because that usually meant owning a boat, or renting a boat, guide, and expensive equipment. Fly-fishing was somewhere in the middle, requiring a car and enough time off to drive to some isolated stream.

Faulkner, who was black, knew bank fishing was sometimes scornfully referred to as "nigger fishing," but he didn't care; it was a peaceful, soulful pastime. Faulkner didn't cheat on the legal limit, but neither did he scorn bottom fishing as a way to help out on the grocery budget.

Bass were predators, which is why they went for lures. Come twilight, feeding time for the bass, Faulkner liked to try out one of his homemade lures just for the fun of it; there was no thrill greater than hooking into a largemouth bass and watching it come firing out of the water trying to shake the hook.

Faulkner didn't have a boat and such lures as he had were ones he made himself; he didn't have the money to pay for expensive commercial lures only to lose them on a snag.

But he had discovered some years earlier it didn't take much to make lures that worked just as well as the expensive models that seemed to contain homing devices that led them straight to the nearest snag. He simply cruised the fishing-tackle sections of Kmart or Wal-Mart to see what outlandishly overpriced offerings were being peddled to fishermen with more money than brains.

Now, as the sun set behind him, and the Potomac lay calm and quiet in the darkening gloom, Faulkner rigged up what he called a Faulkner Flopper, named after a ten-dollar "miracle lure" that was being advertised on the Saturday-morning fishing programs. The Faulkner Flopper had a nifty surface action as it skipped along the top of the water mimicking a crippled fish.

On his fourth cast, as Faulkner retrieved the Flopper with a twitching motion—letting it lie, then jerking it, then repeating the action—a great big old lunker surfaced from the depths and took the lure in a gulp. His heart raced and his blood pumped. This was a real fish. A regular damned shark. Hot damn!

Ellicott City
9:00 P.M.

As they listened to speculation and reports on television, James Burlane and Ara Schott, cups of French roast in hand, studied a map of the Capitol Hill area and the Mall which they had spread out on Schott's coffee table.

Burlane traced the route of the fleeing terrorists with his finger. "They were two or three hundred feet from the shore of the Tidal Basin before the Marine Corps helicopter intercepted them."

Schott took a sip of coffee.

Burlane poured himself some more coffee. "To catch a thief, think like a thief. To catch a terrorist, think like one. What does a terrorist want?" He punched a button on the remote, skipping to ESPN, where the Duke Blue Devils were in a tight hoops contest against the Florida State Seminoles. "ESPN seems to be the only channel left that isn't devoting all its time to the terrorist attacks."

Schott said, "Too bad you didn't get to watch Chet Gorman last night."

"Listened to him on the radio on my way back from Pennsylvania, which was bad enough. Did you note that he wasn't specific about who is supposed to be Isaiah, him or the President?"

"Could be either, couldn't it? A carefully calculated phrase."

"What's he up to?"

Burlane watched the Seminoles drop back into a zone defense. "Gorman? Lamar Gene Cooper would say he just managed to spring a passed pawn." A passed pawn was a pawn with an unobstructed path down a file to the opponent's end of the board, where in a process called queening, it could be changed into the most powerful piece on the board.

"A passed pawn."

Burlane grinned. "Sure. There are eight ranks to a file and eight months until the convention. If Tom Erikson doesn't pin the terrorists before August, then Chet Gorman gets himself a freebie queen."

Schott said, "People would back the beleaguered leader in a time of crisis."

"But if Erikson lets terrorists get away with slaughtering more than a hundred members of Congress and two United States senators, he's dead meat. Chet Gorman knows that, which is why he wants to cancel the primaries. Also, I bet Gorman stands to do better in caucuses or a convention than at the polls, because he's spent the last four years organizing true believers at the grassroots level."

"Nice finesse move."

"Yes, it was. Patriotism cubed, while Gorman advanced his own cause. And remember the rule, Ara: Push passed pawns. If there's nobody blocking your way, go for it. The closer a pawn gets to being queened, the more attention he gets from defenders. Ditto the politician closing in on the nomination."

Schott said, "But if Chet gets the nomination by convention, it might not be worth much. The Christian fundamentalists are with him, but the polls say it's an up-or-down issue with the majority of voters, who are pro-choice."

"Ara, Ara! Those people don't care if anyone says the abortion issue would drag them under. Once they get the nomination, they can manipulate their message to fog the issue. They just want to have their moment of glory. Come November, the Lord will surely provide." The Blue Devils' coach called a time-out; Burlane punched the remote.

The Louisiana populist Lamar Gene Cooper was expressing his opinions on the situation to Larry King.

Burlane looked interested. "Well, look here, the master strategist himself. Democrats in disarray and Republicans ripped in half. What do you think? Perfect time for Lamar Gene to step forward with a third party? Out of the ashes of a discredited past, a new hero steps forth, et cetera."

Larry King, his face solemn, said, "And the terrorists are playing what pieces, Lamar Gene, white or black?"

"My heavens, Larry! White, of course. They moved first, didn't they? The Carter Commission is having to defend."

"The terrorists led with what?" King said. "What pieces?"

"Knights. That's what helicopters do, jump over space. It was a quick, aggressive move. Knights before bishops. Basic tactics. The federal task force has to be very careful here. They have to watch the terrorists don't load up on them before they can do anything about it."

King looked puzzled.

Cooper spoke intently. "Larry, to capture a critical square, you have to have more pieces attacking it than the defender. That's basic to all forms of warfare. Politicians use television advertising to load up on an opponent's weakness. Who can pile the most dollars on any given square?"

King said, "What about white's queen? Isn't the queen the most powerful piece on the board? When will white play his queen?"

Cooper said, "Larry, this is too big not to be a conspiracy. Somewhere there is a terrorist in charge. White's leaving the lady on the back rank until he gets his pieces properly developed. No sense playing her too soon. Plenty of time for the queen." Cooper raised an eyebrow and gave King a hard stare.

"Why is that?" King asked.

Cooper leaned forward. "Why, that ought to be obvious, hadn't it? If you play your queen too early, you have to be careful she doesn't get trapped. An amateur thinks, Lordy, lordy, I've got me this here powerful lady, why I ought to be doing something with her. While he confidently moves his queen around in an attack he can't finish, his opponent quietly develops his pieces. Do you think we're dealing with amateurs here? No, sir! The terrorists've just got our attention."

"How do you beat these terrorists, then, Lamar Gene?"

Cooper said, "You do it with pawns. You move pawns down the board in formation. They have to work together and defend one another, or they'll just get picked off."

"And these pawns would be."

"Members of the United States House of Representatives. We will begin our primaries in another month. We need to choose people who will work together in a unified fashion to capture territory with their combined power. Both the major and minor pieces, the President, the Supreme Court, and members of the Senate need to work together. The enemies of democracy thrive on bickering and disunity."

Ara Schott punched off the set. "Look at old Lamar Gene show off. The rubes in the sticks think all that chess stuff makes him extra smart."

"I don't know about his politics, but Lamar Gene is dead-on right about tactics. Basic tactics is what winning is all about, Ara. That and concentration and perseverance."

Schott grinned. "And not playing your queen too soon."

"Not playing your queen too soon. That too."

"And Lamar Gene Cooper's queen being?"

Burlane looked surprised. "The third party! He's keeping the third party on the back rank until he's developed his pieces and he has a lock on the center."

"Public disgust with both the Democrats and Republicans."

"Sure," Burlane said. "Political parties in this country have gone under before, Ara. The Federalists, the Whigs. Nothing is forever. I say when the polls tell Cooper the board is ready, he'll put his queen into action. Not before."

"You think Lamar Gene Cooper is using chess lingo to tell the public precisely what he's doing? Aw, c'mon!"

Burlane shrugged. "Maybe. Speaking of attacking and defending, I think now's the time to make a little request of our main man in the FBI."

1 0 : 3 0 P . M .

"Well?" James Burlane, having made his request, waited. On the other end of the phone line, an odd sound rumbled up from deep within Frank Coyle's throat.

The FBI? Turn over their data over to Cyberfox? Cooperate with a wiseass hacker who had made a laughingstock of them six months earlier?

"Frank?" Burlane smiled. Coyle was a straight-arrow FBI agent. Burlane knew this was a difficult request for Coyle to accept.

"Cyberfox?" Coyle repeated. He made another noise, then fell silent.

"Frank? Frank?"

"You caught me on my way out of the door."

"Come on, Frank."

"I want to take a look at what the divers brought up today. Maybe they found something good without knowing it."

"She's real good, Frank. She's fun if you know her personally. She knows how to laugh."

Coyle didn't answer.

"You have that kind of information, Frank, I know you do. You have an organized crime unit. They chase mobsters and drug barons. That means they follow money. They have computers. Big ones. And the best software on the market."

"Right. Why don't you have Cyberfox simply steal it from us?" Coyle made another noise. "Ms. Fox of the big brown eyes," he said scornfully. "Blink, blink, blink." In falsetto, he said, *"Who me? Run amok in cyberspace?"*

Burlane said, "Frank, we're dealing with a national emergency here."

"I've got people working with that data to see if we can find any connections that make sense. Believe it or not, Major Khartoum, we've got professionals whose job it is to do that kind of thing. They're on the job this very minute, their happy little fingers going tap, tap, tap on their keyboards."

"They're not as good as she is, and we both know it. Frank."

Coyle sighed. "Ever since your Ms. Griffin had her laugh at us, they've been programming booby traps in their systems to screw over curious outsiders. They've spent a fortune. Just when we think we've wormed our way into their systems, *bam*, they come up with something else. It's a form of game with them."

"You're the FBI, Frank. But we're on the beach, all of us. This is a form of political Dunkirk. We have to push back shits who might not yet be finished. We have to."

Coyle sighed. "I want to pin these bastards as much as you do, Major Khartoum, but I have to clear this with the President. Your foxy lady was a big embarrassment to the administration. Erikson didn't like it any more than we did."

"Call Erikson and Gregg."

Coyle looked surprised. "Erikson and Gregg are in on this?"

"Do it. Call them." Burlane coughed. He remembered his fury at the liar Oliver North standing before Congress, his uniform festooned with medals and ribbons. Now here he was, James Burlane, proposing to blow off the law. He was confident he had decided correctly, but still . . .

"I see," Coyle said. "Say again what you want?"

Burlane said, "I want your current summaries of the activities of organized crime. That's to include Sicilians, Russians, and blacks in New York and San Francisco; Cubans in Miami; Chinese in Seattle, San Francisco, Los Angeles, and New York. All of them. Where possible, I want the names, addresses, and telephones of their leaders, and if you're successfully tapping their conversations. I want to know, specifically, what businesses they either own or are suspected of owning, both in the United States and overseas. If these companies do business overseas, I want the names of their corresponding banks. I also want to know what domestic banks they use and what investment brokers they have. We would appreciate any account numbers you might have collected. The IRS, the DEA, you, whoever has it, I want the data. If you know what security systems they're using or who did their programming, Ms. Griffin wants that."

Coyle said, "I feel obliged to give your wonderful Cyberfox a tip before she attempts to have fun on the insides of their computer systems."

"Sure. Of course. And that is?"

"Tell her before she goes inside, she should anticipate infection by computer viruses."

Burlane said, "You know, Frank, in his farewell address President Dwight Eisenhower warned us about the unchecked power of the military-industrial complex. If he were alive today, he'd warn us about the danger of the military–industrial–hot money complex. That's what we're talking about here, isn't it? A powerful, untaxed underground economy."

Coyle sighed. "Major Khartoum, please. We're both big boys. We both know that nobody wants to stop the action. Too many people are enjoying the goodies."

11:00 P.M.

Frank Coyle peered at the glass table, looking at the numbered shards and bits and pieces of Kiowa helicopters that the Bureau's divers had brought up from the Tidal Basin that day.

Beside him, Marguerite Simson, the tall, middle-aged woman in charge of the computer reconstruction, waited to answer any questions he might have. Simson's technicians had identified everything containing a number or letter except for a twisted piece of aluminum containing a hyphen in front of a capital *D*.

Coyle picked up the piece of aluminum and turned it in his hand. He said, "What is this, Marguerite?"

"Good question. We have no idea," Simson said.

"Have you found anything else with writing in this typeface?"

"No sir, we haven't," Simson said.

FOURTEEN

Carter Commission Exhibit 22-Jan-2M

Transcript of a taped call received at 10:20 A.M., 22 January 2000, by hot-line operator Roberta Jaimeson.

JAIMESON: This is the task-force hot-line for the Carter Commission. We are taping all calls for possible use by our investigators. My name is Roberta.

CALLER: You're the people investigatin' the attack on Congress?

JAIMESON: Yes, we are. Do you have something you think might be of help?

CALLER: Yes, I do. At least I think I do. Maybe. I know this is Sunday and all, but they say we should call any time if we have somethin' we think might help.

JAIMESON: We're open twenty-four hours a day, seven days a week. We do welcome your call, and we hope you do have something that will help. Can you please identify yourself and tell me what you have?

CALLER: My name is Jonas Faulkner. I'm a former master sergeant in the army, now retired. My service number is 18647457. I served in Vietnam. In the Special Forces.

JAIMESON: Yes sir, Sergeant Faulkner, what do you have?

FAULKNER: [Laughs.] Don't "sir" me, ma'am, I worked for a livin'. Late yesterday afternoon I was fishin' underneath the George Mason Bridge on the Virginia side. Now, that's just opposite the entrance to the Tidal Basin on the other side of the river—maybe a half mile away, somethin' like that. Anyway I was usin' a homemade lure, a Faulkner Flopper, ma'am [laughs], and I caught me a beautiful largemouth bass about four or five pounds. A real nice fish, I can tell you. When I was guttin' the bass, I found a little sliver of aluminum inside.

JAIMESON: A sliver of aluminum?

FAULKNER: Yes ma'am. You know a lot of states ban those pop-top aluminum beer and soda cans because people were throwin' 'em out of fishin' boats, and the fish were eatin' 'em. That's likely what happened here. This was a shiny piece of aluminum that wiggles and flashes if you drop it in the water. I know because I checked it out to see. Threw it into a gallon jar. Now it probably wouldn't mean anything to most people, but it does to me.

JAIMESON: Why is that, Sergeant?

FAULKNER: Because it had the words "Leu-Dunston" etched on it. That's capital *L* small *e-u* dash capital *D* small *u-n-s-t-o-n*, ma'am. Triggered old memories in a manner of speaking. [Laughs.]

JAIMESON: "Leu-Dunston"?

FAULKNER: Yes, ma'am. In Vietnam we used to leave a bunch of gear in a campsite after we retreated, pretendin' we were too tired to take it with us. But we'd leave an explosive charge under it, see, and we'd retreat some distance and watch it with binoculars. It was like a sick kind of game, you see. When the VC came in to see what they could scrounge, we'd let as many gather as possible, sort of like bees gathering around a honey pot. Then we'd pop the charge by remote and blow 'em halfway to Hanoi. The lieutenant was the guy who got to pop the remote button, but I was the one who rigged the charges, and that gave me a certain satisfaction.

JAIMESON: And Leu-Dunston is?

FAULKNER: Leu-Dunston was the outfit in Hartford, Connecticut, that manufactured the remote-controlled triggering device that I attached to the explosive charges. You see what I'm gettin' at?

JAIMESON: [Pause.] I'm not sure.

FAULKNER: The piece of aluminum I took out of the fish looked like it had been through some heat.

JAIMESON: [Another pause.] I see.

FAULKNER: [Laughs.] No offense, ma'am, but I can tell by the tone of your voice that you may not see.

JAIMESON: Can you give us a phone number where we can get in touch with you, Sergeant?

FAULKNER: Oh, sure. Anything I can do to help. I'm unemployed now and sort of movin' around, visitin' kin and seein' folks. I'm temporarily stayin' with my cousin, Mike Hoffman, down here in Virginia, Route 1, Box 372, Accotink, Virginia, that would be. He don't have a phone. And ma'am?

JAIMESON: Yes sir, Mr. Faulkner.

FAULKNER: You tell your people that I've popped hundreds of these things in my day, blew many a VC to kingdom come, and I know what I'm talking about. Why I'd just bet you a pretty penny that Leu-Dunston is still in the business of manufacturing remotes for the army. And there's no telling what they've come up with after all these years of making everything smaller and extending the range of the remotes.

JAIMESON: The investigators will get a complete transcript of this call. Is there anything else you want to add?

FAULKNER: No ma'am, I can't think of anything.

JAIMESON: Thank you for calling, Mr. Faulkner.

FAULKNER: Thank *you*, ma'am. We all need to pull together in this awful thing.

1:00 P.M.

Task-force diver John Radcliffe, twenty-four, of Laurel, Maryland, surfaced from the Tidal Basin holding a net evidence bag containing an object that would later bring jubilant cries from the crew manning the dive raft.

Radcliffe had found part of the right hand of a Caucasian female containing an intact thumb and forefinger.

Ellicott City

4:00 P.M.

James Burlane, chewing on his fingernail, stared without seeing at the leafless woods outside Ara Schott's cottage. He listened intently on his cellular phone as Frank Coyle gave him a progress report on the task-force investigation, including the find of body parts in the Tidal Basin and highlights of calls received by the hot-line operators.

Coyle said the FBI had faxed copies of teeth from the splintered jaw, which had belonged to a male, to all state and federal prisons and local jails in the United States. The hands, while not complete, had both yielded serviceable prints. The female hand had a full thumb and forefinger; the male hand had an intact forefinger and middle finger.

Prints taken from both hands were being processed by FBI computers.

Burlane said, "You say you got four calls from people who were driving on the freeway when the helicopters lifted off the flatbed truck. Anything new there?"

"Nope. Two dark blue helicopters. We knew that."

"Helicopters lifting out of a truck four blocks from the Capitol, and it didn't strike anybody as being unusual?"

Coyle said, "We asked them that, but they said no. I guess they've been conditioned by television to expect anything. These were busy people, Major Khartoum. You know how it is. They had places to go and things to do."

"Shit, I guess."

"What do you think about the Leu-Dunston call?"

Burlane said, "If I were you and I had unlimited resources, I would run down everybody I could find who had ever been trained by the military to use remotes."

"People like the caller."

"And anybody in private industry, mining companies and whatever."

Coyle said, "Then see if any of those people have ever had anything to do with religious or political nutballs."

"Or with presidential candidates," Burlane said. "Do you mind if I drive down to Virginia and talk to Jonas Faulkner myself? Maybe the piece of metal with the hyphen *D* is a match to Faulkner's Leu-Dunston find. I'll need the hyphen *D* piece so I can compare them."

Coyle said, "No problem, I'll check it out for you. You've got your cellular phone. I've got your number. If we learn anything new, I'll let you know."

8:00 P.M.

James Burlane was always surprised how the great wealth massed around the mother lode of Washington, D.C.—reflected by what he regarded as the soulless suburbs—yielded so quickly to shacky rural poverty. This was as true in Maryland as it was in Virginia.

In Burlane's opinion the quality of poverty depended largely on the weather. The worst poverty he had ever seen was in Siberia, where the wretched peasants lived in shacks hardly larger than American doghouses, this in winters where the temperature plunged to eighty degrees below zero. The best poverty, if misery was to be so callously rated, was in the tropical Third World.

He felt the poor in rural Virginia probably had it better than those living in northeast Washington because people at least knew one another and the crime was spread out. Better off than either of these were the poor in southern Georgia or South Carolina, say, where at least the winters were bearable. Likewise, owing to the weather, the wretched of Watts had it better than miserable blacks living east of the Anacostia River.

As a teenager in eastern Oregon, Burlane's bedroom had been a seven-foot-long by five-foot-wide renovated chicken coop with newspapers for insulation, with an irrigation ditch a yard in front of the north-facing door. At night he could hear coyotes yelping on the banks of the Columbia River, not two hundred yards away. He had never thought of his family as particularly poor, as he supposed they must have been. But he clearly remembered reading old stories on the yellowed newspapers before he clicked off the single forty-watt lightbulb that hung from the ceiling of his chicken-coop bedroom. He remembered slipping under the frigid covers listening to a howling winter wind whipping out of Canada.

These memories, he felt, were qualitatively superior to those of a suit who had grown up in a well-heated suburban bedroom. He did not envy those who had spent their lives in sterile cocoons of modernity. Envy was a stupid waste of time. Neither did he think it was in any way romantic to be poor. Let the well-off enjoy and buy their toys, he didn't care, as long as Congressmembers and senators didn't walk around with For Sale tags dangling conspicuously from their necks.

The address Jonas Faulkner had given the hot-line operator was typical for the area, a tiny house with peeling yellow paint and a much-patched tar-paper roof. The house had a small porch with a broken overhang. A rusted Oldsmobile with a cracked windshield sat out front of a yard that was a confusion of automobile wheels, fenders, bumpers, and engines. In addition to the greasy, rusted metal, the yard contained a single tree. A tire attached to a rope hung from the largest limb.

A wisp of smoke curled up from a redbrick chimney, and Burlane could see a huge pile of firewood stacked neatly against one end of the house.

Whether it was black poverty or white, the look was the same.

Burlane parked his Cherokee behind the Oldsmobile and threaded his way up a path between the junk in the yard. As he drew near the porch, he could hear laughter inside the house. As he stepped up to the door, he could hear a television set. The family inside was laughing at a sitcom.

Burlane knocked softly on the door, and a lightbulb went on over his head. The door opened, and an elderly black man stood in the doorway. "Yes, sir. Can I help you?"

Burlane showed him his task-force identification.

The man said, "We've been wonderin' if anybody had taken Jonas's call seriously. Come on inside. It has to be getting cold out there."

Burlane stepped inside a tiny, warm room, heated by a wood-burning stove, the floor covered by a threadbare throw rug. It served as a combination dining room and living room. There was a round table at the far end, and at the near end, by the front door, a woman with a large bosom and a nice smile and two teenage boys sat around the table where they had been playing cards. A television set was on in the corner.

On the walls were Nike posters of Shaquille O'Neal, Michael Jordan, and Ken Griffey, Jr.

Burlane's host said, "I bet this is about that piece of metal Jonas found in that bass he caught."

"Yes, it is."

The man studied the ID, then gave it back to Burlane. "Major Khartoum. My name is Mike Hoffman." He turned and called, "Jonas, you got a visitor from the Carter Commission."

From inside a door on Burlane's left a voice called, "In a minute. In a minute."

Hoffman looked amused. "You caught Jonas, uh, indisposed."

Burlane laughed. He gestured at the table. "What're you playing?"

"Hearts."

"Good game."

"I've been sucking up the evil lady all night long."

"That's what always happens to me," Burlane said.

Hoffman said, "Jonas found that piece of metal in the belly of a largemouth bass. Isn't that something? You think it might be from the terrorist helicopters?"

Burlane said, "You never can tell."

Hoffman caught Burlane looking at the posters on the wall.

"You like sports, Major Khartoum?"

Burlane grinned. "Yes, I do. I like baseball best, I have to admit. Basketball has too much home-court nonsense for my taste. The referees play too big a part in the game."

"I know what you mean. Do you have favorite baseball players?"

Burlane said, "Reggie Jackson and George Brett. No ballplayer in history has ever told a jackass owner to sit on it like the Reg did to George Steinbrenner by slugging three home runs in one World Series game. Three homers on three pitches!"

Hoffman grinned. "Wasn't that something? Mr. October."

"I liked it best when the cameras caught him in the dugout holding up three fingers. 'Three, Mom! Three!'" Burlane held up three fingers, mimicking the triumphant Reggie Jackson.

"You met Frank Coyle?"

"Yes, I have. Good man."

"God, wasn't it terrible about those knees of his? Not one, but both knees taken out on one hit. He would have been somethin' in the pros."

"He's not a half-bad FBI agent," Burlane said.

On the television, "The Star-Spangled Banner" played softly. A quartet of male singers, a blue-eyed white girl, a Hispanic man, an African American girl, and an Asian man sang:

"*Oh, say can you see*
By the dawn's early light
What so proudly we hailed
At the twilight's last gleaming."

Elliot Fenn, the hormonal hero of assault-rifle action movies; Stan Johnson, New Orleans Saints quarterback and last year's winner of the Super Bowl MVP award; and Gladys Armstrong, the mayor of Phoenix, Arizona, stood arm in arm.

The music got bolder.
"... *rockets' red glare*
The bombs bursting in air
Gave proof through the night
That our flag was still there."

The national anthem faded.

Elliot Fenn, his face as serious and determined as it was in the movies, looked straight into the camera's red eye. "In this time of national sorrow and outrage our nation must unite and stand firm against conspirators who would bring it under. All Americans can give proof through this dark night of American history by donating to a special nonpartisan fund to elect politicians who are determined to turn the corner on this violent nation gone awry and to secure justice for the martyred congressmen and -women who gave their lives for our country. If you want to be a hero, give, and give freely."

Quarterback Johnson said, "Give Proof Through the Night will support candidates with spine, regardless of party."

The mayor of Phoenix, her face grim, added, "In this national emergency, parties are irrelevant. What the nation needs is courage to do what is right and has to be done. Help us honor our fallen countrymen and -women. Please be generous in this hour of desperate need."

Then the music faded, and the sitcom returned.

Burlane's host said, "This ad, or one like it, is on all the channels, it seems. We can't change channels without seeing it."

Burlane said, "Makes a person wonder how they were able to come up with ads like that so fast."

"Yes, it does, come to think of it," Hoffman said.

Burlane recognized the approach as the practice called "bundling." Viewers sent money to Give Proof Through the Night, and whoever was behind Give Proof would package the various donations into a huge fund or "bundle." This meant they could give as much money to whomever they wished, no questions asked, and no limits on the amount of money they could contribute. In the past, feminists had done this to back female candidates of either party. People who supported the right to have an abortion had used it to elect representatives who agreed with them, regardless of party. The National Rifle Association had done it, too.

Give Proof Through the Night's highly charged emotional pitch for small, individual donations was strikingly similar to the "Win one for Jesus" tactic pioneered by Oliver M. North and copied by Senator Chet Gorman.

Faulkner, a tall, balding black man, stepped out of the john, zipping the fly of his khaki trousers.

Burlane showed him his boxtops and they shook.

Faulkner said, "I bet you know Frank Coyle, don't you?"

Burlane said, "It was Frank who sent me down here. We found a little piece of metal in the Tidal Basin with a hyphen D on it. We were wondering if it might not be a match to the one you found."

"Well, sure. You show me yours, and I'll show you mine." Faulkner grinned.

"Let's do it," Burlane said.

Faulkner dug into his pocket. He held his left fist up and Burlane did the same. "Who goes first?"

Burlane opened his hand, palm up.

Faulkner studied the twist of metal in Burlane's palm. "I do believe we may have lucked out." He opened his hand.

Burlane's hyphen D twist had apparently come from a piece of metal identical to Faulkner's Leu-Dunston find.

"What do you think, Major Khartoum?" Faulkner arched an eyebrow.

Burlane said, "I think maybe somebody used a remote to blow up those choppers."

Faulkner was pleased that he had helped. "Say hey to Frank Coyle for me, will you?"

Burlane took Faulkner's hyphen D twist. "For this, I bet he can be talked into sending you an autographed football."

FIFTEEN

When Frank Coyle's call came, James Burlane was taking a shower, letting the hot water beat on the back of his neck. There was something about a hot shower that encouraged concentration and creativity; he stood, being pummeled by hot water, and thought, a form of intellectual workout.

Now, swabbing himself with a towel, Burlane grabbed his cellular phone.

"Major Khartoum?"

"Here. Dripping. You caught me in the shower, Frank."

"Bingo! We've got two hands with prints, one male, one female. We've got teeth. All total, we're looking at the bones and limbs of eight to ten bodies. Too early to tell how many."

"So the bitch went down with the choppers?"

"Her brother too it looks like."

"Her brother?"

"Both Colombians."

"Uh-oh."

"The female hand belonged to Marta Juarez, the younger sister of Carlos Juarez, a member of the Cali drug cartel who was busted and convicted of cocaine smuggling three years ago. Marta Juarez was captured in the same bust, on a stolen yacht containing three tons of coke, but she claimed she didn't know there was anything unusual on board, and so she was merely deported."

"How long did her brother get?"

"Twenty years. We identified him by his teeth."

"*El hermano de la señorita Marta.* I thought you said he got twenty years."

"I did, but he was released eighteen months later when an appeals court overturned his conviction. The judge was overcome by a tearful plea by the silver-tongued Jaime Cortez."

"Señor Drug Baron Lawyer."

"Cortez argued that the Coast Guard didn't have reasonable grounds to search the yacht, and the appeals court agreed, so he walked."

"Oof!" Burlane said.

Coyle said, "I think I would put it in stronger terms than that."

"How about the other hand?"

"The other hand belonged to Antonio Ceballos. You might have seen his picture in the post office. He was on our ten-most-wanted list. He jumped bail in Atlanta on cocaine-smuggling charges a couple of years ago."

"How about the other body parts?"

"Nothing on them, but we're still checking."

"Have you shown pictures of Carlos and Marta to your bookstore witnesses?"

"Next up," Coyle said.

FBI Building

9:00 A.M.

Elisa Johnston flipped through photographs of Hispanic women.

Frank Coyle, staring at the backs of his hands in his lap, waited.

Upon seeing the eighteenth picture, Johnston immediately set it aside.

"That one?" Coyle said.

"I think so. I need to find her brother to make sure."

She started on the pile of males.

Coyle waited, studying the photograph of the woman.

Johnston picked up the fifth picture. "This is him. Oscar."

Coyle placed the photographs side by side on the table. "These are the ones?"

"That's them. I'm positive."

"They were speaking Spanish?"

"That's right."

"Say again how large they were. Tell me about their bodies."

Johnston hesitated. "Like I said before, I didn't pay much attention to their bodies. They were wearing congressional staff tags, I remember that, and they were well dressed. I remembered them only because they spoke Spanish, and they had those jaws, of course. The woman was . . . I don't know, maybe about my height, and the man a little taller. If it hadn't been for the shooting, Barry and I would have forgotten all about them."

"And you're how tall?"

"I'm five-seven."

Coyle sighed. He stood. "Barry is finished too. You're both free to go, but this is an extremely sensitive matter. We would appreciate it if you don't discuss it with anyone."

"Which ones did Barry pick?"

Coyle hesitated, then said, "Same two."

"Then it's them. Has to be. Are you going to tell me who they are?"

Coyle shook his head. "You'll no doubt see them on television soon enough. If you remember anything more, call us immediately, and don't leave the area without telling us how to get in touch with you if we have more questions."

"You're the former football player, aren't you?"

Coyle gave her a self-deprecating grin and sighed. "I'm the one. Play defense full-time these days."

Capitol Hill Hospital
9:40 A.M.

Terry Donahue, the Capitol guard, had been hit with three slugs in his abdomen and two in his left hip and groin. He had been on the critical list in the hours following the attack, but was now listed as serious but stable. He had tubes in his nose and a needle in his left arm through which clear fluid dropped from a bottle hanging from a portable IV stand.

Donahue was weak but alert. He looked up at Frank Coyle, who was holding something in a paper bag in addition to a folder of photographs. He wanted to do his part. He wanted to help.

"You're sure you're up to it?" Coyle said.

Donahue nodded.

Coyle glanced at Donahue's doctor.

The doctor, a broad-faced woman wearing thick eyeglasses, checked the monitor that registered Donahue's vital signs on a screen. She said, "I'll tell you if I think he needs to stop."

Coyle said, "You don't have to talk, Officer Donahue, just shake your head or nod. Nod if your answer is yes."

Donahue nodded.

"Did you get a clear look at them?"

Donahue did his best to shrug.

Coyle smiled. "And a shrug if you're not sure. Okay. There were a lot of people coming and going. I understand. I'll show you the females first, then the males. We'll see how it goes." Coyle started through the photographs, holding them up one at a time.

Donahue nodded at the ninth photograph.

Coyle set that picture aside and started on the males.

Donahue stopped him on the second picture.

"These two. You're sure?"

Donahue nodded.

"Can you remember how large they were?"

Donahue shrugged.

Coyle thought about that. "Was the man larger or smaller than you?"

He shrugged again.

"Identifying the pictures helped a lot, and that's the truth. Thank you very much, Officer Donahue."

Donahue had a puzzled look on his face.

Coyle said, "Doctor, do you suppose you could leave Officer Donahue and me alone for a minute? For a little cop talk."

"Sure," she said. "But no more than that. He's very weak."

Coyle waited until she had left and said, "You've identified Marta and Carlos Juarez, Colombian coke smugglers. We got a make on them from their remains on the bottom of the Tidal Basin, and two eyewitnesses saw them, in front of Trover's and in Flying Burrito Brothers. She called him 'Oscar' there, but there seems little doubt what his real name is. I don't have to tell you to keep this under your Stetson."

Donahue smiled.

"I know. I know. You're not going anywhere for a while, and couldn't tell anyone if you wanted to."

Donahue tried to talk.

"Easy, easy," Coyle said. "You've been a big, big help. You've done your part. You rest now." Coyle removed a football from the paper bag and autographed it for Donahue.

The White House
11:00 A.M.

President Thomas Erikson sat, resting his chin in the palm of his left hand. He strummed the top of his desk with the fingers of his right hand.

Vice President Douglas Gregg, staring at the floor, rested his forehead on the heels of both hands.

Erikson said, "The Cali drug cartel! Jesus!" He bit his lip. He leaned back in his swivel chair, staring at the ceiling.

Gregg looked up. "Maybe it's not the cartel. Maybe it's just the brother and sister and this guy Ceballos acting on their own. They're pissed, Latin tempers and all that. Get those American cockroaches."

Erikson gave the vice president a look. "On their own? A simultaneous hit in San Francisco and Washington? Perfect timing? Sure."

Gregg looked sour. "You're right, of course. Anybody could have hired them for any number of reasons. We still have no idea who was behind this or why. We don't even know if the drivers of the Wal-Mart truck and car walked away or were in the copters." He paused, thinking. "We'll have to inform the commission."

"We sure as hell don't want to act on our own, that's for sure."

Gregg took a deep breath and exhaled slowly through puffed cheeks.

Erikson said, "We can't keep this secret from the country."

Gregg looked resigned. "No way. I agree."

The Oval Office
9:00 P.M.

As he read his short announcement from the monitor in front of him, President Thomas Erikson felt it was somebody else saying these words, not him. The feeling was similar to those reports by people who had allegedly come back from the dead, later to report that they had watched the doctors working over them.

Those who had been revived after death reported a sensation of being in a tunnel of light. That's the way Erikson felt, surrounded as he was by the intense lights that had turned the Oval Office into a television set.

Colombians. The remains in the Tidal Basin were Colombians. But why? The attack was a form of madness that was beyond Erikson's comprehension.

The red light was on.

Erikson had the sensation of watching himself, the President, a kind of history's puppet, doing what he had to do. His mouth worked and the words came out, and yet, simultaneously, he was a spectator:

"The day following the terrorist assault on the House of Representatives, I announced the formation of the Carter Commission, promising you we would bring the conspirators to justice. I also promised there would be no relevant information withheld from the public such as that which followed the assassination of President John F. Kennedy. I said that when the Carter Commission learned something it could share without compromising its investigation, we would make it public."

Erikson paused for a drink of water. He said, "Well, we *have* found something of significance. Though several reasons might tempt us to keep it secret until more facts are known, we will keep our promise.

"As you all know, two days ago, Carter Commission divers found part of a male hand and a female hand and the lower half of a man's jaw in the waters of the Tidal Basin. We have now identified the deceased owners of the hands and that jaw, and we have corroborating eyewitness testimony.

"I urge you all to remain calm and await the full results of the investigation before leaping to any conclusion as to the full extent of the conspiracy. We don't yet know all the facts. We don't know who planned the attacks. We don't know who financed the attacks. We don't know why the attacks were carried out. We have only identified three of the individuals involved. Let me say that again: We have only identified three of the eight to ten terrorists who went down in the Tidal Basin. That's all. . . ."

10:30 P.M.

James Burlane punched off the television and lay in bed with his head propped up, thinking. Later he would watch what would surely be an inflammatory reaction to Erikson's revelation.

It seemed to Burlane like Give Proof Through the Night had a spot every five minutes, sandwiched in between reactions of public figures who, without exception, were enraged and demanded action. The Give Proof spots featured actors and actresses, sports figures, and people with accents from all over the United States: Texas and Mississippi accents, Boston and Baltimore accents, you name it. Burlane was reminded of the patriotic World War II movies with redneck Southerners and fast-talking Italians from Brooklyn thrown together in a time of national emergency.

His cellular phone rang and Burlane punched the Mute button on the television set.

It was Frank Coyle. "When it rains, it comes in buckets."

"What've you got now?"

Coyle said, "First, the truck was stolen from the Kroger's grocery-store chain. Whoever stole it repainted the tractor and eliminated the Kroger's logo from the sides of the containers and replaced them with Wal-Mart's logo. Each trailer had a false bottom resting under a pneumatic lift. The helicopters rode with their blades just below the open roof. As they approached liftoff, the driver used the lift to push the blades above the sides."

"High enough for the blades to clear the top."

"Right. From there, liftoff was easy. The engines and frames of the helicopters had been scrubbed of all identifying numbers. They were originally red and had recently been repainted blue. The painters sanded the aluminum doors before they sprayed on the blue. They did a thorough job on three of the doors, but got lazy or careless on the fourth. Under high-resolution magnification our lab people could make out, just barely, what appear to be parts of some letters. There aren't any guarantees here, just a possibility. You got a pen and something to write on?"

Burlane retrieved the stenographer's pad that he'd been using to jot down notes as possibilities occurred to him. The first page was covered with doodles and scattered words. "Let me have it."

"Okay, we've got blank space that we can't make out, followed by a small *e*, followed by three spaces and a small *n*. Then we've got a cap *G* followed by a small *j* and four spaces. Then we've got four blank spaces followed by small *c*, followed by five blank spaces, a small *a*, and one space. Then we've got an eight-letter word ending in *g*."

Burlane studied his notebook:

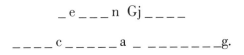

_ e _ _ _ n Gj _ _ _ _

_ _ _ _ c _ _ _ _ _ a _ _ _ _ _ _ _ _g.

Coyle said, "What do you think?"

"The question is what space *e* space-space-space *n*, cap *G*, small *j* and four spaces means?"

"And two more words, one with an *a*, and a second ending in *g*. Any ideas, Sherlock?"

"Let me think about it," Burlane said.

11:00 P.M.

Frank Coyle again.

James Burlane put down his cup of coffee and the pad covered with—in large and small letters—several dozen versions of space *e* space-space-space *n* and *Gj* space-space-space-space. "Jesus, don't you ever sleep, Frank?"

"A black man put in charge of this investigation, a former jock at that, and you think I'm going to sleep? Get real."

"Figure it's third and long. Put your shoulder into it. Lower your head and knock the fuckers on their butts."

"That's precisely what I intend to do," Coyle said. "Sorry to wake you."

"I wasn't sleeping," Burlane said. "Can't figure the *Gj*–four-space puzzle."

"You might have to set that aside for the moment. A half hour ago, Senator Boulanger received a call at her home from a man purporting to represent Guillermo Peña de la Banda-Conchesa in Cali."

"Oh?"

Coyle said, "Señor Peña told her that it's extremely urgent that he talk to someone who is investigating the terrorist attack. He said that Marta and Carlos Juarez and Antonio Ceballos may have once run cocaine, but none of Peña's people have seen them for weeks. He doesn't have anything to do with any attack on Congress, he says. He's been framed."

"Poor baby."

"He said he wants to talk personally to Senator Boulanger or a representative from the task force. He wants someone who has the confidence of the President. He said he will have people waiting for our representative at the airport in Bogotá. He gave her a fax number in Cali for her reply. She called me and suggested that you go. You're a Spanish-speaking operative. You know the ropes."

"And what do you think?"

"I agree. I'll recommend to Erikson and Gregg that the military fly you directly to Bogotá as soon as you can get to the nearest air force base. If they approve, Senator Boulanger will fax your destination and ETA to Peña. We have to hear what he has to say. We can't just blow him off."

SIXTEEN

James Burlane wondered how much it had cost to fuel and maintain the diesel generators that ran the air conditioners and the rest of the modern conveniences. There was no crass and annoying rumbling of diesels; they labored discreetly on in insulated underground chambers at a distance, so that the castle or fortress, or whatever it was, could sit grandly on top of the cliff in blessed, serene silence.

Thanks to the generators there were no barbarous Third World electrical blackouts for Guillermo Peña de la Banda-Conchesa.

Burlane noted that the cannons on top of the battlements were fully restored and maintained. At the bottom of the three-hundred-foot-high cliffs, the Caribbean was azure blue and grand.

The generators also powered the grow-lights in the underground greenhouses where Señor Peña tended to his hobby of growing exotic fruits and vegetables. He did not import Japanese pears or Chilean apples or Swedish lingonberries. He grew his own. In addition to his greenhouses, he had a ranch where he raised wild game, an aviary filled with pheasants and partridges, and aquariums where he grew lobsters, giant prawns, and mammoth scallops.

Although he could not travel without the barbarous DEA swooping down upon him, Peña did not have to live like a fugitive. He had a well-stocked library and a high-tech sound system for his compact discs—he enjoyed classical music and American jazz, but passed on rock 'n' roll.

In short, despite the controversy surrounding his existence, Peña did not forgo the civilized pleasures of the intellect or of the senses, which, in the end, he had told Burlane on their way back from his private airport, was what life was all about.

The mustached, handsome Peña was an elegantly slender man, six feet tall, with intense brown eyes. He passed on what Burlane had come to regard as the Latin American uniform—polished black shoes, black slacks, and white shirt. He was far more secure than that. He wore Birkenstock sandals, pale blue Levi's, and a turquoise silk shirt, open at the throat. Burlane was relieved to note that he did not forgo the gold chains that were ubiquitous for the properly macho drug baron; he wore four heavy ropes of gold around his throat.

Now, in cultivated English that was nearly without accent, he asked Burlane what he would like for lunch. "Anything at all," Peña said. "Anything. If you order something my chefs can't provide, I will be shocked. Truly shocked." He waved his hand grandly.

Burlane wasn't about to order bird's nest soup or corn-fed quails stuffed with truffles. He thought for a moment, then said, "I would like a classic American cheeseburger, with onions, and a bowl of properly made Tex-Mex chili." Should he ask for a bottle of Oregon-brewed Henry Weinhard's? He thought no. "And a cold bottle of Budweiser. If that's possible. If not, you choose, Señor Peña."

Peña laughed. "You're living up to your reputation as an eccentric, Major Khartoum." He rose from his chair. "By the way, you were the gentleman who pinned my man on Senator Boulanger's narc committee, were you not? The pilot."

"It was me."

"Pretending to play the marimba."

"Me," Burlane said.

Peña said, "A pilot of skill, if the stories are to be believed. You could do anything. Except . . ." He looked amused.

"Except for clearing trees at the end of a Nicaraguan runway the size of someone's backyard. Your people have wonderful senses of humor."

"I once vowed to have you skinned alive, Major Khartoum. Did you know that?"

"I can imagine."

Peña smiled. "But now I need your help. Old wounds heal. Times change. If you'll excuse me for a moment, I have to instruct my chef. It's a matter of pride with me that I deliver you a proper cheeseburger and bowl of chili. I wish to be a proper host."

Peña left Burlane with a bottle of Myer's dark rum and a bucket of ice. They were to have their lunch at a white table under a parasol at one end of a kidney-shaped swimming pool. The pool was at the edge of the cliff.

At the far end of the pool, three young Latin beauties wearing string bikinis that were inadequate for their extraordinary bodies lay back on reclining deck chairs under parasols to protect them from the tropical sun.

Behind the air-conditioned fortress with the pool and the beauties rose mountains covered by verdant tropical forest.

Peña, returning from the kitchen, said, "Paco will prepare you chili according to a recipe that won the Tex-Mex chili cook-off in El Paso, Texas, in 1958. Paco said it is *the* classic chili."

Burlane leaned back in his chair. "*The* classic. How does he know that?"

Peña smiled. "Good question. That's actually the opinion of a chef in San Antonio, Texas, a friend of Paco's. Paco gave him a call and he faxed the recipe. Paco has all the ingredients, of course. He'll make it from prime Angus beef."

"And the cheeseburger?"

"That will be from a book called *The Absolute Very Best Cheeseburgers in America* that was published in the U.S. a couple of years ago."

"I see."

"Paco will make you one that's the specialty of a sports bar in San Francisco." Peña, as if discovering the young women for the first time, said, "Some kind of host I am." Fumbling at his chest, he called to the girls, "*Las tetas, señoritas. Las tetas! Las tetas! Ustedes no están en la iglesia!*" (The tits, señoritas. The tits! The tits! You're not in a church!)

The girls, giggling, removed their bikini tops.

"*Dios mío!*" Peña said. "You will of course choose one of the young ladies for your pleasure after lunch, Major Khartoum. Or two. Or all three if you please. Aren't they something?"

"They are indeed," Burlane said.

"*Que grandes tetas! Ay!*"

Burlane raised an eyebrow. "*Me gustan los culos!*" (I like butts!)

Peña looked pleased. "*La comida* followed by *las señoritas* and a nice siesta. *Usted quiera*, Major Khartoum?" (Food followed by the girls and a nice nap. You like, Major Khartoum?)

Burlane, watching the girls, grinned. "*Cuando en Colombia...*" (When in Colombia...)

Peña laughed. "A civilized way to spend an afternoon. We will have supper later on—at ten o'clock, say. I confess, Major Khartoum, that I find it impossible to eat at six like you Anglos. That's time for *merienda*—a drink or two to whet the appetite, and some snacks."

"And some talk."

"Sí, and some talk. That would be a good time to have our talk, I think."

8:00 P.M.

On James Burlane's suggestion, they returned to the table by the swimming pool for their heart-to-heart. A balmy breeze was blowing in from the Caribbean far below.

On Peña's invitation, Burlane chose their refreshment, Jack Daniel's whiskey on ice, and peanuts cooked in oil spiked with garlic.

Peña brought with him a blue folder stuffed with documents. Burlane knew there was something of import in the folder. He also knew Peña would make him wait and wonder before he let him see the contents. But Burlane was patient. He wanted to hear Peña's full pitch.

Peña, munching on peanuts, said, "On a subject like this, it is truly difficult to know where to start, Major Khartoum. How should I begin?"

"Wherever you please." Burlane poured himself a tad more Jack Daniel's.

"First, you should know that the attack on your House of Representatives shocked us every bit as much as it did you, Major Khartoum."

Mildly, Burlane said, "I doubt that, but do continue, señor."

"Please, please, you have to understand. We sell cocaine in your country to make money, not because we hate gringos. Well, okay. You're fun to hate, it's so, but it's always easy for the have-nots to hate the haves. Envy dominates human discourse. Everybody wants more of everything. Is that not true?"

"It's possible to argue the case, I'll give you that," Burlane said.

"Everybody wants to be like the people they see on American television shows. Those cars. Those fancy houses. Everything clean and nice. Those kitchens with all the gadgets. Microwave ovens. Food processors. Blonde girls with pale pink nipples. Now every country in Central and South America wants to be part of the North American Free Trade Agreement. If it all works, the entire hemisphere will prosper: you Americans, the Canadians, the Mexicans, the Chileans and Argentines and Brazilians, all of us. The wonders of free trade and expanding markets."

Burlane smiled. "I doubt if free trade in cocaine is what Washington has in mind."

Peña said, "You are the joker, aren't you, Major Khartoum? But you should look at the drug trade this way: Many are the sons and daughters of drug warriors and Dade County cops whose education has been financed by drug money. We've never resented contributing a little extra to their income."

"The cost of doing business."

"*Por supuesto!* This is what your President Reagan called 'trickle down' economics. When a crooked customs agent buys himself a new house, that provides work for carpenters and electricians and plumbers. And think of the recreational vehicles and speedboats and automobiles that would have gone unsold without drug money. Truly, Major Khartoum, if you were so mad as to end the war on drugs, who would employ all those people who would lose their jobs? DEA agents, customs officials, and federal prosecutors who profit from our bribes, not to mention contractors who build prisons. It doesn't make sense. All those people benefit. We benefit. Where's the harm?"

Burlane said, "The Congressmembers were in the middle of the vote on issuing plastic hundred-dollar bills. You would have had to turn in your old bills for new ones with federal agents watching the action and taking names. Did you like that idea? Hard to believe you did."

Peña cocked his head, looking amused. "So we'd have had to wash our money. It was a onetime shot. Six months. Big deal. Do you really think that would have been anything more than an annoyance? Something to overcome, then on to business as usual. We'd have figured a way. Please, Major Khartoum, give us credit."

"And the two senators killed in San Francisco supported the war on drugs."

"*Caramba!* Major Khartoum! We *want* the war on drugs, don't you see! That's how we earn our living. If it had been us behind the attacks, we'd have killed that *puta* Graciela Boulanger. She wants to end the war on drugs. If you think we want that, you have to be deranged. *She's* the enemy, not the other two senators. Boulanger. *La puta!* Yet she went untouched. Why?"

Burlane shrugged.

"Why on earth would we want to kill Jacoby and Huff? What we want is a *manageable* war on drugs. We *encourage* you to throw your money away on absurd attempts to stop us from smuggling our coke and laundering our money, but we don't want stealth bombers swooping in on us in the dark of night. We don't want an invasion by the United States Marines. *Por Dios!*"

"*Yo entiendo.*" (I understand.)

"What would happen to all the talk of free trade and cooperation in the Western Hemisphere then? We both know what would happen. We would return to the bad old days. Remember the people spitting on Vice President Nixon? Nobody wants to return to that. Please give us credit for having a brain, Major. You may not like what we're doing, but you should know we've not lost our senses."

Burlane said, "I follow your logic, señor. Unfortunately, the teeth and the fingers the task force recovered from the Tidal Basin belonged to Marta and Carlos Juarez, *your* people. Plus, a security guard and two eyewitnesses identified them from their pictures. How do you account for the remains of two known cocaine smugglers corroborated by eyewitnesses?"

Peña poured himself some whiskey and took a shot. He refilled his glass and leaned forward. "Because they disappeared. None of my people have seen them for weeks."

"You were framed."

Peña turned up the palms of his hands. "What other conclusion can you make?"

"Framed. Right," Burlane said dryly.

"Or they did it on their own for reasons that frankly escape me. Or somebody not connected to us hired them. Something. In any event, we didn't have anything to do with it. We're innocent."

Burlane cocked his head. "Innocent? Innocent? Really, señor, isn't that getting a bit carried away?"

"I won't argue that point, Major Khartoum. We may be guilty of a lot of things, but we're innocent of this. We had nothing to do with the *cucaracha* terrorists. Nothing. You must believe me."

Burlane leaned back in his chair. " Okay, Señor Peña. Suppose, for a moment, that I do believe you. The next question, as you point out, is, Who? Who framed you and what was their motive? The public is furious. They want justice. You have to give me motive, solid, convincing evidence for the President and his people to work with. It may hurt a little, but you have to do it."

Peña sighed. "I've been thinking about that a lot, believe me. As you know, the popular assertion is that we control the cocaine trade in the United States. There may be perhaps some truth in that charge."

"'Perhaps'? Please, Señor Peña."

"You want motive, consider heroin. Heroin has traditionally come from Afghanistan, Pakistan, and the Golden Triangle. Owing to pressure from your State Department, there has been less heroin coming from Afghanistan and Pakistan, but it continues to come from the Golden Triangle—smuggled by Chinese Triad gangs who dominate the West Coast market. In the last ten years, we Colombians moved into Miami and New York."

"By 'we' you mean your Cali organization?"

"Uh . . ."

"Go ahead, say it."

"*Sí, señor.*"

"You mean heroin processed in Colombia from poppies grown here."

"*Sí.* Last fall, a two-ton shipment of our heroin was stolen from a Manhattan warehouse minutes before a bust by the DEA and the New York police. We never knew who did this. Two weeks ago, the Los Angeles Police Department busted a nightclub on Santa Monica Boulevard and confiscated two tons of heroin that had been processed in our labs."

"The heroin stolen in New York."

"Almost certainly. We didn't move it in L.A., but the Chinese Triads didn't know that. Then two men with stockings pulled over their faces stepped into a Miami Beach restaurant and murdered my friend Diego Rodriguez and five of our friends. DEA agents who were following Rodriguez saw what happened."

"And your conclusion?"

"Our conclusion is that the attack on the House and the murder of the two senators were part of a setup by the Chinese Triads. The man and woman who killed the congressmen wore ski masks, same as the people who shot Diego."

"Chinese Triads bent on driving you out of the heroin trade."

"Not only the heroin trade, Major Khartoum. You have to remember, if we can grow poppies and process heroin in South America, they can grow coca plants and process cocaine in Indochina. They have mountains there, too."

"Who do you think stole your heroin in Manhattan?"

"*Quien sabe?* Obviously we had a leak in our organization. If the DEA and New York narcotics people knew the dope was in the warehouse, who else knew? All the Chinese knew was that the Los Angeles authorities confiscated two tons of Colombian heroin on their turf. That was enough to make them decide enough was enough."

"Spank your little butts."

"You ask for motive, Major Khartoum, there's motive."

Burlane grimaced. "There's a certain logic to your argument, I have to admit. But the only thing the American public knows is that the money bill, which they've been told you don't like, was in the process of being voted upon. And two senators, whose support of the drug war they assume you hate, were simultaneously murdered in San Francisco. That was a stain on our national honor. People want justice. They're ready to go toe-to-toe to avenge the deaths of the congressmembers and redeem the national honor. Unless something is done quickly, President Erikson won't have any choice but to send in the marines."

Peña stared into the middle distance.

Burlane said, "Mere logic won't cut it, señor. You're going to have to do better."

Peña took a deep breath and slid the folder toward Burlane. "Do you know anything about the financing of political campaigns in America, Major Khartoum?"

"A little," Burlane said.

"Do you know what 'independent expenditures' are?"

Burlane nodded.

"A wonderful system in your country. Any outsider, foreign or domestic, can spend as much as they want independent of a candidate's official campaign—the American Medical Association can do it, the National Trial Lawyers Association, the Japanese government. It doesn't make any difference if we're Colombians; we're not excluded. If we have the money, we're free to spend what we please to buy the American policies we prefer."

"The Brigade of American Patriots can do it."

Peña furrowed his brow.

"Senator Chet Gorman's backers."

"Ah, yes. Well, sure. The Brigade of American Patriots too. Why should they be denied? What's that expression in your country? 'What's good for the . . .'"

"'What's sauce for the goose is sauce for the gander.'"

Peña smiled. "Yes, that's it. Such a wonderful democracy you Americans have. Before, secret money was mere influence. Now one can secretly buy a politician without risk. The more money you have, the more politicians you can buy. The power of television made it all possible." He pushed the blue folder toward Burlane. "I want you to study the contents of this folder, Major Khartoum. No sense going over it here. Read it on the airplane on your way back to the United States. Show it to President Erikson. Show it to the members of the Carter Commission."

Burlane opened the folder and glanced at its contents. It contained a computer printout of numbers. An accountant's report perhaps. Or an audit. "And this is?"

"A detailed, specific account of our discreet intervention on behalf of both Senator Jacoby and Senator Huff in their most recent campaigns. We spent two million dollars on behalf of Senator Jacoby and almost twice that on behalf of Senator Huff. I've included the numbers of those accounts, which were later closed. I'll instruct the banks involved to cooperate fully in any investigation by your task force."

Burlane closed the folder. "Did you deposit the money with the senators' knowledge?"

Peña looked offended. "Certainly not. That would be both dangerous and unnecessary. Unprofessional."

"What was the quid pro quo?"

Peña shook his head. "Please, please, Major Khartoum. No papers were signed. No hands were shaken."

"That's not how such sensitive business is conducted."

"No, it isn't. Your politicians win elections by spending more on television than their opponents. When an unexpected two- or three-million-dollar blessing in independent expenditures benefits a candidate, he or she knows why. We're not competing to see who can waste the most money. We're buying public policy. Senator Jacoby was able to look his voters straight in the eye and tell them his vote was not for sale. That was true in the narrowest, legal sense of the word, but it's absurd to suggest he didn't know where the money was coming from. Now then, if he voted the wrong way . . ."

"If he voted to phase out the drug war . . ."

"*Sí, sí.* Then the millions of dollars from unspecified sources wouldn't be forthcoming the next election. It would go to Senator Jacoby's challenger. Nothing has to be written down for a deal to be made. If Jacoby didn't support us, his opponent would outspend him."

"For you, buying the drug war has been a cost of doing business."

Peña smiled. "Of course, most of the money ends up in the accounts of the television networks. Newspapers make money too, but television is where the action is. To have real reform, you foolish Americans have to make campaigns cheaper, but you'll never do it. You can't even seriously discuss it, or won't. It's impossible."

Burlane looked disheartened.

Peña shrugged. "Well, never mind, Major Khartoum. I like being able to buy your congressmembers and senators."

"I bet you do," Burlane said.

"The most wonderful part is when you *bocas grandes* accuse us of buying elections down here. 'The politics of banana republics,' you call it. You sneer at us. Oh so superior. Such piety, Major Khartoum! Such righteousness. Such blindness! *Ay!*"

"Are you willing to tell us what other Congress members and senators you've covertly supported with independent expenditures?"

Peña shook his head. "Only Senators Jacoby and Huff are at issue here."

"It would help your argument."

Peña looked amused. "I know you have to try, Major Khartoum. But truly, I don't see what's to be gained from overdoing it. The figures on Jacoby and Huff are enough to prove our point. The other Congressmembers and senators we've helped are still alive, aren't they?"

"No use embarrassing them."

"That's right, and if I gave you a complete list, nobody would believe it anyway. If they did, you'd have mobs forming on Pennsylvania Avenue armed with pitchforks and shotguns. All I want to do is defend my source of income and keep stealth bombers from destroying my property."

"I see," Burlane said.

"Which brings us back to the question at hand."

Burlane pursed his lips. "And that being?"

"Why in hell would we want to murder two United States senators we paid good money to put and keep in office, and whose support of the drug war was helping keep us in business? You want motive? You ask your President Thomas Erikson to answer that, Major Khartoum. *Ay caramba!* You Americans! *Dios mío!*"

SEVENTEEN

Governor John Danneman stood, looking at the map of the Chesapeake Bay on the wall of his beach house. He leaned forward and tilted his head so he could look through the bottoms of his bifocals. "You know, Bob, I've always liked the names of these rivers. They have a way about them. A feel. They're lovely. The Susquehanna. The Sassetras. The Patabsco and the Patuxent and the Potomac. The Manokin and the Nanticoke. The Yeocomico and the Tuckahoe and the Choptank. Sounds like Thanksgiving, doesn't it? Make me think of wild turkeys and succotash." He sighed. "My mother put oysters in the dressing. God, was it ever wonderful!"

Looking through the window at the black void that was Chesapeake Bay, Robert Azar, Danneman's longtime friend, took a sip of whiskey. "Choptank an Indian name, do you think? Or did we bring it over?"

"An Indian name I'm betting."

"But not the Gunpowder." The Gunpowder emptied into the Chesapeake just north of Baltimore.

Danneman smiled. "No, not the Gunpowder. You know, Bob, Baltimore used to be a real hole. When people thought of Baltimore all they thought of was East Baltimore Street and sleazy sex."

"The Gayety," Azar said. "Blaze Starr and Gypsy Rose Lee."

"But we changed all that," said Danneman. "By we, I mean people and politicians working together. We cleaned it up. We made the waterfront something to be proud of. Now we have a city that works, not to mention the best baseball park in the major leagues. Remember Ogden Nash:

I could not love New York so much,
Loved I not Baltimore.'"

Azar smiled.

"New York has produced a lot of writers, I know, but we spawned Edgar Allan Poe and H. L. Mencken—not bad," Danneman said. He fell momentarily silent, then said, "Truly, I just can't figure this out. I don't know how it happened. Honest, I don't."

Azar poured himself another drink.

Danneman said, "I knocked off the women, I did. I knew I had to be cleaner than clean to run. And when I made up my mind, I had a physical exam just to make sure there would be no horseshit surprises. That I wasn't packing something I didn't know about."

"And the tests were negative."

"That's right. And I've done nothing, Bob, I swear. No needles, good God! And no men, I don't have to tell you that. No blood transfusions. Nothing." He slumped in a wicker chair beside his friend and stared out of the window. "How? That's what I want to know. Just how in hell did it happen?"

"Maybe you got a false positive. Those things happen. They're rare, I know, but they do happen."

Danneman clenched his jaw. "Now I know why those gay guys are going so crazy, wanting the government to turn the entire federal treasury over to AIDS research. They're desperate. They want somebody to save their lives."

"A false positive. That has to be it."

Danneman stared at the palm of his right hand. "There might be another answer."

"What's that?"

"I gave a speech in Concord the first week of November. There was a crowd gathered around as we came out, and as usual, I went through the handshaking drill. When I got into the car, I noticed I had blood in the palm of my hand."

Azar looked puzzled. "Blood?"

Danneman nodded. "From a substantial cut in the palm of my hand."

"That you got from shaking hands."

"I guess so. I don't remember having a cut on my hand when I left the lodge."

"You think somebody deliberately infected you."

Danneman stared at the palm of his hand. "Here I am the Democratic front-runner, nobody close. I've got the money. I'm moving the party to the center. The nomination's mine. Infecting me with HIV would be like loading me up with a time bomb."

Azar said, "It's possible that you wouldn't have discovered it until after the convention, which would be even better."

Danneman bit his lip, holding back the emotion. He swallowed. "Before or after the convention. It wouldn't make any difference either way. The Democratic Party is already on the ropes. A scandal like this, coming just before the elections, could knock us flat on our ass."

Danneman stood and looked out at the blackness. He could not swallow.

HIV.

He was going to die of a disease the public associated with homosexuals and drug addicts. Humiliated and destroyed.

He was likely deliberately infected.

His stomach twisted with rage and helplessness.

EIGHTEEN

Ara Schott met James Burlane on his landing by military jet at the Baltimore-Washington Airport. This airport, which served Baltimore as well as those people living in the Maryland suburbs of Washington, was once called Friendship Airport. Burlane thought Friendship was a better name, but the marketing people and travel agents prevailed and so a nice touch had been lost.

They said nothing on the way to Burlane's Jeep Cherokee, which Schott had driven to pick him up. As they approached the vehicle, Burlane reached for the keys. "I'm tired of just sitting. Let me drive. Give me a chance to work my arms and legs at least."

Schott flipped him the keys and headed to the passenger's side. "Sure."

Unlocking the driver's door, Burlane said, "Peña says the cartel has been framed. They're innocent."

"Innocent!" Schott rolled his eyes. "Sure they are—them and every felon who ever did time."

"That was my reaction. I've got something I want you to look at. Take a look at this." Burlane gave Schott the large brown envelope containing the details of Peña's anonymous campaign investments in the pro–drug war senators who had been murdered.

Schott studied the sheets of numbers. "Bill Jacoby and George Huff? In the pocket of Peña?"

"I asked him who else in Congress, but he wouldn't tell me. He said this ought to be enough to make his case."

Schott held up the papers. "Do you believe this?"

Burlane shrugged. "I've often wondered if something like that might not be going on. We'll have to tell the President, and Frank's people and Jane can check the numbers." He turned the Cherokee southwest onto the bumpy Spellman Parkway, the principal route between Washington and Baltimore before it had been displaced by Interstate 95 farther north. In five miles he would turn north for the ten-mile drive through Dorsey, to Schott's house in the countryside outside Ellicott City.

They fell into silence for a minute, both thinking about Peña's allegations: to maintain the profitable black market in the U.S., the Cali drug cartel had been secretly financing political supporters of the drug war.

Finally, Schott said, "I suppose you know the country is working itself up for an invasion of Colombia."

"I watched some of the coverage on CNN with Peña. It's got him spooked, and I don't blame him."

"It's on every channel up here. They've got a brigade of reporters assembled over at the Pentagon. They're doing everything short of literally chanting, 'When are we going to do it? When are we going to do it? When? When? When?' The pressure on Tom Erikson must be terrific."

Burlane said, "Has Jane found anything useful?"

"Not yet, she says, but she's working on it. Not to worry, she says, she'll eventually figure things out. She's been working around the clock since Frank gave her the data."

"She doesn't want to go back to Allenwood, and I can't say I blame her."

Ara said, "Who would believe these Colombian cowboys would be sophisticated enough to launder money into the political system itself? Then again, if you think about it, everything points that way. The money goes into legitimate businesses which hook up with in- dependent-expenditure committees. They elect candidates by financ- ing divisive issues. Actually Jimmy, it's easy."

As Schott slowed to park the Cherokee in front of Schott's bunga- low, Burlane said, "I want you take me back to the airport, Ara."

"What?" Schott frowned. "Where are you going now?"

"I'm going home," Burlane said. "I want you to hand-deliver Peña's stuff to Frank Coyle or fax it over a secure line so he can talk to the President."

"Will do," Schott said. "By 'home,' do you mean home as in eastern Oregon?"

"That's it," Burlane said. "Umatilla County, Oregon, near cowboy country."

Point Reyes Station, California
7:30 A.M.

When Ivan Kafelnikov returned to the United States three months after his five-game chess match with Lamar Gene Cooper, he was de- cidedly less visible.

In 1999, he had addressed academics and scholars at American universities and think tanks in Palo Alto, Washington, D.C., and Cambridge, where political scientists, economists, and historians were monitoring and analyzing the unfolding events in the strug- gling Russian democracy.

This time Kafelnikov arrived discreetly in San Francisco, with no advance word to ignite the inflammatory curiosity of the mass media.

Earlier he had quickly jumped at the chance to be interviewed on television and made himself available to any reporter with a pad and pen. He seemingly had an opinion on everything and was willing to express it to anyone and at all times.

He had said the food in Russia, if properly prepared, was better than in the United States. He had said Russians were smarter than Americans and worked harder. The girls were far prettier in Moscow than in Minneapolis. There was hardly a topic on which Kafelnikov was not convinced of the superiority of his countrymen.

Russia, he had said repeatedly, was a country of destiny, recently betrayed by two men seduced by the accumulated largesse of the soft and foolish West: Mikhail Gorbachev and Boris Yeltsin. Russia's talented people, who had demonstrated their superiority in literature and science, had been led astray. He, Ivan Kafelnikov, would save the people from the disaster that had followed systematic treachery, and would restore Moscow as destiny's capital city.

His previous trip had concluded with his beating Lamar Gene Cooper in four out of five chess games in Las Vegas. There was none of that strutting this time. Now, Kafelnikov quickly put an end to speculation that he was seeking another profitable chess match with Cooper. He was not a professional chess player; he was a Russian patriot determined to reclaim his country's rightful place as a world power, and he had returned to the United States to learn. The clamor that would inevitably follow a rematch with Cooper would only get in the way of his more important mission of learning, he said. If he was to lead his countrymen out of the darkness, he had to learn.

Rather than staying in five-star hotels made available by his hosts on his earlier trip, he now sought privacy. In the end, he rented a small cottage at Point Reyes Station, California, thirty-two miles northwest of San Francisco. Berry Patch Cottage, run by a middle-aged couple—Jeri, a good-looking, bookish lady, and Herbie, a bearded, charming little mensch—was a retreat for nature-loving San Franciscans seeking respite from the city. Conceding that there were things his countrymen could learn from Americans, as well as aspects of American civilization the Russians would do well to avoid, he told Jeri and Herbie he was writing a book and wanted privacy;

when they told him the Uncle Remus story of Brer Rabbit and the briar patch, he knew he had found just the place for him—a place to go to ground.

Berry Patch Cottage was located just two miles from the epicenter of the great San Francisco earthquake of 1906, at the head of a beautiful estuary, Tomales Bay, fifteen miles long and one mile wide, that was literally a depression in the famous fault line that ran the length of California.

Ivan Kafelnikov, thus having found privacy in the fishbowl that was America, quickly fell into a routine of morning walks to watch the comings and goings of ducks and geese and shore birds along Tomales Bay and in several small ponds within walking distance of his cottage.

Two weeks after he had moved into the cottage, Ivan Kafelnikov was sitting in the lee of coyote weeds out of the biting wind that was blowing off Tomales Bay. There were several small ponds within walking distance of his cottage. Winter in Marin County was like springtime in Russia, and the rains had turned everything green.

In the pond that he had chosen, a group of two dozen ducks, a mixture of mallards and pintails, swam about on the water.

As a younger man Kafelnikov had been an officer in the KGB, and he still had many friends and supporters there. In the KGB he had learned English. In recent years, as the leader of Russian nationalists, he had had an opportunity to travel several times to the U.K. and the United States, and his English had improved remarkably. Anti-Semitism was part of Kafelnikov's official package of inflammatory opinions that earned him media attention wherever he went, but, under the spell of happy Herbie, he was learning the lesson that the political abstract, the protein of demagogues everywhere, was barbarous nonsense. It was the specific and individual that mattered.

Kafelnikov, being Russian and a lover of language, had an interest in poetry. Now, in his warm coat, he sat back in the soft, long grass, called wintergreen, and tried his hand at a simple poem. He opened his stenographer's pad, and, watching the ducks, wrote:

Every year
When winter comes,
And the sky is as cold as an iceman's eye,
They fly south as always,
Up there, high,
With a leader out front
To point the way.
Come the spring
They will return north again
To sunshine and plenty.
Now, they rest
In the buffeting wind,
Heads bent,
Wary of danger on
The uncertain shore

Kafelnikov was aware of a presence. He looked up at a man with a cleft chin aiming a pistol at his head.

"Sound won't carry far in this wind," said the man with the cleft chin.

Kafelnikov watched the muzzle of the pistol. He said nothing.

"Did you get it right?" the man said.

Kafelnikov blinked. "What's that?"

"Your poem? That's what you're writing, isn't it? Looks like a poem."

"Russian is a better language for poetry."

"You don't like English?"

"I . . ." Kafelnikov, looking at the pistol, hesitated. "English is a good language, too. I thought I'd try my hand at English."

"Russian. English. For you, I suppose it doesn't matter anyway, does it?" The cleft-chinned man pulled the trigger. The impact of the bullet between Kafelnikov's eyes snapped his head back, and his corpse slumped into the comforting embrace of the wintergreen.

The cleft-chinned man, smiling to himself, strolled off, admiring the tall, slender grass swaying softly in the wind.

NINETEEN

This was hilly wheat country just northwest of the Blue Mountains of northeastern Oregon—hard, durum wheat, semolina. Noodle wheat. Farmers outside Pendleton did not like it when Washington offended the noodle-eating Chinese. Farther west lay potato country, where high-capital agribusiness sucked water out of the Columbia River in enormous aluminum pipes to irrigate the desert. Thousands of acres of land where jackrabbits and coyotes once roamed had been transformed by self-propelled combines and aluminum pipes into noodles and fast-food french fries.

James Burlane had grown up along the banks of the Columbia River just outside Umatilla, thirty miles northwest of Pendleton, had known the river before McNary Dam had destroyed the salmon runs. He remembered clearly the yipping and yelping and wavering call of coyotes roaming the stands of willow along the river. His sentimental attraction to the salmon and jackrabbits had always made him question the premise that bigger is somehow better, and that "more" and "quality" were the same thing.

In 1996, any candidate for president had had to start two years in advance and earn $50,000 to $100,000 a day to qualify as serious— that is, electable. That figure had increased to $75,000 to $125,000 a day in the last four years. Burlane did not for a moment believe that political investors were willing to yield that much treasure without expecting something in return.

Where was Governor John Danneman getting that much money? Or Chet Gorman? Or even Lamar Gene Cooper, if he indeed was angling for the presidency? Did he have pockets that deep?

Guillermo Peña de la Banda-Conchesa obviously had the money to invest to protect his business. In a sense, Burlane was not surprised that somebody had opened fire on the House of Representatives; there had long been a form of open season on the notion of democracy as representing anything other than moneyed special interests.

Neither did it surprise Burlane that his inquiries had led him to eastern Oregon. Some twenty years earlier, near Hermiston, some six miles south of Umatilla, there had been a spectacular shoot-out in a potato shed—a huge insulated warehouse where seed potatoes were stored—between the law and passionate members of a gun-loving right-wing militia, Freedom Posse.

The airport in Pendleton—Umatilla county seat and home of the famous Pendleton Round-up—was located on top of a rounded hilltop above the eastern end of town. Below the hilltop, to the left, were the grounds where the cowboy competition was held, and to the right was a state prison that used to be a mental institution before civil-rights lawyers and shrinking budgets had combined to put mentally ill people on the streets.

Once United Airlines had stopped at Pendleton, but no more. Now it was given over to murderously expensive regional airlines that were kept in business by the expense accounts of lawyers and businessmen.

In the airport's modest lobby, the sensational news of the hour on television continued to be the rumors coming from the Pentagon that the United States was preparing for a retaliatory strike on Colombian property thought to be owned by the Cali drug barons. At the end of the newest round of war rumors, the news anchor reported that the famous Russian nationalist Ivan Kafelnikov had been murdered near his retreat outside San Francisco.

Burlane, bag in hand, paused in front of the set—purveyor of all that was presumably worth knowing—to watch a woman give a thumbnail sketch of Kafelnikov's rise to political fame, if not power, in Russia. Early on, he had been an agent of the KGB, which Burlane already knew. During the Vietnam War, Kafelnikov had helped Hanoi in its intelligence-gathering efforts, of which Burlane had also been aware.

Burlane thought Kafelnikov's murder was almost certainly a loop in the logical coil that he was facing. Why was he killed? What had he known and what had he been doing?

The anchor said, "Sources speculate that Kafelnikov may have offended organized-crime elements. They say the Las Vegas bookmakers just didn't accept Kafelnikov's story that he simply blundered in the final game of his sensational chess match with Lamar Gene Cooper—for which they reportedly suffered serious losses."

Chess players of skill said it had been an amateur's error, and Burlane agreed. Surely Kafelnikov, an accomplished chess player, would not have done that accidentally. If it had been a legitimate choke, it had been a horrendous one.

The anchor said, "On this visit to the United States, the opinionated Kafelnikov kept a low profile, declining requests for interviews. He had allegedly been writing a book when he was killed."

As a form of kicker, the CNN anchor said, "California Democrat Dennis Archer died today of complications from surgery following the *cucaracha* attack on the House of Representatives. The death toll now stands at one hundred twenty-four."

Burlane headed for the rental-car window. Was the television speculation correct? Had Ivan Kafelnikov tanked the match with Lamar Gene Cooper and made a bundle on the side?

Had he holed up in Point Reyes thinking he could hide out from the mob?

Burlane didn't think Kafelnikov had thrown his last game with Lamar Gene Cooper. Kafelnikov had been stunned by the consequences of his blunder. It was clear in his eyes.

4:30 P.M.

Joyce Rollin, head of the morgue at the *East Oregonian*, was a graying, fifty-something lady with horn-rimmed glasses and a pleasant way about her.

She looked astonished when James Burlane showed her his Carter Commission identification.

"My questions have to be confidential," Burlane said. "It won't be good if they show up in the paper. We have a national emergency here of grave proportions."

"They will absolutely not show up in the paper," she said. "How can I help?"

Burlane said, "I was born in Hermiston and grew up in Umatilla, and I remember there being a farmer outside Hermiston or Stanfield named Denton Gjerde. I think he may have competed in local rodeo competition. Nothing like the Round-up or anything big-time. He was a roper or steer wrestler. Something like that. I was wondering if you have any clips on him."

Grace Rollin bit her lip. "Could I please see your identification again?"

Burlane showed her.

Rollin studied Burlane's task-force boxtops. She said, "You're talking about a well-known story in Pendleton, Major Khartoum. Denton Gjerde was killed in Vietnam, and was posthumously awarded a medal for heroism. He owned a spraying service over near Hermiston. They sprayed insecticide on potatoes."

"Denton Gjerde Agricultural Spraying? Is that the name?"

"That's right. The potato business has really boomed in the west end of the county in the last thirty years. They pipe the water out of the Columbia for those big circles out in the desert."

"Is the company still in business?"

"As far as I know, but Gjerde's widow sold it a couple of years ago. Gjerde's younger half sister is better known around here."

"Why is that?"

Rollin grinned. "She was the girlfriend of the Spanish tennis star Conchita Rivera for about ten years. Went with her everywhere. Donna Dempsey. She was a famous triathlete, but I think she's retired now."

Burlane remembered—two straight Wimbledons and a U.S. Open with Donna Dempsey in the stands cheering her on. "Did Gjerde have any other interesting siblings?"

"His half brother Tom, Donna's brother, is an interesting one. He was an adviser to the Nicaraguan contras. He's now a mountain man, one of those survivalists, I believe they call themselves. He has a long-standing interest in right-wing militias."

"He does?"

"For a while, he was mixed in with the Freedom Posse. You know about Freedom Posse?"

Burlane felt a rush in his stomach. "I remember there was a shoot-out between the law and Freedom Posse over by Hermiston some years ago. Was he involved in that?"

Rollin said, "I'm not sure. He may have been in Central America then. He's been out of the news for years now except for a couple of run-ins for alleged poaching."

"Where is he now?"

"He lives somewhere in the Blue Mountains, I think."

"And the sister? How old is she?"

Rollin put her finger on her chin, thinking. "Tom's probably in his early fifties by now. Donna's about ten years younger."

"Say, you've got a good memory."

"I've been working here twenty-five years, Major Khartoum. When I started, I used a pair of scissors to cut and file clips for the reporters to use for their research. Now they call everything up on their computers. But if they have trouble figuring things out, they still come to me."

"It's your job to remember things."

"That's right."

"Is Freedom Posse still in business, do you know?"

Rollin shook her head. "It broke up after the federal investigations and turmoil following the bombing of the federal building in Oklahoma City. Several of its members joined a group who called themselves the Riders of the High Country."

"Randolph Scott and Joel McCrea ride again."

She smiled. "If I remember the stories correctly, their membership overlaps with the Montana Militia, which also took a lot of heat after the Oklahoma City thing. But if you believe the rhetoric of the Riders of the High Country, the militiamen in Montana are a bunch of sissies."

"The High Country boys are leaner and meaner, I take it."

"To hear them tell it. Their idea is for the Pacific Northwest to secede from the Union—together with British Columbia and Alaska if they could swing it. If you'll give me a few minutes, I'll give you copies of everything we've got."

"I'd appreciate it," Burlane said. He stood there musing. *Ride the High Country* was an early Sam Peckinpah movie. Scott and Mc-Crea are the last white-hat cowboys, willing to sacrifice themselves if necessary in the fight against the black hats. McCrea is getting on in years but he's determined to go up in the high country on a little demeaning job guarding gold dust—at least it's honest work for an aging deputy. His old partner, Scott, thinks he's crazy. They might as well steal the gold dust themselves. For McCrea it's a matter of integrity and Scott throws in with him in the end. Honor and justice are at stake. If they die, they die. Cowboy samurai. Burlane loved the film and had played the video many times.

"They're no doubt traveling a brick or two short of a full load, but I'm not sure their idea of seceding is all that bad," Rollin said when he returned. "If they sealed off the border to California, I wouldn't object."

Burlane grinned. "Is Donna Dempsey a member of the Riders of the High Country also? I believe even cowgirls can get sore once in a while."

"I don't know, but I bet she could be. She's an antiabortion extremist. You think Tom and Donna Dempsey had something to do with the attack on Congress? They're saying on television that it was Colombians. They have those bones and fingerprints and eyewitnesses."

Burlane said, "I don't have any idea, Ms. Rollin, but if they do, it would be a disaster for everybody if they knew I was asking questions about them."

"I'll get your clips," she said. She added, "I love my country. I told you this would be confidential and I mean it."

"I can see you do," Burlane said. "Thank you."

Rollin said, "Are we going to bomb the Colombians? They say we're moving planes and marines to Panama. Also ships with cruise missiles."

Lake Tahoe, Nevada
5:00 P.M.

As had been their practice for several years, William and Anne Terwilliger—the couple who took the video of Representative Leo Carney chasing the cockroach terrorists down the Capitol stairs—spent Saturday afternoon gambling in Mama's Motherlode at Incline Village on the northwest shore of Lake Tahoe. Since Bill's retirement, they had been going on Fridays to avoid the weekend traffic of Californians coming across the border to try their luck.

Bill liked to play blackjack while Anne was fond of giving high fives to one-armed bandits. For Bill, it was an afternoon of telling a doe-eyed dealer with a low-cut blouse to "hit me, hit me, hit me"; for Anne, it was yank, yank, yank on fortune's cranky handle.

After their gambling, they always had a ten-dollar prime rib dinner—a bargain of bargains that the management of Mama's offered as a loss leader to lure gamblers to the tables and the slots. If they won, the prime rib was a celebratory feast; if they lost, it was a form of consolation.

Unfortunately, they had run into a streak of bad luck over a period of several months, and their markers had been purchased by an anonymous male caller who said he would write them off—plus throw fifty thousand dollars into the bargain—if they performed a simple chore. Well, not so simple. It meant flying to Washington and pretending to be tourists so they could accidentally be at the foot of the stairs to the House of Representatives at a specific time to take some videotape.

The man with their markers told them what to do and what to tell reporters and the police. If they deviated in any way, he said, they would suffer serious consequences.

On the day before they flew to Washington, they found their golden retriever dead in the yard, his head smashed by a bullet. This was a reminder, they knew, that their mysterious caller meant business.

When they had realized they had been hired by the *cucaracha* terrorists, they were too fearful to talk to anybody about it. After all, what had they done that was so terrible? They had taken some video, nothing more.

They returned home, fully expecting to be taken out themselves. But no. Their fifty thousand arrived as promised, and they returned to their old routines.

Now, after their gambling and prime rib dinner, their bellies full, they drove south on Highway 20, aka Lakeshore Drive, through Lake Tahoe State Park to Highway 50, which wound through a mountain passage carved from the north slope of the 7,140-foot-high Spooner. In the summer, when the road was clear, they often took a shortcut, Kings Canyon Road, that forked northeast at the summit and snaked its way to the capital city of Nevada.

But this time the snow in the Sierra Madres was rump-deep to a tall squaw, so William Terwilliger passed on Kings Canyon Road. Bill had won three hundred bucks at blackjack, offsetting Anne's fifty-dollar loss on the slots, and so they were in a good mood. Their Chrysler New Yorker was well tuned. Never mind that it began spitting snow when they left Mama's Motherlode. They had good tires and plenty of time.

Life was good.

Near Spooner Lake, Nevada
5:45 P.M.

The man with the cleft chin waited at a Texaco gas station at the intersection of Lakeshore Drive and Highway 50, and when the black Chrysler New Yorker passed, he pulled in behind it, staying at a discreet distance.

There was nothing unusual in cars traveling in tandem in the wintertime. It was a matter of safety, especially if it was snowing. If one car had obvious problems, there was someone around to help.

The cleft-chinned man listened to country music on the radio as he drove, keeping an eye on the tailights of the Chrysler. The snow was slowly turning into a white blanket.

Usually, he just tapped a remote and a bomb went off. This time, in the interest of sowing doubt and confusion in the minds of investigators, he'd fiddled with the Chrysler's power steering and brakes. He was handy with things mechanical, and it was a form of challenge for him to steal the car and make the necessary adjustments; the Terwilligers had been inside the casino throwing their money away all afternoon, so he'd had plenty of time to do a good job.

The man with the cleft chin believed that life without challenge and meaningful work was no kind of life at all.

Near Spooner Summit
5:52 P.M.

The Chrysler suddenly veered left, toward the canyon.

William Terwilliger hit the brakes. Nothing.

He said, "Hold on, Anne."

"What's the matter?"

Terwilliger didn't have time to answer.

The Chrysler New Yorker shot over the precipice and tumbled down the side of the mountain, bursting into flames.

TWENTY

Pendleton, Oregon

7:10 P.M.

At the Pendleton airport, James Burlane called Frank Coyle. He told Coyle to call him back on a safe phone, and gave him the number of his pay phone. "Be a few minutes, Major Khartoum," Coyle said. Five minutes later, Coyle called back. "And you are where?" he asked.

"The airport in Pendleton, Oregon."

"Find something?"

"Maybe. You can never tell. I want you please to find out everything you can about a former army sergeant named Tom Dempsey, who was an American adviser to the Nicaraguan contras. He's probably in his early to mid fifties. You should be able to get his service record from the Department of Defense."

"Sure."

"He's a survivalist who lives in the Blue Mountains near here. He's a half brother to Denton Gjerde, who was killed in Vietnam. Denton Gjerde ran an agricultural spraying service, which was run by his widow. She sold it a couple of years ago. Gjerde was an odd last name, and it stuck with me."

"Good score, Major!"

"Turns out Dempsey's a nutball who was once a known member of the local branch of Freedom Posse, which went out of business after the Oklahoma City bombing. Do you know about a group of militant nitwits who call themselves the Riders of the High Country?"

"I sure do."

Burlane said, "The woman I talked to said it's likely that both Tom and his sister, Donna Dempsey, are hooked up with the Riders. Donna was a famous triathlete and a former girlfriend of Conchita Rivera."

"The Spanish tennis star?"

"Correct. The baseline whiz. Donna Dempsey is a rabid anti-abortionist, according to the librarian at the newspaper here in Pendleton. She's maybe ten years younger than her brother. Listen, Frank, we're talking Leo Carney's congressional district here."

Coyle was momentarily silent.

"Frank, how old were Carlos and Marta Juarez?"

"He was forty-three. She was thirty-one."

"What do you think? Did Conchita and Donna coo sweet nothings in one another's ear in Spanish or English? The way I remember it, Conchita only spoke a few words of English. She always used English interpreters for her interviews."

Coyle said, "That's how I remember it, too."

"The Dempseys live in Leo Carney's district. Two sets of brothers and sisters, and I bet the Dempseys are both fluent in Spanish. Listen, Frank, I can handle an occasional coincidence, but three coincidences in one isolated part of Oregon is too much."

Coyle said nothing.

"Do you want me to trace the helicopters? Somebody should talk to Denton Gjerde's widow. I've got a flight booked back to Washington, which I can always cancel."

"You come back. I'll have someone out there talk to Ms. Gjerde."

Burlane said, "I've got a flight from here to Salt Lake City at eight-thirty. Ara will pick me up in the morning and take me to his place, and we'll find out what he and Jane Griffin have accomplished on her fancy new equipment."

Coyle said, "I'll have your requests on Dempsey and the Riders of the High Country checked out first thing in the morning, and we'll see what we have."

"The Dempseys are no doubt fit for their ages. You see what I'm getting at?"

"Yes, I do."

"I take it the FBI has some people with a talent for wax."

"We do indeed. As soon as we can lay our hands on some photographs of the Dempseys, I'll put them to work."

8:00 P.M.

As James Burlane waited for his flight, it began to snow. Burlane, looking out at the rounded hills, remembered driving the truck in harvest in July. As a teenager and college student, he had done the harvest circuit every summer, driving a truck in the pea harvest near Walla Walla, Washington, in June, then moving back to Oregon to drive in the wheat harvest near Pendleton in July, and finally pitching watermelons from the fields near Hermiston in August.

He had made sixteen dollars for a twelve-hour shift during pea and wheat harvest, and a dollar an hour for pitching watermelons. There were no days off in the peas because they had to be harvested before they got hard, but he got Sundays off in the wheat—unless it got too hot and the grain began falling off the heads. He had worked with convicts and Mexican aliens in Walla Walla, and hard-bitten loners who drove rice combines in California, and followed the wheat seasons north, winding up in Canada.

Whenever Burlane heard the lyrics *"Oh beautiful, for spacious skies, o'er amber waves of grain,"* he remembered the wheat fields outside Pendleton. He knew what America's amber waves of grain looked like. They were not something he had seen on a television documentary or on vacation. He remembered driving his truck under a combine to take another hit of wheat as the grain fell before the cycle. He remembered, too, the summertime twisters in the one hundred–plus heat.

In his second year driving the wheat truck, a carelessly thrown cigarette butt ignited a fire. A twister hit the fire and sent a funnel of burning chaff and straw skyward to settle on other fields. All the combines and trucks in the area stopped, and their crews raced off to fight the fire. He remembered the awesome fire racing uncontrolled across the wheat.

On that long-ago day a man on a Caterpillar tractor who'd been attempting to scrape a fire lane had been caught in a sprinting wall of fire and burned alive.

Burlane thought the identification of the bodies in the Tidal Basin as former cocaine smugglers was rather like that twister. Now an out-of-control firestorm of emotion was consuming the country.

On the television set in the waiting room, President Erikson, standing directly in front of the firestorm, said, "We're all of us furious about what happened, and we want justice. But we need to get to the bottom of the conspiracy so we can punish the terrorists responsible, not an entire nation. People are saying drug barons are to blame. Well, specifically which drug barons? There are several key figures behind the cocaine trade. Drug barons may have been behind the attack, yes, but possibly not all drug barons and surely not all Colombians. Let's have the names of those directly responsible. Why should innocent Colombians suffer for the behavior of the guilty?"

After Erikson did his best to calm the surging fire, a network anchor said a second suggestive death, or deaths, had been added to the murder of Ivan Kafelnikov. William Terwilliger, the man who had taped the video of the bloodied Leo Carney on the stairs of the House, was dead, along with his wife, Anne. Their car had run off the highway and exploded near Lake Tahoe, Nevada.

Near Ukiah, Oregon
10:00 P.M.

The hills and valleys below were cold and quiet and very, very white. The branches of ponderosa and sugar pines drooped under their mantle of white. It was an awesome, exquisite sight—the mountains of white—the stuff of postcards and tourist brochures.

In the days before satellite monitoring of summertime fire zones in eastern Oregon, the U.S. Forest Service had maintained a series of lookout towers where, in the dangerous months of July and August, when the pine forest was tinder-dry, forest rangers spent their days with binoculars, scanning topography looking for telltale wisps of smoke.

These towers were long ago torn down or sold by the government to recluses, nature lovers, and survivalists. In a cabin at the foot of one of these towers, a man and a woman, with cups of coffee in hand, watched the coverage of the latest development in the *cucaracha* terrorist story.

The rugged, bull-chested Tom Dempsey had piercing, pale green eyes under blond eyebrows and a week-old stubble of blond beard. He had large, powerful hands and a confident, forceful way about him. He wore Levi's, a red-and-black plaid flannel shirt over a turtle-necked sweater, and leather boots.

Donna Dempsey, in her late thirties, bore a distinct resemblance to her brother; she had the same nose, the same forceful set of green eyes, and the same high forehead. They both had a widow's peak. She was tanned and athletic-looking. She had a lean and hard look about her body, more suggestive of a triathlete than someone who pumped iron. Except for the color of her plaid flannel shirt—hers was black and green—she was dressed like her brother.

Tom said, "Well, Orly did his thing."

Donna laughed. "Was there any doubt? Orly's a pro, and they were simple hits in both cases. No problem for him."

Tom, looking at the set, narrowed his eyes. "That can't be Dan Rather's real hair, can it? It's gotta be some kind of plastic or something."

"They make toupees out of human hair, not plastic, stupid, and it's Sam Donaldson that wears the rug, not Rather."

"Donaldson, right." Tom squatted by the set and put on reading glasses. "He should have a surgeon tighten up the skin on his face. They can do that, can't they? Sort of pull it back and stitch it down where nobody can see."

Donna said, "He's got sincerity and presence. People trust him, that's why he's been on there so many years. When he dies, they'll put somebody else in the chair and re-create the head with computers. Make it look like Dan Rather is giving the straight, no-bullshit goods."

"They can do that? Give people a fake Dan Rather every night?"

"This is the twenty-first century, Tom. Of course they can. You're talking virtual reality. They can do anything they want with those computers of theirs. They could probably keep Dan Rather on the evening news for hundreds of years if they wanted. We're on the cusp of history, dear brother. Remember what Erikson said? Grow up."

Tom looked puzzled. "The cusp? Okay, college girl, what does 'cusp' mean?"

"It means a point or a pointed end. The tip of a crescent, say."

"Or the end of a sword."

"Sure," Donna said.

"I guess we showed the cockroaches a cusp, didn't we? A half minute of the biggest point ever made on the floor of the House of Representatives." Tom Dempsey ran his hands over the stubble on his jaw. "I'll be glad when my beard grows back in. I feel naked without it."

TWENTY-ONE

Jane Griffin, her tiny body lost in one of Ara Schott's paint-stained old shirts, was jubilant; her brown eyes shone with pride of accomplishment. "I think I've got something. I think I've got something. God, I couldn't wait for you to get back from your roaming around. Mr. Smart Guy. Calling yourself Major M. Sidarius Khartoum." Cyberfox rolled her eyes in mock disgust. "Give us all a break, man! Right, Ara?"

"You're entirely right," Ara Schott said.

James Burlane, pretending to be suspicious, gave Schott a look. "Ara, has this woman really found something, or is she just full of Cyberfox chickenfeathers?"

Griffin said, "All this talk about me being a full partner in Mixed Enterprises. Sure, sure. I stay home hunched over a computer while you fly around to Colombia and the West Coast. No telling what Peña fixed you up with. Naked, compliant women every time you turned around, I bet. Oh, *Major* Khartoum! You better have yourself checked for diseases, bub."

"I went to eastern Oregon, Jane, not southern California," Burlane said. "You want to learn fieldwork, too? I can teach you the ropes if you want."

Griffin cocked her head. "You're talking Ms. Jane Bond here?"

"Surveillance, weapons, cameras, infrared lenses, parabolic mikes, the works. We're too small an outfit for everybody to be specialists. We have to be flexible. Right, Ara?"

"Right," Schott said dryly.

"I can handle that. You mean it, or are you just jerking me around? Another line. Promise me anything: Sure, baby, whatever you want."

Burlane grinned. "Stick with us, and you're on."

Schott said, "I mined newspaper and magazine files while she worked the deposit accounts and telephone records. We've been working our butts off. We found a whole lot of stuff, but damned if we know what to make of it all."

"What did you find?" Burlane said.

Schott said, "It's best to start with me, I think. Better to understand what Jane found."

"Go for it."

"I began by asking myself, How do you buy prime television time? Turns out, not like a bag of groceries. It has to be reserved months in advance, depending on the market and the time of year if you're doing national ads. There's more flexibility with local affiliates and independents. I started scouring back issues of *Advertising Age*, the advertising industry's trade magazine, and *Campaigns and Elections*, the bible of the political consultants. Two years ago they both reported that the Committee for a New America hired Stohr Timson Williams and Associates, a consulting firm in Washington, to prepare a strategy for establishing a third party this year."

"The New America people being unofficial official surrogates for Lamar Gene Cooper."

"That's right. Last spring, *Advertising Age* and *Campaigns and Elections* both reported Stohr Timson was prepared to spend thirty-eight million dollars of the committee's money on television time beginning this January to launch the New America Party with a patriotic theme."

"Did the New America people raise the thirty-eight million, or did it come from Lamar Gene Cooper?"

"It was Lamar Gene Cooper's money. The *Wall Street Journal* reported yesterday that the day after the *cucaracha* strike, the New America committee sold its Give Proof campaign and its airtime to the Brigade of American Patriots for sixty million dollars. The Patriots have reworked the Give Proof theme to fit the upcoming special congressional elections."

"The ads currently saturating the airwaves."

"Correct. Meanwhile, Cooper's New America people are loading up on prime time during the summer and early fall. Should the New Americans not launch their enterprise, the Brigade has an option to buy that time."

"Who's producing the Give Proof ads now?"

Schott said, "The *Wall Street Journal* says the Brigade hired Stohr Timson's creative team to continue the campaign for them. Give Proof is working quite nicely, thank you. The public is responding."

"My oh my. The money to be made off the blood of patriots! How much are the Patriots raking in, can you tell me that?"

Schott said, "It's too early to tell for sure, but it's apparently coming in faster than they can count it and deposit it in the bank. Let Jane tell you about her money chase."

Griffin gave Burlane a lopsided grin. "I found some fun stuff. The Committee to Elect Chet Gorman, the Brigade of American Patriots, and the Committee for a New America all use the same bank in Washington—International Midlands."

"The president of International Midlands is a heavy contributor to both Gorman's campaign *and* the Committee for a New America," Schott said.

"Fair enough," Burlane said. "He covered his bets, and it paid off. His bank got the business."

Griffin said, "Lamar Gene Cooper's financial empire is controlled by LGC Inc., headquartered in Baton Rouge, Louisiana. Infobahn-Simmons in Boston provides computer security to LGC and its subsidiary companies. If you can decode its current system, you have access to the financial records and transactions of all those companies."

"I see." Burlane said. "And I take it you cracked the code. . . ."

"Yep."

"What did you find?"

"Beginning last spring, LGC began depositing the first of what eventually totaled two hundred twenty-three million dollars into two accounts at International Midlands. The Committee for a New America controlled one account, worth thirty-eight million dollars. A second account, worth one hundred eighty-five million dollars, was used to buy prime time in Democratic districts from the middle of January through April of this year."

Burlane's mouth fell open. "What?"

Griffin said, "Unless Frank Coyle's people were exceptionally skilled and willing to blow off the Constitution, they'd have no way of knowing about the one hundred eighty-five million."

"Oops!"

Schott laughed grimly. "You got that part right."

Burlane scratched his head. "What the hell is this?"

Schott said, "Since the Patriot Brigade is an alleged nonprofit, nonpartisan organization, it can claim to have paid for the Give Proof saturation advertising by public contributions. Donations under two hundred dollars don't have to be accounted for, so the money can be spread out over thousands of phony contributions."

Griffin said, "But that's not all, James. The hundred eighty-five million originally came from a foreign bank."

"Foreign where?"

"Carboni-Senn International, of the Cayman Islands, *the* bank of choice for the Cali drug cartel." She looked chagrined. "Unfortunately, it's probably the most secure bank in the world."

"Carboni-Senn? Are you sure?"

"There's no mistaking the transfer prefix that identifies the country. Unfortunately they change their systems codes from one millisecond to the next in a truly world-class security system. It's the best. That's why it's the bank of choice for crooks."

Burlane gave Jane Griffin a high five. "But at least we know something mighty curious is going on here. Carboni-Senn! Way to go, Zorro!" Using an imaginary sword, Burlane cut a *Z* in the air. *Swish! Swish! Swish!*

11:00 A.M.

James Burlane and Frank Coyle, bundled up in nylon ski jackets and wearing rubber-soled boots, went for a walk in the snowy cold woods behind Ara Schott's stone cottage. Burlane led the way, taking long strides in the soft snow.

Coyle trailed, breathing from the effort. "You may not have heard it yet, Major, but Chet Gorman announced this morning that he wants Leo Carney to be his vice president."

Burlane stopped and turned. "Carney?" He thought a moment. "Congressman Leo Carney gets his picture taken all bloody and becomes famous. Then people who took the famous video of Carney are killed when their car runs off the road and explodes, after which Gorman taps him to be his vice president. Curious sequence."

Coyle said, "And Carney represents eastern Oregon, where Tom Dempsey is holed up. Lotta smoke there." Coyle followed Burlane over a fallen log.

Burlane said, "Nobody sells a two-hundred-twenty-three-million-dollar campaign for sixty million without some kind of quid pro quo."

Coyle said, "Unless a hundred eighty-five million of that is someone else's money. Of course, Lamar Gene might be anticipating us every step of the way. Think of it. That's what a chess player does. He traces and memorizes multiple lines of play. Grand masters can follow and remember extremely complicated sequences. If I make move A, my opponent will make move B, then if I do C, he'll do D, and so on into a logical wilderness."

Burlane said, "We'll learn more if Cyberfox is able to find out who deposited the money in Carboni-Senn before it was moved. What have you learned about the Dempseys?"

"Tom Dempsey lives at a place called Lookout Mountain about forty miles east of Ukiah, Oregon. You know where Ukiah is?"

Burlane nodded yes. "Good deer-hunting country."

"Dempsey, who was a demolition specialist in the Green Berets, is the top hand in the Riders of the High Country."

"A demolitions specialist!"

Coyle, his breath coming in quick puffs, said, "And not the only one in the Riders. His best pal and fellow fireworks artist from the good old days is Orly Lambeau. Look at the MO, Major. Two exploded helicopters. An exploded launch truck. An exploded getaway car. Two limousines exploded in San Francisco. Did Tom Dempsey or Lambeau detonate the car carrying Bill and Anne Terwilliger? They couldn't drive a car up the steps to the House chamber, so they had to use assault rifles for the big hit."

"And the poop on Lambeau?"

"Full name, Orleans Albert Lambeau, born in New Iberia, Louisiana. His cognitive abilities jump off the charts, and he is said to be without remorse—a borderline paranoid in the clinical sense."

"Capable of planning and executing an assault on Congress?" Burlane said.

"Absolutely," Coyle said. "Denton Gjerde's widow said she sold the helicopters to a man named Winston Davis. Turns out Denton Gjerde served with Winston Davis in Vietnam, but Davis's name is with Gjerde's on the memorial in the Capitol Mall."

"Killed in Vietnam."

"That's right. We showed Gjerde's widow a picture of Orly Lambeau. She said the man claiming to be Davis could have been him, or maybe was him. She wasn't sure. In any event, she hasn't seen Davis, the Dempseys, or the copters since then."

"Good work," Burlane said.

"Lambeau bought the choppers," Coyle said.

"I'd bet on it."

Coyle mashed on his lower lip, thinking. "The government sent both Dempsey and Lambeau to the Defense Language Institute in Monterey, California, to learn Spanish before sending them to Central America. They spent nearly twelve years teaching counterinsurgency and guerrilla tactics in El Salvador, Guatemala, and Nicaragua."

Burlane said, "They and Ollie North are probably old pals."

Coyle shrugged. "Dempsey and Lambeau would know plenty of former contras to recruit for a job like this." Coyle sighed. "Donna Dempsey is also fluent in Spanish, owing to her years of traveling with Conchita Rivera."

Burlane said, "The helicopters were only ten to twelve feet off the ground flying when they were above the Mall. Isn't that right?"

"Correct. We have witnesses," Coyle said. "And they were flying just above the water in patchy fog when they exploded."

"They could easily have jumped into the Tidal Basin. Somebody on the ground could have flown the choppers the rest of the way across the water by remote."

"And popped them by remote," Burlane said.

"Right. Leaving the bodies of Carlos and Marta Juarez and Antonio Ceballos or parts of them inside to go up with the blast. There's no current in the Tidal Basin. We couldn't help but find the remains."

"Ten minutes after the explosions over the Tidal Basin Tom and Donna Dempsey were probably ordering crab cakes and cold Budweisers in a corner bar. Orly Lambeau, too, except it would be Irish coffee in San Francisco." Burlane thought a moment. "But it's still only theory. No proof. Have you scored pictures of the Dempseys?"

Coyle said, "We have. And we've got our wax people on the job this very minute."

"Do the makeup people think the Dempseys could have pulled it off?"

Coyle said, "They say yes, of course. Whoever is behind this knew Erikson'd have to tell the public, and predictably, the public demanded action. Send in the stealth bombers!"

"Listen, Frank, under the circumstances, I think I should make a patriotic call on Lamar Gene Cooper and see what he has to say about the movement of money through his accounts."

"Do it," Coyle said. "He's at his estate on the Eastern Shore across from Annapolis."

"Fishing on the Chesapeake. Duck and goose hunting at his private bay. Nice place to practice chess and entertain your guests if you have the bucks."

Coyle said, "And while you do that, I'll have taps put on Gorman and Carney's phones and pull the records of their calls for the last year."

Burlane thought a moment. "And the same for David Enright."

"The Company man?"

Burlane nodded yes. He put his foot on a fallen log and rested a moment, staring into the forest.

1:00 P.M.

Lamar Gene Cooper, having been told by his household servant that his caller was Major M. Sidarius Khartoum of the Carter Commission, was all down-home hospitality on the telephone.

"Why sure, Major Khartoum, I'd be pleased to talk to you. Anything for the cause. I know I can fairly be accused of being a man who loves the limelight and all, possibly gearing up to launch my own party, but I'm sitting on the sidelines with this one. Surely, you don't suspect me of being behind this business?"

Burlane made a clicking sound with his tongue. "Rest assured we're not trying to build a case against you, Mr. Cooper. We're just trying to make sense out of a whole lot of apparently unrelated information we've stumbled across. You don't have to have been an eye-witness to know something we can use."

"You're coming from where, Major Khartoum?"

"Near Ellicott City."

"Okay, well then, your best bet is to take the beltway south to Interstate 97, south to Interstate 595, and go east past Annapolis. You cross the Chesapeake Bay Bridge. When you're about five miles past Grasonville watch for a road south toward Carmichael. Ask anybody in Carmichael where ol' Lamar Gene is and they'll give you directions for the rest of the way to my place on Decoy Bay."

TWENTY-TWO

When James Burlane was a fuzz-cheeked young man, the fabulous Chesapeake Bay had produced some of the best fishing and crabbing in the world. Etched forever in his mind was a large sign outside of a Baltimore fish house that said:

> *The crabs you eat here today*
> *Spent last night in Chesapeake Bay.*

But eventually, because of indiscriminate dumping of human and chemical waste into the many rivers that formed this extraordinary estuary, it had become a celebrated example of human indifference to the environment.

Years later, on Bangtayan Island off the northern tip of Cebu in the Philippines, Burlane had met the American manager of a huge crabbing operation owned by a celebrated and expensive chain of Maryland fish houses. The crabmeat, picked from the shell by Filipina housewives, was cold-packed and flown to Baltimore, where it was fed to tourists and Marylanders giving their out-of-town guests a special seafood treat on the shores of the mighty Chesapeake. Burlane thought of a more appropriate rhyme.

The crab you eat in your seafood stew
Spent last week off the coast of Cebu.

Now, thanks to years of determined cleanup by the state of Maryland and nature lovers, the once proud Chesapeake Bay was staging a remarkable recovery as it entered the new century.

Connected to the Delaware Bay by the Chesapeake and Delaware Canal to the north, the Chesapeake Bay was fed by the Susquehanna, the Potomac, and numerous other rivers; its scores of fjordlike inlets, bays, and estuaries—dotted by dozens of islands—made it the heart of the Atlantic flyway down which millions of ducks and geese passed each year on their way south and back.

The peninsula that separated Chesapeake Bay from Delaware Bay was shared by what Marylanders called the Eastern Shore of their state, and by the state of Delaware. The southern tip of the peninsula belonged to Virginia. The fabulous waterfowl hunting on the bay was not everyone's sport except in the most isolated and inaccessible stretches. The most coveted bays and inlets, those immediately north and south of the Chesapeake Bay Bridge, were privately owned hunting retreats for the wealthy and powerful.

Any lobbyist or millionaire businessman worth his *Forbes* magazine rating owned a hunting retreat to entertain the admirals, generals, senators, cabinet members, and other bureaucrats whose high opinion was earnestly sought. This was a place to have a good time and maybe a drink or two or even occasionally, very discreetly, the favors of a young and willing lady.

No money passed hands, so nobody risked crass and untoward stories appearing in the *Washington Post* or *New York Times.* Outright bribery was avoided; that was the way power was brokered in Washington.

One of these private retreats—with its own bay, boats, duck blinds, even a kennel of retrievers, plus its own cornfields studded with goose blinds, and its own helicopter pad—was Decoy Bay, opposite Annapolis, Maryland. This bit of hunting and fishing paradise belonged to the maybe yes, maybe no presidential candidate Lamar Gene Cooper, who also maintained a city apartment in the Watergate complex near the Kennedy Center in Washington.

James Burlane knew these places existed, but he did not travel in circles where invitations were extended. Now, being given a tour of Cooper's handsome den, he stood before shelves of antique duck decoys. "Nice little bay here. Yours?"

Cooper nodded yes. He was proud of his place.

"I saw your duck blinds out there. Pretty fancy stuff."

Cooper said, "I'm a Louisianan, and Louisiana is a sportsman's paradise. We've got fishing and hunting that you just wouldn't believe. That's in addition to New Orleans with its jazz and all that good food. You can see why this place was a natural for me. By the way, my blinds are all equipped with gas heaters. And they have cooking stoves and little refrigerators. No sense freezing your butt off and eating cold food while you wait for the birds."

"Oh, hell no. That's barbaric."

Cooper picked up an aged canvasback decoy and turned it in his hands. "Isn't this beautiful? I got interested in decoys when I made a trip to Salisbury, farther south. They were holding their annual world decoy-carving championships. They have these big tubs where they generate waves to see how the decoys ride in the water. The judges are all intense, squinting their eyes in concentration, moving this way and that to study the angles. It was a wonderful thing to watch."

"They're gorgeous."

"These are all working decoys, not just carved birds. Do you hunt ducks and geese, Major Khartoum?"

"I did when I was a kid. Almost every day when the season was on. But when I got older, I lost my taste for it. I still love to fish, though."

"We catch a lot of flounder in my little bay here, and farther out we catch sea trout and bluefish. Tell me, Major Khartoum, just what is it that I might know that could conceivably help your investigations?"

Burlane leaned forward to admire a mallard decoy. "I want to know how much you spent on Give Proof Through the Night before you sold everything to the Brigade of American Patriots."

Cooper said, "I put up thirty-six million dollars for advertising and two million for the creative staff. It was all reported in the press. Your people can look it up. In fact, I bet they already did." Cooper looked amused.

"Thirty-eight million? Really? That's a lot of money."

"Think of a political party as a set of players working together, Major Khartoum. A kind of team. I'm putting together a party that stands a chance of dominating the political competition for the next century. That's an expensive and risky strategy."

"But powerful if it works."

"The lay of the board has to be right. This is a rare circumstance, but I think we have it here in the first presidential election of the twenty-first century. And you have to be able to afford the necessary pieces. But no, absolutely, goddamn hell no, I did not have anything to do with the cockroaches who opened fire on the House floor. It doesn't require a conspiracy to buy politicians in Washington."

Cooper had a scattering of shotguns mixed in among the decoys, and Burlane stopped before one of these, an ancient double-barrel.

"You want to take it down and look at it?"

"Sure," Burlane said. He took the shotgun off the wall and looked at it, an old Winchester with a wide bore on the left barrel and a tight bore on the right. Burlane put the butt to his shoulder and swung the barrels as if shooting a bird. "You're sure you only spent thirty-eight million bucks?"

Cooper frowned. "Of course, I'm sure. My God! I'm rich, but I'm not the Sultan of Oman. I sold a thirty-eight-million-dollar campaign for sixty million bucks. That's a handsome profit by any man's standards. Television is power. Power costs money."

Burlane returned the shotgun to its place.

Cooper said, "I may be ambitious, but I try to avoid becoming a complete fool."

"It was a tactical move, then?" Burlane stopped before a large window that looked out onto the bay, where the cold wind was beginning to whip up whitecaps on the water.

"The Committee for a New America has been planning their campaign for more than a year, Major Khartoum. Everything I've done has been open and aboveboard. If we had launched our campaign for a new party on the heels of the *cucaracha* attack, we risked a terrible backlash. And what if Tom Erikson ended up as some kind of hero? The smart thing to do was wait and see what happens."

"How do I verify the thirty-eight-million-dollar figure?"

"Easy. Just ask Bob Stohr. He'll show you the books if you want."

"And Stohr is?"

Cooper looked surprised that Burlane would ask such a question. "Robert Stohr is the chief executive officer of Stohr Timson Williams, the outfit that originally planned the Give Proof campaign. He's planning a totally different New America Party theme for a summer and fall campaign—if we decide we have a go. It's called America Twenty-one, the twenty-one standing for the twenty-first century. The board, Major Khartoum. Remember the board. Always play the board."

Burlane stopped before a handsome chess set on a polished cherrywood table. The queens were a full four or five inches high. "I'd have thought you'd have collected chess sets instead of decoys."

Cooper said, "I've always thought people who collected chess sets were being a little show-offy, if you know what I mean. Pretentious."

NEIL ABERCROMBIE & RICHARD HOYT

Burlane, smiling, picked up the white queen and turned it in his hands. It was filled with lead and so had a satisfying feel. "Decoys are more soulful, I agree. What about the hundred eighty-five million buckeroonies moved through your accounts from the Carboni-Senn branch in the Cayman Islands? Whose money is that?"

Cooper's mouth fell open. "What on earth are you talking about?"

Burlane put the queen back on the board. "I'm talking about electronic transfers, money moved from Carboni-Senn, through LGC, and deposited in International Midlands Bank. Carboni-Senn is the bank of choice for Colombian drug barons."

Cooper looked insulted. "I know what Carboni-Senn is. I read the news magazines same as the next guy. Say again how much money?"

"One hundred eighty-five million dollars."

Cooper burst into laughter. "Horseshit!"

"Fact," Burlane said.

Cooper looked incredulous. "Pure, unadulterated horseshit! I can accept you breaking in here waving the equivalent of a pistol in my face, Major Khartoum. The country is facing a national emergency, and you have an important job to do. But give me a break, for Christ's sake."

"The Give Proof take is being circulated through PACs and used as independent expenditures to back Chet Gorman clones in the special congressional elections."

Cooper pursed his lips in anger. "Please, control your imagination, man. The real question is, What on earth have you been smoking?"

"If Chet Gorman used your accounts to wash drug money through a Cayman Islands bank, his next step will be to knock you off and blame it on drug dealers. Have you ever thought of that, Mr. Cooper?"

"Bullpucky!"

"If you haven't, you better check your board."

Cooper, silent, gazed at Burlane.

Burlane returned to the window overlooking Cooper's bay. "This really is a grand setup you have here."

8:30 P.M.

Jane Griffin and Ara Schott listened to James Burlane's story of his conversation with Lamar Gene Cooper. When he finished, Burlane glanced at Schott. Something was on his mind. Schott looked at Griffin. "Well?"

"Well what?" she said.

"James is wondering if it's possible for the Patriot Brigade to wash hot money through LGC's corporate accounts."

Griffin thought a moment. "If the Brigade had a good-enough hacker and got him or her a job on the inside, yes, it could probably be done. But why?"

Burlane nodded. "To set Lamar Gene Cooper up, knowing somebody like you would eventually discover the wash. One of Ara's old bosses at the Company, a man named James Jesus Angleton, once wrote a book on the intelligence business called *A Wilderness of Mirrors*, a perfect title because it's dead-on accurate."

Griffin shook her head. "I guess."

Burlane said, "If that's the case, we're supposed to conclude that the money came from the Cali drug barons. But did it, really? The next step is for you break into Carboni-Senn and find out who deposited that money in the first place. Can you do that?"

"It would take time. Days maybe, more likely weeks, and then there's no guarantee."

Burlane shook his head. "Is there a shortcut?"

Griffin said, "Sure. The problem is getting into the memory of the Carboni-Senn computers. If I had somebody with an account there who would cooperate with me and make an electronic deposit of a couple of million bucks, I could deal my computer into the loop as a kind of stowaway."

10:10 P.M.

"*Caramba!* You must be mad, Major Khartoum. *Loco.* Have you lost your mind?" Guillermo Peña de la Banda-Conchesa sounded incredulous.

Burlane, examining the fingernails of his left hand, said, "Do you have an account in Carboni-Senn?"

"*Dios mio!*"

"Do you?"

"*Sí, sí.* I have one."

"Have you been watching the news, Señor Peña? You get CNN International down there, don't you? You've got a fancy antenna disk, I bet. The best money can buy."

"*Sí,* I've been watching the news."

"We're moving men and aircraft to our bases in Panama, and we've got aircraft carriers headed your way. We told the President about Jacoby and Huff, but that's not enough at this stage of the game. Have you got a defense against stealth bombers at that fancy place of yours? You've got almost everything else, it seems."

"*Ay!*"

"If you really are innocent, señor, your only defense is the truth, and if you're half as smart as you think you are, you'll help us find the truth. We don't have time to argue."

"*Sí, sí,* I understand."

"We're not trying to steal your lousy two million. We just want you to move the money with our hacker going along for the ride. Even if we did steal your money, it'd be a bargain for you if it helps the President cancel the attacks."

"*Ay!*"

"Just do it," Burlane said. "You Latins, all emotion. Christ! Use your head, man. If you don't help us out, you might as well bend over and kiss your ass good-bye."

"I'll need your hacker's telephone number," Peña said. "How long will it take?"

"A few minutes after the banks open in the morning. If I tried to wake them up, they'd be suspicious. Carboni-Senn will not like this little stunt, I guarantee."

"Screw Carboni-Senn." Burlane gave him Ara's telephone number. "Call as soon as you have made the arrangements, Señor Peña. *Gracias.* Ask for a Ms. Jane Griffin."

"Who?"

"Jane Griffin. Write it down. Got something to write with?"

"*Sí.*"

"G-r-i-f-f-i-n."

"A woman?"

"A smart woman, señor. She knows her computers."

"A handsome mainframe, Major?"

"Her mainframe appears to be in good shape, yes." Burlane said. "But you better pray she's got the brains to go with it, or its *Vaya con Dios* for you, 'amigo.'"

Lookout Mountain
7:30 P.M.

Tom Dempsey, peering through goggles into the fury of snow, powered the Honda snowmobile up the narrow lane that twisted and curved its way up the side of the mountain. The wind howled above the treetops, pushing the snow through the night sky in great, twisting loops and whorls.

When the road turned south and the wind was at his back, the trees on either side acted as a funnel for the wind; there were times when the visibility was so bad that Dempsey had to slow the snowmobile to an idle. But Dempsey didn't mind. He wasn't a wife-and-family, commute-to-work kind of guy. Dempsey regarded himself as an American patriot who truly gave a damn about things that mattered.

In their determination to have their way, a cabal of power-hungry socialists was trying to kiss off the Second, Tenth, and Fourteenth Amendments to the Constitution. In order to keep blacks from killing themselves off, they wanted to trash the right to keep and bear arms; because they loved to issue high-minded edicts, they poached on the rights of state and local governments; and because they were atheistic humanists and women's libbers who feared competition, they pursued unequal protection of the law. They wanted to put the United States of America under the control of the United Nations. Jews, niggers, queers, man-hating dykes, and pope-worshiping

Catholics. The Constitution was clearly on the line, together with hardworking, freedom-loving Americans everywhere.

Tom Dempsey was determined to thwart their ambition with every breath in his body. The feds had done their best to put the militias out of business after Oklahoma City, but they hadn't fully understood what they were up against.

Dempsey was layered to the max, wearing puffy, insulated gloves, wool socks in insulated boots, thermal long johns, a cotton shirt under a heavy wool sweater, all encased in a white nylon snowsuit that would have kept him warm in a Siberian blizzard. He felt cozy, and driving the snowmobile was fun.

When he made the final turn into the clearing on top of the mountain, he saw that lights were on in the cabin. Never mind that it was snowing; the wind that whipped and swirled around the top of Lookout Mountain had the generator propeller turning briskly. The generator didn't mind how cold it was or if the wind was pushing snowflakes through the blades.

He parked the snowmobile in the shed and headed for the cabin with a full backpack slung over his shoulder. Smoke billowed from the chimney, so he knew it would be warm inside. Cozy. Okay!

Dempsey banged on the door with his fist, shouting, "Mailman!" and opened it, engulfed with warmth and the wonderful odor of elk stew. "Does that ever smell good!"

A blackened cast-iron pot hung from a small chain above the fire. Pulling off his gloves, Dempsey walked over to take a whiff of the stew.

"Orly called," Donna Dempsey said. "He said whacking Kafelnikov was easy."

"Oh?"

"He said the stupid Russian was sitting in a patch of weeds writing poetry." Donna thought about that for a moment. "A real Renaissance man."

"Poetry?"

"In English. Orly says he was writing it in English. Dumb ass. Orly just did Kafelnikov with his nine-millimeter and strolled off. No sweat. The Terwilligers were more fun, he said. He said we should have seen their car go up when they tumbled down the side of the canyon. *Ka-boom!* It was a real blast, as they say. Started an avalanche. Ice and fire." Donna looked amused.

Tom threw his backpack at the base of an immense rough-hewn cabinet.

"Did you make your call?"

"I used a telephone booth in Pilot Rock. We've got a definite go. Sunday morning most likely, but maybe not until Monday. Erikson and his people will be meeting tomorrow morning to decide the details of the attacks on Colombia." Tom began peeling off his snowsuit.

"It's a definite, then. Stealth bombers and cruise missiles. No turning back."

"That's it. Not a stick of property belonging to Peña and his amigos will be left standing." Tom grinned triumphantly.

"All right! We did it!" Donna gave her brother a high five.

Tom said, "We're invited to the Nest to watch the fun on the tube. Any time Saturday. Chet and Leo will be there. And Bob Bailey, too. How's that for a well-earned invite?" He gave her a plastic bag of groceries.

Taking the groceries, Donna said, "And Orly?"

"He'll fly to Washington from San Francisco and catch up with us Sunday morning sometime after he finishes his chores."

Donna said, "Okay! Bob Bailey! Boogie time! We'll all get smashed and watch the Colombians being bombed, live on CNN. A righteous, furious nation strikes back. Think of those ratings. Better than the Gulf War because the action will be more compressed." They started putting the groceries on the shelves—coffee, sugar, salt pork, ground cumin . . .

"Who gives a flying fuck about beaners in Colombia anyway?" Tom said. "The truth is they deserve it."

Donna stirred the stew. "I used plenty of turnips, just like Mom. We need to put turnips on our list next time you go to town."

Tom said, "Good for what ails you." He grabbed a spoon from the table and dipped it into the stew. He blew on the spoonful of stew to cool it off for a quick taste. "Hey, this is really good!"

Tom opened another plastic bag and began separating pieces of mail. "No use putting your own president in the White House unless you get a chance to tell him what you want. Isn't that right? What do you say, sis? What's the first thing on your wish list? As if I didn't know already."

"The first thing Gorman should do is put an end to the legal murder of unborn children. There are no moral tweenies: right is right, and wrong is wrong."

"Isn't this what the lobbyist suits call 'quality time'? Get to do a little schmoozing with the new president. Tell him what's on our mind. We can fly out tomorrow and drive up to the Catoctins on Saturday. What do you say?"

Donna said, "I say it's party time for the Riders of the High Country!"

Tom said, "Oklahoma City was like whacking a mule upside the head with a two-by-four. All the government did was blink. The solution was right in front of our eyes. The White House is for sale! Auctioned off every four years! It was all so damn simple." Tom smacked himself on the forehead with the heel of his hand. "Such dolts we were."

"Just like buying a house or a farm," Donna said. "All we had to do is arrange for the necessary financing. Financing's the key."

"Anything's possible in this country if you can arrange the financing," Tom said. "Say, that stew does smell good, doesn't it? Smells like Mom's used to."

TWENTY-THREE

The morning light from John F. Kennedy's Rose Garden flooded the cream-colored Cabinet Room as the solemn figures filed inside. President Thomas Erikson, alone with his thoughts, stood before the left of four eight-foot-tall windows with rounded arches that faced the Rose Garden. On the east end of the garden, just outside the state dining room on the southwest corner of the White House, were a magnolia soulangeana planted by President Kennedy, and President Andrew Jackson's handsome magnolia grandiflora.

Behind him, Vice President Douglas Gregg showed the arrivals where to sit. In addition to President Jimmy Carter and the fifteen-member executive committee of the Carter Commission plus its chief investigator, Frank Coyle, there were Erikson's National Security Advisor, the civilian heads of the army, navy, and air force, plus members of the Joint Chiefs of Staff.

There were nine leather-upholstered chairs on each side of the long, oval-shaped table around which the cabinet ordinarily met. The back of the center chair on the side nearest the Rose Garden was four inches higher than the rest. This was the President's chair.

One week had passed since the executive committee had first met in the Green Room. Now Douglas Gregg cleared his throat and said, "I believe we're ready, Mr. President."

Erikson turned, aware of the eyes watching him. He sat at the table and coughed, glancing at the white busts of George Washington and Benjamin Franklin on either side of the fireplace on his right. Above the fireplace was Edouard Armand Dumaresque's oil painting, *The Signing of the Declaration of Independence.*

President Thomas Erikson looked around the table and adjusted his eyeglasses. He studied his notes. He glanced at General Robert Bach. "After we identified the remains of the Colombians on Monday, I instructed the chairman of the Joint Chiefs of Staff to update whichever of its contingency plans is relevant for a retaliatory attack on Colombia. The general now tells me the armed forces, with the help of the DEA and the CIA, have identified drug cartel assets in Colombia which have been confirmed by satellite photography. They're prepared to destroy those assets if necessary as early as Sunday morning. Is that an accurate summary, General Bach?"

Bach said, "We'll have two aircraft carriers and Marine Corps amphibious units in position within the hour. We have moved stealth bombers and other assets to our bases in Panama. We have submarines with cruise missiles positioning themselves off the coast of Colombia. We've had three days to plan the necessary air sorties. Our targets include Peña's estate overlooking the Caribbean and all properties owned or suspected to be owned by the drug barons outside urban concentrations."

"Why Sunday? Why not tomorrow if necessary?"

"We're still dealing with logistical problems, Mr. President. It will take us a full day to get our support and supply people in place. We need to be assured of proper fuel and munitions to ensure an effective number of air sorties. If we're going to do this, we want to do it right."

"So, then. It's a go for Sunday morning, if we think it's necessary."

"Yes sir."

Erikson looked at Defense Secretary Dennis Fuhr. Fuhr said, "I concur with Bob's assessment. If so ordered, we can go Sunday morning. The network television people have gone so far as to rent hotel suites in Panama City for their headquarters. If we wait longer than Sunday, Peña and his people will have time to disperse anything of value."

Erikson cleared his throat. "If we delay, I'll be accused of coddling drug barons who ordered the slaughter of American congressmen and -women. We've got motive. We've identified the remains of the terrorists. We've got two separate verifications that the man and woman were Carlos and Marta Juarez. What more proof do we need, right? The country wants revenge. The polls say we attack. If I delay, I'll be hounded into action." He waited. "If the polls said the world was flat, I'd have to agree. The precious fucking polls!"

Erikson stopped, thinking. The people in the crowded room sat in silence for a full minute that seemed like an hour.

Erikson nodded at Secretary of State Tom Costello.

"Secretary Costello has been in constant contact with the Colombians. President Salgado and I are new best friends. They and we are in a terrible quandry."

Erikson grimaced. "The economies of Latin American countries are finally turning the corner, and we're making some real export dollars down there. That translates into jobs here in the U.S. It would be stupid to wreck all that progress with a premature assault on Colombia. I'm damned if I attack and damned if I wait. It remains possible that the terrorists acted on their own, independent of the drug barons, or even that they were hired by someone here in the United States. President Carter, do we have any evidence at all linking the Colombians to the terrorists, other than the bones and the photos?"

Jimmy Carter, who had been doodling as he listened, answered without looking up from his pad. "No sir, Mr. President."

"Mr. Mills, has the CIA come up with any further evidence that sheds light on this affair?"

The white-haired Mills, solemn and circumspect, said, "No sir, we haven't, Mr. President."

Erikson bunched his face. "Guillermo Peña de la Banda-Conchesa contacted us Monday night and asked to talk to someone from our government. I sent a personal representative to Colombia to hear what Señor Peña had to say. Peña claims Carlos and Marta Juarez and Antonio Ceballos have been missing for months. If they did attack the House, they did it on their own or for somebody else. He swears neither he nor any of his friends had anything to do with the murders of the senators or the attack on the House floor. He claims he had no motive."

Erikson picked up a stack of papers and passed them down both sides of the table. "By way of proof that he had no motive, Señor Peña offered these documented financial transactions." Erikson waited while those in the room read the summaries of drug cartel contributions to the campaigns of Senators Jacoby and Huff.

Director Mills of the CIA, staring at the papers, wiggled his fingers. "How do we know these figures are for real?"

"Mr. Coyle?" Erikson said.

Frank Coyle said, "We checked the numbers the senators filed with the Federal Election Commission. Sums matching Peña's figures were spent as independent expenditures supporting Jacoby and Huff. Christians United Against Drugs has been Peña's favorite charity, followed by the National Family Alliance, the God and Country Network, the Back-to-Basics Coalition, and the National Neighborhood Watch. In the last election those groups spent close to fifteen million dollars supporting Jacoby, Huff, and other key supporters of the war on drugs. We have to assume that most of that money came from Colombia. If political campaigns were fueled by irony, we'd all be toast."

"Jesus! How did that work?" asked Mills.

Coyle said, "Read the report. Señor Peña's washed it as anonymous charitable donations. Nonprofit religious organizations have high moral ground and unknown numbers of supporters. Family-values groups are cash cows. They're up to their eyebrows in tax-free loot. Have you ever watched those television preachers milk their viewers for money? Except for Jim Bakker, they've been untouchable."

Erikson said, "It makes a person wonder about Give Proof Through the Night, doesn't it?" His question went without answer. He had a faraway look in his eye. "Well, what do we do?" He looked around the table, knowing the final decision was up to him. Nobody wanted to have anything to do with an action that could go monstrously wrong.

11:00 A.M.

Jane Griffin punched up the names on the list of Triad-owned companies given to her by the FBI, the cursor coming to rest on Prescription for Health.

Burlane, watching over her shoulder, said, "Prescription for Health is what?"

"A company that markets homeopathic and Chinese traditional medicines."

"I never see any customers in those places. Are they profitable?"

"They import powders and potions from Asia, so I suppose they're primarily used for smuggling."

She punched up Prescription for Health's credits and debits, and began scrolling through columns of numbers. "They're also used for washing money." Griffin continued tapping on the mouse until the cursor rested on an account number. "But as washes go, they're nickel-and-dimers. They only contributed three million to the account in Carboni-Senn."

Burlane pursed his mouth.

Griffin grinned a lopsided grin. "What we're looking at is an exotic form of agriculture. Poppy seeds planted in the Golden Triangle are ultimately harvested by the American mass media. Political campaigns are just the flowering stage. The crop is stored in bank vaults, not silos."

"That's one way of looking at it," Burlane said.

"The Golden Triangle poppy growers get a nick, followed by Triad smugglers, street sellers in the ghettos, banks like Carboni-Senn, then political consultants and advertising agencies. Finally, the mass media get theirs—all cozy and tidy and well distanced from any hint of guilt. Innocents."

She punched up the list onto the screen. "Which one do you want to try next?" The list of Triad-owned businesses offered among others: Trans-America Health; Cheyne's International Financial Services; Air Cathay; Prescription for Health; Books of America, Inc.; James Stanley's International Maritime Corporation; Continental Movers, Inc.

"What's Trans-America Health?" Burlane asked.

"A chain of for-profit hospitals. They've got overbilling and insurance rip-offs down to an art."

"Piggy-wigs."

"Books of America buys and sells used books in addition to moving current titles. Who's to know how many used titles they buy and sell?"

"And Continental Movers?"

"A trucking company," Griffin said. "Big one, too, used to move hot goods, same as Air Cathay."

Griffin said, "What we have here is Golden Triangle heroin money used to buy television time encouraging Americans to 'Give Proof Through the Night.' This is very patriotic stuff, James. They want to have assurance at dawn's early light that the greenbacks are still there."

Burlane stroked his handlebars, thinking. "We've got mounting evidence that the *cucaracha* terrorists were militia supporters of Chet Gorman. Now you're telling me that Chinese Triads washed one hundred eighty-five million dollars through Lamar Gene Cooper's parent corporation."

Griffin shook her head. "Mmm. Hard to figure."

Burlane said, "But someone like you could pull off the wash deposits through a corporation without anybody knowing it. You have the skill."

"If you have someone like me on the payroll."

1 : 0 0   P . M .

The snow on the East Coast had turned to rain in the night, putting a thin crust on top of the snow. When they walked, the snow crunched beneath their feet. A wind rushed across the icy snow, cutting through them.

Walking *crunch, crunch* on the frozen snow they circled the Washington Monument first, in homage to the first president.

They crunched their way west toward the frozen Reflecting Pool, with the White House on their right, and the splendid Capitol at their backs.

Frank Coyle slipped a handful of photographs out of his pocket and handed them to Burlane. "The wax people finished their work."

James Burlane studied the photographs as he walked. "Good work, Frank. Did you check the phone records?"

Coyle said, "Gorman and Carney have had numerous conversations beginning in September, but that doesn't mean anything. This morning Enright called to tell his wife that he was going to 'tech the nest and turn on the heat.' Do you know what that means?"

Burlane said, "Ara Schott worked with David Enright for years when he was still with the Company. You check your phone taps, and I'll give Ara a call. Maybe he knows about 'the nest.'"

TWENTY-FOUR

With Ara Schott and Jane Griffin respectfully looking on, awed at being in the President's private office, James Burlane and Frank Coyle arranged the six round boxes in a line on the carpet in front of President Erikson's desk. They were slightly larger than hatboxes.

Coyle made no move to open the boxes. Instead, he outlined for Erikson and Gregg the web of circumstance that he and Burlane had uncovered in their investigation: the heroin bust in L.A; the killing in Miami; Jonas Faulkner's detonator scrap; the Dempseys and the Riders of the High Country; the deaths of the Terwilligers; rumors of Chet Gorman's activities during the Vietnam War; the murder of

Ivan Kafelnikov; and David Enright's connection with Gorman and the Chinese Triads.

Finally, Coyle told the President and Vice President about the $185 million in Asian heroin money that had been deposited in Carboni-Senn and moved through the LGC corporate accounts to International Midlands Bank, where it was used to buy Give Proof television time.

Erikson, eyeing the boxes, said, "Are you telling me Lamar Gene Cooper is secretly supporting Chet Gorman?" He shook his head. "I don't believe that for a second."

Coyle glanced at Jane Griffin, her cue.

Griffin said, "It's entirely possible that Gorman's people moved the money through Cooper's accounts without his knowledge, Mr. President."

Erikson furrowed his brow. "How could he do that?"

"By planting a hacker in LGC's corporate accounting office."

Coyle said, "Ms. Griffin's next chore is to identify the hacker, Mr. President. Tracing the money will eventually tell us who moved the money and why. The Dempseys, not Colombians, likely attacked the House floor."

Erikson looked incredulous. "Good heavens, man, we know the terrorists were Colombians. We have physical evidence and eyewitness accounts."

Coyle held up a finger and gave the President a lopsided grin. "Planted evidence, Mr. President. And as to the eyewitness accounts, that's what the boxes are for."

Coyle opened the two boxes on the right and removed a wax head from each. He placed the heads on the corner of the desk. "These are Carlos and Marta Juarez, done by artists at the Bureau working from photographs. You'll note they both have substantial, square jaws." He ran his fingers along the wax jaws of the Juarez brother and sister. "And prominent cheekbones. See there." He tapped the cheekbones of Carlos and Marta.

"I do indeed," Erikson said.

"The near-Asian cheekbones suggest that they might have had

some Native American in their background somewhere. That's common in Latin America. And Carlos has slight temporal baldness."

Gregg held up the wax head of Carlos Juarez and weighed it in his hands.

"But their jaws and cheekbones, in combination, are the most memorable," Coyle said. He glanced at the unopened two boxes.

Coyle opened two more boxes and put the heads on the desk. "These are Tom and Donna Dempsey, also done from photographs." Quickly, he opened the last two boxes, retrieving heads of the Dempseys altered to look like the Juarez siblings.

Gregg's mouth fell open. He grabbed the Carlos Juarez look-alike.

Erikson leaned closer to the Donna Dempsey–Marta Juarez head. He was clearly stunned. "Amazing."

Coyle said, "The hair and hairline were easy, of course. All the Dempseys needed were dye and a razor. The color of the eyes was easy, too, brown-tinted contact lenses. The square jaw and cheekbones were achieved by widely available plastic add-ons used by theatrical makeup artists. No great skill was needed to do the job."

"How about their physical size? Are the sets of brother and sister the same?" Gregg said.

"Good question. No, they're not. Tom Dempsey is two inches taller than Carlos Juarez, and Donna is three inches taller than Marta, but none of our witnesses could remember their height. It would have been far more difficult for a male and female who were not themselves brother and sister to have altered themselves so convincingly."

Erikson looked pale. "My God, was Peña right? Who is behind this, then? And why?"

Coyle said, "Major Khartoum?"

Burlane said. "Mr. President, I think we're looking at David Enright. At least the evidence points that way."

Erikson's shoulders slumped. "I thought you were going to say that," he said. "If we show the public these wax heads and advance the scenario you just outlined, Chet Gorman's supporters will go bonkers. They've been told we've found the remains of Colombian cocaine smugglers on the bottom of the Tidal Basin, and they've fixed on that."

Gregg said, "He's right. The public *wants* to believe the Cali drug cartel did it. They'll conclude that it's all a frame."

"Mr. President, how much time do you need in advance to cancel the big show Sunday morning?" asked Burlane.

"Hours at best," Erikson replied.

Coyle said, "Mr. President, this morning Enright took a call from a man at radio station WFAX in Reston, Virginia, preparing to send a crew to 'the nest' to 'do Bob's setup' and 'turn on the heat.' Enright said it would take all night to get it warm. Ara?"

Schott said, "Enright's talking about the Peregrine's Nest, a former corporate hunting lodge he owns in the Catoctin Mountains, Mr. President. It has six or seven bedrooms, game rooms, and a huge dining hall. The Company has been using it as a retreat and safe house for years."

"In the Catoctins? Anywhere near Camp David?" Camp David was the presidential retreat near the Pennsylvania border.

"Yes sir. About twelve miles south. In weather like this Enright would have to turn the furnace up well in advance."

Coyle said, "WFAX is Bob Bailey's home station, but he likes to broadcast from different locations."

Erikson looked puzzled. "How could Enright afford a fancy place like that on a Company salary?"

Schott shook his head. "Enright has inherited money. His father was for years the CEO of Rabonne-Chalmer, a chemical company in New Jersey, and made a fortune in investments."

Burlane said, "The key to the conspiracy is the money, Mr. President. If we're ever going to know what happened with certainty, it will be the old-fashioned way, by following the money. In the meantime, I think we should do what we have to with the only lead we have, which is the Peregrine's Nest."

"Do whatever you need to do and do it now!"

4:30 P.M.

The two men in KFAX's Dodge van talked about the NBA and listened to the thump of rock 'n' roll as they whizzed along Interstate 270 halfway between Rockville and Frederick, Maryland.

The driver didn't pay much attention when a squad car from the Maryland State Highway Patrol pulled out from a rest area and began following him. He had been driving seventy miles an hour.

Seeing the squad car, he slowed to sixty-five to go along with the unspoken pretense that the speed limit was rigorously enforced.

When the blue light began blinking in the window of the squad car, the driver wasn't worried. At worst, the station might have allowed the van's license to expire. He quickly pulled to the shoulder of the highway and cracked a can of Dr Pepper.

He rolled down the window and took a sip of Dr Pepper while he waited for the cop.

The red-haired, freckle-faced cop looked friendly enough. He gave a polite tip of his hat. He said, "Are you gentlemen by any chance on your way to do a radio setup for Bullet Bob Bailey?"

Near Wolfsville
Frederick County, Maryland
5:30 P.M.

The windows were covered with moisture, so Frank Coyle couldn't see inside, but he could hear the squealing of children. Coyle pulled the collar of his coat around his neck to block the biting wind and knocked on the door.

A round-faced, plump-cheeked woman with a massive, pillowy bosom and elephantine buttocks opened the door. She was twenty-something, one of those big ones Coyle associated with rural poverty. She weighed in excess of 250 pounds. "Yes?"

Coyle showed her his Carter Commission badge. "My name is Frank Coyle, ma'am."

Studying the badge, she said, "I know who you are. I seen you on TV."

"You may have, ma'am."

"The former football player."

"Yes, ma'am. I used to play football."

Her husband showed up, standing behind his wife. He was a big one as well—350 to 400 pounds at least—and wore a West Virginia Mountaineers T-shirt stretched over his biceps, which were as big as ten-pound hams. "Evenin'," he said.

His wife said, "This is Special Agent Frank Coyle from the Carter Commission."

He held out a huge paw. "Name's Don Jones. You were real good. I seen you on TV."

"Edith," his wife said, shaking Coyle's hand.

Don said, "They're saying on TV that we're gonna kick a little butt Sunday morning. Guy down in Panama said we're right this minute targeting our stealths and cruise missiles. Is that the story you folks are getting?"

Coyle said, "That's something we're not permitted to talk about."

Quickly Don said, "Oh, yeah. Security and all. We understand. They had a military guy sayin' it ain't good to let your opponent know what you're going to do in advance."

Behind Don and Edith, Coyle saw two boys and a girl, all under nine or ten years old, playing with a red cocker spaniel. The little girl, the youngest, and the spaniel were tugging at opposite ends of a towel in a form of tug-of-war. The two boys urged their little sister not to give up, much to the delight of the cocker, who wagged the stub of its docked tail.

Don said, "How can we help you?"

Coyle said, "The Carter Commission task force would like to use your house for a day. We can't tell you why, but it's important or we wouldn't ask. We would like to house your family in a motel for the night. We'll spring for a suite of good rooms with a television, and we'll pay for your meals—order anything you want—but you won't be allowed visitors or telephone calls. We'll leave your refrigerator stocked and your house as clean as we found it."

Edith said, "Does this have to do with the terrorists?"

"Yes, it does," Frank said. "Directly. And it is quite urgent." Coyle looked like a quiet, responsible kind of man, engaged in serious business. When he said something was urgent, it must be urgent.

Edith glanced at her husband, who nodded yes. She turned and yelled, "Kids, kids, go get your coats. We're gonna go stay over tonight."

"At Aunt Joy's?" the oldest boy said.

"Shush and get your stuff, Delbert. Get your stuff, the rest of you. Come on. Come on. Scoot!"

Don Jones waved his offspring to action. "Well, don't just stand there, Delbert. Get a move on if you don't want a knock upside the head. Leon! Leon! You, too, if you don't want your brains rattled." To Coyle he said, "I hope our pilots blow them sons a bitches clear to kingdom come and then some. Talk about cockroaches!"

Ellicott City
9:00 P.M.

The corporate headquarters of LGC in Baton Rouge, Louisiana, employing six thousand people, oversaw the activities of sixteen subsidiary companies in Louisiana, Texas, New Jersey, Delaware, New York, Connecticut, and Maryland.

It had been no difficulty for a cyberpilot as skilled as Jane Griffin to negotiate the memory of LGC's mainframe computer in Baton Rouge.

She first instructed her computer to go through the roster of LGC's employees in Baton Rouge, hoping to find a surname that matched any hacker that she had encountered or heard of in her adventures in cyberspace. Most cyberpilots used a pseudonym, but their real names were frequently well known to fellow pilots. Nothing.

But just as it was possible for Griffin to ransack corporate files from the Maryland countryside, Give Proof's hacker could be operating from a remove. Distance in cyberspace was not physical, it was ethereal. It was an imaginary space behind the machine. A place out there, in which solitary hackers roamed and connived like synaptic shooting stars. A mole like the one who had burrowed into LCG could operate from a comfortable cyberhutch by satellite or by fiber optics. As such, he or she was at once nowhere and everywhere.

Griffin repeated the drill, searching the employee files of LCG's subsidiary companies, hoping to find a match. She beamed her inquiries to computer memories in six other states. No luck.

The Internet bulletin board with which she had long been affiliated maintained a list of members of cybergangs. These groups of hypersmart adolescents, brain warriors working separately yet together, roamed the highways and byways of the infobahn, stealing telephone time and prying into other people's business.

Owing to the ability of a properly programmed computer to sort through millions of combinations of letters and numbers looking for a code, key, or password, such formerly inaccessible data as telephone billings, personnel files, and financial records were nothing if not downright boring to these nerds and loners. No challenge.

Ten years earlier, an astronomer-turned–systems manager at the Lawrence Livermore Lab had spotted a seventy-five-cent accounting error which led to a cybergang that had penetrated the Pentagon's worldwide computer network. No military computer was beyond the province of their curiosity. They broke into the Pentagon's Optimus database, the Space Division of the Air Force Systems Command, at El Segundo, California, the White Sands missile range in New Mexico—the works.

One of the famous early cyberwars featuring teenaged cybergangs pitted Erik Bloodaxe's Legion of Doom against Phiber Optik's Masters of Deception. As a sixteen-year-old nerd in 1983, Jane Griffin herself—then logging on as the Hindu deity Shiva—had been a member of one of the earliest gangs, the notorious Cybertribe.

Operating on the theory that adolescents like Bloodaxe—real name Chris Goggans—and Phiber Optik—aka Mark Abene—eventually grow up and have to find employment to support their addiction, she instructed her computer to give her the home residences of identified hacker pseudonyms during the past fifteen years, which dated the effective history of serious cyberwar.

She found an identity, eighteen months old, based in New Orleans. This was Artful Dodger, a freelancer who belonged to no gang or club. The last time Artful Dodger had used his favorite Internet bulletin board was on January 17.

Ara Schott, watching this over Griffin's shoulder, said, "You think this is him. Our man?"

"Gotta be," Griffin said. "But who is he? That's the question."

TWENTY-FIVE

Donna Dempsey navigated, studying the map of Maryland while Tom Dempsey, drinking coffee from a paper cup and feeling good, drove the rented Dodge Caravan.

They had driven northwest fifty miles on Interstate 70 from Washington, D.C., turning north on Maryland State Highway 17, six miles to Wolfsville; at Wolfsville, they had turned east on a winding mountain road that connected Wolfsville with Lewiston, Maryland, ten miles distant.

The Peregrine's Nest was less than two miles south of Cunningham State Park, and ten miles south of Camp David on the edge of the Catoctin Mountain Park, and about twenty-five miles southwest of Gettysburg, Pennsylvania.

Tom, slowing for a curve, said, "These aren't real mountains to my way of thinking. I know they're listed on the map as mountains. And they do have some elevation, that's true. But they're only ridges, the way I see it. They're about as much mountains as New York City is part of the United States."

Donna said, "Real mountains are covered with pine trees or fir, not this ugly stuff. Leaves falling off every autumn."

Tom said, "They debase the language out of stupidity. Their minds have become atrophied from being cooped up in all these ugly cities. They think freedom is not having to do anything for themselves. They want the government to take care of them. Let somebody else foot the bills. 'Gimme my free lunch. Take care of me. Deliver my bastard kids. Fix me up when I get shot or stabbed. Pay my bills.'"

Donna laughed. "Listen, we've been under tremendous pressure. This is a little reward time. Enjoy, big brother. Take it easy!"

Tom stared intently at the road for several minutes. "You know, Donna, I've been thinking about David Enright. He's the kind of guy who runs from sink to sink washing his hands. You ever think of that? Can you imagine how much soap he must go through every week?"

"Maybe he's got a chunk of Procter and Gamble," Donna said, smiling. "Not that we aren't busy little scrubbers ourselves. We scratched seven Nicaraguans all told: two drivers, plus the pilots and little helpers we took out over the Tidal Basin, even Rufino in our copter. They rose happily to contra heaven, fondling their M16s like they were stiff dicks."

"Like President Chet Gorman was going to put them back in power. Right. Let's face it, they were scumbags." Tom looked amused.

"Useful scumbags," Donna said. "Look, we're a team. We're pros—as much as Enright is any day. If anything he needs us more than we need him. We got him this far didn't we? And don't forget, Enright needs Orly to drop Cooper."

Tom pursed his lips. "That's true."

✗ Donna said, "C'mon. We're doing this because we love our country, not just to score a buck. Enright can't trust mercenaries for
something like this."

Tom shook his head. "No way, Jose."

"Enright is smug. So what! It's Chet Gorman who really counts.
That's who we're really going to see, Chet Gorman and Bob Bailey."

Tom visibly brightened. He glanced in the rearview mirror.

Donna said, "It's going to be fun kicking back with Bob Bailey.
They tried to intimidate him after Oklahoma City, but he wouldn't
back down. Orly loves him for that. Orly's pissed that he has to
miss him."

Tom said, "He's got brains enough to know the constitution
doesn't distinguish between BB guns and assault rifles, or between
slingshots and surface-to-air missiles. It says 'arms.' The right to
keep and bear arms shall not be infringed."

Donna smiled. "And if everybody were equal we wouldn't have
track meets and spelling bees."

Tom geared down for a curve. "The Romans tried to destroy the
Christians, remember? And look at what happened. The Christians
didn't give up. They stuck together, little pockets of them. They
fought back."

"They prevailed because they were tough and committed, and
the Romans had become soft."

Ahead, the road branched left, to the north. Donna checked the
odometer. "And you might try turning instead of talking. Here's the
turnoff at mile five."

1:00 P.M.

David Enright, dressed in slacks and a preppy wool sweater of a pale
off-green, was all white teeth and charm as he strode out to meet the
minivan carrying the arriving Riders of the High Country.

He circled quickly to the driver's side, where Tom Dempsey was
getting out.

"Tom! Tom! Donna!" A welcoming, genial host was David Enright. He held out his right hand to shake hands with his guest.

With his left hand, he raised a silenced pistol that was fitted with a khaki-colored grenade the size of a gold ball. He pulled the trigger.

He strode quickly away, upwind, holding his breath. He clapped a mask over his face. Breathing again, he checked his watch, watching the Caravan.

Tom Dempsey's corpse hung out of the door. His sister was flung back over the passenger's seat, her mouth slack, eyes bulging. Tom's corpse managed to look both startled and furious.

5:50 P.M.

Frank Coyle's electronics surveillance technicians—aided by the Maryland State Police—had intercepted Bob Bailey's WFAX radio setup crew and put them on ice; the technicians, dressed in WFAX jackets, had driven the station's truck to the Peregrine's Nest to prepare Bailey's broadcast setup in the corner of the game room.

They also installed miniature surveillance cameras in smoke alarms throughout the compound and inside hollowed-out books in the kitchen, living room, study, and game room—plus they hid microphones under chairs, sofas, coffee tables, and pool tables throughout the house.

They were able to rotate and focus the smoke-alarm cameras from the Don and Edith Jones residence, relaying the action to Camp David.

Chet Gorman, Leo Carney, David Enright, and Bob Bailey were clearly destined to be the stars of a television show that would ultimately be the Gulf War plus the O. J. Simpson trial and the bombing of the Oklahoma City federal building, cubed.

James Burlane and Frank Coyle were in the transmission control room just off Aspen Hall when the first signals from the Peregrine's Nest were relayed from the Jones residence.

Burlane and Coyle watched David Enright give Gorman, Carney, and Bailey a tour of the Peregrine's Nest. He began by showing them the deep freezers just off the large open kitchen where he had kept the mutilated frozen bodies of Marta and Carlos Juarez and their pal Antonio Cebellos. Keeping prisoners was complicated and risky. Frozen corpses and body parts stayed put. No problem to thaw them out for their big helicopter ride.

Burlane and Coyle were disheartened as only those who see their worst fears coming true can be. They had seen enough of this patriotic maggot-who-would-be-president and his cockroach friends to last their lifetimes and more.

Burlane, wondering if Jane and Ara were getting anywhere with their cybersearch, decided to take off. He would watch the Peregrine's Nest tape later if he could stomach it. Frank Coyle and his people could make the collar when the President decided to end the show; they didn't need his help.

Burlane quietly said good-bye to Coyle and hit the road in his Cherokee. He should have felt triumphant perhaps, but he did not. He wanted motion, miles, and music—distance between himself and the political horror that was unfolding at Camp David. He wanted a woman and warmth. A joint maybe. Stoned talk in the night with a hip woman.

He flipped through the radio band, settling on a station where the whiskey-voiced San Francisco jazz singer Little John Tayroon sang:

"Girl! Girl!
What am I gonna do?
You strut downtown,
wigglin' your stuff,
a-talkin' in rhyme
till it's headache time,
And you're so damned sorry
what you went and did.
How many times
do I have to hear the story?
Girl! Girl!
What am I gonna do?"

6:00 P.M.

The fireplace was faced wtih colorful sandstone; these were pale creams and beiges and off-yellow stones streaked with red, and greens and blues. The stonemason had gone to the effort of balancing the stones; those on the right side were matched by those on the left side. The colorful mosaic, when viewed from the far side of the splendidly appointed main hall of the Peregrine's Nest, was extraordinary.

The ruddy-cheeked Senator Chet Gorman looked hale and fit as he warmed his hands against the roaring fire. He wore blue jeans, stylish sports boots, and a sweatshirt with *I'm a Family Kind of Man* printed on the front in red, white, and blue with stars and stripes. He wore pilot-style eyeglasses with progressive bifocals and a haircut that wasn't too fresh—a perfect ten-day trim. "A blazing fire on a cold winter night," he said. "Isn't this the life? Can't beat it." He looked about the hall, looking pleased; he was as happy as Dad at the barbecue—all wholesome and good, surrounded by kids, dogs, Gramps, and Granny.

Congressman Leo Carney wore dark gray wool slacks and a light gray cardigan sweater over a muted blue cotton shirt. He ran his hand over the stone face. "This looks like Oregon rainbow."

"Beautiful stone, wherever it's from," Enright said.

Bob Bailey ran his hand along the top of the immense antique oak table that was the centerpiece of the hall, while Gorman held his hands to the warming fire.

Gorman furrowed his brows and leaned closer to the fire. "What's that?" He looked up at Enright and back into the fire.

Enright looked forward, squinting. "That?" He pointed at the bottom of the fire.

"Right," Gorman said.

"Looks like a lumbar vertebra," Enright said.

"Of a human?" Gorman said.

Enright dropped to one knee. Studying the crusted vertebra, he said, "Belongs to Tom or Donna Dempsey. Undertakers crisp their corpses in an oven when they cremate them. I stripped their flesh with hydrochloric acid, then kept their bones in the fireplace all afternoon. They'll be a layer of ashes in the morning then I'll flush them down the toilet, and that'll be that for those happy Riders of the High Country. No remains, so no victims."

Carney was wide-eyed. "Tom and Donna Dempsey? Man, you're something else. That's cold."

Enright said, "Their creepy friend Orly Lambeau will be next. We'll give him the same treatment after he wastes Cooper. He's out there, waiting for the air strikes so he can do his thing. He's a loner and a suspicious bastard, but he loves you, Chet, and he can't stop quoting Bullet Bob. He'll show up after all this is over, and I'll give him some gas to go with his hot air."

Gorman said, "These cowboys had their use, but let's face it, Leo. For us to take over, they had to be taken care of."

"This is serious business, and you're part of it, Leo. Never forget that," Enright said.

Carney leaned closer to the bones, studying them. "I know. I know. I just wasn't expecting an indoor barbecue."

Gorman laughed. "Hey, Leo, you're all right."

"Can we take care of Lambeau okay?" Carney looked concerned. "He's a professional, isn't he? Isn't that why we recruited him?"

Enright said mildly, "I'm a professional too. And don't forget, four-to-one he'll be intoxicated."

"Drunk?" Gorman looked surprised.

"Suffused with the idea of power. He, Orly Lambeau, one of the President's men. That's how the Riders recruited the contras, remember. Help us put our man in the White House, and we'll put you back in power."

Gorman said, "The drug barons will take the rap for killing Cooper. Turning that punk hacker into a mole was pure genius, David. That was the key, no doubt about it."

Enright smiled. "With the Artful Dodger in cyberheaven, it won't matter whether the public concludes Cooper had a deal with the

Colombians or if people think he was just being used as a laundry by a bunch of out-of-control beaners. The public gets its cues from the movies, television, and talk shows. They've probably never seen a movie that portrayed Colombians as anything except drug dealing monsters."

"It's only right blowing them up," Carney said.

"And the conspiracy buffs will be rabid," said Gorman. "They don't trust anybody, and they'll believe anything and everything as long as it confirms their suspicions. Ain't life grand?" He grinned like a truck driver helping himself to the meat 'n' taters.

Enright said, "The public has been properly conditioned, so they'll know it's true."

Gorman clenched his fists with excitement and punched the air. "We set that idiot Cooper up so sweet. The hot-damn chess master. Mr. Supersmart. Don't you just love it! Beautiful!" He slugged the palm of his left hand. "On my way to the White House."

6:05 P.M.

There was wretched gloom in Aspen Hall at Camp David. The President, Vice President, and the assembled group of Supreme Court justices, congressional leaders, military service secretaries, the Secretary of State, the Attorney General, and Jimmy Carter—appalled and mortified—watched and listened in silence; emotions rocketed between searing anger and dumbstruck mystification throughout the room.

President Erikson's face was at moments stricken, at others flushed with rage. He didn't know how much more he could take. He was afraid he would hyperventilate.

Having Burlane and Coyle's theory and assurances was one thing, but Erikson was determined to hold up the broadcasting of the transmission until he knew exactly what was transpiring. He could not ignore danger of a frame-up—or the accusation of it.

326

It wasn't as if Erikson had to look far for the networks. Reporters and camera crews were swarming on the White House lawn as the hour for the air strikes neared.

When the Attorney General and President Carter concluded they had enough on tape, Erikson would give the nod for the FBI to raid the Peregrine's Nest. After the bust, the Justice Department would feed the tapes to the networks, and Erikson would call off the air strikes. To ensure that the episode would be shown complete and unedited on the first telecast, he would give it to the networks and CNN in a single continuous feed. After that, the producers could cut and edit the action as they saw fit.

6:30 P.M.

James Burlane was driving on Interstate 70, halfway between St. Paul's Church and Hagerstown, when his cellular phone rang. Looking out at a moonlit copse of leafless trees beside the highway, he picked up the phone.

"Jimmy, it's me, Ara. Is it working?"

"Yes, it is. Frank's people did first-rate work."

"I called you because Jane was finally able to break through."

Griffin said, "A hacker named Bobby Dickens living under the pseudonym of Matthew Underhill moved the Carboni-Senn money through LGC's accounts. Underhill is officially listed as an employee of LGC, which pays him a fifty-thousand-dollar annual salary. But his bank accounts show an additional two hundred thousand coming directly from Cooper's personal account."

"And he lives where?"

"*Lived.* Past tense. He worked at home in New Orleans, not in Baton Rouge, and telephone records show that he had been in almost daily contact with Lamar Gene Cooper, apparently working as his personal hacker. A few minutes after the attack on the House of Representatives, Matthew Underhill was driving in his car when his cellular phone blew up in his ear, sending his head in a thousand directions. A few seconds later his house went up in flames and with it his computer and records."

Schott said, "The police think the killer dialed a code to detonate the cellular phone, then called the answering machine at Underhill's home to detonate an incendiary bomb. Smooth work."

Griffin said, "Bobby served time in Allenwood before me. I told you about him, remember."

"The government nailed him, just like they did you."

"He was Robert Lorrain Dickens, Little Bobby to his friends, born in Hartford, Connecticut, in 1977. He called himself Dark Star before he was sent to Allenwood. He was very, very good, James, a little nerd with big ambitions and talent. He was unexpectedly paroled after he had served six months—on condition that he never again operate a computer which had a modem. He agreed to the condition, but there was speculation that a patron had somehow managed to spring him. He returned to cyberspace as Artful Dodger, but with a completely new personal identity."

Schott said, "He had more than just a social security number, Jimmy. He had a driver's license, a birth certificate, a passport. A credit history. Insurance. The works."

Griffin said, "Whoever killed him thought they could scrub his tracks by roasting his computer. They didn't understand that there are people in cyberspace who rent data space like storage lockers. The customers use their own entrance and exit code."

"Their own cyberlock."

"In a manner of speaking. I simply checked all the storage services until I came up with a customer who regularly used his space until January eighteenth. Ordinarily, a customer's data are erased if he doesn't pay his monthly bills. The guy who runs the service is a friend of mine, and when I told him what was at stake, he helped me retrieve the data."

Schott said, "Cooper knew he was moving the money, Jimmy. Enright may have thought he was setting up Cooper for checkmate, but Cooper was following every move. Jane says it's clear from the data that David Enright recruited Little Bobby as Dark Star, but as Artful Dodger, he and Cooper followed the scam from the start."

Burlane said, "Enright thought Bobby Dickens was his pawn, but he belonged to Cooper."

"Correct, Jimmy."

Burlane hung up and called Frank Coyle to tell him what the Cyberfox had learned.

When Burlane was finished, Coyle sighed audibly. "Oh no!" He fell silent for a moment, then said, "Listen, Major, we need to get the details of all this to President Erikson pronto. I'll give you a secure fax-line number. I want Ms. Griffin to send a full report to Camp David now if not sooner."

"The Cyberfox strikes."

"She gets the Heisman for hackers, Major. Unanimous choice!"

TWENTY-SIX

Bullet Bob Bailey had decided to do his three-hour Saturday-night bashing of libby-wimps from a corner of the game room so his companions could shoot billiards or play darts or shuffle-board—that and watch the developing action in the Colombia drama on the tube.

Bailey talked to Enright, Gorman, and Carney as he checked out his gear. "I can do my program from wherever I like. All I need is a setup and an open telephone line. This way, I can take a lady to the beach or mountains or wherever and impress her while I entertain the folks out there in radioland."

He slipped some earphones over his head and settled into a swivel chair that Enright had provided. He wiggled his butt.

"You know how I beat Rush Limbaugh's radio numbers? I do it by being mysterious. I have a good, distinctive broadcast voice and an authoritative personality. I let the readers imagine what I look like. I'm on the air during rush hours in the top fifty markets in the U.S. Have you ever heard a recording of one of those old radio programs that were popular before television came along? 'Who knows what evil lllllurks in the minds of men? The Shadow knows.'" Bailey imitated Lamont Cranston's diabolical laugh.

"See how that works? It feeds off the imagination. Limbaugh can play the clever blimp if he wants. People are getting tired of him while I'm getting stronger and stronger, plus I still have privacy. Okay, gentlemen, we've got five seconds and counting—four, three, two, one . . ."

Bailey, addressing radioland, said, "Well, hello out there, friends. This is your old pal, Bullet Bob Bailey, the human Kalashnikov, here to blow away a few libby-wimps on a most unusual night. Ordinarily, I do my best to answer your calls as soon as possible, but I have a lot of stuff I want to get off my chest tonight."

For the amusement of his companions, Bailey put his hand over his heart and rolled his eyes, a mock lover of country.

"Aren't we all being treated to a sorry spectacle tonight? The sad sack President Erikson, a libby-wimp Democrat in drag, has known the identity of the Colombian bones for six days. He has physical evidence and eyewitnesses. Unspeakable Colombian scumbags opened fire on the chamber of the House of Representatives! Think about that for a moment."

Bailey winked at his comrades. He let his listeners wait for a moment.

"President Erikson is the commander in chief of our armed forces! He could and should act immediately. Yet he strides back and forth like he's trying out for Hamlet in the class play. Dither, dither, dither, 'Oh, whatever shall I do?' What's he waiting for? A proper trial so lawyers can cream off a fortune denying the obvious? Another O. J. Simpson spectacle with the world watching and laughing? Or, just maybe, friends, he's waiting for word from his pals in Colombia, and after they've escaped to safety, he'll pretend to hurt them by dropping a few symbolic bombs. Ever think of that possibility?"

Bailey winked. He let his listeners wait again.

"Let me tell you something, friends, President Chet Gorman would have stealth bombers in the air by now. In a few minutes, you could turn on your television set and watch the smart bombs strike home, knowing they'd been properly targeted. Then we could all stand tall again. We are Americans, and nobody dumps on us like that. We *owned* the twentieth century, and we will not begin the twenty-first century on our knees. The Colombians want to talk about cockroaches, President Chet Gorman would show them some real cockroaches, guaranteed.

"Okay, okay, so we all know timid Tom Erikson is no winner in the courage department. What else is there that's new? Is the Democratic alternative any better? Here's some fun. Have you been wondering why Governor John Boy Danneman has seemed so dispirited lately? The rumor, from sources who are in a position to know—and I do mean in a position to know—is that he has tested HIV-positive. Oh, scandal! Scandal!" Bailey giggled. "But really now, that shouldn't surprise anybody, should it? Didn't the old Bobber tell you a while back that Danneman was up to his old fooling-around ways? Aw, c'mon, Governor Unsafe Sex, come clean. Remember, listeners, you heard it here first. While you enjoy that little tidbit, here's a word from our sponsor, Mother Gilpin's mighty good Chicken Crissssssssssspins! I get hungry every time I run this ad."

Bailey watched the red light turn to yellow, meaning the engineer in Reston was playing the taped pitch for Mother Gilpin's Chicken Crispins.

8:15 P.M.

President Thomas Erikson was grimly pleased that Bullet Bob Bailey was in top form, the better to hone a razor edge on the verbal knife with which he was cutting his throat.

Erikson loathed the talk-show host, not only because Bailey was a Chet Gorman stalking horse, but because Erikson had grown weary of overheated rhetoric by the extremes of both parties. The Democrats believed the mass media were biased in favor of the corporate-loving Republicans; the Republicans were convinced that coverage was dominated by liberal journalists.

President Erikson felt all the mass media wanted were more readers, listeners, and viewers; they were competitors, not ideological players, and the competition, logically enough, was biased in favor of whatever was the most crazy, shocking, or outlandish.

The ancients had understood well the essential question. Erikson remembered the Latin: *Cui bono?* Who profits?

Listening to Bob Bailey on the radio was a bigger kick than reading civilized bores in *The New York Times.*

Therein lay the profit.

8:45 P.M.

The yellow light began blinking. Another Mother Gilpin's Chicken Crispins ad was finishing its run. A digital clock ticked off the seconds in green computer numbers. Ten, nine, eight, seven . . .

Bob Bailey tugged at the belt hidden by his belly

The ad was over. The red light returned.

Bailey said, "This is Bullet Bob Bailey, back again, urging all you listening tonight to back our sponsors. Remember, the folks at Mother Gilpin's spring for the ammo it takes to waste libby-wimps on the radio every night. Chow down on Mother Gilpin's today, and help me take a few more big bites out of a few more layers of hypocrisy. Don't put it off, now. Listen to your mother.

"A PS here for Governor John Boy Danneman. You can stall and stall, Governor, but eventually you're going to have to own up. I, for one, won't drop the HIV story because I know it's true. Out of the whole dimbulb pack of donkey-party candidates out there groping in the dark, you're probably the best of the lot, I'll give you that. But you just couldn't bring yourself to keep your pants zipped, could you? All those big-eyed sweet things out there cooing, 'Oh, Gov-er-nor Dan-ne-man! Are you going to be pres-i-dent? I'll show you mine if you show me yours.' Now you're HIV-positive. Nobody's gonna want an HIV-infected sicko addressing them from the Orifice Off— er, Oval Office.

"Isn't it fun to speculate who the Democrats will run with you out of the race, Governor? Me oh my, whatever will you libby-wimps do? Face yet another rout? You poor, poor babies. Stranded on the moral high ground with blackie-wacks and bull dykes. Not a whole lot to do except play basketball and whine about men.

"You good-time libby-wimps had your fun, coddling crack co-caine addicts and using tax money to support photographic exhibits of queers buggering one another. You sacked the treasury and mort-gaged the future of our children and grandchildren without a hint of modesty—strutting about in your fancy togas like pretend Neros. Spend a million here. Spend a million there. As baggy old Ev Dirk-sen once said, 'It all adds up.' It's been Caligula time in Congress, friends. We've had everything but a horse in the Senate. Well, we've had that too, I suppose, if you count Ready Teddy Kennedy.

"It's all there for us to see on television. We've watched it all. What you freaks don't seem to understand, Governor Danneman, is that people who live by the media die by the media." Bailey did a credible imitation of an inebriated Dean Martin's trademark vi-brato, singing, "*Arrivederci John Boy*: Good-bye! So long! Farewell!"

TWENTY-SEVEN

Jane Griffin and Ara Schott were listening to the Bob Bailey show when James Burlane got back to Schott's small house in the country.

Griffin, sans bra in a too-big Washington Capitol T-shirt, was sprawled out on one end of the couch, joint in hand. Arching her eyebrow, she watched Burlane coolly. "Well, you're certainly looking hip tonight. If it were summer, I bet you'd be flapping about in Birkenstocks."

"You think so? And here I was thinking you look like a terrier that just finished pulling a weasel out of a hole."

"That's about how I feel. Here's what I faxed the President." She gave Burlane a two-page report, single-spaced.

"Thank you." Burlane, reading the summary, said, "I have to admit, you're the master blaster around here, not me. The most powerful piece on the board turned out to be Cyberfox, downloading data instead of firing nine-millimeter slugs."

Griffin looked triumphant. "I fired 'em full automatic. I blasted through Carboni-Senn's security system and ran down Bobby Dickens and retrieved his data. Wasn't it sweet?" She grinned and took a hit off the joint. Looking a bit pale, Griffin got up and went to the toilet.

When she came back, she caught Burlane eyeing her. "Want to tell me what you're looking at, big boy?"

"Nice bones. Good walk," he said. He leaned to one side, examining her. "Sexy. Very foxlike, in fact."

She rolled her eyes. "Right," she said dryly.

Burlane, leering at her, licked his lips.

Schott frowned. "Jimmy! Knock it off."

Griffin laughed. "It's okay, Ara. I don't mind a little fun. No way do I want to work in some uptight place where people can't laugh."

The phone rang.

Schott answered. "It's Frank, Jimmy."

Burlane strode to the kitchen and picked up the phone there. "Frank?"

"Major, the President has read Griffin's report."

"What did he say?"

"I thought he was going to have a heart attack he was so furious."

"I bet."

"He and his people have decided to bust the Peregrine's Nest at eleven o'clock and run the tapes. They're afraid if they show the action in the middle of the night, the paranoids will accuse them of pulling a cover-up. Also, Erikson wants to call off the air strikes in Colombia well in advance of estimated launch time, which is now set for five A.M. our time. If he waits until the last minute, a flight commander or cruise-missile launch chief might not get the word."

"Eleven o'clock will catch plenty of viewers on the East Coast, and it's prime time out West. Good thinking."

"Outside of Ara and Jane, you're the only one who knows about Cooper and the sucker's game he's been playing. The President wants you to go see Cooper. He wants Cooper quietly removed from the board with no one the wiser. Cooper is to understand the President is deadly serious. Cooper gets out now or does hard time in the slammer."

Burlane glanced at his watch. "They'll run the tapes at eleven."

"Correct. That gives you more than enough time to drive to the Eastern Shore."

"Wire the conversation?"

"Goes without saying," Coyle said. "We'll need a record of everything. The President says we should have witnesses as well. He suggests Congressman Mitch Webster and Senator Boulanger, a Democrat and a Republican. He believes we can count on them since they've been a part of the investigation. I called and they're both at Webster's house in Washington. One moment, Major. The President wants to talk to you."

President Erikson was on the line. "Major Khartoum, I have a fractured country on my hands. Cooper can either quietly resign or be mated in public with obstruction-of-justice charges."

"I'll do my best, Mr. President."

"I'll call Congressman Webster and Senator Boulanger and brief them on the situation. By the way, tell Cyberfox I'll write her a full pardon. She's earned it."

Burlane smiled broadly. "Here, you tell her, Mr. President." He handed the receiver to Jane Griffin.

8:45 P.M.

They loaded into James Burlane's Plymouth Cherokee on the street outside Mitch Webster's town house on North Carolina Avenue; Senator Boulanger took the passenger seat beside Burlane, while Webster sat in back, behind Boulanger.

Burlane took Interstate 595 west toward Annapolis, Maryland, a thirty-mile drive. From there, it was another thirty miles across the Chesapeake Bay Bridge to the turnoff for Lamar Gene Cooper's hunting lodge.

As Burlane took the ramp onto the interstate, he said, "You know, Ivan Kafelnikov was right when he said chess mimics warfare and politics. The parallel is essentially correct. The professors have to publish in academic journals, so they dress it up by calling it game theory, but the idea is simple enough."

"How's that?" Boulanger said.

"Well, almost all forms of competition can best be understood by looking at them as games. That's why sports metaphors are so popular. If you alter the game, you change the nature of the competition. Take Cooper's chess, for example. Once pawns could only be moved one square at a time, making the opening a slow affair, so the rules were changed so pawns could advance two squares on their first move."

"That speeded the game up," she said.

"Yes, it did, remarkably. Later, they gave unlimited range to the queen and she became a dominant piece. In politics, polling techniques and television juiced the power of wealthy candidates. If you know what the voters are thinking, you can target your pitch on the tube."

On the backseat, Webster leaned forward. "That's it, Khartoum. Of course! Players buy pieces at auctions that we call elections."

Burlane, grinning, checked his rearview mirror and changed lanes.

Boulanger cocked her head. "My, you two are a couple of Robespierres, aren't you?"

Webster said, "It doesn't take a Robespierre to see the obvious. The public is convinced Joe Montana, Steve Young, and Jerry Rice won all those championship rings for the San Francisco 49ers. But in fact Eddie DeBartolo won those Super Bowls. He was the guy who bought the players it took to win. Look at those murderous scum tonight. Up to their eyes in loot. Secret money on that scale is incendiary!"

Boulanger, laughing, said, "Mitch, Mitch! Calm down. No voters here." She looked around, squinting her eyes, pretending to look for voters.

But Mitch Webster was a passionate man and his button had been pushed. He was suddenly at the stump with a crowd before him, an old-fashioned press-the-flesh, "how do you do, ma'am— what a pretty baby" kind of politician, ready to give 'em hell. "When competitive television spending determines the winners, we end up with negative trash and outright lies. A cancer in the bowel of democracy!" He punched the air with his fist.

Mildly, Boulanger said, "Please, Mitch! We call them attack ads, dear."

Webster sighed. "We wind up with the political extremes."

Burlane moved the Cherokee out of the way of a truck that was tailgating him. He said, "What if we used the cable systems and satellites to beam people simultaneous all-channels debates on the issues by the candidates? To win a seat would be like winning a tournament. How about that, Mr. Congressman?"

"That'd be heaven for us if we could get anybody to tune in."

Boulanger eyed Webster. "You Democrats might really get the stuffing knocked out of you then. You ever think of that, Mitch?"

Webster made a scornful snorting noise. "We'll stand in there and trade blows with you Republicans, idea for idea. Running dogs for millionaires!"

They were now crossing the Chesapeake Bay Bridge, the bay a great vast expanse below them. They could see the silhouette of the trees on the Eastern Shore.

"I say you Democrats love the money as much as anybody," Boulanger said. "You had congressional majorities for decades and not an inch did we move on cutting the cost of running for office. Not a millimeter." She raised her chin, triumphant.

Burlane said, "Gracie has a point."

Webster looked pained. "We've become professional beggars holding our tin cups."

Burlane cried plaintively, "Alms for the love of power! Alms for the love of power!" He thought it was enjoyable to tease the earnest

Webster, and thought Boulanger was witty in addition to being smart and good-looking. "If we opened up the system, maybe a third party would win a few seats," he said. "Put both your parties on the run. Why not? The Libertarians are coming. Routsville! Elephants tripping over their stupid trunks. Staggering donkeys braying wildly."

"The Libertarians?" Webster smiled. "Space travelers. Spare me, please." He looked at Burlane and cocked his head. "You're a soft-core Libertarian, aren't you, Major? A hip-looking, closet space traveler. A nutball logician run amok. But you won't admit it. An agent of Lucifer driving this vehicle. My God!"

Burlane burst out laughing. "The Libertarians are coming! The Libertarians are coming! Eighteenth-century liberals running out of control!"

TWENTY-EIGHT

10:00 P.M.

James Burlane slowed the Cherokee as he approached the private road leading to Lamar Gene Cooper's sprawling hunting lodge. Ahead, lights blazed.

The uniformed guard, one of two in a guard shack by the side of the road, stopped him with the palm of his hand. "This is a private road."

"Can you please tell Mr. Cooper that Major M. Sidarius Khartoum is here to finish the game?"

The guard glanced at Webster and Boulanger. He hesitated.

Burlane added quickly, "Plus Senator Graciela Boulanger of Montana and Congressman Mitch Webster of New York."

"One moment, please." The guard stepped back and called the compound. When he finished talking, he stepped out again and waved Burlane forward. "Go right on ahead, Major Khartoum. Mr. Cooper is expecting you."

Burlane said, "Say, I was curious. What's with all the lights?"

The second guard said, "Perimeter lights. Mr. Cooper's beefed up his security until this thing with Colombia is finished. He says you never know what these crazies are up to."

"Made it Rambo-proof, eh?"

Both guards laughed. The second guard said, "The Terminator might make it through, but he'd have to be running on an updated chip and have a little luck to boot."

10:05 P.M.

Lamar Gene Cooper, looking expansive, met them on the wide, broad steps leading up to that large-screened veranda that overlooked Decoy Bay. "Major Khartoum! Senator Boulanger!" He hesitated. He didn't recognize Webster.

"Congressman Mitch Webster," Webster said quickly.

"Oh?"

"Democrat from Buffalo."

Cooper smiled. "Welcome, Congressman Webster. Pleased to meet you. Now what's this about finishing the game, Major Khartoum? Sounds serious. Well, if there are games to be played, I'm your man. Come on in, the three of you. Let's have some coffee and Irish whiskey and talk about it."

Without waiting for an answer, Cooper led the way inside. "Is the government making sure everybody is tucked in all cozy and tidy on the eve of the big show? Watch those smart bombs strike home?"

Behind him, Burlane said, "Heavens, you sure do have some security in place."

"Until this thing in Colombia plays itself out and we know who did what and why, a man in my position can't be too careful," Cooper said. "What if those cockroaches were helping somebody with a coup in mind? You ever think of that?"

As they took seats in large comfortable leather chairs, Cooper ordered coffee and whiskey from an elderly man who appeared at a side door. Bullet Bob Bailey's insistent voice could be heard on the radio.

Cooper said, "I've been listening to Bullet Bob lately. I'll turn him off if you'd like, although in case you haven't heard, the Bullet appears to have put one in Governor Danneman tonight."

"Leave him on, by all means," Burlane said. "In fact, we were kind of hoping you'd be listening."

Cooper said, "Sounds like you're starting a game, rather than finishing one, Major. Now just what game are we talking about, and do I know the rules?"

"The one you were playing with Little Bobby Dickens against Chet Gorman and David Enright."

"Bobby Dickens?"

"How about Matthew Underhill?" Gracie said.

"Are you accusing me of killing Bobby Dickens? That's preposterous. My people cooperated fully with the New Orleans police. I have no idea why anybody would want to kill him, but I'd be pleased to tell you why I hired him and how he became Matthew Underhill."

"Might be good for starters," Burlane said.

"Well, I was thinking about running for president, and I knew there would be no shortage of journalists lusting for a gotcha. It doesn't make any difference which idiot screws up, if it happens in one of my companies, they'll hold me personally responsible. You know how that works. You have to be cleaner than clean. Am I right, Senator Boulanger?"

Boulanger said, "Hard to pass muster, that's a fact."

Cooper cocked his head. "Congressman Webster?"

Webster adjusted his glasses. "I agree. You have to be careful if you run for president."

Cooper looked vindicated. "I'd have been a damn fool not to have someone I could trust to keep an eye on my corporate accounts and to by God make sure there weren't turds about to hit the fan."

Burlane said, "Don't want a bishop lurking at the end of one of those diagonals, eh?"

Cooper grinned. "I read about this genius hacker up there in Allenwood so I greased a few wheels and sprung him. Hired him to track the financial transactions of my companies and tell me if anybody had been inside the computers snooping around. A piece of cake for him, and he was grateful. Why shouldn't he be?"

Burlane said, "Are you telling me you didn't use Bobby Dickens to do a little prowling on your own?"

Cooper slapped his thigh, looking pleased with himself. "By God, a man would have to be a damned fool to play defense all the time, now wouldn't he, Major Khartoum? Bobby was the Artful Dodger, all right. He was worth every penny I paid him and then some."

They lapsed into silence for a moment, listening to one of Bob Bailey's callers.

"My name is Bat Brainard, from down here in Lubbock, Texas, Mr. Bailey, and I'm just so damn mad I can hardly stand it. What kind of people do we have in our government to allow those Colombians to kill our congressmen and then thumb their noses at us? What can we fed-up voters do to honor our dead heroes?"

Bailey said, *"What you do about it, sir, is turn tragedy into triumph. You replace them with congressmen who have American spine. The Give Proof ads on television are making some good recommendations for the special elections. My advice is to support their choices."*

Cooper said, "You say you want to talk about the game, Major Khartoum? Take another look at the board. Fact is, I have both major parties in discovered check. Do you know what a discovered check is?" He looked at Boulanger, then Webster. "No? Major Khartoum?"

Burlane said, "It's when you move and your opponent discovers you have a hidden piece that has his king in check, so for at least one move, you're free to do whatever you please."

Cooper looked triumphant. "The cockroaches struck on Erikson's watch. Check. John Danneman is HIV-positive. Check. My move." Cooper grinned. "I advance the New America Party to the eighth rank with massive television time next summer."

"What about Chet Gorman?" Webster said.

"Poor player. Won't go with the flow on abortion. Check. The public yearns for a man who understands the game and gets down to the essentials, Congressman Webster. I move my pawns in formation: paranoia, fear, hatred, and disgust."

"I'm David Sonnenberg from Lincoln, Nebraska, and I was wondering, Bob—in view of the current crisis, who do you recommend as the best replacement for that lily-liver in the White House? Still Chet Gorman, I take it?"

Bailey responded, *"Who else but Chet Gorman? If you want to go on sucking up to blackies, dykes, homos, and drug addicts, then vote for somebody else. If you want someone who is disciplined, decisive, and knows what being American is all about, then vote for Chet. He knows Isaiah isn't just the name of a basketball player who whined about not making the first Dream Team."*

Burlane said, "You say you're interested in a game. I say you're the one in discovered check."

"Me?"

"You were one square short of queening your king's pawn, but we had the free move; we were playing a killer queen."

Cooper looked puzzled. "A killer queen?"

"You weren't the only one to spring a hacker from Allenwood. We recruited Cyberfox."

"Cyberfox being?"

"Jane Griffin, a lady who can secretly move along ranks, files, or diagonals as she pleases. She made this move." Burlane handed Cooper a copy of Griffin's report to the President.

Cooper began reading the report.

"I'm Angie Clinger down here in Vero Beach, Florida. Mr. Bailey, my question is this: If the Republicans are split, and if, as you say, Governor Danneman is HIV-positive, won't that open the way for Lamar Gene Cooper's New America Party?"

Bailey said, *"That's a good question, Angie, and I'm glad you asked it. I know the Danneman HIV story for a fact, but I know something else too. . . ."* He paused. *"I suppose I should wait for it to be made official and everything, but under the circumstances, what the hell. Why not? Listen, Angie, we all know the cockroach terrorists had to have an American inside man, don't we? The attack couldn't have been managed by foreigners alone. That stands to reason. The question is who? And why? What's his game?"*

"You know who the inside man is?"

"Well, yes I do, as it happens. I've been told on unimpeachable authority that after the air strikes on Colombia—in maybe two or three days—the Carter Commission will name him, which is why I'm not concerned about the New America Party."

"Lamar Gene Cooper is behind the cockroach terrorists? Is that what you're saying?"

"Ma'am, I didn't say that. My source is in the position to know, I'll say that much. But I try to wait until all the facts are in before talking about something like this."

"You have a source inside the investigation?"

Bailey said, *"This is a sensitive situation, ma'am. Please, I don't want to be accused of fanning the flames. I've got a reputation as a fair and responsible journalist to maintain. You understand that. All I can say is, brace yourself following the attack on Colombia."*

"Lamar Gene Cooper is the man behind the cockroach terrorists?"

"Ma'am, truly, I'm not a cheap-shot artist. I'll let the Carter Commission deliver the awful news. Call me back after it's been made official, and then we'll talk about the future of the so-called New America Party."

Watching Cooper read, Burlane said, "David Enright found out Bobby Dickens was working for you and offered him a deal. If Bobby washed Enright's Triad drug money through LGC accounts for a year, Enright would give him a percentage of it. If he didn't, Enright would blow the whistle on his parole violation."

Cooper put down the report and looked up. "Where did this hotshot queen of yours get this nonsense?"

"But Enright blundered. Little Bobby felt indebted to you and told you about the offer. You doubled him. Gambit accepted. As you can see, it's all detailed there in Ms. Griffin's report."

"If this bullshit was a dollar a pound, Major Khartoum, you could retire. This is not any kind of report. It's pure fiction. Where's the proof?"

"You watched Little Bobby Dickens wash one hundred eighty-five million dollars from Carboni-Senn through your accounts, depositing it in David Enright's account in International Midlands Bank."

Webster said, "You could have gone to the FBI straight off, but you didn't, which makes you an accomplice to the commission of a felony."

"This nonsense is based on what? Bobby Dickens is dead, and his disks are ashes. A hotshot queen, right! She's got a good imagination, I'll give her that."

Burlane shook his head. "Bobby left a diary as a form of insurance in case his play with you was somehow compromised."

"A diary?" Cooper was stunned. "Where?"

"Ms. Griffin found it in an electronic storage locker in cyberspace."

Cooper blinked. Electronic storage locker? Cyberspace?

Burlane said, "A true grand master doesn't spend his whole life playing the Ruy Lopez or the King's Indian. He studies the modern variations. You can't use dated tactics in the year 2000 and expect to win. What this is, asshole, is check and mate. President Erikson would like you to quietly resign from the game."

Lamar Gene Cooper looked out over Decoy Bay.

He had developed his pieces.

He had castled his king early to get him out of harm's way.

He had put pressure on the center.

He had left no hanging or doubled pawns and no open files.

He had figured all potential combinations—except one.

"You should have followed your own advice and paid attention to the board," Webster said.

Cooper's face sagged. He started to answer, then stopped. There was a new voice on the radio, not Bob Bailey's. Cooper furrowed his brow.

Whose voice was that?

Camp David
10:38 p.m.

The picture on the monitor was clear. The man with a cleft chin stood before Chet Gorman, David Enright, Leo Carney, and Bob Bailey, brandishing a huge revolver in each hand. He said, *"Buenas noches, caballeros."*

Thomas Erikson yelled, "Jesus, Mary, and Joseph. Who is that, Mr. Coyle?"

Frank Coyle, sitting to the President's left, said, "That's Orly Lambeau."

"How long will it take to bust 'em?"

"Four or five minutes. We have all the roads blocked, but we've been keeping well clear of the Peregrine's Nest so as not to spook them."

Erikson bellowed, "Do it to 'em now. We want 'em alive. Move! Move! Move! Go!"

Coyle ran from the room, shouting instructions at his subordinates.

TWENTY-NINE

The Peregrine's Nest

10:38.30 P.M.

The four men looked at Lambeau standing at the entrance of the stairwell that led upstairs.

Surprised, Bob Bailey, Leo Carney, and Chet Gorman stared uncertainly.

David Enright looked mystified.

"I'd like to speak to Tom and Donna Dempsey."

Enright started to open his mouth then closed it.

Lambeau said, "Why, I just bet not a whole lot of people are going to be speaking to Tom and Donna tonight, are they, Mr. Enright?"

Enright said nothing.

"Figgers." He spat the word out, and it reeked of disdain and contempt.

"We . . ." Enright coughed.

"I know, you thought you had all night to plan your ambush. I tried to tell Tom that trusting you was like believing in the tooth fairy, but he wanted to believe a deal was a deal. He thought you were on our side, a Rider of the High Country in spirit, simpatico. Say, you guys look like deer caught in headlights. Look at you. You don't know what the fuck to do. Jump left, jump right, or stand there and take your chances—hope you can work some kind of chicken-shit deal."

Enright again started to speak, but stopped, choking.

"Congressman Carney, you said you wanted us to do this job because we're professionals. Remember that? Didn't you know a professional always covers his buddy? And if his buddy takes a ration of shit, whoever gave it to him gets a ration right back with a ribbon on it. That way folks don't dis us, isn't that the lingo?"

Lambeau, enjoying his trapped quarry, sucked in air between his front teeth. "Did you really think I was going to finish this job before I had proof we weren't being screwed? I knew your security system had to be good, so I took my time, but what the hell, I had the best training in breaking and entering that money can buy, courtesy of the United States of America."

Gorman said, "Mr. Lambeau, you and I—"

Lambeau interrupted him. "You want to try to buy me out, appeal to my patriotism? You hyprocrite son of a bitch. Do you think I'm for sale like everything else? All you have to do is peel off a handful of hundred-dollar bills and tuck them in my shirt pocket? Why, you should know better than that! I'm one pissed-off cowboy, amigo. I ride the high country of fury that will not quit." Lambeau smiled, making his baby face look like a mischievous schoolboy's.

"Never underestimate the Riders. When one of us falls, another will saddle up and take his place. We won't give up until you traitorous bastards obey the Constitution and give us our country back. In the meantime, I vote with these." Lambeau gestured with his pistols. "By the way, these big old Smith and Wessons are forty-four-caliber magnum loads with splat slugs. They explode when they hit. Wicked shit." He grinned. "See, I do have mercy."

Lambeau smiled his special smile. "Look at it this way," he said pleasantly. "I'm going to punch your ballot for the big White House in the sky. You can make up all kinds of laws, and issue orders left and right, telling people how to live their lives, and have a good time sacking the treasury. Go for it. Be my guest."

Lambeau shot Enright in the face with his right pistol. The Smith & Wesson bucked in his hand.

He used his left-hand pistol to slam Gorman backward with a slug in the sternum.

He took Carney in the stomach with his right-hand pistol. Carney grimaced in the manner made famous by the video of him chasing the cockroach terrorists.

He looked at the paralyzed Bob Bailey. "I don't think we see eye-to-eye anymore." He shot Bailey in the left eye with his left-hand revolver, splashing his brains against the wall.

Then, to make sure everybody was dead, Lambeau strolled about, delivering an extra slug each into the heads of his victims, taking care to punch out Bailey's remaining eye.

As Orly Lambeau pulled the trigger with his right hand, he fingered the cleft of his chin with his left. This made him look contemplative.

Congressman Neil Abercrombie, a firebrand orator and articulate spokesperson for progressive Democrats, is a champion of human rights, campaign reform, and the American labor movement.

Elected to the Hawaii House of Representatives in 1974, Abercrombie moved to the Hawaii Senate in 1978, where he served eight years. In 1986, he was elected to the U.S. House of Representatives in a special election, returning again in 1990. He is a member of the National Security and Resources Committees, and is the Democratic whip for the Pacific/Northern California region.

Abercrombie has a B.A. in sociology from Union College, an M.A. in sociology from the University of Hawaii, and a Ph.D. in American studies from the University of Hawaii.

Richard Hoyt is a critically acclaimed author of private detective novels and international thrillers. He has been an army counterintelligence agent, a reporter for Honolulu daily newspapers, and a college professor.

Hoyt has lived and worked in numerous countries in Europe, Central America, and Asia—riding trains across the Soviet Union and riverboats the length of the Amazon. He regards Portland, Oregon, as home.

Hoyt has a B.S. and an M.S. in journalism from the University of Oregon, was a fellow in national and international editing and reporting at the Washington Journalism Center, and received a Ph.D. in American studies from the University of Hawaii.